3/8/18

With love
to Paw Paw
from Amber
Marie

WOODSBURNER

This Large Print Book carries the
Seal of Approval of N.A.V.H.

WOODSBURNER

JOHN PIPKIN

THORNDIKE PRESS
A part of Gale, Cengage Learning

GALE
CENGAGE Learning™

Detroit • New York • San Francisco • New Haven, Conn • Waterville, Maine • London

GALE
CENGAGE Learning™

Copyright © 2009 by John Pipkin.
Thorndike Press, a part of Gale, Cengage Learning.

Thorndike Press® Large Print Reviewers' Choice.
The text of this Large Print edition is unabridged.
Other aspects of the book may vary from the original edition.
Set in 16 pt. Plantin.
Printed on permanent paper.

LIBRARY OF CONGRESS CATALOGING-IN-PUBLICATION DATA

Pipkin, John.
   Woodsburner / by John Pipkin.
     p. cm. — (Thorndike Press large print reviewers choice)
   ISBN-13: 978-1-4104-1945-3 (alk. paper)
   ISBN-10: 1-4104-1945-2 (alk. paper)
   1. Thoreau, Henry David, 1817–1862—Fiction. 2. Walden Pond (Middlesex County, Mass.)—Fiction. 3. Forest fires—Fiction. 4. Biographical fiction, American. 5. Large type books. I. Title.
   PS3616.I65W66 2009b
   813'.6—dc22
                                      2009023248

Published in 2009 by arrangement with Nan A. Talese, an imprint of Knopf Doubleday Publishing Group, a division of Random House, Inc.

For Max

— who showed me the urgency of things

■ ■ ■ ■

I
DURING
CONCORD, MASSACHUSETTS
APRIL 30, 1844

■ ■ ■ ■

Fire in the Woods — A fire broke out in the woods near Fair Haven Pond, in this Town, about ten o'clock, last Tuesday forenoon. It extended with great rapidity, and was not subdued until late in the afternoon. The extent of ground over which the fire prevailed is variously estimated, the lowest estimate placing it at not less than 300 acres.

— *Concord Freeman,* May 3, 1844

I once set fire to the woods . . .
It was a glorious spectacle, and I was the
 only one there to enjoy it.
 — *The Journal of Henry David Thoreau,*
June 1850

1
HENRY DAVID

They shall say I ought to have known better.
This is what occurs to Henry David as he
squats on the bank of Fair Haven Bay, a
third of the distance from Mount Misery to
the center of Concord. *The gossips and flib-
bertigibbets, with little else to occupy their
minds, shall call me "wastrel" and "rascal."*
Henry has heard these insults before, dis-
missive whispers trailing just within earshot,
but the words surprise him now, coming as
they do seemingly from the ether, mute and
without cause. He wants only to light a
small fire, enough to cook a simple meal,
nothing more, hardly an undertaking mo-
mentous enough to give rise to premonitions such as these. He tells himself he will
record them later in his journal, along with
the other indiscriminate thoughts that flit
through his head like so much pollen. He is
certain that one day he will make something
of them, or will, at least, belatedly reckon

their import.

The wind sweeps a chattering funnel of dead leaves between his knees and teases the brim of his straw hat and Henry tries to concentrate on what he is doing. Without standing, he lifts his left foot and drags a brittle friction match across the sole of his boot, then watches the red tip flare and expire in the chill wind before he can transfer the flame. It is not unusually cold for the last day of April in Massachusetts, but the wind is strong and there has been no rain for weeks. The trees surrounding Concord and covering the sloped terrain of nearby Walden appear stunned by the drought, reluctant to reveal the swollen green buds still waiting for spring to arrive. Henry recalls the screechings of their little boat as its keel scraped along the riverbed earlier that morning, and he wonders, briefly, if he was meant to heed these sounds as a warning.

He is not alone. Standing above him, Edward Sherman Hoar, his sole companion, holds aloft a string of fish and examines the oily glistening of inanimate scales. A trickle of water drops from the string and lands on Henry's shoulder. Edward grins in apology. Henry had hoped for solitude today — an occasion to explore the uncertainties he has had little time to consider while helping his father make pencils in the long sheds behind their home — but he needed a boat for the excursion, and he prefers not to row alone, lest the loneliness remind him that his brother John will never again take a turn at the oars. Edward Sherman Hoar is several years Henry's junior, the younger brother of one of Henry's former classmates, the son of Squire Hoar (one of Concord's most esteemed patriarchs), and Edward admires Henry, looks to him for guidance. Edward calls himself a disciple of nature and he is an earnest student, eager to benefit from Henry's experience.

In all likelihood, Henry thinks, Edward will never need to learn self-reliance with ax and rope, since the inheritance that awaits him is one to be coveted. But Edward is not entirely without burdens. He has recently returned from California trailing clouds of disgrace, and Henry understands that Edward wishes to put his indiscretions behind him, wants only to resume his life in New England, to finish his final year at Harvard and savor the long, promising foreshadow of days yet unspent. Anxious for Henry's approval, Edward says he will not become a banker like his father, says he will refuse the political legacy that is his due, says he will leave that to his older brothers and will, instead, pursue a life of solemn contemplation. Edward is uncertain of his career, but he at least knows the sort of man he will become.

Henry longs for the assuredness he sometimes sees in the eyes of younger men. His mother, Cynthia, has recently taken another lodger into their crowded home: a young man named Isaac Hecker who, like Henry, appears unsettled as to what manner of life he will lead. Isaac has told Henry how he lived for a time among the philosophers at Brook Farm and then at Fruitlands, but now he says he cannot be driven from the certainty of his books. Isaac is not easily distracted by bright skies or promising winds, and Henry envies the singular attention he devotes to his study of classical languages and the spiritual writings of Orestes Brownson.

Plagued by indecision, Henry still defines his life by what it is not. He is *not* a poet, though he has written poetry. He is *not* a philosopher, though he has spent many quiet nights examining his soul until its clumsy scaffolding seemed but a transparent nuisance. He is *not* an explorer, though he feels more at home beneath a canopy of trees than in the shadows of rooftops and steeples. He has surveyed fields, framed houses, and assembled odd machines for obscure ends, but he does *not* count himself a master of any of these trades. Henry still has no idea how he will employ the life that stretches before him, and today he has come to the edge of the woods to seek respite from his indifferent labors.

Henry and Edward have only three matches, and now two lie black and twisted like question marks in the dirt. Edward forgot to bring the oilcloth-wrapped matches that he purchased for the trip, but they met a shoemaker on the river with enough to spare. Edward watches with interest; fish dangling from one hand, he opens his coat and tries to provide shelter. They agree that it is too windy to start a fire. It seems very likely that they will have to settle for a cold meal after all. Henry frowns and scratches the wild line of beard that faintly circles his chin from ear to ear. Crouching, he is an assortment of sharp angles: elbows, knees, shoulders, nose. Thick lips exaggerate his frown and make it seem as though he were communicating some intuited foreknowledge of the mistake he is about to make. Edward returns to the boat to retrieve a board that might serve as a windbreak, but Henry does not wait. He is a proven outdoorsman; he knows what he is doing. Blocking the wind with his torso, Henry strikes the third match and leans forward over the bowl of a hollow pine stump, half hugging the crude hearth in which he intends to boil their string of fish into a chowder. He whispers to the kindling a sweet and urgent seduction, and the handfuls of dry grass and twigs piled in the stump suddenly ignite and the young fire nips at his fingertips. The wind lifts the straw hat from his head and tosses it playfully into the flames. He understands already that it is too late.

Henry stands and watches helplessly as the small fire he has birthed flows like brilliant liquid over the tree stump's ragged edges and into the dead grass and pine needles that carpet the barren slope from the water's edge to the lip of the woods. It is such a diversion from his intentions that he cannot believe it is happening. For the first few seconds he can only stare at the impossibility blooming before him, and it is at this moment that he recalls one of his earliest lessons, a lesson learned in the prehistory of his youth, when he was still called David Henry, when he still bore his given names so ordered to honor the paternal uncle he would never meet. The lesson was a simple one: *for every cause, an effect.* The edification conveyed from old name to new: *His older brother, John, standing on a chair, holding aloft a dented tin cup brimful with water. John taking unsteady aim — a twist of the wrist and the quivering meniscus breaks. The shimmering water spills earthward, splashes into the bottom of the waiting glass pitcher on the tabletop. For a moment, pitcher and cup are connected by a shivering, silver rope, making and unmaking itself in a sequence of tiny, sparkling miracles. The cup empties, the pitcher fills, the transfer follows itself to its own end, bubbles rise in the churning water and subside. He learns that all things are connected in this way; every result bears within itself the trace of its source, an endless chain linking infinite past to infinite future. Later, young David Henry repeats the experiment on his own — a repetition unsupervised — the objects reversed, glass pitcher held high. The glistening arc of water overruns the waiting cup, misses its mark, splashes over table and chair — the pitcher slipping from defeated fingers, striking the stone floor, shattering into jagged shards. Between cause and effect, intention is but an onlooker. His brother John understands, commiserates. Their mother disapproves. Punishment is duly meted out.*

Henry's recollection returns in fragments, the detritus of experience, a patchwork of truths a priori — that is the graceless name by which his friend Waldo refers to such things. A priori knowledge cannot be learned, only awakened. Such is the essence of the world, the nameless thing-in-itself, a mélange of a priori truths that reside dormant within each man from the moment he is born.

Henry acknowledges the truth of his childhood lesson as he runs frantically along the margin of the knee-high fire in the yellow-brown grass, flapping his arms to no real effect. It seems the right thing to do, that he might shoo the migrating flames back toward the tree stump like so many bright-winged sparrows. He is silent as he does so, as if he thought he might keep the fire a secret and extinguish it by himself before anyone can learn of his foolishness. The fire crackles like a straw broom on cobblestones, but the only sound from Henry is the muffled slap of his coat sleeves. He wants to call Edward back from the boat but is too ashamed of his carelessness. The fire spreads rapidly, a bright wave rolling toward the trees, and Henry pursues the fleeing consequences of his actions with the dogged tenacity of regret itself. He runs and flaps his arms at the flames, breathes in smoke and heat. The fire grows louder, popping and snorting as it gallops up the slope. Henry races around its perimeter, stomping at the edges of the calamity, marking its increasing size with each pass, and he begins to feel the exertion in his chest, feels the sinews tightening like bootlaces woven through his ribs.

Henry knows he cannot contain the growing blaze on his own. At last he cries out for help, but Edward is already there, half hidden by the swirls of dirt he raises with the board he has brought from the boat. Fair-haired and slight of build, Edward is not so long-limbed as Henry, less angular, and his clean-shaven cheeks are bright with the admissions of one who, despite his ambitions, has actually spent little time out of doors. The slightest effort brings his blood to the surface. Henry realizes that Edward is shouting at him, pleading for instructions, but Henry does not know how to respond.

"What should we do? What should we do?" Edward coughs from the smoke, spits at the fire. "What should we do?"

Henry searches for an answer as he kicks desperately at the flames, but the first words that come to mind are *wastrel* and *rascal.*

Edward swings at the burning grass with

the board, and Henry sees that the action only fans the flames, which billow and ripple like an army of yellow flags.

"Use your feet," Henry says. "Like this." He demonstrates, looking a bit like a turkey scratching in the dirt.

"This way?"

"That's it. And there, behind you." Henry points past his companion.

Edward spins about and stomps on the flames that have darted between his legs.

"And there, too!" Edward shouts, and points behind Henry. The fire is suddenly everywhere.

They obey each other's directions as if playing a game, two men hopping about in the dead grass, scattering glowing pine needles like sparks. Henry tries to swallow the panic seeping up into his throat like acid. If he accepts the terrible possibility of what might come to pass, he fears his feet will abandon their useless thrashing. He assumes that Edward thinks the same, and so they treat this as a competition to see which man might stomp the fastest and the longest, each pausing only to check his progress against the other. But the fire does not hesitate, does not pause to catch its breath or check its direction. It does not follow the rules of the improvised game. Encouraged by the wind, it defies gravity and flows up the gentle incline toward the trees.

"Good God!" Edward cries.

Henry looks up, traces the arc of Edward's arm, and sees a host of elfin flames leaping into the air, one upon the other, riding the wind. The flames pitch themselves headlong toward the trees, but they fall short and cannot escape the crush of Henry's heel. The bottom of his boots smolder from stomping on the burning grass; his white shirt is visible through new holes in his jacket, crusted wounds in the coarse fabric marking the landings of flying embers.

Henry thinks of the supplies they brought in the boat: fishing pole, net, blanket, knife, spoon, rope, a hard penny loaf and some potatoes — nothing that might intimidate a fire. Then he remembers the pail and the thought energizes him.

"The pail! Edward, fetch the pail and pass it to me as full as you can carry!"

Edward follows the orders at once. They form a two-man bucket brigade, splitting the distance to the water's edge between them. Fair Haven Bay is little more than a few strides away, and within a minute they have dumped three buckets of water into the blaze, but to no effect. In the time it takes them to refill the small bucket, the flames reclaim the dampened patch of earth and more. Two men with a bucket have no chance against the growing inferno. The fire scorns their efforts, forms a rude phalanx, and marches on the woods.

Henry can no longer ignore the desperation swelling in his chest. It seems they cannot possibly keep up, but he knows they must try to halt the advance before the flames reach the woods. Once the fire is among the trees, there will be no stopping it. It will spread unchecked to Well Meadow Brook on the east, and west to the Sudbury River, a hundred acres or more. And that is not the worst of it, Henry thinks. If they cannot stop it, the fire will race north to Fair Haven Hill, and beyond that Walden Pond, and beyond that . . . *Concord.* Henry David Thoreau has made no mark upon the world and has little aspiration to do so, but he does not want to be remembered as the man who reduced the town of Concord to ashes.

"Well, where will this end?" Edward calls out, as if reading Henry's thoughts.

Henry tries to answer, wants to reassure his young friend that he is master of the fire he has created, that his experience has prepared him for this, but the fear of what may come catches in his throat. Henry throws his arms wide, and the gesture looks more like an indifferent shrug than a reply.

"It will go to town," Henry says, barely audible above the crackling rush.

Edward shakes his head, reluctant to disagree with the man he admires, so Henry repeats his prediction, louder this time.

"If we do not stop it, this *will* go to the town!"

The fire advances in a crooked line a dozen times the length of Henry's arm. The pine needles, though quick to ignite, are easily spent, hardly fuel enough to sustain the flames for more than a few seconds at a time. And the fire knows this; it behaves in accordance with its own set of a priori truths. It must keep moving and consuming to survive. The two men stomp in the grass like animals possessed, but already the fire senses the nearness of the woods. Like flowers turning sunward, the flames reach for the trees.

Henry sees Edward kicking at a burning bush, and he sees the shining bay in the distance, where they enjoyed the flawless morning, floating peacefully beneath guiltless clouds, past whispering bulrushes and dwarf willows, past the alders, birches, oaks, and maples that seemed to stretch and yawn in drowsy expectation of the greener months ahead: a perfect April day. Even now, Henry thinks, somewhere beyond the rising dome of smoke and flame, that day continues unaware, and their day might have continued likewise if not for Edward's insistence that they paddle ashore and prepare a fish chowder for their midday meal. And why not? Henry is a proven fisherman. Sometimes he has felt pangs of guilt over the silver bodies of pickerel and alewives flipping and gasping on the bottom of the boat in unblinking desperation, but he accepts this as an unpleasant inevitability. All things become food for other things, even in the cold expanse of the universe, where pinpoint suns spew planets and consume vast quantities of stellar stuff in their infernal engines. *Sympathy* — that most human tendency to imbue all things with attributes of the self — must bow to *necessity.* But now the fish will go uneaten, a meaningless sacrifice, an irreversible offense to nature.

Edward insisted on the fish chowder, but it was Henry who struck the match. *Cause and effect.* In his twenty-six years, Henry has begotten fires a thousand times before. With no dire consequence, he once kindled a riotous bonfire atop Wachusett Mountain merely to cook a humble breakfast. He has gathered kindling, sparked flints, struck friction matches, but he has never witnessed any disobedience from his flickering progeny. He has no plan for squenching a blaze such as this; he can only think of ways to slow the loss. Should he go for help? It would take a man with stouter lungs than his more than half an hour to reach Concord at a full run, and at least as long for volunteers to assemble and return. How far would the fire spread, unchecked, in that time? Henry's mind wanders, but his feet continue their stomping. Edward shouts at the flames — a guttural, animal cry — and the sound brings Henry back to himself.

"There and there!" Henry calls out, pointing behind Edward. "That's it!"

Edward attacks the colonies of flame where Henry points. His feet leave blackened prints in the dirt as he beats back the swirling disorder.

"I believe we might yet win!" Edward shouts.

Henry is not so certain. He pictures the town of Concord under siege, white clapboard homes and redbrick storefronts ablaze, and he is terrified that he and Edward will fail to halt the flames in time. The fire lurches toward the trees, hungry for the brittle kindling. Henry removes his jacket and beats the flames hissing in the brush. He stops abruptly, retrieves a small book from the inside breast pocket, shoves it into the waistband of his trousers, and resumes. Edward imitates his friend, both men swinging their jackets like clubs, and they convince themselves with nods and grunts that they are making headway. They cling to the lie to keep themselves from surrendering. The flames struggle under the assault, and Henry and Edward redouble their efforts; their backward march slows at the edge of the woods. With his shoulder blades nearly touching the buckled thigh of a towering pine, Henry lashes out at the flames, pumps his arms furiously. His chest tightens, hungry for air. His brown jacket turns gray with ash.

And then a surprise — a momentary shift in the wind and they suddenly begin taking back what the fire has recently stolen. Henry and Edward swing and kick in a pantomime of madness, and the fire staggers back over what it has already burned. Henry's eyes sting from smoke and sweat. The fire is almost at the trees, but Henry sees that it is running out of grass and he begins to take comfort in Edward's naïve hope. The entire slope, from the water's edge to the beginning of the woods, is a charred scab and now the fire has no retreat.

The remaining line of flames must push past Henry and Edward and into the trees if the blaze is to survive. Edward howls, defiant, a soldier's scream of impending victory dearly bought. The flames cower under the relentless thrashing; they dissipate, suffocate, and try to outflank the two men. Henry increases his efforts. His knees feel as though they could shake loose under the vicious stomping; his shoulders ache in their orbits. He grows dizzy from the exertion, but the thought that they might succeed drives him on. A dark space opens as the fire loses momentum, and Henry steps into the breach, stands astride the gap he has created. In the scorched grass, scattered bright tongues of circumscribed chaos sputter, cough, and expire. He swings at the stranded flames and crushes them underfoot.

Within moments their job seems nearly done, and Henry allows himself to answer the exhaustion in his limbs. Around them the blackened earth hisses. Edward laughs, and Henry is embarrassed for having panicked in front of his young friend. Already, in the part of his brain where memory assembles itself, the fierce blaze is becoming little more than an amusing footnote to their day, an anecdote of tragedy narrowly averted, but he shudders when he thinks of what might have happened. Henry hears a splintered shriek behind him, a cackle of triumph. He turns and looks at Edward, but he sees that his companion is not laughing. Henry follows Edward's gaze, looks up into the naked extremities of the woods budding unbloomed, and then he knows. He knows that nature will not be rushed. He knows that each spring comes calling as coyly as the last, for rebirth is always a slow and then sudden transformation. Overhead, he sees a throng of clever flames crouching in the branches of a sleeping birch.

2
ODDMUND

Oddmund Hus sucks on the dead infant tooth wedged alongside his adult incisors like a misplaced apostrophe, and he tries not to think about the thing he saw swinging heavy and damp from Emma Woburn's clothesline. The image has ripened in his mind since the morning, pestering the taut sinews that barely restrain his urges. The air is brisk, but he rolls his sleeves to his elbows, feels the trapped heat rise from his forearms, and pauses to wipe the sweat from the back of his neck. He works alone in the corner field, clearing a patch of ground where Cyrus Woburn's property cuts into the southwest edge of the Concord Woods. Little by little, farms have eaten into the woods. To the south, rolling fields stretch as far as Nine Acre Corner and the Sudbury Meadows. Looking east, Odd figures that only a dozen or so harvests will pass before he is able to see all the way to Boston

27

without so much as a dogwood to block his view. It does not particularly bother him, this impending loss; he knows that things go away.

Odd drags his pitchfork through the heap at his feet: creeping vines in petrified coils, brittle twists of leaves and twigs, and up-rooted saplings dumbfounded by winter's assault. He flings another dry clump into the small fire he has built, and he flinches as it surges to receive his offering. A steady wind whips the busy flames. The sound is like a sheet of paper flapped close to his ear. He feeds the fire slowly, makes sure it does not reach beyond the ring of knee-size stones he cautiously set out — and he tries again to dismiss the bothersome image in his head. Odd has seen Emma Woburn's *inexpressibles* before, and not always by accident like today. From time to time, he finds cause to cross the back porch while Emma is busy at the washboard, her dripping forearms and chapped knuckles bright pink with effort, the woven basket distended with heavy wet knots. Sometimes he lingers within sight of their untangling, watching the clothes catch the breeze and test the wooden fasteners clipped to the line. He is familiar with the limp translucence of freshly scrubbed petticoats and chemises and stockings. But what he saw this morning was nothing so ordinary as that.

Emma probably forgot that he would likely pass near the clothesline on his way to the far corner, he thinks. Or she simply did not think it mattered. He remains certain that she is wholly unaware of the glimpses he steals as she goes about her chores. His head is full to bursting with imprisoned visions of her thick ankles peeking from beneath the hem of her dress and her wide buttocks softly straining against tightly wound apron strings and the weighty pale sway from armpit to elbow as she scrubs floors and dusts shelves . . . He has secreted away scores of other glimpses in the folds of his memory. Sometimes he pictures Emma's full lips rounded in pleasure and he feels a covering shadow between them and a rough edge beneath his fingers, and he cannot tell whether these images are real or something from his dreams. Emma has no idea that he has such thoughts; Odd takes great care to make sure of that.

For a quarter of an hour that morning, though, he stood carelessly in full view, transfixed by what he saw on the clothesline. He watched the miraculous garment rise and fall in the morning breeze as if it were a living, breathing animal. It looked more like a harness for a dray horse than anything Emma might wear next to her skin, but Odd reckoned its purpose right off, tracing the shape of the fabric until the empty outline awakened his longing. He could tell that Emma had stitched it together herself — here a portion of a pleated skirt, there a section of an old corset that she would never have tried to force around her ample hips. At either side were blue wedges cut from one of her husband's handkerchiefs and gusseted to form two large pouches between a brace of curved whalebones. The gentle sway of sagging laces made him shudder, and before he realized what he was doing he began scratching halfheartedly at the butternut wool of his trousers, sending expectant shivers through his limbs, until he stopped himself by picking up a stone and stuffing it into his pocket. Odd could recollect no name for what he saw hanging in the cold air that morning; it was something entirely new, a creation intended to bring some degree of belated support to Emma Woburn's immense and impractical bosom.

Odd squeezes the wooden handle of his pitchfork and tries to sweep away the vision. He hurls a clump of twisted vines into the fire and watches the lacework of desiccated leaves turn to smoke and disappear in the heat. The flames wriggle and spin, dancing to their own crackling music, approximating the languid curves of living things. What he has seen continues to prick at him. Like Emma herself, the garment's presence was irrefutable, its size unapologetic. Odd cannot help imagining the hefty burden it is intended to ease. He leans forward against the rigid shaft of the pitchfork, seeking some momentary relief in the contact, but the sensation is altogether unsatisfying. It is quite the opposite of what he wants, but he has learned that America is a land of ingenuity, a land of invention and resourcefulness, and to live as an American is to make do with what one has ready at hand. If only the woods were a few strides closer, he thinks, he might easily step behind a tree and gratify himself while still keeping an eye on his fire.

Odd has long suspected that something is wrong with him, an imperceptible corruption of sorts, as if the very fibers of his heart and brain daily willed their own misalignment. He cannot define this flaw in his nature, but he knows it is not simply a matter of lacking self-restraint. He has learned to deprive himself of the comforts that might lead him into trouble, but still the yearnings find him, livid sproutings deep in his soul beyond the reach of spade or scythe. He wonders if other men surrender to their base desires as readily as he. He has heard old men snicker wistfully about youthful lusts long since expired, and he wonders if he can dare to hope that his own urges might eventually subside. No longer a young man, at twenty-five he feels he is well past the age at which the desire of his sex should still hold him in thrall. He is old enough to recognize firsthand that all sensations grow dull with repetition — the taste of an apple, the bright relief of cool water on a dry throat, the scent of rain-soaked fields, the crunch of fresh snow. All things excite with newness and fade with routine. Life's many details pale by degrees with each passing season, but his lust alone remains unaltered, unwithered, resilient. It seems a real ailment, one for which he might seek a physician's cure. But he cannot speak of it. He sometimes wishes this hunger would transmute itself into a visible pox, so that he might at least be deserving of some sympathy from the woman who is the sole cause of his suffering.

Odd walks the narrow compass of his fire to make sure there is no danger of its spreading beyond the circle of stones. The smoldering heap coughs a plume of orange embers skyward, where they swirl around themselves high above his head and drift toward the nearby woods. No rain has fallen in more than a month, and today a steady breeze has risen out of the south from beyond Mount Misery, blowing toward the pond at Walden Woods. Odd knows he should have waited for a calmer day to clear away the brush, but he has already put off the chore a number of times, and in the end he really does not have a choice in the matter. Mr. Woburn is resolved that no inch of his land will lie fallow this season, and once the old man decides on something there is no dissuading him. Odd kicks hard at the speckled crown of a rock jutting from the dry earth, but it only wobbles in its hole like a rotting tooth. The soil here in the far corner is diseased with little outcroppings like this; anyone can tell just by looking that it will take a lot more work to ready the field for seed.

Odd's fire chews through the knobbed joints of vines and leaves and roots, spitting out white ash. Another plume of embers soars above him and reaches in vain for the treetops at the edge of the field. Odd knows from experience that it is the nature of fire to burn with a voraciousness that hides the fact of its beginning, as if its fierceness alone might prove its immortality. The unabashed gluttony of the flames frightens him. At the same time, though, he wishes they would hurry up and finish their savage business. There is plenty of other work to be done, and he would much rather sweat over an unwieldy plow — breaking up the soil with the worn-out ox that Mr. Woburn purchased last season for a few bushels of corn — than stand here anxiously watching weeds burn.

Odd suggested carting it all to the edge of the woods, where it might slowly decay under the gentle heat of nature's own invisible flames, but Mr. Woburn wanted it all burned at once. Odd thinks it best to avoid setting a fire. It is not an animal that can be harnessed or tamed. He has never lit a fire in his small cabin behind the farmhouse, although there is a perfectly serviceable cast-iron stove. The stove remains cold and dark even on the most frigid nights, when Odd prefers simply to burrow between extra layers of wool and fur and watch his breath blossom icily in the moonlit room. He likes his bed cold, and on those evenings when he refuses Emma's invitation to supper he is satisfied with cold potatoes and cold meat, which he finds far better for his digestion. But he doubts that a cold meal and a cold bed tonight will erase the image of what he has seen on the clothesline. He has not noticed a change in Emma's shape, but now he will not be able to avoid looking for it. How can he sit at her table, across from Mr. Woburn, and not trace the crescent of whalebones that are sure to be cradling her breasts?

Odd stabs at the fire with the pitchfork; a lick of flame breaks free, leaps over the stones, and hobbles squat-legged across the dead grass. He is on it at once, stamping it out with a satisfied grunt, leaving a scorched divot in the hard ground. He looks for other errant flames to quash beneath his boot heel. Odd has lived in America for fifteen years, and, like other immigrants of his generation, he is smaller than the Americans whose underfed grandfathers landed decades earlier to begin eating their way through the New World's abundance. On the streets of Concord and Boston, where his short stature singles him out as one of the newly arrived, Odd moves with self-conscious hesitation, shuffling crablike through the throngs of tall Americans as if he were not there at all. But here, out in the open, he is capable of explosive movements when necessary.

Odd has often wondered if there are other

people who feel as ill-equipped for this new world as he does. His body is a bothersome thing, laden with unruly wants, and he would gladly have left it behind in Norway with the other things that he and his family had come halfway around the world to escape. His fair skin and the layer of soft fat — which make his nose, cheeks, and chin appear as though they were formed in raw dough — give him ample protection against the New England winter, but his skin blisters in the heat of summer and flushes red at the slightest hint of embarrassment. His hair, white as talc, is too fine to offer his scalp much protection against the harsh American sun, and he has learned never to go without his wide-brimmed felt hat.

Odd envies Emma Woburn. He marvels at the way she shepherds her bulk through her daily routines with pendulous certainty. She is a hand's width taller than Odd and carries half again as much weight on her broad frame. Although she spent the first part of her life in Ireland, she has already rendered herself as imposing as any second-generation American. Odd doubts that he could reach all the way around her, though, of course, he has never tried, but he loves her for this. Odd loves her solidness, loves the deliberate trajectories of her daily chores, loves the way that she fills any open space with her gravity. Whenever Emma is in the same room, there is no corner in which he cannot feel her steady pull. Out in the fields, under the open sky, he feels himself drifting in her direction, sweeping gentle orbits through the rows of corn, over the matted vines of pumpkin and squash and melon, until Mr. Woburn yells at him to wake up and watch what he is doing. He has never had such feelings for a woman, and it should have been simple enough to tell her. He had ample opportunity before, but always something stopped him, a quiet voice whispering to him, a warning passed through generations: *desire unleashed is harder to contain than fire.*

Now it is impossible for him to speak to her of it. When Emma married Cyrus Woburn, there was nothing else Odd could think to do but go to work for her husband. It was the only way he could satisfy himself that she was happy, and it was the only way he could stay close enough to her to ensure that he did not spend the rest of his life adrift, a lifeless planet without a sun.

As he scans the boundary of his small fire, Odd runs his tongue over his teeth and stops at the obscene thing hanging useless where a stronger animal would have sprouted a fang. The small black tooth refused to fall out at the appropriate time with the rest of his infant teeth. From one year to the next it clung to its socket, an indecent thing, a baby's tooth in a man's mouth. His adult teeth pushed it away, choked it, but still the tooth hung on, dying slowly, painfully, turning yellow, then brown, then black. When he was younger, Odd used to soothe the aching tooth by sucking it as it rotted. Now the dead tooth registers no sensation whatsoever, and Odd sucks at it to soothe other things.

He walks around his fire, prodding it with the pitchfork, trying to stir up trouble so that he might have the satisfaction of crushing something else beneath his heel. He pokes at an unburned section of the pile and stops when he hears a squeal. Something dark, unrelated to the fire, moves in the tangled mass. There is a twitch, a flash of pink and gray, and then a terrified mouse clambers out of the smoking heap and perches on a fist of twigs. Odd lifts his foot high and brings his heel down savagely, stamping a small opening in the flames near the trapped animal. He kicks aside one of the stones. The mouse curls into itself and leaps. The flames lurch for it, but the mouse is quick, a dense ball of nervous muscle:

instinct and spasm unhampered by thought. It dashes through the opening and scurries away. Odd smiles, tight-lipped; even when he is by himself he keeps the tiny black tooth concealed out of habit. He watches the mouse run across the field until it diminishes to a speck and disappears into the trees. Then Odd looks skyward and frowns at the pencil-gray line of smoke he sees rising from the Concord Woods.

3
Eliot

It could easily be an October afternoon, he thinks, and not the final day of April.

He stops for a moment and stands in the middle of the empty road, taking in his surroundings as if he were surveying a recently purchased tract of land. The air is brisk, with none of the gray dampness that usually drops into the lungs like wet dough this time of year. Tall trees line either side of the road, and their leafless branches click in the steady breeze like a thousand snapping fingers. Through the trees he can see open fields of quiet, furrowed soil, vague brown humps brought into focus by the small rectangles of glass balanced on his nose. Without his spectacles, the world at a distance is a blur to him, but such is the cost of age and experience. A certain crispness in the light makes him think of his not-too-distant youth, of long afternoon shadows, of the limitless potential spread out before him.

Unharvested frosts of apple-bitten days.

The phrase leaps into Eliot Calvert's head. He pulls out a small pocket memorandum bound in Moroccan leather and secured with a roam clasp (six dollars per dozen wholesale from G. H. Derby & Co. of Geneva, New York, though Eliot sells them for more than twice this) cracks open a gold-edged page, licks the tip of a nine-cent Thoreau No. 2 pencil (the best pencil available at any price, far superior to the greasy Dixon) and jots down the words. The blank book is the most expensive kind he stocks, an outrageous price really, but he has learned not to underestimate the amount of money that people will pay to convince themselves of the value of their purchase. Eliot knows he could get them cheaper in Boston from the likes of Crosby & Nichols or Phillips & Sampson, but he prefers the imitation Russian endpapers and has grown accustomed to the particular weight and feel of the book in his coat pocket. Its retrieval is a gesture rich with intention. *Inspiration, coy mistress, flirts only with those who seek her first.* Eliot licks the tip of his pencil again but decides that this last observation is not inventive enough to deserve a line on one of the creamy-fine pages.

41

It is a perfect day for walking. Eliot instructed Silas Greene, his driver, to deposit him on the Cambridge Turnpike so that he might walk the remaining mile to Concord. He had put on his sturdy boots that morning in the expectation that he might be seized by a notion to wander. Few people use the turnpike nowadays, even though the toll has been suspended. Most prefer the less hilly Boston Road, and this is precisely why Eliot insisted that Silas take the turnpike. He awoke this morning craving solitude. It has not rained since February, and Eliot presumed, correctly, that the roads — usually impassable stretches of mud this time of year — would be hard and dusty, in excellent condition for walking.

Eliot has not packed the valise he usually brings along on overnight business. Today he comes prepared to follow his impulses; he carries a simple bundle, tied up in a tattered plaid blanket that he has knotted around the end of a long stick. Simplicity is the key. He resumes walking down the center of the road with an exaggerated stride. The bundle on the stick bounces on his shoulder, an incongruous accompaniment to his finely tailored blue coat and bright yellow vest. He instructed Silas to return to Boston and inform Mrs. Calvert

42

that her husband has decided to spend the night in Concord. Eliot revels in the near-spontaneity of his decision. Surely Margaret would understand that the few diversions available in rustic Concord are of the most innocent sort. Besides, Eliot is not a man to indulge in reckless entertainments. In fact, the only indulgence he ever seeks these days (though he could never confess it to Margaret) is simply to be left alone.

Eliot follows the Cambridge Turnpike to the Lexington Road, where the wheel ruts of muddier days form faults and ridges that he negotiates with some difficulty. He inhales the tang of rich earth, envisions a bucolic tableau: sturdy men plowing fields, casting seeds, studying the open sky. Boston is the finest city in America, but its streets are so plagued by carriages and trolleys and other horse-drawn conveyances that all one ever smells there is the accumulated dung of transportation. City officials have tried numerous solutions, but they never do more than move the great stinking piles from one side of the street to the other. In Boston, one can no longer smell the earth buried beneath the city. The fresh air of Concord invigorates him. And Eliot finds something more in it today, a soft smell of burning wood so distinct he can practically hear the crackling embers.

Perhaps that is why he is thinking of autumn. There is no reason that the scent of burning wood should not just as well make him think of winter, or of Christmas, or even of a cool New England summer evening, but there is no logic to how the mind answers the senses. He used to consider autumn the most delightful time of year, ripe with the promise of all the things yet to be done. Without the oppressive heat of summer to slow one's hand, grand accomplishments used to feel truly within reach during that magical season. At least that was how he felt as a young man, before dreary poets taught him to regard autumn as the last flush of summer, a harbinger of the season of cold death. Poets, he thinks, are intent on ruining everything. Playwrights, on the other hand, know how to render palatable life's most harrowing moments. A stage play with an unhappy ending can lead one to a much needed catharsis, whereas an unhappy poem simply leaves one, well, unhappy. Far better to write plays, he thinks.

Eliot's last trip to Concord occurred five months earlier, when he answered an invitation to a dinner commemorating issue no. XIV of *The Dial,* that strange and unprofitable transcendentalist magazine, the publishers of which — Mr. Brown and Mr. Little — had obliged every notable bookseller in New England to acknowledge as the pinnacle of American thought. Eliot had sometimes thought *The Dial*'s poetry passable, but he found the philosophical essays — repetitive ruminations on the soul's infinitude, its immanence in nature, etc., etc., etc. — impossible to digest. That was what he told the other booksellers who attended the dinner. Each man at the table had, in turn, been compelled to stand and offer a few words of admiration for the magazine. Eliot thought he set himself apart with his witty contribution: *"I can only say, with deep regret, that the contents of* The Dial, *unlike this evening's marvelous repast, have often proven quite indigestible."* Unfortunately, the other diners were of a humorless sort and did not give his clever quip the appreciation it deserved. As Eliot now recalls, the food and drink truly were the only memorable aspects of the evening.

Eliot had agreed to attend the dinner solely for the purpose of meeting *The Dial*'s distinguished editor, Ralph Waldo Emerson. To Eliot's great disappointment, however, Mr. Emerson was absent, as were the magazine's other principal architects, Margaret

45

Fuller and Theodore Parker. Miss Fuller was said to be out in the Western territories, preaching women's rights on the frontier, and Mr. Parker was pursuing philosophical abstractions somewhere in England. It was no wonder the magazine ceased shortly thereafter. Eliot's disappointment in the evening deepened when he learned that most of the other guests in attendance were also booksellers. The conversation proved more business than literary, and Eliot drank more than was his custom.

So that explains it, Eliot thinks, savoring the Concord air as he negotiates the humps and pits in the road. The night of the dinner had been filled with the heavy musk of harvest. Obviously that is why he is now thinking of autumn, of apple cider, mulled wine, falling leaves, and great stacks of pale yellow squash and bright orange pumpkins.

Eliot stops again in mid-stride, though this time he nearly trips as he braces himself against the slap of memory. *Pumpkins!* He had almost forgotten the appalling sight. He sorts through the foggy recollections of that night, a process that requires him to remain still as his mind lurches backward. He removes his spectacles, twirls the rectangles of glass in one hand and rubs his eyes with the other, his legs wide in the middle of the road, each foot planted on the high crest of a wheel rut.

The memory comes back to him now in full. He had decided to return home directly after the disappointing dinner. Silas had taken ill, so Eliot had driven himself, but he lost his way looking for the turnpike in the gray moonlight. The grog had apparently muddled his sense of direction, though Eliot was certain that he had not consumed enough to invent so gross a vision as what he witnessed from his perch atop the carriage. Eliot recalls the distasteful details one by one, assembling the scene like a stagehand: a dark sky, bright fringed clouds half shrouding a full moon, a field of ripe pumpkins, and the grunting brute, a pale, white-haired Caliban, hunched forward over a large gourd, trousers at his ankles — an onanist in the pumpkin patch, befouling the fruits of autumn. *What could one expect this far from the civilizing influence of Boston?* Eliot is appalled anew by the memory. There is no shortage of perversions in the city, he thinks, but at least in Boston men pursue their unsavory penchants with discretion, and men know well the places to avoid should they prefer not to witness such pursuits.

Eliot returns his spectacles to his nose,

wraps the wires behind his ears, and shakes off the memory. He will not allow the troubling image to interfere with the purpose of his current visit. Another twenty minutes of walking brings him to the edge of Concord. He passes a school set back from the road, and farther on he sees homes with wide front porches, pitched roofs, shuttered windows overgrown with ivy, white picket fences. The Lexington Road takes him past the First Unitarian Church into the center of town, and before he reaches the courthouse on the square he turns left onto Mill Dam Street and walks past both the mill and the dam. A team of four oxen pulling a heavy cartload of timber enters the square and turns onto the Boston Road. The wearied driver does not bother to lift his eyes from the reins. Mill Dam becomes Main Street; white clapboard houses give way to a long block of redbrick storefronts.

Eliot slows his pace. People saunter about at the edges of the dirt road, tipping hats, nodding pleasantly. The sudden blast of a horn sends him scurrying aside to allow the Boston stagecoach to pass. Concord is not so bustling as Boston, but it is a theater of business nonetheless, as the dust and rattle of passing wagons seem to insist. He follows Main Street to the address he has been given, strolling beneath the painted wooden signs that hang above a variety of shops: "Pierce's Harnesses"; "Brown's Clothing Co."; "Mann's Boots and Rubbers"; "John Parkhurst — Druggist Specializing in Pure Wines and Liquor for Medicinal Purposes." There are more taverns than he expected — and at their doors a steady traffic of tradesmen, teamsters, and the Irish laborers newly arrived to complete the rail line to Fitchburg. Here, Eliot thinks, a man might satisfy his every want, and discover a few new ones. He surveys the storefronts along Concord's Main Street, and he is pleased to confirm that there is no bookseller on the block.

In Boston, the business of bookselling is ever-present, a miasma of commerce easily mistaken for culture. Eliot never envisioned a livelihood grounded in ledgers, and lately he has grown weary of the relentless urgency of buying and selling. Boston publishers are forever at his heels, inconstant curs, ingratiating one minute and vicious the next; no sooner are they finished with the collection of one debt than they are encouraging him to incur new ones. In the past week alone, Eliot paid bills and placed orders with Crocker & Brewster, Gould, Kendall & Lincoln, Saxton & Kelt, Strong, Sherburne & Co., and Jenks & Palmer. The upper end of

Washington Street is crammed with publishing houses, twenty or more, and though many have shops of their own, their agents endlessly distribute flyers and notices and catalogues, proffering their newest books to other shop owners, boasting improved editions, promising discounts and bulk pricing and generous terms of credit. And near the top of this clamoring row, where Washington Street stumbles past School Street, William Davis Ticknor sits confidently on his publishing throne above the Old Corner Bookstore as if he were king.

Eliot wonders if Ticknor will ever understand that he is in no small way the reason for this visit to Concord today. As far as Eliot is concerned, the thriving Old Corner Bookstore should really be *his,* and not Ticknor's. Sooner or later, Eliot is certain, he would have been made a partner in the firm of Carter, Hendee & Co. if not for Ticknor — a man with little experience in the world of books — who came along and snatched up the business: shop, stock, and publishing house. The great injustice Eliot suffered has all the elements of a fine melodrama — a tragic tale of promise withheld, a moral for the common working man — and Eliot would happily write it himself were it not for fear of the unseemly vitriol that would surely spew from his pen. Eliot has decided instead that if he cannot compete with Ticknor in Boston he will take the competition elsewhere. Here, in Concord, out from under Ticknor's shadow, he has good reason to hope that a second bookshop might finally purchase him the liberty he has so long sought.

Walking down Main Street, Eliot passes the Shakespeare Hotel, where he will spend the night; he passes Concord's carriage factory, a dry-goods store, a haberdashery, and pauses in front of a jeweler's window, where gold and silver watch fobs hang from delicate chains. It amazes him, the effort people expend in creating objects for the sole purpose of ornamenting other objects. Watch fobs, hat pins, tie tacks, snuffboxes, cigar cases, opera-glass chains, wallets, reticules, the whole lot of *things* that people use to coddle their other *things.* He has seen men with a half-dozen fobs — commemorating everything from political campaigns to wedding anniversaries — dangling from their watch chains like military medals, as if by decorating themselves these men might convince others of the fullness of their lives.

One of the fobs on display in the shop window is cast in the image of an open book roughly the size of a silver eagle dollar. It sits next to a campaign fob bearing the likeness of the unfortunate William Henry Harrison, "Old Tippecanoe," whose presidential campaign three and a half years earlier proved more successful than the four-hour inaugural speech he delivered to the cold, wet crowd gathered on the Capitol grounds beneath a raging snowstorm. As a result of the infamous speech, longer than any in presidential history, Harrison fell victim to a severe ague, which sent him directly from the inaugural podium to an early grave and catapulted the uninspiring vice president, John Tyler, into the highest office of the land. After months of hearing campaign slogans for "Tippecanoe and Tyler Too," the country now had only Tyler. Eliot has read editorials claiming that President Tyler's vehement support of states' rights during the past three years has deepened the rift between the Northern and the Southern states, but Eliot does not concern himself with such matters. As a man dedicated to the art of the written word, he believes that he needs to rise above the quotidian, to aspire to something more universal than the time-bound debates of politicians and abolitionists.

Eliot stares at the fobs on display and fingers the watch chain drooping naked between his buttonhole and his waistcoat pocket. He does not think the book-shaped fob is large enough to hold the inscription that appears on the recently amended sign above his Boston storefront: "Eliot R. Calvert, Purveyor of Fine Books, Maps of Impeccable Quality, Stationery and Writing Supplies, Toy Books, Games, Apparatus for Schools." There are more items listed on the sign, now, than there were when he first opened his shop a decade earlier. The last part of the list, in particular, depressed him. He hated the fact that he desperately needed the measly profits from primers and pocket maps and copybooks and writing papers and cheap nibs. No one had warned him that a bookseller is little more than a well-read hardware salesman. The sign above Eliot's shop expanded over the years, advertising an increasingly varied stock, but it still does not, of course, mention the other, highly profitable materials that patrons might also acquire by arrangement. *Discretion Assured.* He has considered simplifying the sign, now that he is about to open a new location. "Calvert Books — Boston, Concord, and Beyond." That would easily fit on the fob. Perhaps just "Calvert Books" would suffice. He pictures the fob hanging from his chain, a counterweight to the gold watch he consults with dramatic flair whenever one of the Washington Street publishers refuses to settle on a reasonable price.

A small paper tag hangs from the fob in the window. Eliot stoops, but the tag is facedown. Out of the corner of his eye, he sees the proprietor watching him. If he wants to learn the price, he will have to enter the shop. Eliot knows the tricks shopkeepers employ to lure a customer across the threshold, the necessary prelude to getting said customer to draw forth his purse; he has used such ploys many times himself. Eliot straightens and turns to leave, but he catches his reflection in the window, the bright flash of his spectacles, and stops to study it. His face has changed considerably over the years, but the ambition is still there, tucked away behind the well-fed softness of middle age. His once sharp jaw is now buried under an extra layer of flesh, but these changes do not worry him. The engravings of the great tragedians in his bookshop show the same changes. His chest is still sound as an oak barrel, even if his shoulders have begun to slump forward under the invisible burdens that no man can hope to escape. His hair is still thick and dark, and, though his vision is not what it once was, the blue of his eyes suffers none of the cloudiness that afflicts some of his best customers, who no doubt spend too many nights sighing over candlelit pages. Eliot gives his reflection a nod of approval. *Happy is the man,* he thinks, *whose countenance is reflected thus.*

Eliot turns from the window, scribbling this last thought in his expensive pocket memorandum. If he loiters any longer at the window, he knows he will not be able to resist the temptation to enter the shop and examine the fob more closely, discuss its craftsmanship with the jeweler, feel its heft, dangle it from his own watch chain experimentally. Eliot walks on past other storefronts, taking note of the goods available and the size and lettering of the signs hanging above. He nods politely at a young couple strolling past. He observes the cut of the man's clothes, hopelessly out of fashion, and he can tell that the woman's jacket is too thin for such a chilly day, but with no parade of children behind them the young man walks tall, shoulders back, and the young woman clings weightlessly to his arm. The day is theirs to use as they wish, the world wide open to them to explore or ignore as they see fit.

Eliot shakes his head. He has no reason to feel ashamed of such thoughts, has he?

There are men who would run from the duties that he accepts without complaint. He sees these fugitives every day on the streets of Boston, nameless men at easels mixing watery paints with bristly nubbins, skinny young men outside dark-windowed taverns, writing on scraps of paper, muttering in rhyme, veterans of forgotten jobs strung together to support their stubborn devotion to fiddle or flute, penniless old men who refuse to abandon the fruitless dreams of their youth. Yet sometimes, beneath his contempt, Eliot wonders how it would be to switch places with one of them for a day, to be a man whose sole purpose in rising from bed was to make manifest the airy shapes that populated his imagination.

And that is the real reason for his coming to Concord, is it not? If all goes as planned, the additional income from the new bookshop will afford him that which he covets most of all: *time.* He pulls a card from his coat pocket and checks the name of the man he has come to meet. It distresses him to think that his lot could be bound to such a person, but the world is indeed a vast stage with a great variety of players. In business, such liaisons are regrettable but necessary. If his new bookshop succeeds, he will hire another clerk. As the owner of two bookstores, he could not possibly be expected to involve himself in the daily details of receipts and ledgers, and he might even give over management of both shops to a trusted employee for one, or two, or even three days a week. *Three days* in which to sit and work on his plays! Given such a luxury, surely he might at last finish his most recent play, *The House of Many Windows.* The manager of the Boston Museum, Moses Kimball, has all but agreed to produce it and has encouraged Eliot to complete the manuscript, but Eliot thus far has found himself at an impasse. He needs time to revise. And there are financial matters to consider: the play will conclude with a great conflagration, an unheard-of and expensive spectacle. In the third act, an entire house will be burned to the ground, right before the audience. Moses Kimball made the suggestion himself, but there remains the question of cost. There is always the question of cost.

If his new business venture proves profitable, Eliot will finance *The House of Many Windows* himself; he might even rent an apartment with an inspiring view of the new Public Gardens, where he can sit alone with his notebooks. Eliot has not mentioned this part of his plan to Margaret. She would likely voice opposition — but what of it? He should not need to have her approval. He knows of other men who secretly rent rooms at midday for far more ignoble endeavors.

Eliot reaches the empty storefront on Main Street, where, as the agent informed him, the previous owner worked doggedly until the day he met with an untimely accident. Eliot takes another deep breath of the crisp air. The smell he detected back on the turnpike has grown stronger, as if all Concord's residents conspired to pack their stoves with green wood today. Eliot steps back from the empty storefront and imagines his name hanging from the signpost; he thinks again of the watch fob bearing the same inscription. He studies the windows, the red door, the peeling paint and broken glass, and then he looks up to the roofline and raises an eyebrow. In the distance, a thick finger of smoke floats ominously into the perfect blue sky.

4
CALEB

They will think the light is for them.

The Reverend Caleb Ephraim Dowdy sees the miraculous light in the woods before the others do. He sees the beginnings of it, as if time slowed for him alone so that he might mark the infinitesimal motions of things in the open field around them: a beating insect wing, a budding plant, the lengthening of an eyelash, the eruption of a match head. He watches the leading edge of the light slicing through the air like the prow of a ship, and he barely resists the urge to drop to his knees.

Filtering through the barren interstices of limb and branch, the unmistakable glow of benediction falls upon the believers gathered under the clear, cold sky, a fitting sign for those craving affirmation. They gasp when the light touches them, and they believe they are feeling nothing less than the hand of God.

Suspicious at first, Caleb reassures himself that this is not a dream. In his dreams, he is free from the headaches and the shaking hands and the leaden remorse that hangs like a pendulum in his belly during his waking hours. Caleb rubs his temples, tries to wipe away the cloying perfume that addles his brain. His short black hair is plastered to his forehead, held in place by the sheen of sweat covering his round pale face. It makes him shiver in the cool air. He is a thin, nervous man, but the robes he wears lend him some bulk and help to hide his trembling. He slides his fingers from his temples to his eyes and presses them gently. He briefly thinks that he might press harder, drive his thumbs in all the way and thus bring an end to the torment. There is no discernible cause for the constant pain behind his eyes, nothing that can be leeched or blistered. He can find temporary relief in only one remedy, but it has the unfortunate effect of doubling the discomfort afterward.

Caleb tries to hold the attention of his followers, thirty or so in number, but it is hard to compete with the flickering light that grows stronger by the minute. He knows each of them personally. He knows their histories, some better than others. At the edge of the gathering, he sees the widow

60

Esther Harrington and the reformed drunkard Amos Stiles standing next to each other, elbows touching, and for no particular reason Caleb wonders if they have begun sharing a bed. He imagines the savage cries issuing from the widow's dry lips under the rutting weight of the drunkard. Caleb presses his eyes again with thumb and forefinger and tries to focus on the reason they are all here.

They stand in a field that runs right up to the edge of the Concord Woods. In the middle of this field, the stone foundations of an old farmhouse squat knee-high in the overgrown grass, and scattered among the forgotten rows of dried corn stalks are the remnants of shingles and rotted timbers and the bald spokes of a wagon wheel. Among the crumbled foundations, a few charred beams outline the decayed skeleton of the house that burned over a year ago. No one ever returned to the land, and Caleb has told the men and women gathered before him that today they will reclaim it in God's name. Caleb's followers huddle together against the sharp April chill; it is hard for them to believe that tomorrow will be the first day of May. A man wearing the soiled canvas overalls of a carpenter paces off dimensions in the dry yellow husks and points to the ghosts of future steps, doors, and windows. He carries the tools of his trade — hammer, saw, measuring tape — swinging from loops sewn at his waist. His lip bulges with a plug of tobacco, and every few steps he spits into his hand and rubs it on his sleeve, out of respect for the soon-to-be-consecrated ground.

Caleb explains to them that they are far enough from Boston to elude the taint of corruption, but not so far as to invite the temptations of the wilderness. He is disgusted with the city: the fetid open sewers of the Back Bay, the greedy merchants, and the decadent homes at Pemberton Square and Beacon Hill. Caleb spent most of the night preparing his sermon, readying himself to preach to his followers and fill them with the trembling passion that is more dependable than faith alone. He feels the excitement of a soldier about to charge into battle, and he will not allow his moment to be stolen by the light coming through the trees.

Caleb takes a deep breath, raises his arms, and shouts, "Scripture tells us, *'Ye are the light of the world. A city that is set on a hill cannot be hid.'* Our fathers and their fathers before them came to build that city, the city on the hill. And yet what has become of it?

What have we allowed to happen? Boston is no longer a beacon of righteousness. Our great city has fallen into the hands of corrupt men sated to distraction by the bountiful rewards that heaven bestowed upon their forefathers."

Caleb watches his followers nod in assent, but he sees them steal sideways glances at the flickering light. He will not be able to hold their interest much longer. They are faithful, but he knows that they have been waiting for a sign.

The field where Caleb and his followers intend to build their church abuts the last remaining bit of woods in Concord, a few hundred acres of untouched forest stretching from the edge of town to Walden Pond and the river. Most of the trees in Concord have been chopped down to make room for the growing town. Where there had once spread a dense crown of pines and oaks and sugar maples, now the rich soil of New England lies exposed to sun and sky, furrowed by plow, bought, owned, and sold by men. And this, Caleb believes, is as it should be. He has not brought his hatchet today, and his hands feel empty and useless as he eyes the surrounding trees. When men allow God's gifts to go unexploited, they show contempt for the Almighty's plan. Far better to cut down all the forests in America than for man to think that he might create his own Eden here among the trees. He is disgusted by utopians like George Ripley and Bronson Alcott, who think they can re-create the world in their own image. Caleb points to the empty branches in the woods and waits until he has the congregation's attention. He decides to improvise.

"You are right to gaze at the barren trees yonder. Why are they not festooned with greenery? What do they tell us? *Depravity!* Everywhere we see signs of man's depravity. The seasons, in which some men erroneously find cause for celebration, are evidence of man's wickedness. Why do we not have eternal summer? Because our first parents chose sin. They chose knowledge over obedience, and every generation since has made the same choice. The changing seasons are evidence that we are a fallen people, evidence that in this world we will find neither perfection nor salvation."

Caleb knows that there are men who think otherwise: the mystics and the spiritualists, the Swedenborgians and the Fourierists, and the so-called transcendentalists — pagans all of them. These men claim to look no further than nature for their comfort and reward. They seek the infinite in every bud and leaf, find revelations in birdsong and thunder, and pretend to read the mind of God by watching the wind blow. They fail to realize that it was nature, bountiful nature, that led men astray in the first place, so much so that God has entirely given up on them, allowing them to do as they please without recrimination or punishment. The Methodists and the Unitarians and the Trinitarians are all too tolerant of the pantheists, who disguise their idolatry as poetry and hide in leafy shadows at Brook Farm and Fruitlands and Hopedale, living like animals among the trees.

"And thus," Caleb continues, "it is only just that we come here to lay the cornerstone of our new church at the doorstep of Mr. Emerson."

Caleb's followers are aware that they are not among the elect. They cling to the hope that they may as yet be chosen, but they do not know that it is Caleb Ephraim Dowdy alone who will do the choosing. He has revealed nothing of his plan to them, and he does not tell them his true purpose in founding this new church. These simple people cannot comprehend the dark mystery that has taken him a lifetime to realize: that the path to revelation lay through damnation.

Caleb opens his Bible and holds down the annotated pages with his thumbs. The breeze ruffles the edges of the thin paper. He worked late into the night, rewriting the Latin benediction into a blasphemous tangle. None of his followers will understand a word of what he is about to say, but it is not them he means to offend. This patch of earth will be more than the bedrock of their new congregation. It is here that Caleb will put the Almighty to the test, here that he will at last tempt God to give evidence that He is not some pitiful illusion.

Caleb looks up from his text and feels a cold hand seize his heart. There, at the edge of the field, he sees two old women; he guesses that they are sisters by the similarity of their mannish features and their close-cropped silvered hair. He thinks he might have seen them once before, but only from a distance. They speak to each other behind cupped palms while mimicking the gestures the carpenter made earlier, outlining imaginary steeples and doors. And after each gesture they point to a different part of their bodies — an elbow, a thigh, a forearm — as if they were casting a spell. He starts to tremble as they approach. Absently, he reaches for the hatchet he has not brought today. He thinks of Revelation, the Gospels, Genesis, but he recalls nothing about the Devil assuming the form of two old women.

His followers take no notice of the women, so enraptured are they by the light in the woods. It grows brighter, as if moving closer. The women hobble toward Caleb with agonizing slowness, and he fully expects their ancient faces to be his last vision in this world before their curses send him spiraling into a realm of indescribable suffering. He braces himself for judgment and whispers, *"Therefore thou art inexcusable, O man, whosoever thou art that judgest: for wherein thou judgest another, thou condemnest thyself; for thou that judgest doest the same things."*

The old women stand before him, withered faces, twisted bodies; their demeanor gives belated credence to the fears of an earlier generation in Salem. They mumble to each other in a strange language; then the taller of the two speaks in fractured English.

"Prominte!" Her eyes are black, her blind companion's milky white. "We are begging your pardon."

"This is to be *kostel?*" the shorter woman with milky eyes asks impatiently. She turns to her dark-eyed friend, seeking out her shadow, whispers a question, and then says again, "*Kostel!* Yes, *kostel* — ah, church, yes? You build church?"

"How do you know this?" Caleb sputters. He notices that the others have begun to drift toward the light, leaving him alone. Thus does the hand of the Almighty rescue the faithful, he thinks. The Lord is shepherding them from the chasm about to open beneath his feet, guiding them away from the thunderbolt about to fall from the sky.

"We are hearing of this," says the blind woman.

"We are wondering," the dark-eyed woman adds. "You are making with bones, maybe?"

"Yes. Yes," says the other woman. "You will build for us church of bones?"

Caleb's hands tremble as if they will fly from their wrists, and the empty field seems to move away in all directions. He becomes conscious of his skeleton, brittle beneath his skin and muscles, a flimsy frame for an unworthy soul.

The dark-eyed woman swings her skinny forearm from the elbow and points emphatically to her wrist. "*Kost.* Bone. Bones. *Rozumite?* Understanding you? Yes?"

"Like trees, to build with bones." The blind woman crosses her forearms in a

68

pantomime of stacking firewood, and she holds Caleb with her milky-white stare. "In old country. In *Kutná Hora.* We have beautiful chapel made from the bones. The altar with beautiful ornamentings from bones. All bones. Not animal. People bones. White, beautiful bones."

"Sedlec Kostnice," the other woman added as an explanation. "It is what you call *Beinhaus,* yes? Full with bones."

"You will build here a new church like this, with people bones?"

Caleb closes his eyes and holds his breath. He waits for the cataclysm. He waits to be smashed, swallowed, pulverized. He waits for his bones to be ripped from his flesh and stacked before him. He waits to feel the grip of God's vengeful hand, waits for his heart to burst under the pressure. He waits for proof, confirmation in the form of condemnation. But nothing happens. Caleb opens his eyes and exhales. The women are still there, and now they do not seem like witches or devils any more than did any of the old women he regularly met on the steps of his former church. He starts to say something but is interrupted by the astonished cries of recognition from the members of the congregation. They point to the woods, and their astonishment mingles with disappointment. The light is not a benediction, not a miracle of the Holy Ghost at all, but something even more unthinkable. The woods are on fire.

Caleb hears the old women mutter sadly behind him.

"Strasny. Strasny."

He looks at the smoke curling above the treetops, hoping that he might still find some sign, something to acknowledge his trespass, but what he sees forming in the rising smoke is nothing so encouraging as that. What he sees staring down at him is the same terrified visage that has been plaguing his waking dreams for years.

5
HENRY DAVID

David Henry (now Henry David) runs as fast as his lungs allow. He stumbles over roots extruded like fat gray knuckles, swats the low branches scratching his face. They wasted no time discussing it. Edward took the boat, paddling downriver toward the center of town, and Henry set off on foot, running through the untouched woods, the fire crawling behind him, taking its time, taunting him. Whoever arrives first will rouse the citizens of Concord. The unthinkable loss of the woods will surely spur their fellow Concordians to action, Henry believes. At the very least, he feels confident that the venerable name of Edward's father will wield authority enough to summon volunteers. Aided by the current, Edward's route will likely be faster, but they hope that Henry will encounter someone along the way who might help hold back the flames until Edward can return with more men.

After running a quarter of a mile, Henry is already gasping for breath, but he does not stop. Desperation pursues him, driving him over uneven terrain thickly cluttered with moldering leaves and twigs and fallen branches, the composts of seasons past. And as Henry runs, chest heaving and arms flailing, the effort reminds him of another moment of instruction, not a childhood punishment, this, but a penalty incurred by his own misjudgment. His third year at Harvard — a place where he stood out in his old green jacket while all others wore the required black that he could not afford — lonely for the company of his family, he left Cambridge and set out for Concord on foot. The way was long, and before he was halfway home his feet were swollen and blistered so badly that he removed his shoes and continued the remaining miles in tattered stockings. He arrived with feet torn and bloodied. He limped for weeks afterward. Yet this did not diminish his affinity for walking, did not at all lessen his ardor for life in the wilderness. If there was a lesson to be learned from his blistered feet, it was only that punishment could exist independently of guilt, in which case it was simply misfortune. But the lesson of misfortune is a portion of knowledge like any other, likewise awakened by experience and etched upon the tabula rasa, which is not quite so blank as many have thought.

What lesson then, Henry asks himself, is his current experience awakening? He knew when he struck the match that there had been no rain for weeks. He knew the wind was strong, the grass dry, the woods asleep. These are not bits of innate wisdom; these are not universal truths that transcend experience; these are the lessons that one pieces together from living. To not know them is not to be guilty or reprehensible, only ignorant. But at what point does ignorance become *culpable?* A man so inclined might avoid experience entirely, he thinks, might leave his society behind and live alone in nature, thereby preserving the animal innocence that any act of knowing dispels. But are there not times when it would be inexcusable *not* to know?

These thoughts are not helpful to Henry at present. He keeps running, imagining that he can feel the heat of the fire at his back. He looks over his shoulder and the smoke is no longer visible, but he can smell it; he carries it with him. He is an able wanderer, a vigorous walker, but not at all adept at running great distances. His lungs protest, but he ignores their viscous whimper, forces his legs to rise and fall. He runs through tangled underbrush, through dried snarls of huckleberries, blackberries, barberries. Earlier that morning, in a marshy recess near the river, he and Edward found skunk cabbages already in bloom — *Symplocarpus foetidus* — and he now thinks he sees a cluster of mayflowers, but he dares not pause to confirm whether he has indeed spotted the first *Epigaea repens* of the year. He can identify by name every plant and vine and withered berry that he crushes in his panicked stride, and he recalls the classifications he learned in natural history from Harvard's librarian, Thaddeus William Harris, a man from whom he would have liked to learn more about the emerging science of entomology, if only that he might be able to curse with accuracy the nagging insects flitting about his eyes and sticking to the sweat on the back of his neck.

His legs grow tired, and he feels heavy breaths scraping the bottom of his lungs, dredging up a coppery paste. He contracted a sickness nine years earlier, and as a result his lungs are often feeble things, unwilling to tolerate the exertions he demands of them. They are the reluctant engines of his excursions, sometimes weighing on him like stowaways. He has to pamper them during the days of cold and damp, but not today. He imagines his chest is made of tempered steel. He forces himself to run faster than he feels capable of running, through thickening woods, past budding oaks and birches and white pines, past alders and maples — two more miles to town, by his estimate. In all likelihood, Edward will reach it first by boat, but there is still a chance that Henry will find help along the way, someone who might sound an alarm or carry word ahead of him by faster means.

On his left, the woods begin to thin, then open onto a cleared field, and Henry sees a man behind a pair of oxen, plowing his dry fields. The man pauses and watches him stumble through the undergrowth. Henry waves his arms above his head as if he were drowning. Urgency does not permit him to consider his appearance.

"Help! Fire!"

That is what Henry yells, but the words come out thin and damp, with hardly a breath to ride on; they sound more like coughs than discernible bits of language. The farmer does not leave his oxen; he is not interested enough to come nearer, but curiosity keeps him from plowing on. He waits for Henry to trip out of the tangled brambles and half run, half hobble up to him, pausing every few steps to catch his breath.

"There . . . is . . . a . . . fire . . ."

The farmer looks at Henry's head as if it were a tree stump to be cleared from the land.

"You are trespassing, sir," the farmer says, casting his eyes possessively over the woods abutting his field. Henry follows the farmer's eyes, knows that the man must be able to see the smoke behind him. With each passing moment, the fire claims another tree, and Henry cannot fathom why the man is so slow to offer aid.

"Please." Henry can hardly breathe. He sees brilliant flashes of color at the corners of his eyes and is afraid that he might faint. "It is moving . . . rapidly. I require your assistance . . . at once."

The farmer makes a show of squinting, as if he were trying to decipher a message scrawled above the horizon. He removes his straw hat, the wide brim frayed like a collection of loose matchsticks, scratches at his long gray muttonchops, then draws a line through the air with hat and hand.

"The land from there to there belongs to me. My trees, my property."

Not quite understanding, still dizzied from his exertions, Henry points to the faint wisp of smoke beyond the invisible boundary.

"The . . . woods . . . are . . . *burning.*"

"I see no fire in *my* woods," the man says sharply. "Whatever lies beyond is not mine."

Henry is dumbfounded by the absurd possibility that the man will leave him without promising aid. He feels he can run no farther; his lungs will not tolerate it. He waves his arms weakly and stomps the ground with tired feet, trying to circulate some life back into them. He can hear the regret in his own voice and wishes he did not sound so like a child.

"I have set a fire, sir . . . and it is spreading. I must have your help."

The frayed hat returns to the farmer's head. He grabs the reins decisively and barks something to the oxen, which resume pulling the plow's heavy blade through the baked soil.

"Your fire is none of my stuff," the farmer says. "Please keep it, and yourself, off my property."

Henry's fear is realized then. He can think of nothing he might say to convince this man of the dire threat looming in the woods. What this man cannot claim as his own, he appears content to disregard. The farmer turns and, without so much as a glance at the darkening plume, resumes his work. Henry is astonished. He had not thought he would encounter indifference, had not considered that he might have difficulty finding help. When these woods are lost, Henry thinks, the loss will be felt by all, not just by the man who wields ownership of the land.

Back through the woods, Henry must keep running, heavy legs swinging like upright scissors, cutting half successfully through knotted vegetation and dried effigies from the last season: calyx, flagroot, thoroughwort, cinquefoil, tower mustard, nightshade. A few months hence, he would normally expect to see a profusion of trumpetweed, honeysuckle, Virginian Rhexia, drooping Neottia, and the bright yellow button buds of tansy, but he doubts that the charred earth behind him will adorn itself with such a display this summer. Even now, the hopeful roots and seedlings of summer's fruit lie curled expectantly beneath the cold soil, unaware of their dismal future. Henry trips, falls, scrapes his knees through the coarse fabric of his pants, and is up again and running. He does not stop, though it strikes him as useless, this desperate flight. With each step, the fire claims another inch of woods. Henry can do nothing to halt its progress as he runs toward uncertain aid.

And what is to keep him from walking away? The fire cannot touch him where he is now. Nothing prevents him from disavowing knowledge of the fire and its origin. He and Edward could have entered into such an agreement and then set out in different directions, feigning ignorance, keeping their agency to themselves, leaving their reputations unscathed.

He cannot help but wonder how he came so suddenly to be in this predicament, after such a peaceful morning. If he were to stop running and stand still in this quiet part of the Concord Woods, there would seem to be no cause for concern. As long as he tells no one, the tragedy seems as yet not quite real. Then he thinks of Edward, paddling with the current, carrying the news to an unsuspecting audience. The fire exists only for the two of them, for now. How many people, Henry wonders, must recognize a thing for it to be real?

They will say that only a fool would have struck a match on a day such as today. An accusation to which one might retort that only a fool would consent to give a match to a man who announced the intention to use it on a day such as today, and yet they had found just such a man. Strange fortune. Henry and Edward possessed no match when they started. At the day's beginning, they had no means to cause this tragedy. The insignificant events that occurred to make the fire possible were few compared with the multitude of conditions that might have prevented it. What if the shoemaker they happened upon near the river had not possessed a match? What if he had been unwilling to give them one? What if the matches had been damp? What if it had rained? What if Henry had simply told Edward that he did not have a taste for fish chowder? How rapidly the unplanned cause produces the unexpected effect. It takes only a moment to reverse all the moments that have come before.

Just a day earlier, Henry felt certain that he had arrived at the solution to his lifelong indecision. Should he teach, or farm, or write, or take up a trade? Should he be an observer of men, a philosopher, a chronicler of the world in which so many live and that so many ignore? Should he build things? The young country needs homes and roads and bridges and machines of all sorts in order to advance and improve men's lives. Henry's untested skills are many and they vie for his attention, but, only yesterday, he believed that he had at last conquered their dissidence, and he thought the occasion a fit cause for taking a holiday on the river. The result is not what he envisioned, but his determination is unchanged. When he returns home from this misadventure, he thinks, he will solidify his new commitment in the journal that he began seven years earlier. He composes the new entry in his head as he runs. He will write this down to ensure that he does not drift from his true purpose:

Having passed the greater part of my life mired in indecision, I have decided at last how I intend to pass the balance of my days. *The Dial* is finished, and so is that corner of my being. There will be no other magazine to publish my simple poems and wandering thoughts. The world before me is of too much consequence to be merely observed. I must spread roots in it and become a man of practical concerns. Henceforth I shall sign my name *Henry David Thoreau — Civil Engineer.* The world does not want for another self-assured scribbler, possessed of a surfeit of words and little of necessity to say. What use has our world of another such man? What progress can be hoped from these labors? To have a tangible effect, to feel the weight of one's accomplishment in the palm of one's own hand — progress with heft! — this is the divine union of invention and reward. I have decided! I shall make pencils, still. I shall make their manufacture and perfection my work. The drill, the saw, the lathe — these shall be my tools. Plumbago and Bavarian clay, minerals from earth, galvanic batteries, baked pencil leads — these shall be my trade. Far better than the ungrounded ideas and airy pursuits that frustrate those men who would call themselves my contemporaries.

It was Edward who had insisted on a fish chowder, and Henry might have refused, argued against it. But he did not, so he cannot disburden himself of the responsibility. He cannot wriggle free from the logic that has clamped shut upon some guilty lobe of his brain. Every second of every day, a man is the sum effect of every second that has touched him before; he routinely encounters influences that will produce changes and actions that he cannot begin to predict or understand. And yet to acknowledge the complexity of these causes and motives was not to disallow agency. In that, all men are equal, even the cloistered monk — equally innocent, equally guilty. A man is not wholly responsible for what he becomes, but he is absolutely accountable for who he is.

Henry keeps running, though not so fast as before. His legs have become heavy posts, and his chest feels as though it is about to collapse under its own weight. His heart pounds against his sternum as if it might burst from his chest. Henry begins to worry that he will not make it to Concord, that he will expire right here, alone, and be overtaken by the flames. And then he sees that he is not alone in the woods after all. There is another wanderer ahead, a stout man with a crooked walking stick. Henry drops to one knee; not in supplication, he simply can no longer stand. The stout man approaches, and Henry again makes his breathless plea. His panting comes in a deafening rush, and he cannot hear himself speak. To his own ears the words sound like choking. But the other man understands; his reply indicates as much.

"A fire, you say?"

The stout man tries to keep an eye on his dog — a spotted hound of some indiscernible origin, the bastard offspring of immigrant dogs. The man looks around for verification of Henry's claim.

"Where is this fire?"

"A mile . . ." Henry can hardly sacrifice

the breath needed for speech. "A mile or so . . . perhaps more."

The man whistles for his dog, contemplates the direction Henry indicates.

"You are certain?"

Henry nods emphatically, still kneeling, greedily gulping air, hoping he will not need to run farther. "Yes . . . yonder . . . it is a furious beast."

"Impossible. I was there this morning. There was no fire."

"Believe me." Henry pleads between heavy breaths. "It is very large . . . and moving with great speed."

"It cannot be," the man says, though he sounds unconvinced by his own reasoning. "There is, in the direction you indicate, a sizable plot of land belonging to me. And I lit no fire there this morning. Why would any man set fire to trees not his own?"

Henry has neither time nor breath to argue that the converse would appear equally illogical. "We did not intend to do so . . . we only lit a small fire . . . but this wind . . . I am certain it has spread the flames . . . halfway to Fair Haven Hill by now . . ."

"Fair Haven Hill? If that's true, it will go to Concord. What kind of fire have you started? Do you mean to burn down the town?"

The stout man calls to his dog, and together the three turn back in the direction Henry has come, eight legs leaping over roots and vines. The stout man is surprisingly agile, and he lends Henry a supportive arm more than once. They smell it long before they see it. They hear a roar that reminds Henry of the deafening crack of spring ice on Walden Pond, and they feel the rush of heat carried on the wind. The man whose woods are becoming ash mutters as they run. *Lord Almighty! Lord Almighty!* When they reach the first tendrils of smoke exploring the untouched woods they come upon a terrified old man with an ax and an empty sack, hurrying in the opposite direction. His eyes are wide, his face streaked with soot, and his few gray hairs float about his head like cobwebs. He tells them he is a carpenter, come to collect dead wood, but the fire chased him away. He says the blaze is fierce and spreading quickly. He urges them to turn back, and then he runs away.

The stout man watches the carpenter flee, looks at Henry, and says only, "Lord Almight-y!"

They continue on, but they do not need to travel as far as Henry has come; the fire graciously meets them halfway. The dog runs at a syncopated gait, as if the ground were hot, and barks ecstatically, not at the fire but at the legion of woodchucks and squirrels and rabbits racing toward them, a rippling carpet of brown and gray fear.

When they finally arrive, they cannot believe that they could not see it before, cannot believe that there are not flames reaching to the heavens. The fire has spread out along the ground, and its path seems at least a half mile wide. The woods beyond are obscured by dark smoke, and they can hear the sounds of chirping birds fooled into thinking it is dusk. Henry and the stout man stomp along the leading edge of the flames thinking they can fight it back, slow its progress. It is only a grass fire among the trees, they lie to themselves, an ankle-high intruder. Henry's foot is large and leaves a substantial black imprint. The other man's feet are smaller, but he works with apoplectic determination, short legs pumping high, elbows flying. The dog is of no help at all. Henry remembers a centuries-old woodcut he once saw reproduced in a book: a line of grinning skeletons dancing knock-kneed amid orderly tongues of flame — *Der Totentanz.* Together they perform their own death dance, hopping madly over the burning earth, before admitting that it is a hopeless job for two men and a well-meaning dog.

The stout man says that he and his dog will go for help since, after all, his property is a part of the land engulfed. Henry agrees to remain behind to keep an eye on the fire. He is momentarily relieved; spent from running nearly two miles, he can barely lift his legs, and his chest feels as though it were being squeezed in the steel jaws of a trap. The stout man suggests that Henry retreat to higher ground. Fair Haven Hill is near and will provide an excellent vantage point from which to observe the destruction and wait for aid. On his own, Henry can do nothing to deter the fire's advance, but both men agree that it is best not to leave the cunning flames unwatched.

6
ODDMUND

"*Odd*-mund!"

Her voice, when it finally reaches him, has its usual effect, makes him feel as though he is already drifting toward her. His body responds without waiting for consent, shifting its center of balance forward, and he leans on his pitchfork to ride out the dizzying current. He tries to acknowledge her call, but the shout catches on his tongue. Emma Woburn hollers for him again, her voice high and clear in the crisp air, stripped of its Irish lilt by the distance it travels from the weather-beaten porch of the white house, and in the far corner field Odd feels his throat constrict. He knows why she is calling. He knows she sees the smoke rising from the woods. It is a heavy cloud now, impossible to miss, no longer something that might be mistaken for morning vapors. Odd sucks at his tiny dead tooth and twists his pitchfork in the brushfire. Emma will want him to look into the cause of the smoke, or worse.

Odd wipes his brow with the back of his hand, checks the flecks of ash smeared like drops of ink across his knuckles. Sweat darkens his shirt unevenly, making him look as though he had spent the morning napping on his side in a patch of damp grass. Parts of his body are dead at the surface, stiff as untanned leather. His left forearm and the left flank of his chest no longer perspire, not even when he is hard at work under the summer sun. As he watches the menacing smoke thicken in the distance, the whorled skin from elbow to wrist begins to tingle, restraining what lies beneath. There is no denying it. Something has sparked a fire among the trees. Emma calls out again, and Odd wishes he could cup her voice in his palms, scoop it out of the air like so much water, and hold it to his ear behind locked fingers, a sound to be heard only by him.

Odd lays the pitchfork on the ground, picks up a shovel, and throws a heaping of dirt onto the small fire within the circle of stones. He grimaces as the impact sends forth plumes of expiring cinders like swarming gnats; he watches how eagerly they fly overhead, weightless fragments of disorder floating impossibly far, darting erratically toward the trees just as the frightened mouse had done earlier. Surely his cinders could not have drifted all the way to the woods, he thinks; surely he is not the cause of the smoke hanging above the trees. But he knows people will look for someone to blame, and he can already hear the accusations. It was too dry, they will grumble, much too dry to burn brush safely, and only a fool would do so in such a wind. He should never have agreed to clear the far corner today, even if it meant suffering Mr. Woburn's unpredictable anger.

Odd heaves more dirt onto his fire. Flyaway sprigs ignite, but there is little to sustain the fire now; he has doomed it to expire from hunger. Still, he dares not leave it unattended. He will make sure it is dead before he answers Emma's call. Perhaps he can pretend not to have noticed the smoke rising from the woods. For a moment he hopes that she has not seen it, that she will not ask him to go looking for an explanation. He rehearses what he will say to her, observations about the morning, the condition of the fields, and perhaps a compliment for her appearance. No. That will never do. He will make no comment on how she looks. He must be sure he takes no notice of what she is wearing. Any expectant pleasure is blunted now by the thought of the unmentionable thing on the clothesline. There will be no way for him to resist looking for hints of it beneath the contours of her dress. He shovels dirt onto the fire slowly, taking his time, trying to delay the inevitable. If Emma asks about the smoke above the woods, he will not make excuses. *He set out a circle of stones, kept the fire small, fed it slowly, extinguished it as soon as the wind became too strong.* He will simply do whatever she asks of him, and he will not let his eyes wander in search of the undergarment. Odd tamps a smoldering tangle with the back of the shovel. He cannot understand why the troubles life throws at him do not arrive one at a time instead of by the handful.

He wants to close his eyes and sink back into the dream he awoke from that morning. Already the exact details have left him. He remembers only a large ship and a bright sea and a suffocating calmness. The dream is familiar, but there are many others. His dreams are vivid, and on occasion they are so very like his real experiences that they confuse him, mingling with his memories until he cannot tell them apart. Emma is in them, though not always. Sometimes his dreams are lustful, and he wakes in need. Sometimes the dreams themselves bring satisfaction. And in his dreams his understanding of the world and its mysteries often seems greater than when he is awake, as if he were too simple a creature for daylight. He has only brief glimpses of this understanding. It is more a feeling than a knowing, a vague sense that there are truths sleeping within him, waiting to be roused.

Faint ribbons of smoke, final, desperate gasps, push through the little mounds of earth Odd has piled within the stone circle. He throws more dirt onto the last bit of smoldering brush and drops the shovel next to the pitchfork. He will have to finish the burning later. He waits a moment longer, then turns slowly and walks toward the farmhouse, stopping every few steps and glancing over his shoulder to see if the fire has only been waiting for him to leave before it crawls out of hiding.

Woburn Farm sits on a low rise that looks as though a giant elbow were gently pushing upward from beneath the carpet of rich soil. The house and barn sit at the southern edge, hidden from the far corner by the swelling at the farm's center. Odd trudges toward the swell, rehearsing what he will say to Emma, reminding himself of the things he cannot say, reminding himself not to think of what he has seen hanging on the clothesline. He unrolls his sleeves as he walks. One sleeve clings more tightly than the other. He buttons the cuffs, lowers his head left and then right to wipe his face against his forearms, looking for a moment like a cat cleaning itself.

Odd runs his fingers through his hair, only half believing he might render himself presentable, while he sucks at the dead tooth behind pursed lips. Even alone in the field, he tries to keep it out of sight. Teeth are tiny blunders of creation, he thinks, brittle bits of unrealized pain, one of the many flaws in the human animal, like the soft exposed belly or the tender heart encaged by narrow ribs. He never bares his teeth unless effort or discomfort gives him fit cause to grimace, but it is not just the tiny dead tooth's appearance that bothers him. By itself, it is hardly a thing to make him stand out from other men. He has seen far worse, and most people in Concord revealed missing or broken teeth whenever they smiled. The dozen or so tobacco-stained teeth still left in Mr. Woburn's gums lie sunken in the shadows of his mouth like a clumsily harvested field. And Emma's teeth were scarcely better, gray and square, overlapping as if there were simply too many for her small mouth. When she smiled, though, Odd saw only her happiness; she appeared exactly as she should be, which made Odd all the more intent on hiding his own flaws.

What vexes him most about his rotted infant tooth is the way it draws attention to his other teeth, which appeared unnaturally flawless, straight, white, and intact. Years earlier, he cracked a molar on a buckshot pellet in a shank of venison, but this mishap left behind a void noticeable to no one save himself. He makes no extraordinary efforts to care for his teeth, aside from scraping them clean once a month with the splintered end of a chewed stick. They were bestowed upon him like an inheritance, unasked for, unearned. Every Hus in the Old World likewise possessed a broad and brilliant smile, one that seemed as if it bespoke a flawless soul, a smile that surely aided the disreputable ones in their wicked pursuits. People might estimate a man's character by his eyes, Odd thinks, but they will gauge his intent by the shape of his smile every time.

Odd has tried to work the infant tooth loose on more than one occasion, but its sinewy resistance always made him think of meat pulled from the bone, and the sensation forced him to abandon every attempt. The roots of the dead thing would not let go. A barber once asked him where he had obtained such masterfully carved dentures, finding it unbelievable that a man entering his third decade of life might retain all of his natural teeth in so remarkable a condition. Upon realizing his error, the man offered to extract the dead tooth for free, but as he demonstrated the gleaming forceps and the practiced yank Odd swooned.

"*Odd*-mund!"

Odd hears Emma call for him again, and he quickens his pace. He knows she will see him once he reaches the top of the rise. He can already picture her: knuckles rolled inward against plump hips, rounded shoulders thrown back, one foot turned outward. He brushes away the crumbs of dirt still clinging to his shirtfront, slaps his thighs and knees, checks and rechecks his trousers, making sure there is no cause for embarrassment. His clothes are mottled with dirt and grass and animal stains, greasy imprints of manure and feed, dried outlines and dark patches of fresh sweat. He sees nothing shameful.

Odd mounts the gentle swell at the farm's center, and with every step the horizon rocks up into his line of sight, a little more each time, until the house pops into view: first the chimney, then the weathered gray roof, then the white shingles and the second floor windows, and at last the green door and the crooked porch with Emma before it. The farm's chickens are gathered around her feet in worship. She is almost as he has pictured her. The sun lights her hair, single strands bright as fire straying from the mass of dull orange curls hanging to her shoulders. She stands with hands at hips, feet together at right angles, head thrown back, as though she were trying to balance the weight of her cheeks on her short neck. The sight never fails to make Odd catch his breath. He feels his steps stutter as his feet suddenly grow uncertain of themselves.

Emma's voice is soft and confident, like the hum of swarming honeybees, a voice capable of achieving distance-conquering volume without becoming harsh or grating. Her accent carries no remnant of what she suffered before leaving the famines and plagues of her native Ireland. When she calls him, she stretches out the first syllable like an invocation: *Odd*-mund. She is the only person who uses his full name. She listened with interest when he explained to her that his name was rich with meaning. He told her how *Odd* came from *Oddin,* meaning "the point of a sword," and *mund* from *mundin,* meaning "protection." Emma seemed to accept this as true. He knows that his name sounds like an American word, but the similarity is only an accident of language. No one but Emma has ever seemed willing to believe that his name could be a different thing altogether, a word unto itself. His father told him that it was the name of kings, but most people in the New World uttered the first syllable like an accusation.

Emma's voice traverses the shrinking space between them and settles gently in his ear. "*Odd*-mund *Hus!* There you are. Mr. Woburn said he set you at clearing the far corner, and in such a wind as this. I cannot reason with that man. Not when his mind is fixed I cannot."

Odd feels his feet lose the rhythm of walking. He moves toward her awkwardly, stepping between the chickens pecking at the pale yellow kernels sprinkled in the dirt. Only now does he notice the noisy clucking.

"Did you eat breakfast this morning?" Emma asks as if it were the most pressing question of the day.

"I did."

"There's always something for you in my

97

kitchen, you know. Bacon and biscuits today. Hot coffee, too. Why you don't come in every morning I'll never understand. It does no good to put something cold in your belly the way you do. I thought surely you would come in to warm yourself at the stove."

Odd wades through the chickens, and he almost trips to keep from lumbering right into Emma, headfirst like a goat. He imagines falling into the warm folds of her flesh, wrapping his arms around her, tumbling to the ground, and the very thought prickles the skin up and down his legs. Emma is staring at him, as if waiting for a reply, and Odd wonders if she can tell what he is thinking.

"This morning I had much to do," he offers.

Emma folds her arms and taps her foot. "I know what you were doing."

Odd sucks on the dead tooth and tries to avoid her stare.

"I saw you this morning, Oddmund Hus, standing out there for a half hour."

Odd sucks harder on the little tooth, almost hard enough to pull it from its socket. He knows she saw him staring at the clothesline. His eyes dart toward the neckline of her dress and he drags them away.

He looks instead at the porch, the sky, the chickens. To his amazement, despite the rising panic and embarrassment and the noisy clucking, he feels a stirring, a warm, heavy rising.

"I . . . I . . ."

Emma holds up a chapped hand. The wedding band is outlined in red where the finger has swollen around it. "I know what you were about. I saw the glow at your cheeks. . . ." Odd feels the urge to run, wishes he could hide. "Staring off into space, deep in thought, you were. Looking right through this world. It's a philosopher you are, Oddmund Hus. I've told Mr. Woburn a thousand times, what he's hired is no farmer. I told him he's got himself a philosopher in his employ."

"Mrs. Woburn . . . I . . ."

"Don't think I don't comprehend. I've met plenty of deep-thinking men. There's no shortage of them hereabouts. Something in these parts does it to a person, gets him thinking on the things he cannot hope to see."

Odd's eyes dart over Emma's face, drop to her shoulders, her arms — sneaking, creeping, fighting against his own will — across her wide bosom, and back up to her face. He does not see any signs of straps or laces, but he knows they are there.

"You are a thoughtful man," Emma says, her final judgment.

She stoops to brush away a chicken perched on her toe, and Odd cannot pull his eyes away from the inviting cleft at the neckline of her dress — the soft skin, the dark recess, all right there before him. He cannot let her catch him looking, but he looks anyway, a short fugue of quick glances. The urge to run away comes upon him again.

"Why did you call for me, Em— Mrs. Woburn?"

"Oh." She straightens and points over his head. "What is that?"

Odd follows the line of her finger, and the tingling in his legs ceases; the heavy warmth dissipates. She is pointing at the tower of pale smoke, which has doubled in size since he last looked.

"Ah . . . *skog* . . ." Odd shakes his head. The old words sometimes creep back. "*Ja*, the woods."

"I've never seen them do that before," she says. "You're sure that isn't any of your smoke, then? With this wind, might be hard to tell."

"No, ma'am. No. It is none of my smoke."

Emma nods. "Well, I told Mr. Woburn

you'd not get smoke such as that from burning off a field. I told him it was trouble, to be sure. But I knew you had nothing to do with it. I told Mr. Woburn if there was any trouble out there in the field, you would already be seeing to it."

Odd swallows. He knows his fire is not the cause. He watched it carefully, and he extinguished it before the wind could spread the cinders.

Emma laughs for no reason, a soft, apologetic laugh. "Mr. Woburn said I ought to send you into Concord to tell someone, if I was still having apprehensions about it once I talked to you." She repeats the concerns she voiced to her husband without letting the slightest hint of worry cross her face.

Odd can never tell when she is upset or angry or disappointed. Her smile never diminishes to anything less than a placid crescent, like the faint wisp of the new moon, a suggestion of fullness to come. From the bits of stolen glances in his memory, he can compose the soft details of her face, her shifting expressions, the generous proportions of her arms and legs and back, and the way her dress struggles over certain curves, but he cannot puzzle out the feelings hidden beneath the expanse of flesh standing right before him.

"Seems to me we might be needing help if the wind changes and it comes this way," she says. "Mr. Woburn would have seen to it himself, but he told me he had business in the other direction. He says I worry too much. Still, it would put my mind at ease if you could tell someone in town. Oh, I suppose you'll have to walk to Concord, as Mr. Woburn took the wagon. I hope you don't mind."

Odd checks the front of his trousers; it has become almost a reflex. He sees Emma make a face when he does so, then he nods.

"*Ja, ja.* I will go, then."

Emma turns and gestures toward the kitchen door with a heavy arm. "I baked a pie . . ." she starts to say, but when she turns back she sees that Odd has already picked his way through the cluster of chickens and set off toward the center of Concord.

Emma calls after him, "You might as well take something to eat."

Odd waves, a long, slow sweep of the arm, but he does not stop.

7
ODDMUND

Emma is not wholly incorrect. He does not believe himself so deep a thinker as she suggests, but in his dreams he is indeed a philosopher. In his dreams he is eloquent, no awkward stumbling after the American words that still feel like stones in his mouth, no grasping after the ideas of wiser men. When he is asleep, his mind awakens to the truths he has somehow always known but cannot fully recall in daylight. When his thinking self lies dormant, his dreams explore the profundities of his adopted home.

Before it was a place, the New World was an idea. Before *desire* found its object, *regret* knew what it would willingly leave behind. The only world men had ever known was once so old that they could not imagine a time when it might have been young, a time when civilizations might not have marched blindly toward collapse in order to avoid slipping into the gulf of history. The citizens of the Old World longed for boundless, level plains, and out of this longing was born the idea of the New World, a pesky half-thought hiding in the shadows of disappointment, haunting the margins of laboring hours when futility acquired the numbing power of an opiate. The idea survived the onslaughts of religion and history, a vestigial hope, a footprint of want from previous generations, eroded but intact.

The continent that would bear the weight of these expectations had always been here, for as long as continents had floated on the oceans, crashing into one another with remorseless mountain-making force. The first explorers came in the name of primitive desires: gold, jewels, spices, slaves, trade. Those who came later wanted less, wanted — above all else — to discover the one condition that promised unimpeded possibility: *nothing.* Men would have been satisfied to find the land barren, as long as it contained absolutely nothing to remind them of the past, nothing to limit the horizon.

The wonders of the New World did not disappoint, but they were unlike the strange marvels that previous centuries had foretold. The plants and animals were somehow familiar, like an unfocused reflection of the Old World projected and inverted through a pinhole; the flora and fauna were wonders in kind but more so in number, for America's true wonder was a wonder of plenitude. What need had a starving man for a rare parrot of bright plumes, when he might easily grasp a hundred gray sparrows simply by swatting at the teeming skies? What fascination did a scaly monster from the deep hold for a simple man who might dip his net into silvery flashes and snare enough unremarkable fish to feed his family for a month? Wonders of abundance!

But this new world held disenchantments, too, and the greatest was that men were already here. What disappointment to learn that the promised land had been promised to someone else! *Oh, epic jealousy,* the old poets would have cried had they not been among the most reluctant to leave the Old World behind. This garden already had ample Adams and Eves, blissful spoilers, a people whose crude weapons and forthright manners seemed to serve no purpose other than to remind the newly arrived that nothing in the world was new. The native inhabitants were far less exotic than what one might expect to find peopling the land of one's fantasy. None of the bronze Indians spoke through yellow-fanged navels; none sprouted feathers instead of hair; none stood on cloven hooves or carried more than one head upon their shoulders. But, wonder of wonders, these men and women had been here for generations, daring to walk upon the soil of the New World like somnambulant trespassers in a centuries-old dream. The explorers of the New World turned to the machinations of the Old to preserve their illusion; history had not forestalled the discovery of Eden, and they would not allow it to disrupt their dream. And so began the infection of the New World with the ways of the Old. In the end, desire would not be sated; regret would go unreconciled. The Old World would not be left behind, after all.

Oslo, Norway, 1829. Oddmund Hus's father, Lars, insisted that the large trunk belonging to Oddmund's grandfather accompany them on the voyage that most travelers made with little more than what they might tie up in a quilt. Over the protestations of Oddmund's mother, Lars Hus paid the crew extra gilders to bring the heavy thing up the gangplank and down into the hold. Ingrid Hus had little patience with impracticality, and though she fully realized the significance of their leaving, she had no interest in hidden meanings. She had cut her hair stubble-short the day before, not as a symbolic gesture — though Lars mistakenly admired the act as such and dramatically razored his own head of blond hair — but for entirely practical reasons: as a deterrent against fleas and lice. They were not a wealthy family, but neither were they as poor as many of the other travelers lining the docks at Oslo, willing to barter themselves into servitude for passage to America. Lars Hus had no need to seek fortune in the New World, but he had reason enough to leave the old one behind. Ill fortune took many forms, and, among them, the affliction of a family name was by far the least uncommon.

The large trunk sat solidly in the corner of the cramped hold, half hidden by the barrels and crates brought on board at every port before they turned westward. The other passengers found it a sturdy source of gossip; with little else to do for weeks at sea, they speculated on what it might contain. Loose bits of straw hung from the lip of the lid, a sign that whatever the trunk contained was valuable enough to have been packed carefully for the voyage. Everything from gold coins to guns to an alchemical apparatus was rumored to occupy the trunk. Those passengers who knew something of the history of the family Hus whispered that the trunk no doubt concealed a stolen treasure or a pair of entwined corpses. Lars told them that the trunk held what he was leaving behind, and no one realized that he meant this quite literally.

When it was too cold or wet or rough to play on deck, Oddmund and his sister climbed onto the trunk, feet scraping the riveted sides, he reaching the top first and extending a hand to pull Birgit up before she started whining. He was ten and she was younger by two years. Sometimes they pretended they were riding an elegant carriage through the streets of their destination, a city called Boston. At other times they imagined they were sitting in a jeweled chair on the back of a lumbering Indian elephant. *Were there wild elephants roaming the green forests of America?* Oddmund and Birgit knew they were going to a place where no one would understand them. Neither could remember how they had first learned to speak, but they knew they would have to learn how to do it all over again. As they sat together on the trunk, they sounded out the strange new words, letter by letter, stenciled on the barrels and crates around them: VINO, GUNPOWDER, LINEN, TEA, LAMP OIL. Lars lowered his bulky length into the dim hold at noon each day to check on the trunk, as if he were afraid it might fall through the rotting bulkhead unnoticed. He did not unclasp the lock to look inside. He patted the trunk like a favorite pet, whispering to it, as if to reassure himself and what was inside that they were all still there.

The voyage was no more and no less arduous than other sea crossings: the ship too small to accommodate the number of passengers, too little food, too little water, too much sickness. For some travelers, the Atlantic proved to be their final destination. Death trailed them from the Old World, nipping at their heels, snatching passengers at random, sending their shrouded bodies to the ocean floor. Two weeks from America, a mottled sickness seized Ingrid Hus, just as it had unceremoniously taken hold of others, and slowly squeezed the life from her lungs. Oddmund and Birgit watched the health drain from their mother's cheeks. While their father forced tin cups of rank water between her pale lips, brother and sister mounted their fierce elephant belowdecks to chase away the demon tormenting their mother. After a weeklong siege, death released its grip, miraculously returned their mother to them, and seemed, if only for a while, to retreat to the safety of the Old World, where it might prey more easily upon the crowded cities.

When they at last sighted land — the Cape of Cod, it was unbelievably called — Lars had the heavy trunk brought up from the hold. The bold white letters of their grandfather's name, V. HUS, shone like the standard on a flag. It was a struggle to bring it up the narrow ladder, and once it was on deck they left it next to the open hatch. Lars sat on the edge of the trunk near the starboard rail and watched America approach as they cleared the cape and sailed through the waters of Massachusetts Bay. When they could see the clusters of masts and sails marking Boston Harbor in the distance, Lars retrieved the key from his boot and worked at the stubborn lock, barnacled with glittering mushrooms of rust from a month in the salty dampness. Those few passengers who still had energy enough to remain interested gathered around and watched quietly, too tired to remind one another of the wagers made weeks before. Oddmund winced under a shower of flying sparks as a man behind him lit a clay pipe filled with the cheap tobacco that was mostly straw and lint. Each puff sent another cloud of bright orange cinders spilling over the pipe's bowl. Lars checked the horizon again before opening the trunk, as if to make sure that America had not drifted away; he ignored the impatient grunts from curious passengers.

As their father lifted the lid, Oddmund and Birgit stood on their toes to peer inside, and they understood at once why the other passengers hissed. Nothing in there was worth the extra gilders Lars had paid to bring the trunk halfway around the world: a moth-eaten overcoat, a curled pair of boots with peeling soles, a spineless book, a broken clock, a flaking portrait in oil, a spade, papers, curios — *junk.* The rubbish had been carefully packed in straw like precious trinkets. Lars watched his children's reactions while Ingrid watched America loom measurably larger with each passing minute. Oddmund fingered the curled toe of the boot, furred with mildew. *This,* their father said, *is what we are leaving behind.* They had heard him say this before, but they were surprised to hear him speak Norwegian instead of the clumsy American words he insisted they practice during the voyage.

Lars grabbed the boot, and as he lifted it

from the trunk the other boot followed, tied to its mate by knotted laces. *These belonged to your great-grandfather,* he said. He held them in front of Oddmund and Birgit long enough to ensure that the two children registered the significance of the rotted leather, then, swinging his arm like a catapult, he hurled them back over his shoulder and into the ocean. Oddmund heard the twin splashes seconds after the boots disappeared over the rail. Lars did not take his eyes off his children as he reached into the trunk for another object. *Your great-grandfather wore those boots on the day of his trial. Thanks be to God he did not live to teach his sons how to help themselves to the contents of other men's pockets.*

Oddmund moved closer to the ship's rail, where he could see the waves slapping against the hull. Then Lars lifted the battered oil portrait from the trunk and frowned scornfully; the face on the canvas smiled back with straight, white teeth, and a lower lip pointed like an inverted *V*. Oddmund watched his father spit on the face and curl his lips in a silent curse. *Your uncle, Søren Hus,* Lars said. *He fled his fate; some say the ocean took him, else he would have suffered a punishment worse than your great-*

grandfather's. This portrait he tossed like a dinner plate, sending it spinning overboard. Next he retrieved a cracked magnifying glass belonging to a counterfeiting Hus; this, too, Oddmund's father threw over the rail. Oddmund watched a wedge of the broken glass fall from the lens and trace its own path to the water, slicing into the waves like a hard piece of the ocean itself.

A spade came next, with clumps of foreign soil still clinging to the blade. Lars rubbed the grit between his fingers. A smooth stone the size of a knuckle dislodged from the spade and landed at Oddmund's feet. *Through good seasons and bad, our family worked the fields. Only by the grace of heaven were we more fortunate than most. But now you are free to choose your destiny.* Lars flung the spade over his shoulder. It entered the water silently and then shot back to the surface, buoyed by its wooden handle. Oddmund bent and picked up the smooth stone, gray with a coppery vein running its length, and slipped it into his pocket. It seemed sad to leave it on the deck after it had tenaciously made the journey halfway around the world.

Overboard went the broken pocket watch of a murderous nephew, a leather satchel belonging to a horse-thieving cousin, a pair of spectacles used by a lock-picking brother-in-law, a bonnet worn by an adulterous aunt, the pewter flask of a debauched great-uncle. Most of what Lars discarded sank immediately, but some of the objects formed a crooked trail of flotsam behind the ship, and from the rail Oddmund could still see the blond knob of the spade, bobbing in slow pursuit.

Then Lars pulled out a flattened roll of parchment, the last item in the trunk; he unrolled it and held it wide between his arms. There were names and dates written by several different hands; the names were scattered around the branches of a crooked tree, which appeared to have grown too expansive for its gnarled, shallow roots. Here and there, some of the names were blotted out; others had been scratched away so that it looked as though a portion of the tree were being attacked by blight. Lars let one end go, and the scroll curled back around itself by memory, but this he did not throw into the sea. Ingrid took her husband gently by the arm and whispered something to him, but he shook his head; he insisted that he would finish it. *We are leaving this behind,* he said. *We will begin again.* He pulled a small tin box from his coat pocket, removed a phosphorus match wrapped safely in a bit of brown paper, struck it against the strip of sandpaper on the box's lid, and touched the flame to the end of the scroll.

Lars held the burning scroll at arm's length. The wind fanned the flames, spread them along the length of the scroll and over Lars's fingertips, and he dropped the scroll into the trunk, where it lit the loose bed of straw. The fire spread quickly, consuming the scroll in a flash. The passengers who had previously lost interest in the trunk's worthless contents returned now, drawn by the expectation that something spectacular was about to happen. Clusters of burning straw took flight, whirling about their heads and up into the sails and the rigging. Oddmund and Birgit laughed and jumped up and down and swatted at the flying bits of fire. Then Oddmund looked up and saw something that didn't seem to fit with his father's plan; a clump of straw must have landed high up in the basket they called the crow's nest, because *that* was burning now, too, a bright orange ball at the top of the tallest mast. A sailor was climbing up the rigging, lugging a bucket of water, but soon one of the sails caught fire. Lars tried to close the lid of the trunk, but the fire lashed at his arms and lit up his face; burning straw was flying everywhere, dancing across the deck and down into the hold. The captain shouted something in words that were not in the American primer Lars had given his children. Flashes of light from the hatch told them that the fire had found its way below, carried into the cargo hold by the burning straw.

A loud rumbling shook the deck, and then a fiery blast threw Oddmund skyward. One moment he saw his father standing in front of him, feathers of glowing parchment from the burning scroll fluttering about his head, the teetering masts of Boston Harbor visible in the distance. In that same moment, he saw his sister Birgit twirling on her toes and laughing at the spiky flames leaping from the trunk and the sparks swarming over the deck like a frenzied host of fireflies. He was almost certain that he saw his mother raise her eyebrows and cover her mouth in astonishment, and in the very next moment he felt himself take flight, lifted by a hot cloud, chased by blinding white light. As he tumbled into the sky, Oddmund glimpsed the people below him, scurrying over the disintegrating deck of the *Sovereign of the Seas* like beetles on floating dung. He rose higher, propelled by the force of a second explosion, and he thought that he was going to fly straight up into heaven, that his mother and father and sister would soon be following him into the peaceful blue sky. Then there came a sickening, bottomless feeling in his stomach followed by nothing but cold, wet midnight.

Trusting chance and the tide to cast ashore treasures from Boston Harbor, the scavengers patrolling the wharves were the first to see the bright fist of light smack the flat sky. Boots in hands, pants rolled to knees, the fortune-seekers crouched at the water's edge, assumed Herculean poses beneath the piers, and speculated that the fiery plume on the horizon was the exhalation of some as yet undiscovered leviathan. A halo of gray seagulls fled the exploding light, and at its fringes the clumsy birds twirled and tumbled; moments later the scavengers realized that the birds were people and the leviathan an ordinary ship.

Those working the docks shrugged. Such things were not extraordinary, they said. Ships that looked too large to float, too small to brave the open sea, too heavy, too old, too rotten, too battered — sometimes such ships made the impossible journey across the Atlantic only to smash their hulls on the rocky coast of New England. Within sight of land, ships swollen with cargo and overladen with passengers — ships that had survived pounding waves, vicious storms, drunken captains — shuddered in the presence of the New World and sank beneath the cold waters of Massachusetts Bay, as if that dramatic finale were the reason for their voyage. The scavengers saw these things, walked the beaches looking for survivors, and fought one another over what the ocean no longer wanted.

Most had never seen a vessel explode the way the *Sovereign of the Seas* did, but they had seen others burst into flames. They had seen sea-soaked timbers catch fire under the ministrations of whale oil, watched sailcloth turn to ash, witnessed the chaos a spark could unleash in an airless hold packed with barrels of gunpowder or dusty bales of cotton. They knew that water, even an ocean of it, was no deterrent when a fire was determined to do its business. They had seen strange tragedies, and they had heard stranger tales of ghostly ships that disappeared and reappeared up and down the coast but never came to port.

Some who saw the end of the *Sovereign of the Seas* spoke of it as if they had been standing on the doomed ship's deck and could verify the cause. There was mention of an old cannon in the hold, forgotten from the last war with the British; there was talk of a lightning bolt thick as a man's arm splitting the vessel's hull; there was speculation that witchcraft was to blame. Some fishermen claimed to have seen smoke before the explosion, and they surmised that something volatile in the cargo hold must have come into contact with an open flame. There was little else to be said. The fishermen returned to their nets. The newspapers had plenty of other wrecks to report. The bankers who had invested in the ship's cargo wanted only to forget their loss. Scavengers found nothing salvageable among the wreckage that washed ashore later in the day. The only survivor was a ten-year-old Norwegian boy, whom they found sprawled unconscious on the sand amid charred bodies and blackened remnants of sails and masts and decking.

The scavengers carried Oddmund away before the tide could reclaim him. In his pockets they discovered nothing that might tell them who he was, nothing of any value except for a small, smooth stone shot through with a coppery vein. They left the worthless stone with him, thinking it might remind him of his home, his family, his name, in the event that the sea had stolen those memories along with the rest of the cargo.

Oddmund had no recollection of what happened to him once the fiery cloud let him drop. When he finally awoke, he expected things to be as they were before he left his home. He expected to see his mother leaning over him the way she did whenever he shivered with fever, expected to feel the thud of his father's heavy footsteps in the next room, to hear Birgit's chirping laughter, to smell a salty chowder of salmon or yellow peas bubbling in the pot. Instead, the first thing Oddmund saw upon opening his eyes was fire and blood. The blood fell in large red drops from grievous wounds, from a heart swollen and red, immersed in flames but unburned, somehow continuing to beat outside the chest of the soft-smiling man whose unblinking eyes held him in their gaze. The vision terrified him. He had seen the man before, he thought, though never with the burning heart. Oddmund squeezed his eyes shut. He thought of his mother's gentle voice. He tried to wish her face before him. He found the small stone someone had placed under his pillow, and he clutched it tightly in his little fist until his knuckles turned white and his hand felt as though it had become hard as the stone.

He drifted away again, but every time he opened his eyes the man was still there; he seemed to be waiting for something, his disembodied heart still bleeding, still burning.

On the fourth day of his convalescence, Oddmund realized that he was looking at a large painting on the opposite wall, and then he remembered one of the man's many names. Oddmund's mother had taught him to memorize prayers to the solemn statue of the Savior in the small church near their home, but if the statue he prayed to had held a burning heart it had been hidden somewhere beneath the thick folds of its marble robe. Oddmund wanted to ask his mother if this was the same gentle God in the stories she read aloud, but he knew that she was not going to come to him. He understood that she and Birgit and his father had gone away. For a while, the painting made him hope that they might have come through the flames without being consumed, burning yet unburned like the miraculous heart. He hoped they might somehow have drifted back home unharmed, even if this meant that he would never see them again. But, no matter how hard he wished it, he could not convince himself that it was so. The painting, he decided, was a cruel trick, the fanciful strokes of an artist's brush, and after his recent glimpse of heaven on the cloud of hot air Oddmund decided he would prefer to keep his eyes fixed solidly on the earth for as long as he walked upon it.

A woman in a black hood with a stiff white brim spoke to him in a kind voice, gave him gentle commands that he followed without really knowing what the words meant. The scavengers had left him on the steps of the Saint Vincent Female Orphan Asylum. The Catholic Daughters of Charity bandaged the burns on his arms and chest; they set his broken shin. They prayed for him. The nuns fed him salted cod, told him how fortunate he was. In simple English, they said that God had smiled on him. They reminded him that he should be thankful that he had arrived. Eventually, he understood their meaning: *Just think how much worse it would be to find oneself orphaned in the Old World, with no hope of reaching the shores of the promised land.*

The nuns could not refuse to help a child so terribly injured as Oddmund, but they dared not jeopardize the innocence of their girls by keeping a boy among them at the Purchase Street asylum. Once his fever passed and it was clear that he was beginning to mend, they sent him back out to sea. Oddmund could not communicate the panic he felt as they carried him, swathed in bandages, back to the docks, placed him on board another boat — a small one, with no sails — and began to take him away from the New World where he had only lately arrived. Such a small boat could not possibly survive the ocean, and Oddmund believed that they were only going to row him out to the wreckage, to return him to his family. The journey took an hour, by his reckoning. They docked at an island in Boston Harbor, and they delivered Oddmund to the Boston Asylum and Farm School for Indigent Boys. He recovered from his injuries and, with the hundred or so other orphans and street Arabs and guttersnipes, he was given a blue uniform and taught how to be a farmer.

The other boys found him amusing, for all the wrong reasons. Oddmund did not understand why they snickered whenever his name was called, and it perplexed him that their sneering did not diminish even after he had learned enough English to be able to explain the significance of his name. The other boys, brutish and dull, found his name immeasurably funny, and Oddmund learned his first lesson in the New World:

one must never underestimate the persistent convictions of the ignorant.

Oddmund held on to the smooth gray stone that he had rescued from the deck of the *Sovereign of the Seas*. Aside from his tattered clothes, this was the only possession that survived with him. One afternoon, wandering alone along the edge of the island, Oddmund found two short wooden tubes half buried in the sand. The tubes were so arranged that the smaller slid into the larger, and he decided that this may very well have been the spyglass used by the captain of the *Sovereign of the Seas.* Though the lenses had fallen out and the brass rings at either end were missing, Oddmund clutched the useless spyglass as if it held forbidden secrets, and looked through its empty tunnel, comforted by the confined perspective it offered. He carried it everywhere, hidden in his pocket with the stones he collected from the grounds around the asylum. From the window of the dormitory, he surveyed the harbor, the masts of the tall ships at the wharf, the steeples of the churches of Boston, and, when he dared, he scanned the dark surface of the water where, to the best of his knowledge, the *Sovereign of the Seas* had disappeared. His nightly searches with the useless spyglass only added to the mirth of the other boys, who believed his puzzling behavior confirmed the meaning of his peculiar name.

For almost three years, Oddmund remained at the asylum on Thompson Island while his Unitarian caretakers circulated his name through the surrounding counties. They had reunited other families. They printed his name in newspapers. They posted bills. They wrote letters and knocked on doors in search of a Hus who might take him in. There was a *Hoss* family in Connecticut. There were *Hooses* in Vermont. There were *Hesses* in the Berkshires and *Hasses* in the Appalachians. But these settlers were not included on the family tree that Lars Hus burned on board the *Sovereign of the Seas.* The Hosses and the Hooses ignored the letters. The Hesses and the Hasses turned away inquiring visitors. Those who did respond swore ardently that they were not related to the poor boy's family; they insisted they had never heard of the father; they said they already had children enough, and some confessed that they wanted nothing to do with an orphaned Hus from the Old World.

But it was only a matter of time before someone retrieved him. Oddmund might eventually have found himself alone, to fend for himself on the streets of Boston, had it not been for the well-dressed man with hard sweets in his coat pocket who drifted up the orphanage steps one day and knocked gently on its doors. The man conferred with the ministers in hushed tones; he said he came as soon as he learned of the possibility, and one look at Oddmund told him that his suspicions were correct. When he smiled — a mouthful of white, even teeth — his bottom lip contracted into an inverted *V* at its middle.

"You must be Master Oddmund," the man said. "How delightful." He presented Oddmund with a peppermint lozenge in his open palm. "I am your uncle, Søren Mikkel Hus. I have long hoped someone would come."

Thus did something discarded and forgotten by the family Hus reappear, washed up by the inexplicable undercurrents of fate.

8
ELIOT

Eliot squints through his spectacles at the fat pillar of smoke rising in the distance and wonders if there is cause for concern. It is possible, he thinks, that his heavy glass lenses are making the plume appear larger than it really is. No one else on Main Street seems to take notice. He slips the spectacles into a coat pocket, then pulls a key from another pocket and works it in the lock of the shop's door. He has heard stories of men who thought they had purchased a property only to learn that they had pro- cured nothing more than a counterfeit deed and a phony key, and he is relieved when the bolt reluctantly gives way. Of course, he will need to replace the lock with something more modern, he thinks, and the cracked pane of glass in the door will need fixing as well. Once inside, he is disappointed to find the space smaller than he expected, nar- rower and darker than his Boston shop. And the smell surprises him. It will take some effort to expel the pungent aroma of boot polish and mildew and rotted stockings. But here, at least, he will not find himself in daily contest with the Old Corner Bookstore, will not have to compete for the attention of the customers who frequent Ticknor's cluttered rooms, which, as Eliot recollects with some consolation, are not without their own malodorous history.

The building in which William Davis Ticknor runs his bookstore has stood at the corner of School and Washington Streets since 1718, when it began as Thomas Crease's Apothecary, and patrons of the Old Corner Bookstore can still smell the abrasive chemical perfume beneath the more alluring scent of leather bindings and ink and slowly moldering paper stored in the printing house on the second floor. But the stink does not keep the eminent writers of New England from gathering there for readings and conversation. Eliot knows his Boston shop will never become a meetinghouse for the likes of Longfellow and Holmes and the other literati who lounge about Ticknor's as if it were a public drawing room. But he also knows that a customer with a full purse wants something more than the privilege of mixing in famous company; he desires items that cannot be found anywhere else, and Eliot has become proficient at attending to these needs. He would happily open his doors for a lone, paying customer before letting in a hoard of poets with empty pockets. Still, he cannot help believing that things should have turned out otherwise, that the Old Corner Bookstore should, rightfully, be his.

He has worked through the fantasy a thousand times, and though he tries not to dwell on it, the suspicion that he was swindled out of his destiny claws at him from within, like a tiny spur of bone at the base of his skull. A decade earlier, Eliot fully expected that, in due time, he would be made a partner in Carter, Hendee & Co. He had, after all, given five years of loyal service to Timothy Carter and Charles Hendee, who then owned the Old Corner Bookstore and the publishing enterprise on its upper floors. Eliot had envisioned what he would do at the helm of the company; he made imaginary lists of the great literary works he would publish and the new authors he would discover. He never dreamed that William Davis Ticknor — a man with little experience in publishing — would take over the business with the help of Carter's older brother. When Ticknor, Allen, and Carter purchased Carter, Hendee & Co., they announced that, henceforth, they would publish books of medical interest only. Eliot foresaw a dreadful future for himself, editing the cramped scribblings of ghoulish surgeons, surrounded by tedious engravings of frog bladders and misshapen tumors. So he set out on his own, certain that Ticknor's shop would founder within a few months and that the Old Corner Bookstore would soon be placed on auction. But Eliot had been wrong.

William Davis Ticknor unexpectedly turned his attention to literature and began publishing poetry and novels, respected works by masters and new works by famous Americans. Next to the latest editions of *Collins's Treatise on Midwifery, Lisfranc's Diseases of the Uterus, Bigelow's Manual of Orthopedic Surgery,* and *Tuson's Dissector's Guide,* Ticknor crammed his shelves with handsome fifty-cent editions of Alfred Lord Tennyson, William Wordsworth, Leigh Hunt, Oliver Wendell Holmes, Bronson Alcott, and Henry Wadsworth Longfellow. The writers whom Eliot once imagined would gather at *his* store — to discuss their work, to weigh the merits of the newest author venturing into print, or to hear Eliot himself read from his latest play — flocked instead to the Old Corner Bookstore.

The injustice was made complete when Ticknor promoted Eliot's former assistant to full partner in the new company; James Thomas Fields, a mere junior clerk at Carter, Hendee & Co., had shown the sheepish foresight to stay on after Eliot departed. And, if all *that* were not intolerable enough, Mr. Ticknor and Mr. Fields, like a pair of insufferable schoolboys on holiday, began to fancy themselves poets. Poets! The audacious booksellers even held readings of their own work in their shop. It is all too much for Eliot to bear, to think that these men stood between him and financial liberty.

There was a time, Eliot reminds himself, when money was something that he had neither sought nor possessed in any significant quantity. In his youth, wealth held no communion with his literary ambitions. Yet now he often lies awake at night, wondering if the next day's business will be slow enough to allow him a few moments alone to work on the next scene of *The House of Many Windows*. During busy hours he hopes for such moments, though he knows that he will not actually use the time to write; he will sit hunched over his unfinished play, worrying about the day's receipts and hoping that an increase in business the next day will compensate for the deficiency. That is the paradox of the modern age: a man needs to make a healthy sum of money in order to pretend that money does not matter to him. Some nights it surprises Eliot that his wife, sound asleep in the bedroom next to his, cannot hear the loud worries buzzing through his head. He knows it is foolish to suppose that anyone might remain unaltered by the passage of years, but he wonders if Margaret can detect the slow changes that he daily identifies with staggering disappointment.

The first time he saw her was in the old Federal Street Theater, a year before it was sold as a meeting hall to the Baptist Church. Margaret Mahoney was a dark-haired beauty then, slender and fair-skinned, a warm and breathing portrait of the kind of woman Eliot thought only inhabited sonnets. He had followed her through the lobby, thinking she was an actress until he saw her take a seat in the box to the right of the stage, next to an older man with a pointed nose similar to her own. Although the stage was only partially visible from where Eliot sat, his view of the beautiful woman was unobstructed, and the flickering lamps on the stage cast enough light to illuminate her face, which shone with the spectral beauty that drove men to do ridiculous things. She did not cast her eyes about the audience like so many of the other women, looking for familiar faces in less expensive seats or checking to make sure that her dress was of the latest fashion. Her eyes, remarkably enough, remained fixed on the stage throughout the entire performance, as if she were truly engaged in the unfolding drama.

Eliot watched the forgettable play from his usual twenty-five-cent place in the gallery. He saw no need to spend more. He had learned from the example of his father's strict household economy, and he budgeted his own meager income carefully. His father was a tutor of classical languages, and though Ambrose Calvert enjoyed no small degree of respect in the community, that respect stopped short of providing him with the financial means to participate in the city's more refined pursuits. It had angered Eliot to think that his father, who spent his days deciphering the subtleties of classical drama to the dull sons of moneyed Bostonians, could ill afford to attend the theater packed with the tea merchants and bankers and other men of business whose broad backsides barely fit into the seats.

Eliot remembers the relief that he was

certain he saw flit across his father's brow when he explained that he had taken employment as a typesetter's assistant at Carter, Hendee & Co., where he intended to earn a living until his talents as a dramatist delivered him to fame's doorstep. Eliot wanted a job that left his imagination untapped for his own use. Setting type and inking plates required a good deal more effort than Eliot had at first estimated, but he managed to keep his wit untaxed, and he lost himself in the romance of assembling other men's ideas with his hands. When he returned at night to his shoddy room near Mount Vernon, his hands and face stained with ink, his clothes reeking of chemicals, he was overjoyed with the image that he cast: the struggling artist, stained with the ink of other men's writings, laboring by lamplight over the manuscript of his own unrecognized masterpiece.

At the time, his modest income more than met his needs. His lodgings were simple, as were his clothes. He kept only one good waistcoat and jacket for attending the theater, and he sat in the least expensive seats so that he might attend as many performances of as many plays as possible. When a performance enjoyed an extended run, he went to the same play several times to study how the same lines could be delivered with a different emphasis every night.

Working by candlelight late into the night, he finished his first play, *The Forgotten Brother; or The Search for Light.* He felt allied with his main character, Horatio Standforth, a writer whose genius went unappreciated by a callous world. Eliot was particularly proud of the play's opening speech.

HORATIO: Oh, what a confounded fretfulness is this life! I stumble in darkness tangible toward a distant light. I feel my pulse quicken at the promise of a brighter morrow, while, alas, my soul trembles behind me, lost in the shadows like a forgotten brother of my own true self. Is it by sword or pen that I shall thrust my way through this utter black world? I pronounce boldly — by pen shall I conquer this new American land!

Horatio died spectacularly, leaping from a cliff at the drama's end, but when Eliot performed all parts of the play for himself in his room he judged its theme too solemn for the stage. He determined that his second play would not rely so heavily upon soliloquies three and four pages in duration. His next effort, *The Rebirth of Europa; or America Found,* proved too large a theme, and he put the half-finished first act aside to begin a third play, a farce about ill-suited lovers. He thought *Am I Your Husband?* held great promise at first, but then he seemed to run out of things for his characters to do and say.

At Carter, Hendee & Co., he was promoted from his position as a typesetter's assistant and was no longer required to clean the type in the large vats of concentrated urine that fouled the air on the second floor. He continued working among the ink and chemicals for several months more before Mr. Hendee himself decided that his skills were put to better use behind a desk as an editor's assistant. An increase in pay came with this, but Eliot kept to his simple tastes, afraid that an improvement in the comfort of his circumstances would distract him from his mission. He bought a new suit and a box of fine writing paper, but he remained in the same lodgings, frequented the same taverns, and still bought only the cheapest tickets to the theater.

And then he met Margaret Mary Mahoney.

■ ■ ■ ■

Eliot knows it is foolish for him to revisit his past as often as he does, rooting out mistakes and regrets that cannot be edited away. He can only assume that it is in his nature as a writer to think of his life as a story that might be endlessly revised, but today he is determined to concentrate on his future. He paces the length of the vacant shop, listening to the echo of his steps, trying to picture the quiet space crammed with books and, more important, customers. A single, feathery cobweb hangs slack from the center of the ceiling to a crooked shelf at the back. Eliot tests it with his finger and the strand drifts lazily down along the length of his arm. Yellowed slips of paper, old bills and receipts that once composed the daily details of the previous owner's life, lie curled in corners, swept into piles by fastidious drafts.

The edge of a warped floorboard catches Eliot's foot, and he prods the offending surface with his toe, adding its repair to the list of expenses he silently tallies. Eliot fumbles at his waistcoat pocket and yanks out his watch by its chain. He thinks of the book-shaped fob he spied in the shop window earlier that morning. There was at least one practical purpose that a fob would serve: it would give his blunt fingers something to grasp so that he might retrieve his timepiece more gracefully. Eliot checks the time and frowns. He slips the watch back into his pocket, rubs the smooth gold chain between his fingers, then pulls a card from his breast pocket and checks the date and time written on its obverse. He wonders if anyone in Concord knows Seymour Twine, the man he is to meet today. He would prefer that his dealings be kept discreet. Truth be told, he would rather avoid this sort of man altogether, but just such a man had provided wares that proved to be the salvation of his Boston business. Eliot can see no other way to guarantee his speedy success in Concord.

Eliot walks back outside and again tries to picture his sign hanging above the storefront. He thinks he might have the sign cut in the shape of a stack of books, a giant version of the fob in the jeweler's window. For the second time today, Eliot examines his reflection, this time in the dirty windows of his own shop. He retrieves his spectacles and taps them, folded, against his lips. He likes what he sees — the profile of a man pondering days yet to be. He stares at his contemplative twin until they are both startled by a loud voice in the street.

"Can't get your boots mended there!"

The voice belongs to a short bald man in an unbuttoned vest. His tiny eyes are set close in his round head, and his mottled skin and rumpled clothes give him the appearance of having recently been boiled. He carries a broom and points its bristles at Eliot's shop. Although this man is not quite what he had pictured, Eliot is nonetheless relieved that he has finally arrived.

The boiled man keeps talking as he approaches, sweeping the air with the broom, and as he gets closer Eliot notices a pattern in the mottled red patches covering his bald head, shapes reminiscent of a flock of birds, or perhaps a large bat.

"Dropped dead where he stood," the man says. "Mr. Saintsbury, hammer in one hand, lady's boot in the other. They say he had his hand deep down inside it, the boot. Had a time getting it off on account of the stiffness having already set in. She won't wear those boots anymore, Mrs. Mullins, and I can't say I blame her."

Eliot resents the fact that his livelihood seems tied to such men as this, and he is pleased to see that, if nothing else, this man is not quite so odious in appearance as he had reason to expect. In fact, he looks as ordinary as an honest shopkeeper. Eliot waits until the boiled man comes closer, and then says quietly, "I am pleased to see you are a punctual man."

"Eh?" The boiled man smiles broadly, revealing crooked yellow teeth, widely spaced. It is what Eliot has come to expect from such men.

"We are to meet at noon," Eliot says, checking his watch. "You are right on time."

The man's yellow smile shrinks. "I'm afraid you've mistaken me, sir. You are new to Concord?"

"Indeed, I am," Eliot says, chagrined that his usually impeccable judgment of character seems to have failed him. He slips his watch back into his waistcoat.

"I'm Otis Dickerson," the man says. "Sole proprietor of Dickerson and Hapgood Dry Goods and Hardware."

Eliot nods, enough to take the place of a bow. "Eliot Calvert — I'm pleased to make your acquaintance. I will no doubt come calling on Dickerson and Hapgood's once I've inventoried the necessary repairs here."

"Of course, there's no Hapgood now," Dickerson says with a note of apology. "And you'll find I stock more hardware than dry goods these days. But I try to sell what

140

people need, and their needs are mighty changeable."

"I was just entertaining that very thought, Mr. Dickerson. I have been told that Concord is a hospitable place for business."

"So it's true, then? You're taking Saintsbury's place?" Dickerson shifts around to the open doorway, inserting his boiled head into the empty shop as if he expected to see the place already transformed. "Are you the new cobbler? These brogans are about to give out. I can practically see my toes."

"Oh, I don't cobble. I plan to —"

"Not hardware or dry goods you deal in, is it?" Dickerson interrupts. "There was talk of another hardware man coming. Mind you, I'm not afraid of a little competition, but I'd rather know sooner than later."

"I can assure you, Mr. Dickerson, I am not a hardware merchant. I am a purveyor of the printed word."

"Oh. Well, good then. Whatever your trade, though, you'll want to manage better than your neighbor."

Eliot looks where Otis Dickerson points. The windows of the shop next door reveal an assortment of junk piled floor to ceiling. The paint is peeling from the sills and shutters. There is no sign over the crammed windows or above the door. Eliot holds his spectacles in his hand as he scans the storefront, and even without them on he notices that the blurry line of smoke rising above the rooftop has grown thick enough for him to make it out as a dark smudge against the sky. He is about to ask the boiled man if he knows anything about the smoke when he spots a marked slant to the doorway of his shop. He'll need to have that righted, possibly have the lintel replaced as well, if not the whole frame. This might prove a more expensive undertaking than he thought. Eliot begins wishing that Mr. Dickerson were indeed the man he mistook him for.

"I see people carrying stuff in there on most days," Mr. Dickerson says, still pointing next door, "though I hardly ever see them bringing anything out."

Eliot puts on his spectacles and glances up and down the length of Main Street, but he sees no one who might be the dilatory Mr. Twine. It is not absolutely necessary that Eliot meet him today, but if not today what guarantee can he have that the man will show in the future? It is possible, Eliot thinks, that he might stock his new bookshop without this man's assistance; such an arrangement had not been among his intentions when he first opened his Boston shop.

Still, Eliot's dealings in Boston had proved so lucrative, he can scarce imagine doing without similar arrangements in Concord.

Dickerson waits for Eliot to take an interest in his neighbor, and when no questions come he provides the answers in advance. "Stubbins is his name, if you're curious. Humphrey Stubbins. Quiet fellow. Runs a pawn in back. Mean business that, if you ask me."

"I see," Eliot says distractedly. He is reluctant to ask Otis Dickerson if he knows of Mr. Twine's whereabouts, and at the same time he wishes he were not so quick to feel ashamed. Distasteful liaisons were oftentimes a necessary part of business. A man needs to have the will to do what is necessary if he expects to make his way in the world.

"It's not another junk shop you're planning to open, is it?" Dickerson asks.

"No. Certainly not. As I said —"

"Well, whatever you're planning, you just let me know what you need. I'll see you get quality."

"Actually, Mr. Dickerson, it is a bookshop I plan to establish here. A bookshop. I hope you will find it a welcome addition." Eliot hears a certain meekness creeping into his voice, as if he were already apologizing for

143

the question he wants to ask.

"Books?" Dickerson considers this for a moment, rolling the word on his tongue as if to determine its flavor. "Books. Yes. Fine, fine. A fine business."

"I also write myself," Eliot adds. "For the stage." He thinks it important that Dickerson know this. After his play is a success he will be able to look back with fond chagrin at the lengths to which he has gone to make a living while struggling to produce his art. All will be forgiven. "In fact, it is my hope that you will see my latest work performed within the year."

"I don't attend the theater. I take it you'll sell ledgers and bankbooks and the like?"

"Well, yes, and literary works of the highest quality — fine bindings, decorative endpapers. In fact, I am confident this location will prove an attractive gathering place for like-minded patrons to discuss recent events and publications."

"What about card games — something educational, for the children? You'll be selling those, too?"

"Those as well, yes." Eliot tries to hide his disappointment. "I guarantee you will find all that you might expect in any fine bookshop, and more."

"Well, I can see you'll want new shelving,

and that lock there won't hold long enough to baffle a squirrel. You be sure to come to me, whatever you need."

Eliot taps the card in his pocket and wishes that he could conduct the unpleasant business boldly, without embarrassment. "As a matter of fact," he ventures, "there is a small matter in which you might be of assistance."

"If I can't help you," Dickerson says, "you'll be hard pressed to find one who can."

Eliot pulls out the card and makes a show of being unfamiliar with the name. "Do you happen to know where I might find Mr. Seymour Twine?"

The boiled man takes a step back and Eliot sees his eyes flicker back and forth between Eliot's face and the vacant shop.

Eliot immediately regrets mentioning the name. "I only . . . we have some small matters of business to conduct, and I thought you might have some knowledge of the man's whereabouts."

"I thought you said it was a bookshop you were opening?"

"Yes, but there is a separate matter I need to discuss with him, you understand."

"No, I do not understand." Dickerson holds his broom upright, stares squarely at

Eliot. "This is a town of good people, Mr. Calvert, God-fearing people. But we cannot be held accountable for the likes of what passes through from time to time."

Eliot wishes he could say that he is mistaken — that in truth he has no need for the likes of Seymour Twine, that this is all a misunderstanding. He feels as though someone were staring at him, and he sees that the young man and woman he passed earlier are now standing on the far side of the street pointing in his direction. Then Eliot realizes that they are actually pointing at the sky above his storefront and are most likely staring at the smoke rising from the trees.

Dickerson clears his throat before saying quietly, "I'd avoid this Twine fellow if I were you, but if you must, I hear he might be sought some afternoons at Wright's Tavern. An otherwise respectable place, mind you."

"I appreciate your candor," Eliot says. He wants to show Dickerson that he is not embarrassed, that he is a man well acquainted with the wide world and its great variety of commerce. "You may very well have saved me an afternoon of waiting in vain."

Dickerson purses his lips. "I suppose you'll conduct your business as you see fit, but I must insist that you refrain from mentioning my name in this matter."

"Of course," Eliot says. "And, likewise, I would be most grateful if you, in turn, would avoid mentioning this to, well, to anyone else. I would not have my intentions misconstrued."

Dickerson works his tongue in his cheek, grunts in assent, and makes his way back to his shop with the broom over his shoulder. His feet kick up little whirls of dust in the street. Eliot turns and stares through the dirty window of the empty store, pretending to take inventory of the crooked shelves, the warped countertop, the bent nails and scraps of shoe leather scattered about the floor. He can see Dickerson's reflection in the glass and he watches him scuttle away, looking just as boiled as before but somehow less certain of his stride. Eliot sometimes hates himself for the things he feels he must do, simply because there seems no other way to achieve the end he deserves. Every man undergoes transformations, he thinks, some great, but most so small as to be imperceptible, until that day when the sheer number makes their reversal improbable.

The first time Eliot spoke to the beautiful and unapproachable Margaret Mary Mahoney, his legs were very nearly numb from more than an hour of standing in restless anticipation. When he arrived earlier that evening, he found that all three tiers of the Haymarket Theater were sold out, and the twenty-five-cent gallery was crammed with spectators standing shoulder to shoulder. There seemed little reason for the crowd, since the play was known to be mediocre at best. He decided to leave and come back on another night, but then he saw the woman from the Federal Street Theater make her way up the wide stairs on the far side of the Haymarket's lobby. As if by reflex, Eliot surrendered the coin he was about to return to his purse, hurried through the doors, and squeezed into the last bit of remaining space in the gallery. Though he could see only a corner of the stage, he had a clear view of the private boxes hovering above, and through most of the first two acts he watched the dim light from the stage lamps flicker shadows over the woman's graceful expressions.

During intermission, Eliot spotted her alone and within reach in the crowded lobby — coincidences he dared not ignore. For months he had been secretly rehearsing what he would say to her if given the chance, but until that moment he had never seen her without the imposing gentleman he assumed was her father. Once more, silently, Eliot practiced his greeting and the bon mots he had prepared especially for this encounter, and he almost lost his nerve, almost gave in to the churning sensation in his stomach. As he wove his way around the prattling knots of gray-haired men and bejeweled women, Eliot marveled that she had not already attracted the other potential suitors in attendance, men in possession of far greater prospects than his own. He fully expected a handsome gentleman of obvious wealth to step to her side at the last moment, and then he suddenly felt that he could not shuffle through the unyielding crowd fast enough. It surprised him that he was even attempting so audacious a maneuver. He would never have considered doing such a thing a few months earlier, before his rapid advancement at Carter, Hendee & Co. Eliot still chose to sit in the cheapest seats available despite the rise in his wages, but tonight he wore a new suit of clothes, and in his coat pocket his purse hung heavier than usual. Its weight gave him an unexpected confidence.

Up in her private box, the woman had seemed to him to exist in a world far removed from his own, but as he pushed his way toward her in the lobby she surprised him by deigning to look up from her playbill and nod, as though he was just as deserving of her nods as anyone else. It struck him as too generous an acknowledgment. Emboldened by her attention, he drew close, bowed politely, and introduced himself. She said her name was Margaret Mahoney. When she smiled, fine lines bloomed at the corners of her eyes, giving her an air of intelligence that made her appear a bit older than he'd expected, perhaps several years beyond his own twenty-three, but this only made him marvel that she was not already on the arm of another gentleman.

"And what is it that you do, Mr. Eliot Calvert?" she asked. It was a natural enough question, but her directness took Eliot by surprise. It was not what he had rehearsed.

"I am a playwright," he heard himself announce, and he watched how the words made her knowing eyes sparkle. He had not meant to reveal his ambitions from the start, had intended only to say that he was a senior clerk at Carter, Hendee & Co., but her reaction made it impossible for him to take the words back.

"A playwright? How wonderful. I have never before met a playwright. I daresay that Father will be most, ah, intrigued."

150

Eliot had no idea how he would explain his position to her father if the man did not share his daughter's enthusiasm. He tried to remember what he was supposed to say next.

Margaret Mahoney looked at him expectantly, and then said, with what seemed undue excitement, "What a lovely shade of lilac."

Eliot nodded, and nodded again. His mouth had gone completely dry.

"Your coat," she prompted him.

Alone in his room, Eliot had imagined the phrases spoken by the kind of man accustomed to addressing such a rare woman. But now he had completely forgotten his lines. He feared he would have to improvise.

Margaret Mahoney continued, untroubled by his silence. "It is a fitting coat for a man of creative endeavors." She seemed to speak in smiles. "If I were to venture a guess, I would say State Street? By the Common, yes?"

"State Street," he repeated, with some effort.

"Studemeyer's on State. I believe I saw that lilac fabric in the window last month, and it too-soon disappeared."

"Oh, yes, of course. That is most perceptive." Eliot self-consciously brushed the darker lavender of his lapels. His pulse quickened as he sought the right words, pressed his tongue against his teeth, and forced out one of the bits of dialogue he had prepared.

"May I ask what you think of tonight's performance, Miss Mahoney?"

"It is no worse than some, though no better than most."

"A polite judgment."

"You wish something more caustic? Well, then, our hero, I think, lacks direction."

"Perhaps it is intentional?" Eliot watched as a richly attired man examined Miss Mahoney's profile from across the room and then caught Eliot's eye and nodded. It was the first time he had ever possessed, however temporarily, an object of another man's admiration. The rush of blood in his ears made it hard to hear what she was saying.

"And our heroine," Margaret Mahoney said with an air of disdain, "if such she may be called, seems utterly incapable of speaking her mind. If she is waiting for our hero to speak it for her, we shall be imprisoned in this theater for quite a long time."

"You are splendidly harsh."

"And as for the title, I should think that *A Conflagration; or The Lover's Chance Meeting* would necessitate the inclusion of, shall we say, a bit more *heat.* Is that judgment enough?"

"Bravo, Miss Mahoney." Eliot could not believe his good fortune — wit and beauty together. He began to worry that he was even more ill-equipped for the task at hand than he had at first suspected.

"So then, Mr. *Calvert* . . ." Her smile changed, almost imperceptibly, the cordiality replaced by something more calculated. "Is this the moment at which you confess your nom de plume, reveal that you are indeed the author of tonight's entertainment, and upbraid me for my presumption?"

"Oh . . . no . . . no." Eliot felt that he was about to stammer. He took a deep breath and lowered his voice in a masquerade of confidentiality. "I give you my most solemn assurance that I bear no responsibility for tonight's wreckage."

"That is fortunate." She laughed politely. "Else I would have to choose between prolonging my embarrassment and finding other company."

Eliot believed he understood her meaning clearly. She *chose* to remain with him, for this moment, and he had to resist the temptation to fold his arms across his chest, as if to cradle the privilege.

"Is it possible, Mr. Calvert, that I have already had the pleasure of seeing one of your plays?" she asked.

Without considering the consequences, Eliot leaped upon the opportunity to display his wit at last. "No, I am afraid not, Miss Mahoney, unless you have found your way into my imagination." *Was that too bold?* He saw her brow wrinkle, but she was still smiling.

"What an unusual thing to say." She laughed again.

Well played! Eliot thought to himself, growing more confident. "What I mean to say is that I have yet to subject my dramatic works to the public, as they are still in their drooling infancy."

"Your plays, or the public?" she said quickly.

"I, ah, I beg your pardon?" Eliot felt that he had advanced well into the conversation, had in fact turned a corner, only to come upon a wall of stone.

Margaret Mahoney held him in her stare, the way he imagined she might appraise a piece of jewelry on first glance, before picking it up for further consideration. He was distracted by the silky blackness of her hair, by the way the coiled ringlets at the sides of her face bounced gently when she shook

154

her head.

"Who or what is doing the drooling, Mr. Calvert?" she said.

It took Eliot another few seconds to gather her meaning, and then it seemed to spark before his eyes. "Oh, yes, of course. My plays or the public, you mean. I was referring to my plays, certainly, though I suppose, as you wisely suggest, one might indeed say the same of the public."

"Then perhaps we should hope for the swift maturation of both."

"Yes, yes." It was all he could think to say. He felt he had been bested, but he thought he detected a note of encouragement, perhaps even a compliment, in her quip. Never before had he taken such delight in being outwitted.

"I envy you, Mr. Calvert," she said. "I should think the most delicious part of success is the moment just prior to fulfillment."

Eliot tried to choose his words carefully. "I am confident, Miss Mahoney, that even now I stand at the very precipice of fame." As soon as the words left his lips, he thought they sounded childish and boastful. He saw her eyes drift over the crowded lobby and feared she was seeking better conversation. It was only with great effort that he was able to keep from stammering, "I-I-I hope that I do not strike you as a braggart."

Margaret Mahoney turned her attention back to Eliot, and the dark ringlets bounced at her ears. She looked him full in the face for several long seconds. He had not lost her, not yet.

"Mr. Calvert, I find nothing unbecoming about confidence in a man of artistic temperament. One never hears a man of business apologize for his pursuit of wealth. It is an odd measure of success, is it not, having at one's disposal a greater number of the same coin that every man carries in his pocket? I would not count hardship as an accomplishment, but the dedicated avoidance of it is an unromantic goal upon which to construct one's raison d' être. Although" — she paused and let her eyes wander again before returning to Eliot — "I suppose we women must be grateful for the men who are content to do so. We cannot all be wed to struggling artists, else who would attend the theater?"

Eliot wanted to match her sudden philosophizing with an observation of corresponding depth. He thought he might quote an appropriate passage from one of his plays, but then Margaret Mahoney sighed and he found that he could not recall a single line of his own writing. She waved her playbill at the crowded lobby, as if the room of silvered heads and glittering necks proved her point.

"I should think it far easier to instruct an artist in the ways of amassing a fortune than it would be to instill a banker with a love of poetry," she said. "Would you not agree?"

Miraculously, a swift reply came to Eliot, and he delighted in hearing the words slide from his tongue as if their delivery required no effort at all.

"I cannot say, Miss Mahoney, as I have attempted neither."

She laughed, and Eliot watched the lamp light play over the cluster of diamonds and gold filigree at her neck. He felt emboldened and decided to venture an observation of some complexity, one that he had come to some time ago. He brought his lips close to her ear, almost close enough to feel the silky black curls against his cheek — a daring move — and spoke softly.

"I suspect that many who attend the theater little comprehend the depth of humanity represented onstage, but they would be quick to judge the full measure of a man's worth solely by the girth of his bank account and waistcoat."

She nodded. "Then I daresay Father's own success is easily measured by tailor and bookkeeper alike."

Eliot jumped back and saw that her father was making his way toward them. Other men stepped aside to make room for the rotund patriarch, who pushed forward in the confidence that a path would be made for him. The man's cheeks shone with the exertion of lugging around his bulk, and the bare top of his head glistened with sweat between the crests of gray hair that tumbled over his ears. Something stuck in Eliot's throat. He had forgotten himself; he had let his wit outrun his sense.

"I meant no insult," Eliot whispered.

She ignored him and opened her arms to greet her father. He lumbered toward her, and she leaned forward to kiss him on the cheek. The large man patted his cheek where the kiss landed and looked at Eliot critically.

"Father, I was beginning to fear you had abandoned me. Fortunately, Mr. Eliot Calvert has entertained me in your absence. Mr. Calvert, this is my father, Patrick Mahoney."

Before Eliot could say a word, Margaret Mahoney winked at him and said, "Mr. Calvert is a playwright, Father."

Eliot felt his heart race.

"A writer?" Mr. Mahoney was intentionally loud. He spoke with the confidence that anyone within earshot would want to hear what he had to say. "I hope it is none of your nonsense we are suffering tonight."

"Father!"

"You cannot expect politeness," Mr. Mahoney barked, "as I mourn the loss of another hour that might have been spent in the enjoyment of a good cigar."

"Honestly." She playfully patted his arm. "The ushers will begin turning us away at the door if you continue to play the rogue."

"They'll not turn me away as long as they have dollar seats in need of selling." Mr. Mahoney jerked his head upward, indicating the balconies, before looking Eliot directly in the eyes.

"To be honest, sir," Eliot said, "I cannot claim the title of *playwright* just yet —"

"Wait!" Mr. Mahoney held up a soft, thick hand and curled the fat index finger beneath the tip of his nose. "I'll warrant you're a Washington Street man, am I correct?"

"Well," Eliot said, relieved at the tone of approval he heard in the man's voice. "Ah, yes, as a matter of fact. How did you know?"

Eliot heard Margaret Mahoney laugh, saw her roll her eyes and offer an apologetic smile, as if she knew what was to follow. He could hardly pay attention to what her father said, so entranced was he by the way she placed her splayed fingertips to her pale throat.

Mr. Mahoney grunted in satisfaction. "You see, Calvert, it is my business to know men — their motives, their ambitions, their shortcomings. I knew straight off by the cut of your coat that you were more than just a writer, though I did not doubt that you were occupied with the printed word in some fashion. The ink beneath your fingernails gave you away. Where on Washington Street do you ply your trade?"

"Carter, Hendee & Co."

"*Carter and Hendee?* Ha! Then I'll wager it's *Ticknor and Allen* you'll be working for soon enough, once they've acquired the capital. Mark my words, Messieurs Carter and Hendee will be bought before the year is out."

"I had not heard this," Eliot said. There were always rumors, and he had learned to ignore the whispers that periodically sent Mr. Carter or Mr. Hendee (or sometimes both) into pencil-snapping fits; still, he found Mr. Mahoney's matter-of-factness disconcerting. "Are you certain?"

"It's no secret. Scarcely a month passes that one publisher is not swallowing another. I have reliable eyes and ears, as it were."

160

"You are in the publishing business your-self, then?"

"No. Far from it," Mr. Mahoney said. "Finance. Opportunity. I make it my busi-ness to detect opportunities. Intriguing developments in your corner of the city, so I am told."

"Yes, well, the publishing world presents a most tumultuous drama," Eliot replied.

"Drama indeed!" Mr. Mahoney practically bellowed as he stabbed the air with a thick forefinger. "And that is what makes any business more profound than the empty entertainments of the theater, eh? We think alike, Calvert. A man of business is a man of endless interest. I have told my daughter so a thousand times."

"A thousand times at least," she said, and squeezed her father's arm.

Mr. Mahoney cast his eyes upward again. "The trials we men endure, eh, Calvert? The tallest theater in Boston, and she persists in calling it her favorite." He eyed the stairs and cleared his throat. "At the prices we pay, they should be obliged to carry us. Shall we accompany you to your box?"

"Thank you, sir, but, no, I am waiting for . . ." Eliot noticed Margaret Mahoney taking an interest in his response and he stumbled for a convincing conclusion. "For a colleague."

Mr. Mahoney eyed the stairs again, as if he had forgotten they were there, and grumbled, "Well, let's get on with it, my dear. Calvert, a pleasure to meet you."

Consumed with the thought of the task ahead, Mr. Mahoney turned to begin a slow, arduous waddle toward the sweeping stairs, and the crowd parted as before; then he stopped, looked over his shoulder, and called out, "Calvert, we should have a serious conversation about the hurly-burly world of publishing. I have a growing interest in things bookish."

Margaret Mahoney smiled and shook her head. "Please excuse me, Mr. Calvert. I must accompany my father, or the stairs will utterly confound him."

Eliot bowed, trying to remember what he had practiced saying, the perfect line to end their first meeting. But all he could think of was his inadvertent reference to Mr. Mahoney's girth.

"Miss Mahoney . . . your father . . . truly, I meant no insult."

Margaret Mahoney dropped her chin, coyly, and looked up at him with raised eyebrows. "Mr. Calvert, not all that may be insulting to my father is necessarily insulting to his daughter."

She turned and followed the large man. She was truly the most beautiful woman who had ever spoken to Eliot, and he thought he might be happy to spend the rest of his life repaying her for this act of kindness. He watched the imagined outline of her hips sway beneath the layers of crinoline. He sighed when he saw her place her hand upon her father's arm, and in that moment Eliot believed that he had indeed become a playwright, a man for whom the drama of life unfolded beyond the confines of the stage. As Margaret Mahoney climbed the grand staircase, Eliot made his way back to the gallery and found a spot in the shadows where he would not be seen from the boxes above. In the darkness, he thought of Miss Mahoney's swaying figure on the stairs, and he decided that it might not be so great an indulgence to buy a ticket in the upper tiers from now on.

9
CALEB

Caleb Ephraim Dowdy stands alone in the lifeless yellow field, waiting. Nearby, the remains of the old farmhouse trace a jagged rectangle in the dirt. An hour earlier, his voice seemed to fill the ruined space, as if the nave of their new church already enclosed the air above them, but now the only sound he hears is the wind huffing through dry stubble. After the final prayer, the others returned to their homes and shops and farms and street corners; some paused to praise his vision, but now they, too, were gone. Caleb waits until he is certain that they are all out of sight, then he removes his black topcoat, drapes it over a corner of the farmhouse's crumbling foundations, and crawls under.

Over his black shirt and black trousers, he wears the white surplice that he has not put on since leaving his Boston congregation, and the robe spills around his feet as he crouches beneath the tent of his coat and squeezes himself into a ball. He reaches up into his coat pocket and retrieves a slender wooden box. It holds everything he needs. He flips the clasp, and the wind whips the edge of his coat against his face and scatters the contents of the box over the ground. Stiff blades of dead grass prick his fingers as he scratches in the dirt. He finds the pipe easily, but it takes him longer than it should to collect the matches, and he has to stop twice and press his hands flat on the ground to keep them from trembling. Sitting knees to chest, he strikes a match and watches the flame claim a corner of the semidarkness. The sliver of wood curls into a whisker. The flame hiccups, disappears.

This very spot is where his new church will rise — his *church of bones,* the old women called it. So be it, he thinks. Caleb licks his singed fingertips and selects another match. He could waste the dozen or so matches in the same way, and that would put an end to it. He allows ample opportunity for a heavenly power to intervene and drive off the demons that torture him. He strikes another match, holds it a few inches from his nose, and watches the flame crawl toward his fingertips.

These are crucial moments, each pregnant

with the next, each an opportunity to expunge future remorse. The actions men regret — actions they can do nothing to change — live always among things yet to be done. At any moment, a man might forestall the conception of deeds that will later torment him with their irreversibility. Caleb delivers powerful sermons about that very fact. He makes the faithful weep with his descriptions of remorse. He knows how to make them feel the mortality of their fragile bodies and fear for their souls. He makes them see the terror in a pocket watch, the merciless progression of gears, the indifferent sweep of hands, the incremental loss, second by unobserved second. He fills them with guilt for things they have done or contemplated or failed to do. He makes them regret the simple comforts they so easily enjoy in a land where their lives are inexcusably less miserable than they would be anywhere else. And whenever he speaks to his congregation he sees the haunting face, the eyes rolled back, the open mouth and distended tongue, swollen, purple, like a fat bruise. The face gives no sign of recognition. It neither accuses nor forgives; it is simply there, an indifferent, irreversible fact.

Caleb angles the match downward, coaxing the flame toward his fingers. He places his long-stemmed pipe between his teeth and waits. It is not genuine deliberation, this momentary hesitation. The flame sputters, waits for him to make up his mind. It squats into itself like a dog crouching to defecate, and the blackened matchstick glows red, then white, seeming to burn without being consumed, a modern miracle between his fingertips. He holds the match to the bowl of his pipe and then pulls it away, as if prolonged contemplation of the sin will somehow blunt the inevitable transgression. He wants a witness to his struggle, wants God to see his soul's discord played out. Again Caleb brings the flame to his pipe, and this time he inhales the hot perfume that curls off the sticky ball in the pipe's bowl.

The smoke sinks into his lungs. He closes his eyes and thinks of the fallen city on the hill until he can see it hovering before him. He thinks of sin and punishment, of vengeance and condemnation, of lakes of molten ore and everlasting fire, but none of these certainties fill him with the holy dread that has kept generations of the faithful on the straight and righteous path. It is not damnation he fears. What frightens him more is the possibility that these horrific visions merely hide an unfathomable darkness. More terrible than the sentence of eternal suffering is the incomprehensibility of eternity itself, a blank, empty, measureless abyss. What if this fearful nothingness — which men so desperately cram with painted fantasies far better and far worse than the world they know — what if this void is all that awaits even the most devout?

He has spent countless dream-riddled hours staring into the darkness. No longer can he recognize the religion of his forefathers. Their one faith has shattered like a pane of glass, each narrow fragment clear and pure and edged with dangerous points — Unitarians, Trinitarians, Methodists, Presbyterians, Quakers, Shakers, Baptists, and the rest, never again to be reunited into a bright whole. As if revelations fell like spring rains, the fertile soil of New England seems to sprout new faiths, each promising nourishment beyond what their corrupt fruit could ever hope to yield. Caleb finds none so poisonous as those recent heresies that seek to deify America itself, and yet, though he has awaited a fitting response to this sacrilege from heaven, he hears only silence; the profane continue to walk upon the New World with impunity. Faced with such evidence, how could one not find just cause for doubt? Caleb wants to pose this very question to the man who has shown how easily a pagan can walk without fear in God's light. If Caleb could blame one man for showing him heaven's indifference to earthly folly, it is the Unitarian minister — the *ex–Unitarian minister* — Ralph Waldo Emerson, who has demonstrated how carelessly one might progress from believing in Christian redemption to worshipping trees. And has heaven objected to this blasphemy? Do the old women who cursed Caleb's church also beleaguer *Mister* Emerson with their talk of bones? Do these witches stalk the tree worshippers of Concord and remind them that their bones will soon lie in the earth to feed the roots they venerate?

Caleb exhales, watches the bluish smoke coil like snakes into a floating pair of eyes and open-mouthed astonishment. He swats the visage away, then lifts a corner of his coat and surveys the empty field, making certain he is still alone. The old women stayed well after the others, chattering excitedly, poking through the crumbling foundations, comparing bits of brick and mortar to the knobby joints visible beneath the flesh on their skinny arms. They are gone now, but he can still hear their voices. *You will build a church of bones, yes?* Yes, indeed, if that is what is required to force God's hand, then he would build a church from his own bones and place a clapper in his skull to toll loudly from the belfry. Caleb lets the corner of his coat fall, and returns his attention to the shiny black pipe with red-gold dragon lacquered along its length.

He thinks he has seen the two old women before, though he knows he has never heard them speak. He would have remembered the halting accents, the voice of the blind one like a dog's growl, the voice of the other like a wet finger on glass. Despite his fervent hope, they did not prove to be angels dispatched to cast him into the fires of perdition; they did not comport themselves like angels at all, unless, perhaps, they were agents of another rank, seraphim entrusted with gathering evidence to ensure that his damnation, once decreed, would be incontrovertible. Heaven's justice is said to be swift, but it is also said that eternity for man is but a second in the eyes of God. As far as Caleb knows, his trial might be under way this very moment, a court of angels debating his soul's fate. The thought gives him hope.

It was not unthinkable that the women came as messengers from that other place, heaven's opposite. Caleb realizes that if his plan has even the slightest chance of success, Satan himself would certainly want to interrupt its machinations before it brought forth proof. Caleb has not thought of this before. Failure or success will give him an answer — yea or nay — but if his plan goes unexecuted he will have nothing to dispel his doubts. Another thought restores Caleb's trust in his plan. In the event that the old women — if not angels, then witches to be sure — succeeded in foiling his plot, would not this intervention itself prove the existence of Satan and, therefore, the existence of eternity, of a world beyond this? At the very least, he thinks, surely it would disprove the absolute emptiness of the void.

Caleb holds the burning smoke in his chest. The small bowl he imbibed early that morning had muted his crushing headache but had not been enough to sustain him past noon. He is relieved that today none of the members of his congregation tarried the way they usually did, waiting sheepishly to ask him for special prayers or advice. Whenever they stand before him, describing their doubts and trials and infirmities, he feels as though he were perched on the point of a steeple. How small these people appear, with their self-important worries, wholly unaware that even now they stand cheek to jowl with oblivion; at any moment they might disappear and never be missed. And yet they turn to him for benediction, as if he possessed magical powers to bring them closer to God. If only they could see what he sees.

Caleb inhales deeply, feeling the smoke grow hotter as the contents of the bowl diminish; he rolls onto his side and peers out from under his coat again. He can see distant flashes from the fire churning in the woods. From the size of the dark cloud rising above the treetops, he guesses that the fire will not die out on its own, and this simple epiphany makes him smile. He wonders what *Mister* Emerson and his followers will think when they see their hapless deities reduced to ashes. He imagines their despair at having the mutability of their frail beliefs rendered palpable. Will they weep for every tree that falls? Caleb does not expect them to weep for him when his plan at last succeeds, but will they shudder at what his proof reveals? Caleb sucks, drawing out another wisp of poison, and the truth of things assumes the clarity that he finds only when he is at his pipe. The logic of his argument is as strong as a tightly woven rope, mathematical in its precision, philosophical in its simplicity, a proof deserving comparison to those of Descartes or Spinoza. Caleb knows that only one question remains: will the Almighty, who surely foresees the design and intent of his clever plan, allow him to follow it through?

10
ANEZKA AND ZALENKA

Long before the two ancient women with cropped silver hair took up residence in the small cottage near Concord, Massachusetts, they lived for many years on opposite ends of the exhausted silver-mining city of Kutná Hora, in Bohemia. They were born before the newly independent American colonies drafted their Constitution. They met when one was in the third and the other in the fourth decade of life, and during the fifteen years immediately preceding the arrival of Anezka Havlicková and Zalenka Duseková in the New World they each occupied one of the tiny cells in the prison at Krivoklát Castle. Thus did the two women embark on their life together at the advanced age when most expected only to tend the warm ashes of expired love. So had their jailers thought as they turned their heavy keys, releasing the women in the belief that time and slow decay had diminished the desires that the law could not erase.

Zalenka had first been attracted by the buttery apple *koláče* that issued from Anezka's oven at summer's end, when bright apples seemed to drop from the trees in pairs and roll into waiting palms as if they had been planning to do so since the first buddings of spring. One September afternoon, with an apple in each hand, Zalenka followed the sugary smell through a narrow alley in Kutná Hora until she found Anezka sifting flour in a hot kitchen, laughing playfully at the pixie clouds she stirred. Anezka looked to be a decade older than Zalenka but was surprisingly youthful for a woman of nearly forty years. Zalenka watched through the open window, a thief of glances, gathering impressions before making her own. Anezka's fingers were long and thin, and they moved lightly through the sifted flour as if she were experiencing a snowfall for the first time. Zalenka looked at her own hands, thick and calloused; wide enough that she might have carried two apples in each if she had tried.

Zalenka lingered at the window, bathing in the delicious smells, until Anezka invited her in. Awkwardness melted into something else, an unfamiliar comfort. Zalenka stood close, watching the thin fingers work the dough, and in the space between the women there arose more than curiosity, something closer to need. Anezka explained that she was baking for her husband, and Zalenka declared that she wished she could bake such delicacies for her fiancé, but neither confession abated the wanting. Zalenka offered the apples in exchange for instruction. They shared information. *The flour must be carefully sifted. The dough must be rolled thin and kept moist. Bruised apples, just past ripe, were best. The husband was miserly and difficult. The fire in the oven must be spread evenly. The fiancé was conceited and impatient. The apples should be peeled and sliced into wedges. Sugar and cinnamon and a dab of butter on top. The husband was angry that there were no children. Then the edges are folded over, like this. The fiancé wanted as many children as there were apples on the trees. Neither man spoke often of love.* A breeze blew through the kitchen, conjuring a storm cloud from the flour barrel left uncovered, and they laughed at the tempest they had precipitated indoors.

The *koláče* that formed under Zalenka's fingers were lumpy and misshapen, pimpled by pockets of unmixed flour, but her heavy hands were not without skill. They were more accustomed to wrapping bandages, setting splints, sewing gashes, and returning displaced joints to their proper orbits. She had once mended her brother after a hunting accident, removed the bullet, stanched the flow of blood, and made repairs with needle and thread without flinching. He lived to hunt again, though one's aim is never as good after something like that. From her mother, Zalenka learned the art of midwifery, and by an early age she was well acquainted with the terrors of childbirth, long before she became familiar with the cause. Zalenka noticed a fresh burn on Anezka's forearm where she had brushed the hot bricks of the oven; she recommended a salve, and promised to bring an ointment for the older burns already scabbed. Anezka did not ask her for a remedy for the tender, fist-size bruises hidden beneath her corset.

Zalenka and Anezka settled on a place and a time where they could meet without attracting suspicious stares; people readily questioned furtive errands, but no one doubted the propriety of two women bringing flowers to the dank ossuary at Sedlec. The crowded Cistercian graveyard where the ossuary squatted half underground was hardly a spot that anyone would think suitable for trysts. Five centuries earlier, the promise of silver in Kutná Hora had lured men by the tens of thousands; they tunneled into the dirt for the precious metal and remained until plagues and wars swept through the region and filled the earth at Sedlec with their bones, as if in recompense for what they had taken out.

Once a week, sometimes more, Anezka and Zalenka walked between rows of teetering headstones, descended the steep steps into the dark ossuary, and took refuge amid the thousands of bones stacked in pyramids beneath the vaulted stone ceiling. Huge wooden crowns hung above each pyramid, the sides of which were decorated with bones lashed into crucifixes, and at the corners of the ossuary bones festooned the walls in long, drooping chains. In front of the small altar, four Baroque candelabra shaped like towering darts held a procession of skulls gnawing on leg bones, and, at the top of each, fat candles flickered and spilled wax from the laps of trumpeting cherubs.

Anezka and Zalenka knelt before the altar with fingers interlocked; they spoke in whispers that might have been prayers. They shared stories of the parts of their lives that had begun to seem as insubstantial as the stories themselves. They exchanged rings.

There was no need to hide their friendship. Acquaintances admired their sisterly devotion to each other and praised the kindness they showed to the nameless, forgotten remains in the cold, dark chamber. Anezka and Zalenka left flowers at the altar. They carried in brooms and swept the powdery dust that had accumulated on the steps and floor. They gathered the loose bones that spilled from the pyramids and arranged them in straight rows against the ossuary walls. Sometimes they found a tidy pile of bones stacked like firewood at the entrance, bleached white and tied with string, waiting to be laid to rest. Anezka brought a length of cord, and Zalenka helped her string together a garland of skulls and drape them from one pyramid to the other.

For two years, Anezka and Zalenka found sanctuary among the bones, until the day that Anezka did not arrive at the usual hour. Zalenka waited in the gloom, worried that something terrible had happened to Anezka, that her husband had learned the true purpose of their devotions. Zalenka watched the dim candlelight invent shapes and usher shadows between the restless bones. She did not believe in visions, was much too practical to pay attention to the waking dreams that sometimes masqueraded as premonitions. As a child, she had scoffed at her grandmother's earnest tales of fairies who harvested fields in the night, of saints who protected the miners in their tunnels, and of the clay behemoths who guarded the Jews of the Josevov ghetto in nearby Prague. But, despite her skepticism, Zalenka beheld a vision as she waited for Anezka in the animated darkness. She glimpsed what was to come: the bones taken from their piles and rearranged in an elaborate chandelier at the center of the ossuary ceiling, ribs and skulls and tibias, an intricate masterpiece of interlocking pelvises and femurs and vertebrae, candles nestled in knuckled joints, blinking in empty eye sockets. The ghastly spectacle hung before her in the flickering candlelight, swaying in the jittery shadows, and Zalenka thought she could hear the hollow wooden clink of the bones swinging against one another.

And when Anezka finally arrived, weeping, her scarf barely hiding the plum ripe bruise swelling beneath her eye, Zalenka knew at once that they would never see her vision made manifest. Zalenka held Anezka's head in her hands, felt the hardness beneath her cheeks, and kissed her softly in the shadow of the bones. She took her hand and led her up the uneven steps into the

180

light of the cemetery to get a better look at the bruise, and there, beneath the bright sky, she kissed her again.

The holding of hands, the embraces, the whispers and smiles, all these could be overlooked, but there was no overlooking the kiss — the long pressing of lips, not an abrupt veneration of chaste friendship but a kiss full of longing and intent. No written law prohibited what everyone knew was unnatural. One might as well pass laws against flying, they said. But where punishment was wanted there were always laws to be found, charges to be brought.

Anezka and Zalenka were accused of holding intercourse with the dead, of casting spells with whispers and furtive glances. Witches, their accusers hissed. Some said that the two women had taken bones from the chapel, that a skull was found under a bed, a rib in a flour barrel. Their husbands charged them with theft and betrayal and argued that they had at last found the cause of their childless marriages, for God would certainly not permit the propagation of evil. Vows and promises were voided. In an earlier, less enlightened time, the women might have been tortured and burned for their witchery, but instead they were granted the vicious mercy of indefinite imprisonment. The cells were crowded, but they were kept apart. Sometimes a compassionate guard, a frail, soft-spoken man, fearful himself of unwritten prohibitions, would accept scribbled notes and deliver them with an understanding nod. Some of the other guards delivered only slaps and kicks.

Though few survived so long an imprisonment, Anezka and Zalenka each refused to die alone, knowing too well the bleak rest that awaited, and when they were finally released, a decade and a half later, they returned to Sedlec, to the graveyard that seemed destined as their final home. The ossuary had grown more crowded still, and disease had already delivered both husbands to the hulking pyramids. The women's crimes were known by everyone in Kutná Hora, but no one cared if two old women embraced to hold each other upright as they hobbled down streets more heavily trafficked than they remembered. Faces vaguely familiar turned away from the two women — one bent, one half-blind — who now resembled the witches they had once been accused of being.

In prison, they had heard whispers about the New World. They had heard about the new towns and villages, the shining city built on a hill, a place where it was said that men had not yet written unjust laws or built cruel prisons, a place where one might look forward to a peaceful rest, unmolested in an uncrowded grave. After they emerged from their cells, they heard the New World discussed openly in the streets and in cafés, a place where simple wants could be met, a place where the only currency one needed was the sweat of honest labor, a place where one need not hide one's wants in silent desperation. So Anezka and Zalenka turned away from the chapel of bones and boarded a ship bound for America, to the land that promised the blessed absolution of anonymity.

11
HENRY DAVID

Henry wants to do something but cannot. It is a conundrum familiar to him.

He lies on his back, splayed flat across the crest of Fair Haven Hill as if he had been dropped from a great height by a startled bird. He is clutching the ground, trying to catch his breath, when he feels an urgent prickling along his limbs like hot sparks, feels the muscles in his arms and legs contract in spasms.

Henry ignored the stout man's advice at first; after the man and his dog ran to get help, Henry continued the fight, tried to wrestle the flames on his own. He stomped at the smoldering grass. He kicked waves of dirt. With bare hands, he ripped up vines and bushes in the fire's path. He yelled at the flames, but his voice was a hoarse whisper compared with the pure, thunderous rage moving through the trees. It burned on without remorse. It scorched the earth, felled trees, devoured animals whole — a brutal, reckless harvest. Henry was helpless. Starved for cool air, barely able to lift his legs or swing his arms, he at last turned away from the fire, climbed Fair Haven Hill, and collapsed at the top until the hot sparks of his conscience began to agitate his limbs.

He raises himself onto his elbows, but his legs do not respond to the prickling. His calves quiver in phantom convulsions of running, but he is too exhausted to move. His face and hands are black with soot, and his fingers, slashed and crusted in a dozen places, are so swollen that he can no longer clench his fist in defiance. He is grateful that the stout man and his dog agreed to carry word to Concord, for he realizes that he could not have made it himself, not without stopping to rest. He wonders if the river has carried Edward to Concord by now. Edward must be tired as well, Henry thinks, though Edward has not run for two miles through the woods. Surely Edward will not need to rest, but what if the boat runs aground or takes on water or capsizes? How much more time will pass, Henry wonders, before help finally arrives?

He pulls himself to a sitting position, and from the hill he can almost see the distant spot where the fire started. He tries to massage the life back into his legs as he stares at the fury below. The bright swirling plumes inspire unusual thoughts, and his unfortunate likeness to the emperor Nero in this regard does not escape his notice; he is glad that he left his flute at home today. The fire crawls along tree limbs like a luminous fungus, hopping onto frail branches barely able to support the infinitesimal weight of flame before burning into nothingness. Henry examines his rough hands, the very hands that gathered the kindling and struck the match, and he rubs the tips of his thumb and forefinger together, grinding the hard grain of guilt between them. He wonders if it makes a difference, if blame can be ranked and parceled out, if one can ever be *less guilty* or *more innocent.* Where can one ultimately assign the first cause? It was his hand that struck the match, but there are any number of preconditions that made the act possible, perhaps unavoidable. He wonders if he might convincingly argue that pencils helped cause this tragedy.

He was a boy when his father began manufacturing pencils in the small room at the back of their rented house. It is still an honest enough pursuit, Henry thinks, a humble and forthright occupation. Its absolute impunity is compromised only by the observable fact that his father conducts the business at no small profit. Henry grew up amid the smells of wood shavings and glue, learned the grammar of pencil manufacture along with mathematics and history, and he has worked in his father's little factory, off and on, for years. But only recently has he come to accept that his filial service to John Thoreau & Co. may very likely constitute his defining labor as a man.

Henry assumes that chance played no small role in the early success enjoyed by the Thoreau brand of pencils — chance and a lode of exceptionally compliant graphite. American pencils were generally regarded as impotent tools: greasy, gritty, easily smeared. For years, the Munroes and the Dixons and the other pencil-making families of America sought the proper mixture to improve their dismal stores of the twinkling black mineral. Glue, bayberry wax, spermaceti, and graphite were all to be found in the most popular concoctions. But American pencils remained temperamental things — glutinous in summer, brittle in winter. Some pencil-makers sealed their boxes with forged foreign stamps to make their pencils easier to sell, since everyone knew that pencils of real quality were to be had only from Europe — *crayons* from Pannier &

Paillard of Paris, *Bleistiften* from the Fabers of Nuremberg — and the very best came from London, made with superior English antimony from Borrowdale. But European pencils were an expensive luxury, and in times of conflict and embargo they could not be had at all. Americans needed pencils of their own.

And so it seems to Henry that fate must have been at work when his maternal uncle, Charles Dunbar, stumbled upon a rich vein of graphite — what some still called plumbago — near Brixton in the hills of New Hampshire. Charles persuaded Henry's father to open a pencil factory after John Thoreau's attempts at coaxing a living from the soil had proved fruitless for yet another season. Henry's father was earnest in his new trade, even if he was disheartened to find that making pencils was a dirty business. The New Hampshire plumbago crumbled at the touch. It smeared, left greasy smudges on his hands, clothes, face. The walls and doorframes of Henry's childhood home collected black fingerprints; at dinner a loaf of bread bore the leaden mark of his father's hand where he tore off a piece for his gravy, and customers complained that their documents left traces of the words and figures they recorded. But, even so,

Charles Dunbar's plumbago proved to be superior to anything else available, and in no time the pencils that issued from the little factory of John Thoreau & Co. were regarded as the finest in America. Some shopkeepers in Boston proudly displayed the award-winning Thoreau pencils — which did not need the masquerade of forged foreign stamps — as if they were fine cigars, ribbon-bound in handsome wooden boxes.

And then fate intervened again, Henry thinks. He wonders how often his life will be affected by accidents, by the chance occurrences that outweighed the impetus of his own intentions. Henry did not want to spend his life making pencils. He gave up working in his father's factory so that he might devote his energies to writing and teaching. He traveled to New York to pursue a writing career and to tutor the sons of William Emerson, brother of Henry's good friend Waldo, in whose home he had been living for almost two years. It was Waldo who encouraged his writing, insisted that he begin keeping a journal, urged him to move to New York and cast himself into the wider world. The arrangement was, at first, all that Henry could have hoped for. But he soon found life in New York a wholly unpleasant and lonely affair, unless one enjoyed the companionship of the wild pigs roaming the city streets. Even the weather displeased him; it seemed, if possible, colder and wetter than in New England.

And there it is, Henry concludes, as he watches another leafless maple succumb to the flames. *There is the distant cause that has resulted in this calamity before him. Cause and effect.* If New York had been more hospitable, if he had found a publisher there for his poems and essays, if tutoring the Emerson boys had brought him more satisfaction, if he had found another friend like Waldo, if only *one* of these things had transpired, he might happily have remained in that great American city, and the Concord Woods would not now be aflame.

But Henry did not stay in New York for long. Homesick and disappointed, he returned to Concord, a route he seemed destined to travel again and again. Determined to be useful to his family, he resolved to help his father improve his pencil-making business. Henry experimented with new blends of plumbago paste in search of a better filling. He mixed plumbago with boot polish. He stirred in ash and tallow and spit. He added silt from the bottom of the Sudbury River. He sprinkled in manure. And then he mixed the graphite with Bavarian clay and found that, by carefully varying the ratio of the two, he could control the hardness and darkness of the resulting paste. He designated pencils of varying hardness with *SS* or *S* or *H* or *HH.* He made pencils in Carpenter's Large, Round, and Oval sizes, black or red. The new blend left a rich mark, smooth and smudgeproof; Thoreau pencils gave testimony that American pencils need not crumble under the pressure of a nervous hand or change consistency with the weather. Within months of developing the new filling, he heard that men of discerning taste — men who appreciated the qualities of a fine line well drawn — refused to write with anything else. Henry found some contentment in knowing that he was providing Americans with pencils worthy of their grand ambitions.

John Thoreau & Co. began supplying the new lead to other pencil-makers at considerable profit, while Henry turned his attention to the machinery of the business. It was tedious work. The wood had to be split into thin fingers, the halves grooved, the hollows packed with lead paste, and the halves glued back together, all by hand. The monotony of the process was surpassed only by its wastefulness. But Henry knew that his special mixture tolerated fire and could be baked into cakes hard enough to withstand cutting. He invented a machine to slice the hardened lead cakes into thin rods. He invented another machine for drilling holes in pencil wood. To better grind the plumbago into the finest possible dust, he built a churnlike device that operated on its own once his sisters, Helen and Sophia, wound the clever spring. He devised a method for tamping the hardened lead rods into the hollowed wooden shafts. The shop overflowed with cords of pencils piled high, like a miniature forest laid low; Henry and his father walked among the little fallen trees like gargantuan lumberjacks. For the first time in their lives, the Thoreau family could begin to think about purchasing a parcel of land on which to build a home of their own. No longer would they live in rented lodgings. With little forethought, Henry became an engineer of sorts; after years of failing to choose a career himself, he found that circumstance had chosen for him.

Then, wearied by his industriousness, he decided to take a holiday, to stretch his legs and clear his lungs. His pencil work kept him indoors, bent to the workbench, breathing the heavy air of graphite and sawdust. He and Edward Sherman Hoar set out to wander under the open sky, a day of gliding over noiseless waters, bothering no one save the occasional bittern nesting along the river's edge. They caught a mess of fish and thought to boil a chowder. They forgot matches, but fate interceded, yet once more, and a shoemaker near the river gave them three red-tipped marvels that they could strike anywhere. The matches were a great improvement over the phosphorus locofocos notorious for erupting in their boxes. Henry struck the match against a hollow tree stump; everything was as it should have been, but the grass was exceedingly dry and the wind exceptionally strong.

Henry hugs his knees tightly, watches the half-mile-wide fire, and considers the many individual acts that led to this moment. He has gone over this again and again. Is blame elastic, or can it be confined to a single point? He watches as the southwest wind continues to push the flames away from the river, away from the hollow stump at Fair Haven Bay, over Shrub Oak Plain, toward Fair Haven Hill, Bear Garden Hill, and Concord. The fire continues its dizzying climb into the uppermost reaches of the trees and beyond, hurling itself upward, reaching for the clouds. On the far side of the fire, the newly laid Boston–Fitchburg rail line will create a firebreak, Henry thinks. Although the trains will not begin their journeys between Boston and Fitchburg until the summer, Henry already despises the railroad for the ruin it will bring to the serenity of the woods. Now he wonders if there will be woods left to disturb.

Henry slaps his thighs, kneads the muscles with his knuckles, begins to feel life slowly returning. He will be ready to rejoin the battle when the men finally arrive from town. But he has begun to worry. He expects to see scores of men running through the trees, but it already seems that an hour or more has passed since he and Edward parted ways. Has it been longer? What if Edward cannot convince the people of Concord that the fire is of a magnitude that warrants their concern? What if the stout farmer and his dog have been overcome by smoke and cannot corroborate Edward's alarm? At what point, Henry wonders, should he conclude that he has been abandoned on the hill, left to face the flames alone?

He knows it is of no real use, his sitting and watching, but he cannot turn away from the raucous fugue. Viscous sap bubbles from blackened bark with greasy hisses. Pinecones squeal and pop. Leaves whistle and disappear. Trunks crack open, limbs burst, tiny buds snap with tiny cries. Other cries are unbearable. Birds lost in the smoke, unable to fly upward without knowledge of the sky, call for direction; squirrels stranded in the attics of trees chatter fiercely at the invisible ground. Nothing emerges.

Henry rubs his legs vigorously. He drives his knuckles deep into the muscles as if he might force the regret from his limbs, wring out the hopeless desire to undo what he has done. He wishes now that he had taken no holiday. He wishes that he had remained in the workshop today, shut away from the natural world, hunched over his geared inventions, blackening his lungs with clouds of powdered pencil lead.

12

ODDMUND

He follows the narrow cow path called
Corner Road and crosses Hubbard's Bridge
and does not pause to watch the Concord
River sparkling in the gaps between the
loose boards. In summer the bridge is
slippery with moss, but today the boards
are as dry and dusty as the fields. Under his
footsteps they clatter loosely against the
worn crossbeams. Now and again he thinks
he can smell the smoke behind him, but he
does not turn to look. He takes short,
explosive strides, and in no time he passes
Bear Garden Hill, nearly halfway to town.
He would rather not go. He is, at best, a
reluctant messenger, and he worries what
the people of Concord will think when he
delivers the news. He avoids them whenever
he can. It is easier to shun their company
altogether than to bear the little disappointments of their polite indifference. They are
always uneasy with him, always unsure what

to make of his quiet, solitary manner. He wonders if they will be suspicious when he tells them what is happening in the woods. Will they accuse him of causing the fire through his own carelessness?

If Mr. Woburn himself had asked him to go to town, Odd might have found a reason not to, but he never refuses Emma. He cannot stand the thought of disappointing her. Odd counts his steps. He knows the number the milelong walk requires, give or take a few strides. He travels this road frequently and can reckon the extra time needed to make the trip ankle-deep in mud or knee-deep in snow. Today, with the wind at his back, there is nothing to slow his pace but his own dread; he will make the trip in less than half an hour.

The first time he wandered down Corner Road, he did not expect to return. That was just after his uncle Søren's death, a decade earlier, when Odd found himself abandoned once more in the strange new world. He no longer remembers exactly how many years he lived with Søren Hus in the tidy house on Court Street near Boston's busy Scollay Square, though he can vividly recall how it felt to step through the doorway that first time, like being wrapped in a thick blanket smelling heavily of spices he could not identify, a scent of sweet and bitter confusion. It is easy for him to summon vague impressions such as these; they linger on his senses like an aftertaste of experience, but the facts themselves never survive so well. Most of the nutshell-hard memories from his childhood, the demonstrable tokens of a life lived elsewhere, have all but vanished. He can no longer recall the sound of his father's voice, but he remembers the sensation of the deep baritone resonating against his breastbone, and he has no trouble at all remembering the tickle of stiff whiskers against the back of his neck, or the oily smell of his father's hair. Odd can still feel the soft, blubbery fatness of the pink mole on his father's wrist; he could not resist poking it in fascination whenever his father fell asleep in the chair by the hearth. But Odd can recall none of the practical advice that might have helped him find his way through this foreign land on his own.

Odd's memories of his uncle Søren have already faded in much the same way; a few specific details remain, and most of these he would gladly forget. Søren Hus made his living by importing cinnamon and nutmeg and cloves and tea and coffee and other profitable things from distant places. It was not a business that required him to have anything to do with the arduous work of loading, sailing, and unloading ships. As far as Odd could tell, Søren Hus achieved these tasks by shifting long columns of numbers in the thick account books that filled his study. He spent endless hours fretting over the tallies. He traveled often, inspecting newly arrived cargo, appraising the seaworthiness of ships, meeting with merchants in Connecticut, New York, Maryland, Virginia, and sometimes as far away as the Carolinas. The loss of any one ship at sea, his uncle told him, could cost him everything he had earned over the years, including the house at Scollay Square. Odd could not understand why his uncle acted as though something might be done to preclude such inevitable loss. He had seen that all things eventually disappeared, and it surprised him that men struggled tirelessly under the illusion that they could change this basic fact.

Odd cannot recall precisely what he felt for his uncle at the time. He was happy to be taken from the Boston Asylum and Farm School for Indigent Boys, happy that someone had come looking for him. In the house at Scollay Square, no aspect of his care was overlooked, and his uncle even arranged for private tutors to see to his education. But Odd was not convinced that his sudden good fortune was anything more than a temporary accident. He always suspected that he would be abandoned again, and it did not seem at all unlikely that his uncle would one day simply go away. Odd could not understand what he had done to make people leave him, or why it was that he was sure to be left behind when those he cared for were taken, but he knew that if he bothered to care too deeply he would find it that much harder to deal with the loss when it came. Still, he was drawn to Søren Hus, this man whom his father had so reviled, his only blood relation in the New World. At the time, Odd did not fully grasp how his uncle had found him or why he had even bothered. Søren Hus had no wife, no family of his own, and he usually had few words for Odd, seldom communicated at all aside from patting Odd awkwardly on the head. Sometimes Odd felt that his uncle looked at him as though he were surprised to see him in his home, and it made Odd wonder if the man had simply collected him like one of the knickknacks cluttering his shelves and curio cabinets, another piece of gimcrackery that the man had picked up on his travels to show his guests the richness of his life.

Odd saw more of the housekeeper, Mrs. Galligan, than he did of his uncle, and she daily told him how fortunate he was to be looked after by a flesh-and-blood relation. Mrs. Galligan, a slight woman with sharp features and steel-colored hair, had no living family. She said she had watched them die one by one in the rebellion that ravaged Ireland in 1798. She came to America alone. The blood that flowed through her veins was the last of an unremarkable vintage. She never married, but everyone called her "Mrs. Galligan" out of respect for her age. The day was approaching, she frequently told Odd, when she would depart this earth and there would be no more Galligans of Dun Laoghaire. She seemed more relieved than saddened by this fact, and she did not let an opportunity pass without reminding Odd that no bond was stronger than the bond of family; nowhere would he learn more about who he was and what he was likely to become.

Odd never mentioned the objects that his father had thrown from the deck of the *Sovereign of the Seas.* He never mentioned how his father had consigned to the ocean the small portrait of the man with an inverted *V* for a smile. He never told how his family whispered Uncle Søren's name back in the Old World, how they shook their heads and clicked their tongues after he disappeared. In the house on Court Street, Odd found no evidence of the unspoken transgressions that had so provoked his father. He saw nothing that set Søren Hus apart from the mass of well-intentioned men, nothing that should cause him to scorn the man who had come looking for him. Still, he would not permit himself to feel anything for his uncle beyond gratitude, so certain was he that a stronger feeling might trick him into believing that he would never find himself alone again.

Uncle Søren brought him gifts from his travels up and down the coast: a shark's tooth bearing a scrimshaw schooner along its length, a wooden box with a hinged lid and a clipper ship carved on its side for Odd to store his collection of stones, a new spyglass to replace the broken one that Odd nevertheless preferred. From an Indiaman loaded with cinnamon, Uncle Søren brought a polished teardrop of amber with an insect inside; he explained how this marvel came to be, but Odd felt sorry for the tiny fly, imprisoned for simply alighting on the wrong tree at the wrong time a thousand years ago. It struck him that no creature walking the earth was safe from the accidents of fate, but this knowledge was not enough to prepare him for what was to come.

In the summer of Odd's sixteenth year, Søren Hus was hung from his neck in the courtyard of the Leverett Street Jail for offenses that everyone knew he had not committed, and Odd became the last Hus in America.

A week before Uncle Søren met his grim end, Odd lay hidden in the tall, fecund-smelling weeds near the head of the Charles River with Sarah Middlebrooke, a skinny girl who sold flowers in Scollay Square, and they each tested the boundaries of recently discovered wants. He had not found the skinny girl particularly attractive or interesting, aside from the curiosity of her hopelessly crooked teeth, but she had paid him attention, and that seemed enough. Hidden among the overgrown grasses and top-heavy cattails, Odd kissed her uncertainly. His first kiss was a distant imitation of the kisses he had seen his father grant his mother, chaste gifts of affection, a grudging acknowledgment of presence. Odd heard the weeds whispering disapproval as they bent and swayed, rubbing against each other under the pressure of the breeze. He touched Sarah's shoulder, her elbow, her hair, uncoordinated explorations, as if he were trying to convince himself that she was there, that the clumsy, prodding hand was his. Her touch was more practiced. He sensed that she had been to the weeds before, and it made him embarrassed for his inexperience. Her hand seemed certain of its path. Starting at his face, her fingertips glided over his cheek, across his shallow Adam's apple, down his shirtfront, and then, without the slightest hesitation, into the front of his trousers.

Sarah leaned into him, whispering something into the back of his neck while her fingers worked against a rough seam. Odd felt himself rise to her touch; he clutched at the tangled roots on either side, anchoring himself, declaring this spot the center of his world. But in the next moment he was overwhelmed with disappointment as he felt himself dissolve and drift away. Though the skinny girl was on top of him, she was so light, so insubstantial, that it seemed she might be carried away by the breeze rustling through the tall weeds, leaving him alone with his discovery. As if the girl were in no way connected to the slender fingers urgently working in his trousers, Odd felt himself float right through her, rising on an expanding cloud of heat, and then a roaring wave of pleasure swept him from this cloud and he plummeted into a cold, wet blackness. When he opened his eyes, he found the skinny girl crying and clawing at his hand where it clutched her thin arm. At the moment of his crisis, he had desperately reached out for something to keep himself from floating away, and he had caught her arm in his fist with such force that her pale skin was already showing a ring of bruises like a blue bracelet.

Panicked, Odd ran from the crying girl, promising himself that he would never again return to the weeds. When he arrived at the house on Court Street, he found Mrs. Galligan sitting on the front steps, and he was confused at first to see that she, too, was in tears. For a moment he thought that she had discovered where he had been, but then he saw that the front door hung crookedly on its hinges, the lock shattered. Through the gaping doorway, he could see that the inside of the house was in shambles. Odd knew right away that he had somehow caused this disorder, that the punishment for his indiscretion with Sarah Middlebrooke had lighted upon his uncle's house. He told himself how it must have happened: the skinny girl had arrived home before him, had shown her father and her brothers the bruises, and they had come for him. Odd hung his head in shame as he approached, and he was about to confess his guilt when Mrs. Galligan placed her hand on his shoulder and held him at arm's length.

"You must go at once," she said. "It cannot be true, but you must go at once."

Odd thought she was telling him to flee. "Where will I go?"

"To Leverett Street. To your uncle." Her tears, he understood then, had nothing at all to do with what had happened in the weeds. "They have taken your uncle Søren to the jail."

Odd found his way to the Leverett Street Jail just as Mrs. Galligan had instructed. At first, he was not as alarmed as he thought he might be to see his uncle imprisoned. The communal cell looked palatial compared with the dark cabin Odd's family had been forced to share with two other families during the crossing. Odd remembered how his mother had shared all of their sugary potato *lefse* with the other children that first night, though he had hoped there would be enough to last all the way to America. There was no food in his uncle's cell, but there was a square window near the ceiling and piles of clean straw and no dead flies floating in the water bucket. Odd saw that a number of other men occupied the cell, and they appeared to be keeping their distance from his uncle, squatting on the straw and leaning into the corners. Odd tried not to look at them. Søren Hus retained an air of offended elegance — as if he had been slapped for brash words at a dance and needed only to return home to sleep off his rejection. His vest and coat were torn but still buttoned, his cravat still tight at his throat. A purple bruise spread beneath his right eye, and flecks of dried blood sat at the corners of his mouth. Odd thought he smelled cloves and cinnamon.

Søren Hus tried to tell him what had happened. Odd watched his uncle's tongue flicker through the jagged gap where teeth had been broken. The story spilled out in jumbled fragments; it involved a young lady, he said, a very young lady. Odd was struck by the look of shock in his uncle's eyes, as if he had abruptly been awakened from a terrible dream to find it real. The details made no sense at first. The story had to be repeated, enlarged. The girl, his uncle explained, a child really, had resisted his advances and in the ensuing scuffle he had used more force than he intended. He had, in fact, very nearly killed her, but the child escaped his grasp and spoke of what had happened. She might not have been believed, but there was a witness, and within days other witnesses came forth. He had been seen with other girls. He had been seen in the company of young boys as well, ruffians and guttersnipes, unfortunate boys without families. The women of the Boston Female Asylum said he had pretended to be the uncle of one of their destitute girls before they sent him away, and he confessed to Odd that he had visited the Boston Asylum and Farm School on Thompson's Island more than once. Søren Hus seemed relieved to have been found out. He said that he would willingly have confessed, but before he could be properly arrested angry men marched on Scollay Square and dragged him to the jail. He denied nothing. He made no excuses to Odd. His only explanation for his deeds was that he could not do otherwise.

Odd listened, silent, bewildered. Nothing in his uncle's demeanor — his quiet speech, gentle manners, fine clothes — had ever suggested that the man might be capable of what he described. Odd thought of the portrait sailing from his father's hand, and he loathed himself for not trusting his father's judgment. Then he thought of Sarah Middlebrooke. He thought of the urges that had rushed through him, and he wondered if he himself had narrowly avoided a similar end. What violent acts might he have committed if Sarah had not been so willing from the start? At that moment, a strange sensation rose from the pit of his stomach; it was not hatred or disgust for his uncle but, rather, abhorrence for the blood in his own veins, the blood he and his uncle shared. Odd felt as though he had been plunged into a murky pool; his vision blurred and he felt that he could not breathe. And then something his uncle had said, a small detail, bobbed to the surface. Odd formed the question slowly, already saddened by the answer that he knew would come.

"When you came to the island, it was not to find me?"

His uncle shook his head slowly.

"You wanted a different boy," Odd said. "*Sturen gutt, dårlig gutt* — any boy."

"I did not even know you had come to America," his uncle said. "It was an accident, my finding you there. Chance. Fortune."

Odd puckered his lips and sucked at his dead tooth. He realized, then, that since his arrival in the New World he had always been alone.

"Oddmund," his uncle muttered through swollen lips, shaking his head ruefully, "you were to be my atonement."

Odd closed his eyes and tried to pretend that none of this was happening. He wished he could lay claim to his life as a thing untouched by others, a solitary, singular fullness that he might cleave to himself and carry off into the wilderness.

"I see you are disgusted with me," his uncle said. Odd wanted to protest, but he could not explain what it was that had taken the place of disgust.

"It is easy to condemn my weakness," his uncle said, lisping through his broken teeth. "But one day you will understand."

Odd wanted to ask his uncle a hundred things. He wanted to know how he might avoid a similar end. He wanted to beg him for guidance. Most of all, Odd wanted to be reassured that whatever willful perversions had seized his uncle would not, one day, enthrall him as well. Odd thought of Sarah lying on top of him in the weeds, and he began to fear for her safety. He thought of the cravings that she drew out of him, and he knew he must never see her again. Sarah had not resisted, but there had been nothing to resist. He had been too nervous to do anything. He had only to let it happen. But what if he had wanted more? What if she had denied him? What would he have done?

Odd's uncle rummaged in his coat pocket and came toward him. "They will, no doubt, take everything. There are debts, of course. But this is for you."

Søren Hus slid his fist between the bars of the cell door, uncurled his fingers, and a small weight dropped into Odd's palm. It was shaped like a flattened egg. The silver was badly tarnished, but the clasp worked and the hinge opened to reveal two thumb-size portraits of Odd's parents.

"My brother forgot me. Understandable. A family must rid itself of what it cannot explain. But, still, he was my brother."

The trial, the conviction, the hanging — all followed a week later.

Odd wanted to see for himself, to make sure, but executions had ceased to be public spectacles in Boston; the old, portable gallows was no longer wheeled into the Common before a jeering crowd. So, on the appointed day, Odd climbed up into the branches of a sturdy oak and peered over the edge of the prison wall. He saw that no one else was in the yard or on the street. Some said that the anti-gallows societies would eventually eliminate the dispatching of criminals altogether, but Odd had heard that even those who wanted to abolish the ugly practice fell mute when they learned of

Søren Mikkel Hus's crimes. Odd carried the broken spyglass with him, and from the tree he scanned the empty prison yard. He did not expect to be able to see it happen, but he hoped that there would be some way to make sure that Søren Hus took his weakness with him. Odd could not bear the prospect of facing it alone in the New World; he was not strong enough by himself to defeat whatever demons had tormented the family for generations.

Like the officials gathered on the scaffold in the prison yard, Odd knew that his uncle had not done the things they said out loud. No one dared speak of his true crimes. Instead, they called him a thief and a murderer. *A thief of virtue, a murderer of innocence.* It was said that several years earlier another man had paid for the evil that Søren Hus acknowledged as his own. The minister attending the previous execution had refused to ask God to have mercy on the unfortunate man's soul, and now the condemned man's spirit was said to wander Leverett Street at night seeking vengeance. But no one regretted the tragic error. Some crimes were so heinous that an accidental sacrifice seemed a small price to pay to ensure that evil was purged from the society of decent men.

Odd perched in the branches, looking through the broken spyglass, and he thought he saw his uncle grin as the noose was placed around his neck. Odd saw his uncle scoff at the men too weak to name his transgression, saw him mock his executioner as his false sentence was read out loud, saw the pride he took in the fact that he alone committed acts that other men dare not even speak aloud. When the trapdoor swung open, he saw his uncle drop through the black hole, saw his back arch and twist in the shadow of the scaffold. Once the struggle stopped, once the man's last breath carried off his life and his pants darkened with the final issues of the dead, Odd watched for some sign of the departure of his uncle's soul. His eyes watered as he strained to see what was not there. Was it possible for a soul to remain with its mortal shell and molder in the ground? And, if not, where would it go, unwanted, unwelcome, unrepentant? Odd stared. He cupped a hand to his ear and listened. He cannot remember clearly what happened next, but he was certain he heard something, muffled and distant at first. And then it was coming for him in a great, howling rush. The sky moved around him. Trees and buildings shuddered under the blow. Odd dropped his useless spyglass and clung to the branches of the oak, and he felt the force of it lifting him, driving him up through the branches and out over the scaffold, offering him to the tortured spirit that death had unleashed below.

As he hurries up Corner Road toward Concord, Odd notes that the sun has already begun the slow creep from its noontide height. The fire in the woods has been burning for at least an hour, he guesses, and he dares not imagine how far the wind has spread the flames in that time. He is afraid to look back at the dark plume that he knows has grown steadily since he set out.

At a shallow depression in the road, Odd comes to a raft of logs set into the hard dirt. The logs are a recent improvement, leveling the very spot where Odd first met Emma Woburn a few years earlier, when she was still Emma Manning, when the possibility still existed that he might make his feelings known to her. He imagines Emma's weight pressed against him, and the very idea makes him catch his breath. Another twenty minutes of walking will bring him to the center of town, but he hesitates here at the raft of logs. The whole of Concord could burn to the ground, he thinks, and still he would not be able to tell Emma how often she is in his thoughts.

By the time Odd met Emma, he had lived by himself in a small cabin in the Concord Woods for almost five years, longer than he had lived with his uncle, longer than he had stayed at the orphanage on Thompson Island. After his uncle's death, Odd's first thought was to run, to change his name, to forget the man and his deeds entirely. But he was also old enough to understand that there were things he could not escape. He knew he could not run from the perversions that surely flowed through his own veins, just as it had flowed through the veins of Søren Hus and every Hus whose relics his father had thrown into Massachusetts Bay.

Instead of running, Odd drifted. He wandered the streets of the city that still seemed strange and new. For a few weeks, he lived among the scavengers at Boston Harbor, huddling in the narrow spaces between warehouses at night. The scavengers ignored him. He walked the piers, watched the arrival and departure of ships, waited for the Atlantic to disgorge some remnant of his past, some artifact that might indicate the nature of the crimes he feared he was destined to commit. But the ocean kept its secrets. He watched men and women spill from ships, stunned by the sudden fact of their arrival. He watched families arrive intact — weak, ill, imperfect, but whole — watched them set foot in the New World without suffering through the flames that would have purged their flaws, culled their frailties, transformed them into stronger animals. He imagined himself among them, holding Birgit's hand and clutching his mother's dress, standing in his father's protective shadow. In his loneliness he envied these new arrivals, undeserving survivors of the world's grotesque unfairness. They had no right to bring their weaknesses with them, he thought. What right did Søren Hus have to carry his flaws to the New World? Why had flames and accidents spared his uncle's ship and not the *Sovereign of the Seas*? Odd was frightened by the rage he felt building in his breast as, day after day, he watched one ragged traveler after another stumble down the gangplanks. He hated himself for wishing upon them the same misery he had endured, hated himself for feeling that he should be somehow stronger, somehow better for having borne fortune's random cruelty.

Odd did not stay at the docks. He turned inland, drifted westward through the growing city that was busily wharfing out and leveling hills and filling bays and rivers; he drifted out into the untouched forests between Boston and Concord. Odd never returned to the house on Court Street at Scollay Square. He never visited Mrs. Galligan, and he never again went to the tall grass with Sarah Middlebrooke or any other girl. He could not risk satisfying one unruly appetite lest it awaken unknown hungers. Odd cast his eyes to the ground whenever he passed another person on the road, fearful that the encounter might summon whatever weakness he carried in his blood. From Concord he wandered south along Corner Road, and then he stepped from the road into the sheltering trees. He drew a large circle in the dirt with the toe of his boot, stood in the center of this circle, and then drew a smaller one inside it and erased the first.

He walked back to Concord and described his plans in as few words as possible to the gray-haired dry-goods merchant, Shebuel Hapgood, who would not be dissuaded from demonstrating how, despite his rheumatism and his crooked back, he could still swing an ax in one and and a hammer in the other.

"I am to live in the woods," Odd told him.

"A respectable endeavor," the old man

replied. "You'll need this ax and hammer to start. And you tell your wife, anything she wants, Dickerson and Hapgood's Dry Goods and Hardware will see to it."

"I will live alone."

"No wife, then? Well, I suppose you'll still be after something in the way of domestic comforts. We've got cloths for your table, and a doormat and window coverings in back."

"I'll have only what is needed, naught else."

What little money he had he spent on an ax, a hammer, a box of nails, three hinges, and a coil of rope. On credit he bought a shovel, a cup, a plate, a large spoon, a blanket, and a useful knife. He built a small cabin from the wood of fallen trees; his walls were painted with green mosses, egg-white freckles of mildew and mushrooms, and soft dark cavities of arrested decay. When this wood ran out, he chopped down as few trees as he absolutely needed to complete his roof. He made a single door, and a single window with a shutter hinged at its top. There was no chimney and no hearth, since Odd had no intention of ever lighting a fire. He took on small jobs at nearby farms. Later, he added a small porch to his cabin, so that he might have a place to sit when the weather turned pleasant in the spring. He brought nothing with him from his uncle's house, not even the collection of stones that began with the one he had pocketed on board the *Sovereign of the Seas.* He gathered new stones; he adopted rocks and pebbles as if they were orphaned bits of the earth. He was especially fond of stones that bore feathery veins of contrasting hues trapped like frozen thunderbolts. It made him sad to think that these small fragments of beauty went unnoticed, scattered on the ground, trampled underfoot.

Once, when he was looking for interesting stones near the road, he came upon a box turtle with its shell staved in. A carriage wheel had crushed the black-and-orange dome into a broken puzzle. Odd thought of burying the turtle in the woods to spare it the indignity of swarming flies, but when he lifted the ruined shell a wrinkled head drunkenly emerged and the creature cast a brittle-hooded eye at him. Odd carried the turtle back to his cabin, and after picking out the jagged bits from the soft crater he tried to bandage the wound as best he could with a long strip of burlap. He brought the turtle seeds and dead insects, and though he never saw the creature emerge to take what he had left, he could tell it was eating by the small dark pellets that piled up beneath its tail. In a few weeks, the turtle began to claw its way slowly around the cabin, but the slightest sound sent its head snapping back into the damaged shell. Odd understood. After a few months, the turtle began picking at the knotted burlap with its beaked jaw, and a few weeks after that Odd found the crumpled bandage by his cabin door, and in the dirt he saw a shallow trail of claw marks, like swimmer's strokes, leading away and disappearing into the undergrowth.

Odd had sought only to remove himself from the paths of other people, but he had not expected that he would find in the woods companionship of a different sort. He walked among the trees at night, in the pitch black, not half so apprehensive as when he walked among people in the city. He was grateful to the woods for providing him with the means to build his simple cabin, and he knew that he was only its caretaker, that someday someone else in need would arrive and give him an opportunity to repay his debt. Odd did not want for company; he found that the rustling leaves provided adequate conversation. He listened to the winds agitating the trees, and he found a corresponding spirit in the sound. He imagined each gust as a great wave beginning on the other side of the world, rearing up on the coast of his native land, sweeping up portions of all it traversed, and depositing the collected wealth at his door. He needed only to walk around his cabin to feel as though he were traveling the globe. He learned that the smallest woodland animal lived a life of great complexity, and as he watched the creatures scurrying and flitting about he realized that they were part of a vast whole, a complication far greater than the combined complexities of its parts. There was much to study, much to learn from the woods, and he decided that he would live out his days alone, simply, quietly, without fear of doing harm to anyone, and for a while this brought him some measure of peace.

But still, Odd continued to watch for signs of his uncle's unquenchable appetites. The sound of his own laughter sometimes frightened him with the way it took control of his breathing and his speech. He wondered what glance or word or deed had first awakened the urges that led Søren Hus to his miserable end. And what of the disreputable relatives they had left behind in Oslo? Had they intended their misdeeds, or did they stumble into wrongdoing, following instincts until they could no longer fathom an existence uninvolved with swindling or cheating or inflicting injuries of a kind Odd dared not imagine.

Odd had hoped that living alone would free him from the sinister temptations that seemed the sole remnant of his family inheritance, but he was wrong. He still felt the restless desires stirring beneath his skin, refusing to be ignored. Each morning he awoke to yearnings that seemed to have renewed themselves overnight, urges breeding like gnats as he slept. It shamed him to awaken stiff and protruding, as if his body were trying to push its way out of itself. Sometimes he tended to his need before getting out of bed, lying on his back, watching the thin plumes of steam rise from between his clenched teeth into the cold morning air, hoping the curl of his own hand would alleviate the hunger that otherwise dogged him throughout the day. But the release was always temporary, the satisfaction never complete.

And then, one day, as Odd was returning to his cabin after working the fields, he came upon a carriage stuck axel-deep in the pool of mud that would later be covered by logs. Three men toiled in the slippery muck, trying to free the stranded vehicle. The exhausted horses stood to the side, hides splattered with crusted earth. For a while, Odd watched from a distance as the men struggled. Backs hunched, shoulders touching, they looked as if they had been freshly dipped in batter. Odd hesitated before offering to help, not wanting to risk the consequences of pressing up against another human being, not wanting to be drawn into the conversations and handshakes and future obligations that such exchanges unavoidably incur. But he could not simply walk past without offering assistance.

Odd set his bundle at the side of the road and nodded silently to the others. He saw the recognition in their eyes, but they did not utter his name. They moved aside, creating a space for him. He placed his shoulder against the rear of the carriage and leaned forward, putting his full weight into the effort. He strained against the immovable mass, felt the exertions of the other men, and sucked hard at his dead tooth. The carriage rocked on creaking springs, but the wheels did not move. Odd pushed again, slipped forward, and sank to his knees alongside the carriage. He stared down at the spot where the spokes disappeared into the mud and then, before he could right himself and try again, something large and heavy fell on him from above.

She had decided to exit the carriage to lighten the load. The wheels shifted just as she stepped from the doorway and she lost her balance and tumbled onto Odd's back. He collapsed under her weight and landed facedown in the thick mud. The nimbler men jumped clear and howled with laughter. Odd felt the soft bulk of the large woman on his back, and he was powerless to push her away. The more he struggled, the deeper he sank, until he realized that he was in danger of suffocating. His only choice, if he wished to continue drawing breath in the time it would take for the other men to finish laughing and help them up, was to stop struggling altogether. He lifted his face from the mud, spat a mouthful of the brown soup, craned his neck as far as he could turn, and found himself face-to-face with Emma Manning. She had the most significant proportions of any woman he had ever seen, and Odd could not tell whether his shortness of breath was due to her pressing weight or to his astonishment at being trapped beneath such an exquisite creature.

Her features were delicate, her skin as fair as an eggshell, her hair a dazzling auburn flecked with deeper hints of ginger, the color of an October sugar maple, her eyes brown and gentle. And she was laughing with the other men, an embarrassed laugh, a sound as sweet and fragile as falling rose petals. Odd was conscious of the contours of her soft body; he felt the heavy flesh of her thighs straddling his waist, felt the flat bones of her hips pushing on his back, felt his shoulders pressing up into a vast warm tenderness. His excitement defied the cold mud, and he could do nothing to halt or relieve the building sensation. He was held fast beneath her, utterly incapable of moving. And that was the moment he fell in love with Emma Manning. She was not married then, and he might have made his intentions known on any number of subsequent occasions, but it would have taken the combined weight of three Emma Mannings to keep him from fleeing the expression of his own terrifying desire.

After that day, Odd continued to live in his simple cabin, entertaining fantasies of how he might confess his love for her, up until the day he learned of Emma's unfathomable engagement to Cyrus Woburn, a man who seemed to Odd to be old in a way that suggested he had never been young. Odd understood why Emma did not warm to his own silent proposals, but he thought her wrongheaded and reckless for giving herself over to someone who could not possibly love her as he did. Cyrus Woburn had purchased a large farm at the far end of Corner Road, and Odd knew from the moment he heard of the engagement that he would go to work for Mr. Woburn on a permanent basis. When the time came, Odd left the door to his little cabin propped open, an invitation to whoever needed its shelter next. He did not feel that he owned the cabin any more than he owned the woods. He took the time to build a simple hearth of stones and clay before he left, so that the next inhabitant would find it as hospitable a home as he had.

And now the woods where Odd once found refuge are burning to the ground, and he is afraid that it might be his fault. He knows he was careful beyond reproach. He laid out a barrier of stones, and he fed his fire slowly. He kept the flames of his small brushfire in check. He never looked away, not once. But it would have taken only one ember, one errant cinder. Odd stares at the raft of logs in the hardened earth a moment longer, and then continues on to Concord at a faster pace than before. He thinks he can hear the flames chewing through the trees behind him, but it is only the crunch of his boots grinding out their cadence against the dusty road. He cannot stop thinking about lying beneath Emma in the mud. Even now, years later, when he recalls the moment he feels as though there were a hive of bees buzzing somewhere behind his stomach. He wonders if he might step into the woods and right there, in the splintered shadows of the leaf-less oaks, relieve himself of the longing that has crept forward from memory. It is the second time today that he has nearly given himself over to such a thought. If there was some connection between love and the base act of copulation, he has not found it. He has searched for a safe means of quelling his longing, a release without consequence, but nothing ever brought him the satisfaction he sought.

The previous autumn, Odd paid a number of midnight calls to the fat pumpkins ripening on the hairy vines that covered Woburn Farm. But the relief never outlived the fleeting pleasure. He tried to picture her face when he was at it, hoping he might conjure up some semblance of intimacy, but it never worked. The pleasure and release echoed all the more loudly in the absence it was meant to fill. He might have continued at it night after night had Mr. Woburn not discovered the ruined pumpkins and vowed that he and

Odd would spend every night until harvest in armed watchfulness. It was the only time that Odd ever held a rifle. Under cover of darkness, he sat next to Mr. Woburn on the small rise near the field, cradling the cold steel barrel between his thighs while Mr. Woburn aimed at phantoms and cursed the vandals whom he believed had senselessly corkscrewed bungholes in his pumpkins and left them to rot.

Odd did not return to the pumpkins after that, though he still considers it from time to time. The indulgence was no more disappointing than any other, but the risk proved too great. Still, he thinks he might be less careless in the future. He knows there are ways he might hide his tracks were he to try it once more. He promised himself that he would not resort to such foolishness again, but he is already beginning to look forward to the approach of autumn and the ripening of a new crop. He imagines the bright, moonlit field, the scattered rows of orange humps, and allows himself to consider how he might do a better job of it next time, urged on by the kind of crippled nostalgia that compels other men to yearn for a second chance at their first mishandled loves.

13

EMMA

After Oddmund left, Emma Woburn stood among her chickens and watched his diminishing shape until he finally disappeared around the far bend in the Corner Road. From behind he looked like an old man — white hair, bowed head, stooped shoulders — but there was no mistaking the strength in his step. He is not tall, and she can only guess that he must weigh less than she does by at least three stone. But he is a hardy one, to be sure, solid of limb, and she has seen him lift a calf more than half his size and sling the creature across his broad back without so much as a grunt. If he only chose to, she thinks, he could easily puff out his chest and claim as much space in this world as any other man.

Emma sprinkles a final handful of feed over the chickens pecking at her shoes and slaps her palms on her skirts. She has been daydreaming, staring at the column of smoke above the woods, and it has taken her three times longer than it should have to complete her morning chores. Her husband would have scolded her had he not departed shortly before Oddmund did. Emma does not know for certain where Cyrus has gone. He seldom tells her. He muttered only that he had "business" to tend to, though she suspects that the trip involves a bottle. It is a worriment to her. She has seen the drink ruin good men, and she never thought she would be married to one with the weakness. Her mother had warned her about the ways of men, and Emma would be deeply ashamed if her mother could see her now with the likes of Cyrus Woburn. Emma always suspected that the good in men would not be easy to find, but she had not thought that the bad would be so hard to avoid.

Emma reaches distractedly into her apron pocket and pops the last bit of a hard biscuit into her mouth. She flicks the crumbs from her fingers and trudges off toward the clothesline to check on the undergarment she left drying with the bedclothes. On the way, she scoops up the empty wicker basket from the back porch and swings it at her side and thinks of Oddmund making his way toward Concord with his eyes downcast and his chin tucked into his chest, hiding the handsome line of his jaw.

Oddmund Hus is a riddle to her. Try as she might, she cannot twig the discomfort he wears like an apology. He strikes her as no more surprising or disappointing than the middling sort of man, and yet there is something separate about him, a holding back of sorts. Even a gesture as simple as a nod seems to come only after he has taken the time to work out the hidden consequences. From what Emma has seen, most men tend to carry on as if they owned the tiny patches of earth they trod, but not Oddmund; he moves through the world as if he believed it was a place created solely for other people. She has watched him working quietly in the fields, has seen him stop to put a hand to his brow as he thinks through some complicated trouble he keeps to himself.

Emma is convinced that his head is bursting with notions of one kind or another, but he is no great one for talking. It sometimes amuses her, his awkward speech, the way he sounds as if he simply has not spoken enough in his life to be comfortable with the words that fall from his mouth. He never utters more than a few words in a row, and sometimes he gives the impression that he would rather save his breath to blow the dust off his shoes. Emma knows better, though. It is not arrogance. She can sense a yearning in him that he is simply too timid to satisfy. He never asks anything of anyone, never acts as if he had the right to, and Emma knows he has not a clue that there was a time when she might have considered giving him whatever he asked.

When Emma reaches the clothesline, she places the basket at her feet and takes hold of one of the posts Oddmund hammered into the ground to support the line. The crooked post wobbles under the weight of the laundry, and Emma reminds herself to tell Oddmund that it needs fixing. He is a wonder at remedying little problems like this. She plucks the stiff sheets and pillowcases from the line and folds them into the basket. Then she reaches for the undergarment that took her two weeks to stitch together. It is a hodgepodge of scraps and is still damp in spots where the fabric is heavy. She smoothes it between her thick hands and leaves it to dry a bit longer. This is her third attempt at making such a convenience; the others were ill-begotten creations, tight and loose in all the wrong places. Emma rubs the sore creases beneath her arms, where the skin is chafed from the long strip of muslin she winds tightly over her chemise every morning, and she smiles as she considers the relief her improvised patchwork will bring.

If men only knew the discomforting tug and pull of her heft, she thinks, it would surely dampen their curiosity. She has felt them staring at her heavy breasts, at her broad backside, has felt their sidelong glances stroke the fullness of her thighs, as if these parts were set out before them for their merriment. It is not merely lust that drives these men to gaze at her so intently; something close to wonderment and disapproval is there, too. She has felt them dismiss her with their eyes after they have had their fill. She has grown accustomed to being ignored once they have thought through their wicked little fancies, and it angers her that they can think her so easily disappeared. And yet she cannot help feeling cowed by their reproachful looks when she dares to look back.

Men had not always treated her this way. In Ireland, she had been regarded as a pretty girl, slender like her mother, with delicate features and dark eyes. Her ma told her that she would soon enough attract a herd of young men from which to choose a fit husband. For a time, Emma's family had been better off than most in County Donegal. Her pa held a lease on a small farm in Tawnawilly Parish, where Emma and her two brothers were born. She recalls no unhappiness between her parents before things turned bad. Emma remembers her ma's laugh. She remembers her cleverness with needle and thread, and how she mended clothes long past the point where new stitches outnumbered those that had turned to dust. She remembers the animal satisfaction her father seemed to take in a day spent sweating in the fields.

Their family had survived rebellions and poor harvests. They had lost land and regained it. But the real trouble began in 1830, when the potatoes in Donegal came out of the ground small and soft and black. Long after the harvest was over that year, a fetid-sweet stench of vegetable rot hung over the fields in Tawnawilly and in nearby Killymard Parish, and her family struggled through the winter like everyone else in that part of the island. They butchered the few skinny animals they owned; they ate the feed they had stored for the chickens. They watched wagonloads of grain clatter toward Donegal Quay to be loaded onto ships and taken away. Emma watched her pa's thick arms and chest shrink beneath his baggy clothes.

He was a proud man and refused to resort to outright begging, as many of their neighbors had done, but he walked into Donegal Town every Monday — the day that the local shopkeepers had declared Help Day — and stood in line at the grocer's to collect a few handfuls of corn or oatmeal or whatever was being doled out that week. He was given a paper badge showing his name and parish and told to wear it on a string around his neck so that the starving families in Killymard and elsewhere could not abuse the generosity of the Tawnawilly merchants. On Mondays her pa walked the streets of Donegal Town until late, and brought back stories of what he saw in the shop windows. Behind the glass, the buying and selling continued. When he could not put food in their bellies, he put stories in their heads to help them forget the dull, empty ache. He was a great one for telling stories. He could describe a sack of grain such that Emma could feel the bread crumbling on her tongue. He invented stories about the ladies he saw in town, buying fine hats and boots, and the men lugging away sacks of nails and armloads of lumber and bricks and carefully boxed panes of glass bound for unknown inland estates. He described in great detail the huge sides of blood-fresh beef hanging next to the puckered carcasses of birds of all sizes.

Emma still clearly recalls the evening he told them about the table-size books on display in a shop window; the books held etchings of sailing ships and fish and flowers and animals of all sorts. He described pages that looked as if they were sliced from giant slabs of butter, and bindings of leather so rich it seemed they could be eaten with gravy. He conjured up the printed pictures for them as if he were holding one of the big books in his hands, reading it to them in the dark cottage by the cold hearth and the empty pot. The sound of his voice called forth images of slippery eels cooked into stews, partridges baked into pies, and loaves of coarse bread piled high next to mounds of bright-colored fruit. And Emma promised herself right then that she would one day have beautiful books of her own. She might go without stockings or a bonnet; she might want for better shoes or a heavier coat, but she would always have books.

Her father was confident that things would improve. But the potato crop failed again the next year. Even the untainted potatoes they rescued from the lazy beds and stored in the shed soon wore the slippery pale fur of blight. Emma had heard it said that the trouble in County Donegal was not widespread, but this news offered little solace. She had also heard that it was only a matter of time before the rest of the island felt the bitter sting of famine; they said that this was but a taste of a greater horror to come. But it was hard for her to imagine that anything could be worse.

The hunger came first; it prepared the way, left their withered bodies and wilted spirits easy prey. Then came the sickness. Consumption took one brother, then the other, and then Emma's ma. Their deaths seemed a gradual disappearing, and in the constant dizziness of hunger Emma found it impossible not to dream that they would all reappear in the spring, sprouting from the sick earth. Her father was too worn out to grieve, too hungry to care about his pride. He took to begging in the end. The sickness had seized him, but he was not too weak to stagger from one house to the next. Some days he was well enough to stumble for miles. He pleaded at the doors of well-off farmers throughout Tawnawilly. He threw away his name badge and went begging in the neighboring towns of Killymard Parish until at last he could rub together coins enough to buy Emma passage to America. He reminded her that she was of marriageable age, and there was every reason to believe she might find better prospects in the New World. It was easier to imagine a life in a world they had not seen than it was to forecast the portion that awaited Emma in the misery they knew. In America, her father told her, the heavenly Father bestowed riches equally on all his children. He insisted that Emma leave at once, since she, too, was little more than skin and bones kept upright by some mysterious force of will.

Emma refused at first. She did not want her pa to die alone, another unnumbered death, but he had been a strong man and he clung to his life for months, the flesh taking its time to melt from his bones. And, when he was finally gone, it was as if he had never been. So many had passed in this way, unmarked deaths that left no room for grief, for the dying had vanished long before they actually passed on. The dying were everywhere, wraiths barely taking up the spaces where they lay, as if they feared their lingering presence might be seen as an insult to the earth.

Emma determined that, once she arrived in the New World, she would root herself firmly in it. Like the rocky islets that held fast against the current of the River Drove near her home, she would not allow herself to be swept away. She would leave a mark upon the earth. She would marry and fill herself with children, spread herself across the new continent that would have no choice but to surrender to her claim. She would not wither and fade like everyone she had ever known in her homeland. People could turn away when she approached, they could spurn her friendship and whisper mean names when she passed, but she would never permit them to deny that she was here.

In the weeks after she first set foot in America, Emma wandered the streets of Boston in a daze, huddling in doorways, hands cupped, just another emaciated girl from across the ocean looking for work or charity, anything that might put a crust of bread in her mouth. Men pitied her. They paid attention to her — if only briefly — as a soul in need of rescue. Some few sought to take advantage, saw in her frail and wasted form something that aroused un-nameable thirsts. Some promised her measly fortunes in exchange for awful favors, but most simply let a coin or two drop before stepping past. She refused to surrender to her hunger; in this new land such a yielding seemed wholly needless. At every square and intersection in Boston, she heard shouts from vendors hawking oysters and fresh fish and hot corn and raspberries and milk and sweet doughnuts fried in pig fat. Everywhere the air smelled of cooking, as if America were one vast kitchen, and it seemed she need only breathe to fill herself with food.

She tried to get work as a seamstress, but, pale and thin as she was, no one would hire her for fear that she would faint before her first shift was out. Instead, she took a job as a book folder for a printing house, making a penny for every hundred sheets of paper she folded into rectangles eight layers thick. She rubbed the words and pictures covering the pages as she halved the sheets again and again, and she renewed her promise that one day she would have books of her own. In a boardinghouse near Dock Square, she found a cheap room and shared it with two German girls, square-faced and braided, who spoke no English. Sometimes she took in piecework, imitating the quick movements of her ma's fingers in the dark, and when her strength returned she found a second job at night making boxes and sewing sacks.

Passing down Change Avenue one after-

240

noon, she happened to notice a man get up from a long wooden table outside the Bite Tavern and leave his meal unfinished to hurry back across the square to Quincy Market. She returned the next day and, peering through one of the tavern's open windows, saw the same thing happen again, only this time a dozen apron-wrapped market men leaped from their half-eaten meals to return to their stalls across the square. She saw unwashed platters stacked at the counter, plates and tankards scattered about the empty tables, trampled remnants of meals strewn across the floorboards. Without hesitating, Emma entered the Bite and talked the owner into hiring her as a table girl. She saw to it that the leftover food did not go to waste. As she worked, she furtively stuffed her pockets with half-bitten biscuits and gristly rinds of steak and the hard ends of sausages. Within a few months, her dress no longer hung empty from her shoulders and she felt the earth begin to tug at her with more urgency than before. Month by month, she grew large on the abundance of the New World, until the same men who had once shown pity for her when she first arrived found her bosom and buttocks to be of unseemly proportions, her thick arms and legs swollen with an indiscreet surfeit of life.

Six years after arriving in Boston, Emma left for Concord, taking with her a valise holding a pair of boots, a bonnet, three dresses, and five times as many books. She had grown weary of Boston, and she longed for green farms and open spaces. She also knew that there would be fewer people in Concord than in the city, fewer eyes to stare at her in disapproval. She found work as a barmaid in Wright's Tavern. Within the year, she had learned the name of everyone in town, except for the curious white-haired young man she first saw on the road into Concord; she was passing in a carriage and he was standing at the side of the road, holding a length of twine tied to a turtle whose shell was wrapped in what looked like a dirty bandage. She saw the white-haired man again on Mill Dam Street, hands in pockets, shuffling hesitantly toward the center of town as if he felt he were trespassing, but she did not speak to him until the day she fell on him in the thick mud of Corner Road.

It was not the introduction she would have wished, but he seemed to take an interest in her, despite being nearly smothered. A few days after their folly in the mud, he came into Wright's Tavern for a tankard of weak ale, which he drank diluted with hot water. He sipped the drink slowly, spoke to no one, but made a point of wishing her a good day before leaving, offering her an embarrassed smile that revealed a tiny blackened tooth set prominently in the front of his mouth. Then he began coming to the tavern for supper, never more than once a week, and always he sat as far as possible from the open fire. That was when Emma first felt the weight of his stare. She sensed it like a gentle hand on her shoulder. From across the room, she could feel his eyes follow when her back was turned and she found it reassuring, a reminder that she had not disappeared. It amused her that he seemed to believe she was blind to his attention. She saw how his head snapped away whenever she glanced in his direction, saw how he jumped as if prodded with a hot poker whenever she called his name.

She tried to tease him into conversation, and through half-finished sentences she learned that he lived alone, collected pretty stones in the woods, and worked as a laborer on nearby farms, doing whatever needed to be done on any given day. Most often he took on jobs for Cyrus Woburn, a regular patron at Wright's Tavern, whose stern face at first reminded Emma of her pa. Though she knew little else about Oddmund, Emma half expected the strange young man to seek her hand. He always seemed on the cusp of asking a question or making a statement that required more courage than he had in store. Emma knew that some people were not made for marrying or raising children, and she supposed Oddmund might possibly issue from this mold. Emma was certain that she had not mistaken Oddmund's quiet interest, yet she suspected he might be the sort who would prefer a tiny, prim woman half his age for a helpmeet. But, to be sure, Emma knew little of what brought men and women together.

Emma Manning was up to her elbows in dishwater at Wright's Tavern when Cyrus Woburn surprised her by muttering his sensible offer of marriage. As he spoke, she watched his reflection squirm on the washing barrel's greasy gray surface. His calloused hands were clasped behind his back, and he was staring at a clump of blond dirt he had scraped from his boots. It was a wholly practical proposal. He owned a large farm and had no children; Emma was approaching the end of her childbearing years and had neither suitors nor any prospects other than the wearisome future that her heavy, chapped arms bespoke. Cyrus

Woburn delivered his proposal in the same tone of voice he might have used to offer a begrudging price for a field of shallow, rocky soil.

Emma knew that this was very likely her only chance at companionship, her only chance at children, but she had one demand that would need to be satisfied by the man who would be her husband. Emma had heard the patrons recount how Wright's Tavern had seen desperate strategies worked out during the War of Independence, and so it seemed to her a fitting backdrop against which to negotiate the terms of her future with the old farmer.

"If you've a mind to have me as your wife, Mr. Woburn, then there is one condition to be met."

"A condition?"

"I will have books."

"I got the Bible if that's what you're after."

"Books of poetry. Stories. Pictures. That sort."

"Reading books, you mean?"

"It is all I ask. I fetch one book every month out of my wages. I can leave the tavern, if you require it, but I'll not give up my monthly books."

He did not even mull it over. He only shrugged, as if someone were telling him that a particular head of cattle on auction came with its spots.

"Well, all right, then."

Emma did not tell him that she had never actually read an entire book on her own. She recognized hardly more than a bushelful of words in the books she bought. She mouthed the letters in the printed shapes she did not recognize, and often the resulting sounds did not match anything she had ever heard in conversation. Mostly, she liked the feel of the type beneath her fingers. She knew she held something worthwhile in her hands, and she liked nothing more than to sit on the porch at dusk or by the fire in the evening and cast her eyes over the lines of print, thinking of her pa, his gravelly voice describing the things he had seen on his hungry wanderings. If her ma would be disappointed to find her shackled to the likes of Cyrus Woburn, she thought, her pa would be proud to see the small library she was building for herself in the narrow bookcase off the kitchen.

When Cyrus Woburn proposed, Emma knew little of how her own parents had satisfied each other's needs, but she found something wanting in the way that he offered his reluctant smiles as small surrenders to the fact that he had taken her as his wife. He seemed willing enough to take what other men had spurned, and she was grateful for his attention. She only wished that he had not so readily accepted her gratitude as proof of his charity.

After readjusting the damp undergarment on the line, Emma trudges back to the house, the half-full laundry basket cradled beneath her arm. She sees that the smoke has thickened above the treetops like a mounting thundercloud, spread out flat at the bottom, swollen at the top. She worries that the fire might come this way, after all. It would not be able to cross the barren fields, but it might easily leap from tree to tree along the farm's boundary and nestle in the cluster of apple trees next to the house. Mr. Woburn has warned her not to worry so, but she knows how things can simply go wrong. She watches the immense cloud's dark shiftings, and she tries to calm herself with the notion that it might move in the other direction. All will be well, she tells herself. She has sent Oddmund for help, and she decides that the best thing she can do now is stay indoors and wait for him to return. Her morning chores are almost complete, and she is looking forward to stealing a few restful moments with her new book, a collection of tales by the brooding Virginian Edgar Allan Poe. She keeps the book hidden at the back of her bookcase. She asked Cyrus to purchase it for her, but she does not want visitors to find the scandalous little volume on her shelves.

On the back porch, Emma shifts the basket from one hip to the other and turns away from the looming cloud to look in the direction that Oddmund has taken, as if he, too, might have left a trail of smoke. She knows he will probably find himself drawn into fighting the fire in the woods, despite his noticeable dread. She assumes that his fear of fire has something to do with the scars on his arms. He has never spoken about what happened, though she has asked him directly more than once. He is a good man, she thinks, this Oddmund Hus. There are not many men like him, certainly not among those she has met.

Her husband is nothing at all like Oddmund, and she cannot keep from drawing comparisons, though she knows it is wrong of her to do so. Oddmund always shows an interest in the books she pretends to read, always asks politely, in as few words as possible, what new books she has collected for her little library. Someone taught him to read English, but she has never learned how this came to be. She can sometimes persuade him to read a few sentences aloud for her, when she finds one especially difficult to decipher, though this is a rare accomplishment. She wonders what it would be like to have Oddmund read to her all the time, after supper, near the fire on cold nights, to hear him speak the words that covered every single page of every book on her shelves. What would her pa think of that? Surely even her ma would approve of such an arrangement.

Emma does not entirely regret her marriage. She is confident that she need never again want for the necessities of life, and she might still hope for children, but she cannot help feeling that her satisfaction would be increased if she could somehow supplant the coarser attributes in Cyrus with the sweetness in Oddmund. She retreats into these guilty imaginings on those nights when she lies awake next to her snoring husband, sore from his abrupt, efficient attentions. It is wrong of her, she knows, terribly wrong, but she sometimes wishes she could take the best portions of the men she has come to know and piece together a better man, a superior animal deserving of this new world they have come to inhabit.

14

CALEB

The light finds its way to him through naked branches, fracturing into complex mosaics of yellow and orange, geometric patterns like stained glass. The similarity does not escape Caleb's notice. Huddled beneath his coat, he peeks out at the edge of the woods and draws on his pipe, lets the smoke transport him to the stained-glass window in his father's church. He finds cause to think of it a dozen times a day, for it was this magnificent window that occasioned the first of many signs revealed to him. He inhales the fumes from his pipe and leans back against the farmhouse ruins, feels the colors radiating from the glass, sees the loud fires roiling in its design.

The panes had arrived packed in molasses. One hundred stout oak barrels stood in two neat ranks along Court Street at Adams Square, their rims encrusted with translucent-winged insects, lured to entombment by sugary promise. Ingenious, he thought. There was no end to the clever feats man could achieve when guided by the hand of heaven. Not a single colorful pane of stained glass had broken during the arduous voyage that had begun three months earlier at the Glasgow Glass Works and ended in Boston in the spring of 1820.

Caleb Ephraim Dowdy, fourteen years of age, eldest son of the Reverend Marcus Ezekiel Dowdy of Court Street Unitarian Church, sat wiping a deep blue pane he held sandwiched between his spindly legs. The coarse tow cloth of his trousers drank in the molasses until the fabric was heavy and slow. He stood to retrieve another section from the barrels, and he had to hold his pants at the waist to avoid tripping over the sodden cuffs. The molasses clung to whatever it touched. When his father was not looking, Caleb could not resist touching a syrupy finger to his tongue. He had no idea that the amber splotches at the corners of his mouth gave him away, and he did not reckon the significance of his father's indulgent smiles. Luscious warmth filled his mouth, and he surmised that the paradise awaiting faithful Christians could hardly be sweeter.

It was to be the most glorious window of

any church in Boston; not even the Cathedral of the Holy Cross, swollen with the idolatrous French and Irish Catholics and their love for gilt objects, would boast anything so sublime. Caleb had marveled at the drawings on his father's desk. The window held eight scenes recounting the creation of heaven and earth, the fall of the angels, Adam and Eve, banishment from Eden, the birth of Christ, his death and resurrection, the discovery of America, and then the most glorious scene of all: Judgment Day. There was to be no representation of God the Father or the Holy Spirit as separate entities, nothing to suggest that deific power issued from anything other than a single, unified whole.

As a young man, Marcus Ezekiel Dowdy had worshipped at the Park Street First Anglican Church, a staid structure of clean white walls, sharp lines, and windows of watery glass. The church had been built two centuries earlier by order of King James II, who had seized a small corner of the Park Street Cemetery from the Puritans so that the Church of England might have a presence in the New World. But as a young man, hopeful that the advances of science and industry — wondrous manifestations of man's reason — might find a place in God's creation, Marcus had marched into the swelling legions of Unitarians. And now, close upon the midpoint of a new century in America, he believed that the time had come for bold gestures where matters of ornamentation were concerned. The window was an epic undertaking, and Marcus had at first encountered no small opposition from the members of his congregation, but he persuaded them by citing the natural beauty of the land. "Our Puritan roots run deep, but everywhere we see its fruit withering on the vine," Marcus reasoned from his pulpit, gesturing toward the empty pews at the back of the small church. "God so adorned this land that man might marvel at his wondrous creation; thus, is it not fitting that America's churches should celebrate his glory by doing the same?"

The pane Caleb held showed a portion of the sky, clouds suffused with heavenly radiance. He watched the images emerge as he scraped away the tenacious molasses with a wooden spatula like the one he vaguely remembered his mother using when she made griddle cakes. She had died when Caleb was eight, after a brief illness, and he had not eaten griddle cakes since. The smell of frying batter still made his stomach ache with the sadness of not seeing her at the stove. When Caleb told his father how much he missed her, his father explained that this sorrow was brought on by the sinister workings of doubt. Marcus assured his son that there was no cause for grief, for his mother would one day return, and Caleb tried to imagine her sitting in a straight-backed chair on a cloud, hands folded in her lap, quietly waiting for the appointed time when she could come back and cook breakfast.

Sometimes the doubts returned, but Caleb was having no difficulty thinking of his mother seated on her cloud as he happily dragged the spatula from top to bottom, leaving smooth, even trails on the glass. If his hand wavered, he repeated the motion, straightening the lines in the molasses before moving on to clean another row. Caleb was more careful than the other workers, more diligent, as if the manner in which the molasses was removed might in some way affect the purity of the overall work hidden beneath. His father had taught him that everything he did, the simplest act, should be undertaken as if it were being performed for a heavenly audience. Even when he worked alone at his mathematics, Caleb made sure that his fraction bars and equal signs were perfectly straight. God was watching, always, and Caleb did not want to disappoint him in a task so simple as a straight line.

Once he had gotten the top layer of molasses off, he worked at the remaining syrup with a rag, then placed the section of window next to the others, propped against the church steps. The workmen were using a special mixture of ash and lye to remove the remaining stickiness from the panes before the glaziers began installing them in the gaping hole that had been opened in the church's nave.

The stagecoaches bound for Cambridge slowed as they passed through Adams Square, horses sniffing the sugary air, passengers craning their necks to view the curious spectacle. The molasses ran in great, heavy gobs, soaking Caleb's shirt until it clung to his forearms like ill-fitting skin. It ran down his legs, into his shoes, pooled on the dirt at the base of the church steps. It dripped in wispy filaments. Long, spidery threads stuck to his face and landed in his hair, and it was not long before the sweetness attracted a host of eager insects. Bees and wasps flew straight into the amber globs and stuck fast, immobilized by their greed. Caleb saw the lesson in this.

He surreptitiously ran his finger over the face of the angel Gabriel, traced the length of his trumpet, and then slipped the gobbet of molasses into his mouth. It was a small transgression, one in a series he had committed this afternoon in the service of a noble purpose. Caleb looked at the angel seated on the golden cloud, and he held the sweet glob on his tongue until it melted and ran along the insides of his teeth, stinging his molars. He knew then that, were anyone to ask him when he had decided to follow his father into the ministry, he would be able to identify the exact moment. How could such artistry, such craftsmanship, such skill in transport and installation, such perfection — how could any of this exist were it not for the existence of God? If heaven held but a portion of the intense color, if its sweetness were only half as cloying, if the ingenuity of angels came close to the genius before him, then it was indeed a destination to be pursued above all others. It made him happy to think that his mother waited in so marvelous a place, and he wondered if she would truly want to return to them.

Caleb looked at the bottom panes waiting to be installed first. They depicted the fallen, damned to the flames, preyed upon by serpents and insects, skeletal arms raised in vain supplication, mouths agape in fleshless astonishment. Caleb judged these panes to be the most realistic, and he had good reason. He could not know if the window's portrait of heaven was accurate, but he had once found a decayed body when he was just a boy, and he knew death's true visage. A year after his mother's passing, he had stumbled upon the body while walking in the woods on a bright spring afternoon. Beneath the trunk of a fallen tree he saw the toe of a boot and a flattened pants leg. Nearby lay a hatchet, its blade rusted, its long handle speckled with blue paint. Until that moment he had seen bodies only at wakes, lying in silk-lined coffins or on pillows of hay in simple pine boxes, but they had been prepared for viewing, the first patina of death wiped away, washed and dressed as if they had never been part of this world but were just passing through. The body he had found in the woods was a different thing altogether. He had tried to roll away the log hiding the dead man's face, but the wood no longer owned the hardness of its shape; it came apart in spongy handfuls. He pulled on the dead man's boot, felt something give way with a slippery pop, felt the hard outline of bone and little else. Caleb stepped to the other end of the log and rolled away a sizable chunk. Underneath, he found a wide-brimmed hat, a faded blue shirt, and a flattened, outstretched arm, the white bones poking through the frayed fingers of a glove. He took a closer look. It was not a glove at all but the hand's empty skin, greasy leather no longer able to cover its frame. Caleb hesitated, then lifted the black brim of the hat.

From behind the mask of leather, the white skull stared back at him. A fat beetle pushed its way up through the dirt in one of the eye sockets, paused as if confused to find itself exposed, then waddled down over the shirt and entered the log resting on the body. A few seconds later, the beetle re-emerged and crawled beneath the shirt. Caleb saw that scores of insects were shuttling back and forth, inhabiting wood, flesh, and soil indiscriminately. He did not think that there were insects in heaven, but he suddenly feared for his mother. He remembered what his father had told him — that one day the dead would triumphantly arise — and he was terrified at the thought that he might encounter this rotted body alive again and walking among them. Caleb knew that he needed to save it from further desecration. He clawed at the soft wood with his bare hands until he could not tell where the tree ended and the desiccated flesh began.

He seized the old hatchet and swung wildly at the decaying log, exposing more of the human remains beneath. Caleb saw that flesh and wood had melded together, but he refused to believe it possible that God would allow a man to become as common to the earth as a fallen tree. He fled the woods in a panic and was nearly home before he realized that he was still clutching the rusted hatchet and that it had shed flakes of blue paint over his palms.

Caleb later told his father what he had found, and Marcus Dowdy explained that his discovery was neither evidence of God's callousness nor a sign that man was a soulless portion of nature.

"My son, I am certain the body was that of a heathen," Marcus explained. "The native tribes of this land believe themselves one with the soil, so it is only to be expected that when death comes to them it comes as commonly as it does to the animals of the field. God would never allow a true Christian to arrive at so inglorious an end."

There was, however, one detail about the dead body in the woods that Caleb had not shared with his father, because he feared it would have marred his father's explanation and, worse, jeopardized his mother's peaceful abidance. Around the neck of the dead man had hung a small leather wallet, and stamped into the decaying leather was a simple cross. Caleb had seen Catholic scapulars before, dangling from the scrawny necks of the superstitious Irish, and he knew it contained a small scrap of paper, a fragment of the Bible. There was no doubt in his mind that the rotting body had once housed a Christian soul.

Caleb thought of his father's explanation as he continued to scrape molasses from a pane of bright blue sky. The Judgment Day panes would be the brightest, most colorful of all: brilliant reds and yellows, great fugues of intertwined flames, arms belatedly outstretched for forgiveness lost. The sunlight pouring through these sections would make those who stood before them feel as though they were immersed in a burning sea. Caleb grew excited as he thought about the effect, the very air palpably stained with the brilliant crimson and gold of damnation. In his enthusiasm, he ran two fingers over the clouds pushing the ships of the faithful to America's shore. He raked a furrow through the dark molasses, contemplating the window's perfection, but as he placed dripping fingertips reverently onto his tongue something caught his eye. He looked closer at the stained-glass clouds, doubted, and looked again.

Alongside one of the lead seams that joined the colorful fragments, a web of fissures spread through the glass. A flaw! Caleb grabbed the rag and rubbed at the square of glass to see if the crack had spread. It seemed impossible that any damage could have occurred during shipment. The molasses was so thick that it would have forgiven even the harshest seas. Caleb leaned in close to examine the pane, and slowly the realization settled in. The cracks must have occurred in the assembly of the window. Caleb found where the glazier, too lazy to replace the broken piece, had tried to cover the mistake with an extra layer of lead along the seam. It was hardly noticeable, but Caleb would forever know that there was a flaw hidden by another flaw, the second sin greater than the first. When the sun shone through the window, he would know that the bright sparkle in the clouds was the effect of cracks acting as a prism. It was unforgivable. Unlike his father, who doled out absolution like a man drunk with his own munificence, Caleb thought that some things, laziness among them, were inexcusable.

Caleb saw a bee struggling in the molasses on the glass, and he pressed his thumb into the syrup and squashed the imprisoned insect. He could see that in the years to come the great window of the Court Street Church would be a sign to him. Where others saw the sparkling brilliance of Providence, Caleb would see man's failure. It was the duty of every son to improve upon his father's deeds, Caleb thought, and though he knew his father was a good man, he thought him too lenient, too forgiving. Caleb knew that it would fall to him to root out and squash the flaws of the New World, lest the new be tainted by the degradations of the old. He had a great task before him. He was suddenly proud and happy and thankful, gravely thankful, for having been born in America, unburdened by the complacency of the past; there was simply too much work to be done.

15
HENRY DAVID

Truth be told, it is a glorious spectacle, if one can part the burning from the burned. This is what comes to Henry as he appraises the destruction from the top of Fair Haven Hill. In the midst of terrific loss, he thinks, there is yet beauty to celebrate, for nature is never chapfallen. He feels life return to his spent legs, feels the cramped tingling subside, and he pushes himself to his feet. He is invigorated by the thought that he may find means to recuperate this day; the fire is a wonder to behold, and he is almost sorry that he alone is present to appreciate the awful force he has unleashed.

He skids sideways down the hill to be closer to the heat and smoke. The way is awkward and steep, and he stumbles, boot heels braking his descent, plowing up small stones like arrowheads and shallow, spidery roots. Halfway to the bottom he stops, crouches on the slope, and listens to the fire, trying to decipher its brute, rapacious language. He reckons the flames are distant by two hundred yards or so, close enough to reach Fair Haven Hill before help arrives. But Henry is no longer panicked by this possibility. He has stopped hoping that the woods might be saved. He has given up denying the truth of what has followed from his hand. He decides instead that he must endeavor to make the most of his regret; it is the only lesson to be taken from the tragedy. He tells himself that, henceforth, he will no longer turn from guilt; he will pull regret to his core, feel it deeply, and be happy for it.

Though he so often courts solitude, right now he would gladly welcome the company of Edward, or Waldo, or Isaac, or some beautiful specimen of Young America, that he might demonstrate to another how the bright orange flames mimic autumn's vibrant decay, how swirling cinders pay homage to celestial majesties, how the fire's roar echoes the flying tumult of the cataract. To be here in the final moments of the woods is consolation and privilege. The fire is close enough for Henry to hear its labored grumblings, feel its muted thunder against his breastbone, and it comes in waves, a slow throbbing, like the dying pulse of a giant.

Henry squats lower, wraps his arms around his knees, and wonders at the beauty of the flames.

And then he hears something else, an exhalation issuing from the trees like an angry whisper, and the sound forms itself into a word, clear and distinct and impossible: *woodsburner.* The accusation wakes Henry from his reverie. He reels from the slap, bracing himself on backward-flung arms, then scrambles to his feet and peers into the shrubs nearby to see if someone is there, hiding from the flames. Henry holds a finger to his lips — on occasion he has caught himself muttering out loud when he is alone — but still he hears it, a voice begotten by the wind, a haunting in his ears: *woodsburner, woodsburner, woodsburner.* He turns and scrambles back up Fair Haven Hill with long, low strides, elbows fluttering, and the words pursue him. He glances over his shoulder, expecting to see his mysterious accuser a few steps behind.

When he reaches the crest, Henry puts his hands over his ears and shuts his eyes and tries to ignore what he has heard. He revisits the many insignificant causes that have brought him to this moment, but his thoughts cannot drown out the hissing indictment from the woods. He presses his palms hard against his head until his ears make their own roar. He sits, hunched forward, hands at his ears, and searches for a way that he might parcel out responsibility for what has happened — Edward wanted a chowder, the shoemaker at the river gave them matches, the woods were unusually dry, the wind unusually strong — and next his thoughts alight upon someone else who might shoulder a portion of the guilt, a writer he met a year and a half earlier, then newly arrived in Concord: Nathaniel Hawthorne.

Long-faced, clean-shaven, carefully buttoned, Nathaniel had at once struck Henry as a man poorly suited for life outdoors. Over dinner with Nathaniel and his wife, Sophia, Henry learned of his host's miserable rustic experiment at the Brook Farm community, where shoveling manure had proved far less agreeable than tallying weights and tariffs at the customs house in Boston. Nathaniel praised Henry's love of nature, and he professed his eagerness that they undertake a river excursion together, though Henry detected in him a reluctance to dirty his clothes or hands.

Henry thinks of Nathaniel's pale fingernails, trimmed and clean, tidy hands for writing stories and novels, better suited than

Henry's for bright papers squarely stacked, slanted desktops, and well-cut nibs. Then Henry looks down at his own chipped fingernails underwritten with soil, fingertips blunt like broken sticks, accustomed to scrawling in notebooks with nubbins of discarded pencils. As if to prove his thoughts, he claws a primitive design in the dirt and wipes his hands on his pants. Despite their differences, Henry had been attracted by the graveness in Nathaniel's eyes, and they formed an immediate friendship without forethought of what that friendship might bring. It is not wholly unreasonable, Henry thinks, to conjecture that their relationship has, in its own small way, contributed to the present tragedy. After all, had Nathaniel not been a friend, Henry would not have offered to sell him his boat — the very boat that Henry and his brother John had built with their own rough hands. Henry had only sold the *Musketaquid* because he could not take the heavy boat with him to New York when he left to tutor Waldo's nephews. But now he suspects that if he still owned his old boat the Concord woods would not be burning.

Long before they drove the first nail, Henry and John had decided that they would name their boat *Musketaquid,* after the Indian name for the Concord River. For years, they had discussed taking a trip on the river, and each season the waters beckoned to them impatiently, asking when they were coming. Henry did not understand the urgency then; they were young men, and there seemed an endless reserve of long summer days in which such an adventure might be taken. Yet the river called as if each summer might be the last. Even in winter, Henry felt the frigid current tugging at him, and all he need do was look at his older brother staring out the frost-etched window to understand that he was feeling the same pull. When they finally committed to the journey, they decided that their old boat, the *Rover,* was too ordinary for the task. A trip on the Concord and Merrimack Rivers required a superior vessel, and they set about selecting each plank with this journey in mind, as if they were consecrating stones for a cathedral. They gave the new boat wheels and a set of sturdy poles for transport over land; they gave it two masts, two sails, two sets of oars, and room enough to store a tent and all the supplies their adventure would require. Henry and John had agreed on every detail down to the green and blue paint. And the boat performed admirably on their journey, taking them past hundreds of brooks and farms and hills and men whom they had never heard of before and whose names they never knew.

Henry still thinks the *Musketaquid* a dignified, manly name. But Nathaniel Hawthorne apparently took it for granted that his seven dollars also purchased the right to rechristen the proud boat the *Pond Lily*. Henry did not believe that any man could possibly imagine himself destined for adventure in a boat called the *Pond Lily*. And what further disheartened Henry was that Nathaniel simply did not appreciate the fine vessel he had so cheaply purchased; he did not connect with its obedient temper. All Henry ever had to do was will the boat this way or that. But, even after repeated lessons, Nathaniel complained that the *Musketaquid* was sluggish, heavy in the water, and impossible to steer.

If Nathaniel had not renamed the once noble vessel, Henry might have considered borrowing it today; instead, he embarked in Edward's small boat, and Henry deferred to his young companion in the choice of where to come ashore. Had Henry been at the helm of the *Musketaquid,* he might have chosen not to stop so early in the day, might have insisted they not cook a chowder at all, or he might have been bold enough to suggest that they ignore their hunger and continue on until dusk. By then, the wind would certainly have lessened. With the *Musketaquid* beneath him, he might even have elected to make the excursion by himself.

A loud crash signals another fallen tree, and as Henry watches blood-red embers coil skyward he admits that these are foolish thoughts, the desperate overreachings of his troubled reason. He cannot blame Nathaniel Hawthorne any more than he can blame Edward or his brother, though he wishes he could have spent this day with John instead, paddling the *Musketaquid* as they had done five years earlier. There had been no disagreements between them on their trip down the Concord and Merrimack Rivers, and in the span of an immortal summer week they had garnered experiences to fortify them for a lifetime of winters. What a piece of wonder it was, those days spent on the river together. In no time before or since has he felt greater contentment, or companionship as complete. He is still nourished by memories of the sheer volume of life everywhere on display — swaying alders, birches, oaks, and maples, scurrying mice and moles and splashing muskrats, floating cranberries and wheeling gulls, and John behind him at the oars, smiling quietly in the bright flashes from wind-driven waves. Henry meticulously recorded every detail of their journey in his notebooks, and he sometimes believes he might work his notes into a proper book, given the time. He wishes he could abandon his pencil-making duties and live alone with only his notebooks, so that he might finally write the book he has long had in mind. If John were here to help guide him, Henry knows he would at last find the time and the means to finish the project. John always seemed at the ready with solutions.

After all, Henry thinks, it was John who had come to his rescue when it seemed that his Concord Academy would fail, and together they made a success of the little school for almost three years. Henry still considers it one of his happiest periods, among his few real contributions to the world, though he knows the students always preferred John to him. Henry was not jealous of his brother in this regard. John was warm and encouraging where Henry could sometimes be stern and demanding. Henry was content in the knowledge that their students respected him, even if it was John whom they loved. Another tree crashes to the ground, and it makes Henry wonder what his brother would do in this predicament. Nothing like this would be happening if John were here, he thinks.

But John Thoreau is dead.

Two years have already passed since John's death, and Henry's loneliness, far from dissipating, has grown deeper. Henry thinks that the only remedy for the loss of his brother's love is to love more, but neither new acquaintances nor the companionship of old friends can fill the absence. Together, Henry and John had dared swift-moving waters, hiked trails where a single misstep might have sent them tumbling. Together they had slept out of doors, exposing themselves to cold and rain, taunting illnesses that preyed on human carelessness. They had fired guns, swung axes, climbed unreliable trees, mounted unruly horses, ridden carriages over uncertain roadways. They had offered misfortune a thousand opportunities to seize them.

Then, on New Year's Day, 1842, John cut himself while stropping his razor and died of lockjaw ten days later. Might today's events, Henry wonders, be blamed on a rusted edge of steel? How quickly, how easily, a man moves from one state of being to the next. The language cannot keep up. "My brother John *is* dead," Henry shouts at the distant flames. The present tense of the verb

272

invites him to think of his brother inhabiting a different state, lying cramped in a pine box, staring at the lid, bored and lonely, as if the tragedy of dying were simply that one must tolerate conditions considerably less pleasant than those enjoyed by the living.

John is dead. It is a fact so difficult to grasp that shortly after John's death Henry began experiencing the same symptoms. Some inquiring part of his brain — the part dedicated to the acquisition of impossible facts — determined that only by experiencing the same condition as his brother could he claim the requisite information. Henry had not cut himself; for days after his brother's accident Henry would not go near his razor. His mourning kept him confined to his room, away from the pencil works, far from the garden and the woodshed and the river and the forest, far from any setting where he might encounter a sharp edge. Nonetheless, Henry began suffering the unmistakable symptoms that had delivered his brother to the grave. He knew he was not truly ill, but there was no denying his condition. He awoke feeling miserable, he complained of uncertain pains, a stiff neck, and a spreading numbness in his limbs.

The doctor was perplexed. He could find no cause, no visible wound or mortified flesh. Henry sank deeper into the vague malaise. His flesh grew cold. Days passed, and he could not rise from his bed. He found it difficult to speak; his words came out slurred and stupid. His jaw went slack in open-mouthed astonishment at its own capitulation to a phantom affliction. The doctor recommended they trickle water onto his tongue, enough to quench thirst, but not too much, lest he drown in his bed. For days, Henry's grieving mother squeezed a sponge over his open mouth. She changed his bedclothes and rearranged his pillows. Henry rolled his eyes in panicked submission, fearful that he would soon be joining his brother in death's semiconscious prison.

But Henry's sympathetic lockjaw did not outlive his sorrow. The symptoms passed on, but he did not. One morning his jaw swung shut, and he found himself returned to the living world. The doctor could explain neither the illness nor the cure and blamed Henry's overly sensitive disposition. Henry emerged from his ordeal without the satisfaction of having conquered a real disease. And John was dead, still.

Henry knows that his brother would have stopped him from committing so tragic an error as striking a match on such a day as this, but his brother will never again travel with him down any of the rivers of New England. It is almost unbelievable to Henry that he still cannot determine what to make of the long years stretching before him, when none remain for his brother. After twenty-six years, Henry has accomplished little, and the burden of his empty history weighs heavily on him. He cannot determine how to order the life that still feels as new to him as a stiff pair of boots. Yet his brother's life is complete. John has already become all that he will ever be.

Henry no longer expects to find a love that might take the place of what he felt for his brother. They had once even proposed marriage to the same woman, Ellen Sewall, within days of each other, and afterward they commiserated in their rejection. Henry has felt admiration for other women, but not having a wife is not something he regards as a loss. He knows there is a divergence between love and the entanglements of wedlock, though sometimes the two concur. He knows that the insatiable yearning for physical touch so confounds heart and mind as to reduce a man to animal bewilderment, a dog chasing its tail. He has come to prefer the love he finds in nature, and in this he has never been disappointed. He has been moved to soft tears by the generosity of spring and the unexpected gifts of autumn. He has taken comfort in the embrace of dappled moonlight beneath a crown of oaks. The woods are full of more varied personalities than he could ever hope to find in Concord. He observes now how every tree burns with a signature distinctly its own as the intense heat releases saps and resins hoarded in its concentric heart. A pine bursts into flame from trunk to crown, a gigantic matchstick with a blue-white fist of heat at its center. Trees hiss and whistle at different pitches, some burn like coal, blackening and crumbling beneath a thin aurora, some flare like lanterns filled with oil.

If John were alive, Henry thinks, this day would have turned out differently. He considers how he and his brother prepared scores of meals under the open sky, and never once had they started a fire they could not control. It is clear to him that one man's death erases not only that man's possibilities but all the possibilities that might have ensued from those, like the wake of a boat slicing through waves that might otherwise have reached the shore. Every man lives among the deaths of all who came before. What consequences would he unleash, Henry wonders, if he were to walk down

the hill into the burning trees? What unforeseen series of events might his sudden
demise cause or forestall, ten, twenty, a
hundred years from now? How would his
non-being ripple through the seasons to
come?

Henry runs his open hand over his whiskers, feels the hard edge of the jawbone
beneath, and decides that there is something
quintessentially corporeal about the jawbone. Here is the definition of a man, he
thinks. A man is a composite of bone and
deed. About the first, one can do nothing,
but it is through deeds that one makes
oneself a man, a creature distinct from the
nameless mass of jawbones.

He steps to where the downward slope
begins and studies the furrows he left on his
last descent. He considers walking back
down, but first he listens for the whispers
that chased him here. The fire is close, but
its advance has slowed; the flames lash out
and retreat, like a cat suspicious of the dish
of milk it demanded. Henry expects the
flames to take a half hour or more to reach
the base of Fair Haven Hill. He knows it
should not take as long as that for the men
of Concord to assemble and come to his
aid. And they will bring with them more
than shovels and axes; they will come with

angry stares, furious accusations, and thoughts of retribution. His regret, he understands, will not be so easily embraced after all. His guilt will not be so readily mastered. Henry steps back from the slope. Remorse presses down upon him heavy and full, like the lowering sky of an approaching tempest, and he admits that he is grateful, after all, to be alone here above the burning earth.

16
ELIOT

Eliot checks his watch, fingers the slack chain, slips it back into his vest pocket. The small sample of Concord visible through the dirty storefront window seems half-asleep. The breeze drifting through the open door carries the charred scent that has grown stronger since morning, and every now and then Eliot sees a passerby stop and point at the sky before continuing on, unconcerned.

It is already half past noon, well past the time Seymour Twine agreed to meet. Eliot has not communicated with him directly. He arranged their meeting through a mutual business associate, a man in whom he places only a modicum of trust. It seems to him that his life is populated by unreliable men — merchants, tradesmen, salesmen — men whom he knows only by a last name, men identified by the wares they carry. Eliot is as ignorant of their personal lives as he is of the cobbler, who, according to Otis Dickerson, died in the very shop where Eliot now paces impatiently. How, he wonders, have his days come to consist of one petty negotiation after another?

Eliot is not a diarist and has never felt the need. Those experiences worthy of recollection — food for reflection when he is working on his plays — always seem to lodge themselves in his memory. Sometimes, though, he wishes he had kept a diary as a young man, if only that he might now have a document detailing the indiscriminate decisions and digressions that have ushered him here. Eliot had thought only of love when he pursued Margaret Mahoney; he had not considered that he was wooing a father-in-law and business partner as well. He remembers the first time he ventured to take Margaret's hand, trembling at the touch of her cool, delicate fingers. He remembers their first kiss, stolen in the shadows of the Tremont Theater balcony after Mr. Mahoney was called away on an important matter of business, and he can recall other isolated moments, conversations, walks, dinners. But now, looking back, he cannot mark the incremental progression that brought him from romance to love to something more prudent, if less inspiring.

Eliot's first visit to the Mahoneys' parlor came not in the name of courtship but in response to an invitation from Mr. Mahoney himself. When Eliot arrived, he learned that Margaret was not even at home but was in Philadelphia visiting a cousin. The two men were alone, seated on facing serpentine sofas, when Mr. Mahoney made his intentions known.

"Calvert, I can see you are a man of the world, so I shall speak plainly."

"Thank you, sir," Eliot said, flattered.

"My daughter, as I am sure you have discerned, is a strong-minded woman, as well she should be, considering the sum I have exhausted on her schooling. But her willfulness has at times proven a frustration to those men who did not feel up to the challenge."

"I should think such men fools."

Mr. Mahoney grunted and tugged at his tight-fitting waistcoat. He slid back into the sofa, seeking a comfortable position on the fat green cushions, and his great stomach rose before him like an island. "The fact is that you, my boy, are not the first dog to come sniffing at our door. There have been suitors before, and most had an ample supply of the one thing you do not: *money.*"

Eliot sat still, uncertain whether he should take offense. In the theater, dissemblance and misdirection were the preferred paths to truth; he was not used to dealing with men who spoke bluntly.

"Nevertheless," Mr. Mahoney continued, "you have advanced further than the lot of them. Most fled as soon as they realized they could not match my daughter's wit. As for the others, I refused their entreaties because *they* lacked what you possess: *ambition.* And what is ambition but a desire to be something more than what you are? Tell me that I am not mistaken."

"You are not mistaken, sir."

"Certainly not. I know men. It is not the *having* that makes a man what he is to become. It is the *wanting.* Young men raised on their fathers' money do not understand the necessity of wanting what they do not already have."

"Yes, sir."

Mr. Mahoney tugged at his snug waistcoat again and unfastened the lowest button, which practically jumped from its hole.

"Nothing is more important to me than my daughter's happiness."

"Of course."

"But" — Mr. Mahoney held up a thick

finger — "she has, upon occasion, associated with men of artistic temperament — men of little or no accomplishment to speak of — and I know that she does so simply to confound my interest in seeing her settled with a husband of sound finances. She gets her rebellious spirit from her dear departed mother, and it comes as no surprise to me. But I fear she does not always act in her best interest."

Eliot fidgeted nervously. "Am I to understand that you disapprove of my attentions?"

"Not at all. You miss my point entirely." Mr. Mahoney struggled against the cushions for a moment and then settled back into them with a deep sigh. His immense head, with it sparse crests of gray hair, looked as though it were slowly being swallowed by his chest. "That is why I have asked you here, Calvert. Something in your nature sets you apart from the others. I wish to know more about your plans."

Eliot held on to the armrest to keep himself afloat on the wide sofa as he studied Mr. Mahoney's face, looking for some indication of how he should reply.

"Plans for what?" Eliot asked.

Mr. Mahoney cocked an eyebrow and stared at Eliot over the rise of his stomach.

"Why, for life! Your plans for life! I can tell that you are not a man content to wander aimlessly through his days."

Eliot hesitated. "Well, I am working on a play of some merit —"

"Yes, yes. Margaret has told me as much. I have written a little poetry myself. A man of business needs recreation to sharpen the mind. But I want to know about your *real* work. What of your business plans? Your expectations for the future."

"I have reason to believe," Eliot said, trying to sound confident, "that there might yet be a place for me at Carter and Hendee, after the sale is complete."

"You cannot expect to blacken Carter's boots forever, Calvert. Besides, we both know Carter and Hendee will be blackening Ticknor's boots soon enough." Mr. Mahoney twisted another button on his waistcoat but could not dislodge it. He gave up and regarded Eliot with disapproval. "You strike me as a man who wants something more."

"Well, yes, I do indeed." Eliot watched Mr. Mahoney's hand return to the strained button at his waistcoat, and he felt an urge to leap up and unfasten it for him. "I should think there will be new opportunities for advancement once Mr. Ticknor is in charge, possibly."

"You are aware of the type of books Ticknor intends to publish?"

Eliot nodded. "Medical books — they may prove to be a lucrative offering. There is always a demand, and such publications command no small price, especially those with engravings."

"And you do not think that a man of your ambitions will grow weary of dissection manuals?" Mr. Mahoney abandoned his efforts at undoing the button for a second time. "And what then? When your weariness turns to desperation, what then? Will you become one of the mass of men, forgotten in middling jobs, too uninspired to advance, too debt-ridden to quit altogether? What then, Calvert?"

Eliot was not prepared for the assault. He did not relish the future Mr. Mahoney described, but he could think of no plausible alternative.

"Your concern is not unwarranted," Eliot said, stalling for an answer that did not sound naïve. "But my position at Carter and Hendee . . . well, it is truly only a means to an end. As soon as I finish my play, I shall immediately strive to have it produced on the stage. All I need is one good night to attract investors, and I expect that once I leave my position I shall be able to devote all my energies to writing . . ."

"All your energies, you say?"

"Well, certainly —"

"Can you possibly expect your plays to generate income enough for my daughter?"

The boldness of the moment nearly struck Eliot dumb.

"I . . . I had not thought on it."

"Of course you have," Mr. Mahoney pressed. "Margaret is wholly entranced by the world of the theater and its romantic nonsense, but at the end of the day she will need to be kept in the manner to which she has grown accustomed. It is no small wonder that she has not yet found the man who can guarantee her happiness. However, in this I believe I might offer you some assistance."

Eliot's eyes darted about the handsomely appointed room, taking in the mahogany Hepplewhite furniture, dark paintings of stormy landscapes, ornamented corner chairs, statuettes and candlesticks and miniature portraits in tiny gilt frames. He became suddenly conscious of the close, dusty air. If he could have intuited what Mr. Mahoney wanted him to say, he would gladly have uttered it so that he might conclude the conversation and leave the suffocating parlor.

"Mr. Mahoney, please do not think me impertinent for saying so, but I see no reason that I should not hope to sustain your daughter's happiness on my own until I achieve fortune on the stage."

Mr. Mahoney regarded Eliot with the cold stare of a man accustomed to negotiating other men out of their money.

"This is your final offer, Calvert?"

"I was unaware that an offer was being made."

The large man rolled his eyes toward the ceiling and broke into laughter.

"Ho! You are a good one, Calvert. It has taken me a lifetime to acquire this wealth. How can I expect the same from a young man like yourself? No one has ever dissembled so well under my stare, and I have broken tougher nuts."

"I am not dissembling, sir."

"Enough! Ho! You have won. And I cannot say that I do not deserve the abuse. Margaret must have told you something of my plan already. I cannot trust the girl to keep a secret. Oh, you will make her a fine husband indeed."

Mr. Mahoney shifted his bulk and the sofa creaked beneath him, while Eliot wondered if a proposal of marriage had just been made and accepted on his behalf.

"We can work out the details later," Mr. Mahoney said, "but it should suffice to say that I have excess capital that I must put to work."

Eliot was not sure if Mr. Mahoney was referring to his daughter or to his money.

"I have decided to invest in a bookshop, Calvert. Timothy Carter and Charles Hendee will soon be out of the game. William Davis Ticknor is a formidable businessman, but he shows no interest in literary stuff. That leaves us with little competition."

"Competition?" Eliot had never met Mr. Ticknor, but he knew that the man had arranged for considerable backing to support his venture.

Mr. Mahoney paid Eliot's reluctance no heed. "I know opportunity, but I know nothing of the publishing world. You understand the people who read and buy books, but you have not the means to put your understanding into action. We shall wed our advantages each to each. I shall buy a bookstore, and you shall have the running of it."

"I am flattered, truly," Eliot said, hoping to slow the advance of what seemed to him an utterly absurd scheme. "But I fear your investment would be at risk."

Mr. Mahoney dispelled Eliot's doubt with a sweep of his thick arm.

"Have you heard of the *Sovereign of the Seas*?"

Eliot shook his head.

"No reason you should have. Norwegian ship. It was said to be a good investment — well built, valuable cargo, certain profit — but I had a bad feeling, and I always follow my gut." Mr. Mahoney respectfully patted his stomach. "And what happened? The doomed ship exploded in Boston Harbor. No survivors, a terrible loss of capital."

"Remarkable instincts," Eliot said, only slightly reassured by the man's confidence.

"I never doubt them. And now my instincts tell me that a bookshop is the thing."

Eliot rubbed his jaw. He felt numbed by the possibilities suddenly opening before him. "I have never given any thought to running a bookstore."

"You'll learn how to balance the accounts in time, easiest thing in the world."

"I . . . well, I am without words."

"Ha! Without words! That wit! Soon you'll have plenty to sell, at great profit. Margaret has convinced me that you are the perfect man for the job, and my *gut* agrees."

"Margaret knows of this?"

"Well, certainly! It is practically her idea."

289

Eliot could not have felt less certain how to respond. Margaret had never hinted at the possibility of such an arrangement. He felt it discomfiting to think of the two of them, father and daughter, discussing his future as if it wanted planning. But he did his best to summon a weak smile, and nodded slowly without actually meaning to.

"When do you require an answer?" Eliot asked.

"Your expression has already given your answer," Mr. Mahoney observed. "Ha! Besides, you really have no choice in the matter. How else could you expect to afford the wedding gift I have in mind for my daughter?"

Eliot Calvert's bookstore opened for business a year and a half before Margaret Mahoney became Mrs. Eliot Calvert. Once the sign was hung and the books displayed, Eliot found that running a bookshop had far less to do with books than it did with ledgers and receipts. Patrick Mahoney promised not to intervene, provided that the shop turned a profit, and he was true to his word.

Eliot was free to fill the shelves as he saw fit, and he sent orders to publishers and printing houses with the avarice of a nouveau riche collector. Books that he longed to read appeared by the cartload; writing instruments and exquisite papers arrived in carefully packed crates. He became the temporary caretaker of expensive folios that he could never have hoped to afford. He looked forward to the possibility of slow afternoons when he might sit on the high stool in the front window, reading the books in his trust, a living advertisement for the pleasures offered by his shop.

The wooden sign that swung above Boylston Street glittered with twelve-inch gold letters crowned with a pair of reading spectacles, "Eliot Calvert, Purveyor of Fine Books." The sign was visible to clear-eyed readers from all the way across the new Public Gardens. Eliot thought of the tiny handprinted block letters on the white card tacked to the door of the cramped basement office that his father was sometimes permitted to use at Harvard. He brought his father and mother to the shop on the first day of business, and as they walked side by side beneath the sign he observed their reflections, multiplied across the checkerboard panes of glass at the shop front. No longer a timid observer of other men's accomplishments, Eliot stood square-shouldered to show that he had as much right to walk the streets as any man, an owner and shaper of the world in which he lived. Eliot's father walked stooped, hands clutched behind his back, and his mother clung to her husband's arm for support. Edna Calvert suffered from grievous bunions that forced her to take quick, short, painful steps, which made her appear as though she were forever running downhill.

"Faust," Ambrose Calvert said appreciatively, as he rubbed the leather cover of the book Eliot had purposely left on the counter.

Edna ventured between the closely set bookcases, marveling at the packed shelves. "How do you afford so many fine books?" she called out to her son.

"They belong to the shop," Eliot answered. "That is how a business works."

His father looked around thoughtfully. "Still, I should think a man must first own what he intends to sell."

"Mr. Mahoney has been most generous in his support."

Eliot's father tapped the cover of the big book on the counter. "And does Mr. Mahoney support your other efforts?" he asked.

Eliot picked up the volume of Goethe and placed it on the empty stand in the window. "If you are referring to my plays, Father,

Mr. Mahoney has shown great interest, but my writing requires little in the way of capital." Eliot spotted his mother on the other side of the shop, running a finger along the shelves, checking for dust.

"Capital?" His father chuckled. "That is not a word I ever expected you to employ." He placed a hand on Eliot's shoulder, and it struck Eliot that his father's jacket and waistcoat were identical to his own — gray and black, the cut and color of apology. "I suppose you'll have no choice now but to marry this man's daughter," Ambrose said.

Eliot smiled. "Only if she'll have me."

His father looked out the window at the immense sign creaking heavily above the street.

"It would appear that she already does," he said.

The next morning, Eliot promptly bought six new coats and waistcoats in contrasting colors. Never again would he stare at the ground as he walked. The years that he had spent with downcast eyes, ruminating on plots and characters, had done little to advance his success as a playwright. He could see no reason to adhere to that public performance of introspection, as long as he remained faithful to the exercise of writing itself. He considered moving to new accommodations, but then decided against it, unwilling to alter the circumstances of his creative life. He would be a successful businessman by day and a struggling play-wright by night.

Eliot harbored a loyal affection for his simple room near Mount Vernon, Boston's westernmost hill, once dubbed "Mount Whoredom" by British soldiers, for obvious reasons. Eliot's room was furnished with all that he had ever needed in his pursuit of fame: books, a desk, a chair, and a bed. Most important, the room's location on the top floor, with one narrow window overlooking a small garden instead of the busy street opposite, provided him with solitude and silence. There were few places in the modern world, he thought, with its emphasis on speed and efficiency, where a man could sit undisturbed and undistracted, accompanied by nothing more than his own thoughts.

After they announced their engagement, Margaret insisted that he at last show her something he had written, and Eliot reluctantly allowed her to read the incomplete draft of *The House of Many Windows*. It lacked not only a conclusion, he explained to her, but a beginning as well, and some of the middle parts were in need of attention, but he was confident that he had produced some spirited dialogue. He sat across from her in the Mahoneys' parlor and watched her turn the pages of the manuscript as she sat on the same sofa where Mr. Mahoney had made his business proposition. Eliot studied her shifting expressions, and he fought the urge to snatch the pages away before she finished.

ACT V, SCENE 2
[At center stage, a house, engulfed in flames.]

DEMONTE: He is lost!

REYNALD: There is hope still.

DEMONTE: Here sit my wife and daughter, forlorn, lately pulled from the inferno by daring, reckless hands. The boy is lost.

REYNALD: My young friend, you might yet act! Were it not for these aged limbs, I myself would fly into the flames to save your newborn son instead of sacrificing the innocent one to hesitating discourse.

DEMONTE: Oh, my son! My infant son, asleep above encroaching flames!

REYNALD: Have faith. He lives yet, and yet might he be rescued.

DEMONTE: What fool charges into the

conflagration to save what is already lost?

REYNALD: One who willingly risks all to preserve what he holds dear.

DEMONTE: You speak of demigods and simpletons.

REYNALD: No. I speak of men!

"What do you think?" he asked as soon as Margaret looked up from the last lines. "It is not, as you can see, complete."

"Will this end well?"

"I have not yet decided my hero's end. But do you like it, thus far?"

"Well, yes, certainly, but . . ."

Eliot's heart sank. "But what? You would like something with more coherence, no doubt, but I should remind you that this is only a draft. And you should know that I do intend to provide something more in the way of action in future drafts."

"No, no. That is not it. I . . . well . . . I think you should consider leaving your dreary rooms at Mount Vernon. A brighter prospect might fill you with thoughts less . . . gloomy."

Eliot found no cause for disappointment in Margaret's critique. He did not expect her to comprehend that his writing was explorative of man's graver humors. Nor did he think she would appreciate the conditions he found conducive to summoning inspiration.

"I understand your concern, my darling. But I can assure you that my rooms are not so gloomy as you think." He took her hand. "Not when they are brightened by my thoughts of you."

"Oh, Eliot," Margaret said, laughing. "The things you say."

Eliot had forgotten Patrick Mahoney's allusion to his wedding gift until the day he asked Eliot and Margaret to meet him at an address on Beacon Hill. Identical redbrick façades, bowed fronts in the Bulfinch style, stretched before them, their purple-flushed windows glowing brilliantly in the reflected sunlight. Patrick Mahoney stood at the foot of a short flight of steps, and his bulk seemed to fill the entire street. He welcomed his daughter with open arms, and the gesture made Eliot fear that Margaret might disappear beneath the immense curtain of his open coat. Margaret ran to her father — like a child, Eliot thought — and for a second he wondered why she did not rush so breathlessly into his embrace. Mr. Mahoney handed his daughter a key tied with a bit of ribbon.

"Father, you are far too generous," she said happily.

Mr. Mahoney nodded and pointed to the door. "Shall we go in?"

He took hold of the iron railing and began pulling himself up the steps hand over hand. Eliot did not move. Margaret turned to the street and grabbed Eliot by the arm.

"What are you waiting for?" she asked.

"Who lives here?"

From halfway up the steps, Patrick Mahoney overheard him and wheezed. "Ha! That wit. I am always unprepared for it. Please, I am already winded."

Margaret understood what her father did not. She lowered her voice and squeezed Eliot's arm firmly. "*We* do, Eliot. This will be *our* home as soon as we are wed."

"This?" Eliot drew back, as if stung, and he saw his mistake in Margaret's eyes.

"Isn't it wonderful?" she said, without smiling.

"It is . . . unexpected."

She tugged his arm, but Eliot remained rooted in the street while her father unlocked the door and entered the house.

"The wedding is but three months away," she said. "Where did you think we would go afterward?"

"I have given it some consideration," Eliot

said quietly, once he was sure that her father was out of earshot. "Honestly I have, though I did not think the need quite so pressing. There are only two of us and —"

"You did not expect me to share your dismal, cramped rooms at Mount Vernon, did you?"

"We might have moved into rooms at Alexina Fisher's until —"

"Fisher's? The boardinghouse? With the actors? You cannot be serious."

"I would have found us a place, Margaret. Certainly nothing so grand as this, but do we really need something this large? Two or three rooms would have sufficed."

"Eliot, please! Where would I receive guests? Where would we entertain? How would you write amid the chaos of a household? Here you can have your own study, a whole room to sit with your books." She leaned closer. "And if you get lonely you can refresh yourself with the knowledge that I am always just beyond your door."

Eliot craned his neck and cast his eyes up to the roof; he thought he could already hear the deafening echo of so many large, empty rooms.

"Do we own all three floors?"

"Eliot, really," she chided. "What use would we have for half a home?"

Eliot's mouth was dry, and the back of his throat felt as if it were covered with a layer of grit. He tried to swallow but could not draw enough saliva.

"Of course, of course." He forced himself to laugh at his own misunderstanding. "It is only . . . well, I cannot imagine how we will ever begin to furnish such a place."

"I am sure Father has taken care of everything."

Eliot felt like an intruder when he stepped through the front door. Carpets of red and blue covered the floors, filling the close air with a heavy musk. The rooms were already stuffed with maple furniture in the American Empire style, and the walls held paintings of hunting scenes and sea voyages. Eliot turned and found himself staring into a large pier glass.

"Eliot! Do come here!" Margaret's excited voice reached him from somewhere above.

"I believe the master of the house is needed," Mr. Mahoney said.

Eliot hurried up the stairs. His father-in-law-to-be watched him take the risers two at a time with an expression Eliot judged to be a mixture of longing and recollection. When he reached the second floor, he looked into two fully furnished rooms before realizing that Margaret was calling from above. He bounded up two more flights, ignoring the dark paintings that hung at the landing. On the third floor, Margaret motioned excitedly. She stood in a bright doorway, and from the hallway Eliot could hear the noise of people and carriages in the street below.

Margaret walked to the middle of the room, her dark silhouette surrounded by a nimbus of bright light alive with swirling dust motes.

"Oh, Eliot, look. Here is your study."

Eliot remained in the doorway, stunned by the room's brightness. A green carpet filled the expanse, and two armchairs sat before bookcases that covered the walls from floor to ceiling. The shelves were already crammed with books; the dark leather of their spines swallowed their titles.

"And here, look." Margaret pointed to an empty bottom shelf. "Father has left a space for you to put your books. He really is too kind. Oh, Father!" She ran from the room, and Eliot heard her soft footfalls on the carpeted stairs.

A scalding torrent of light poured in through the huge windows, and from below the din of the street intruded with impunity. Eliot felt dizzy. He stepped uncertainly toward the enormous mahogany desk that perched on heavy, pointed legs and braced himself against its corner. The noise in the street seemed to grow louder. He held his hand at his brow to shield his eyes from the glare, but it did no good. It was too bright to see, too loud to think. Eliot closed his eyes, felt the room spin, and winced as a loud pain pierced his temples like the sharp clap of a slamming door.

Eliot's first child was born in the third-floor bedroom one year after he and Margaret moved into their new home as husband and wife. The child was a boy, and they named him Josiah Edward. Eliot acknowledged that a firstborn son was the wish of nearly every man since Adam, and yet, despite his gratitude toward whatever forces of nature or heaven were responsible for fulfilling this most fundamental yearning, he nevertheless felt a concentrated hollowness beneath his heart. He tried to fill this space with the language assigned to the presumptions of fatherhood, but no matter how solidly he attempted to pack the heavy void with simple words like *pride* and *duty* they seemed only to pass through the space, slip away, as if carried off by the coursing of his blood. What he felt along the circumference of the hollowness seemed more closely related to some sense of remorse — a nameless, illogical sorrow for having forced this child into a world that he himself had not yet mastered.

The emotions that dared flit across this void were unexpected. Eliot found himself moved to incredible sadness one afternoon as he watched Josiah Edward, at only six months, straining for a shiny object beyond his grasp. The infant sat on a sky-blue blanket, and just past the blanket's edge a bright ninepence sat on the red carpet. The child grunted softly, rocking forward onto his chubby thighs, breathing hard through a mouth wide open in expectation of tasting some new fascination in the ever-expanding world. The struggle could not have lasted more than a minute, but to Eliot it seemed the quest of an hour's duration, an example of preternatural tenacity in so young a mind. Eliot watched his son rock back and forth, straining, resolved, increasing his reach by a hair's breadth each time, pudgy fingers scratching at the blanket. Eliot felt utterly powerless to intervene. By stages the child pulled himself onto his soft round knees, stretched too far, and slowly toppled forward. His forehead struck the carpet with a harmless thud. Josiah Edward lay facedown, confused and unable to right himself, his fingers still wiggling in an ineffectual grasp. And then, quietly, the infant began to whimper.

Eliot roused himself from his chair and lifted his son with a sweeping motion, as if this act might banish the recent disappointment. He felt a deep melancholy on the boy's behalf — for the nature of things, for the arrangement of the world, for the structure of what passed for reality. And then he realized that the cause of his sadness was not the futility of his son's determination, not the boy's inability to recognize that what he wanted was beyond his reach but, rather, the fact that the shiny coin, once grasped, once tasted, would have proved unworthy of the effort. At that moment, Eliot wanted to pull his son into the heavy, empty space in his chest, so that he might fill himself with his child and replace his confused feelings for the boy with the boy himself.

How suddenly Eliot's life had changed into an utterly foreign thing. Even when his bookshop was thriving, the profits never seemed enough. The house on Beacon Hill, while a generous gift, to be sure, was a burden to maintain. And though the bookshop's profits met his household expenses, the bills were steady enough to make any missteps unthinkable. The house had demanded attention from the start, and it had not occurred to him — not until Margaret pointed out with her tinkling-chandelier laugh — that such a house could be properly maintained only with two servants, at the very least.

And then came more children: after Josiah Edward there was Abigail Marie, Nathaniel Thomas, Humphrey Joseph, and, finally, Samuel Titus. Margaret seemed to have the names at the ready, as if she had known in advance each child's inevitability. Eliot was not sure why he allowed himself to feel surprised every time. He had not thought that he would be childless, and he believed he welcomed the idea of children. But he had not thought their arrival, one upon the other, would be quite so swift, quite so relentless. He knew of playwrights who had children, but he had never encountered fathers who wrote plays.

With the children came additional expenses, and he raised the prices on his most valuable books. If he could only generate slightly higher profits, he reasoned, he might employ a clerk to oversee the shop in his stead, freeing himself to devote an hour or two each day to working on his plays. He expanded the range of inks and nibs he carried. He imported expensive Faber pencils but later replaced these with the superior ones manufactured by John Thoreau & Co. He tried stocking unusual items: reading glasses from France and bookmarks studded with jewels. In an effort to attract wealthy collectors, Eliot devoted an entire wall to exquisite books he ordered from Hatchards bookshop in London. Yet, despite his best efforts, he seemed able to outpace his debts only by the barest of margins, until the day the account books revealed that he was gradually slipping into debt.

Eliot took note of what interested his patrons, what books they bought, what books they examined and returned to the shelves, and tried to vary his stock accordingly. He had always made careful observations of the people who visited his shop, but it was not until his financial difficulties began to mount that he noticed a peculiar, pock-faced man nosing through the stacks, fingering books, staring at the other customers. The man came in every week but never bought anything. He introduced himself as Punch one day, and then set about his usual practice of examining Eliot's wares without another word. Eliot did not ask whether Punch was a first or last name or something entirely fabricated to suit the man's demeanor. The man's nose was permanently mashed to the side, one nostril twice as large as the other, and his breath wheezed noisily through the smaller opening. He bought nothing, spoke to no one, and seemed more interested in Eliot's customers than in anything on the shelves. Whenever Eliot asked him if he needed assistance, Punch merely smiled politely and shook his head, as if he did not understand what Eliot was saying.

Punch finally broke his silence one evening when Eliot was preparing to close. As soon as Eliot pulled down the shade on the front door, he was startled by a voice that sounded as though it had bubbled up from a thick pool of phlegm.

"I believe I may be of some service, Mr. Calvert."

Eliot had thought that the shop was empty. He turned and saw the pock-faced man standing at the counter. Though Punch usually kept his hands hidden in his coat pockets, today he carried a canvas bag that bulged with flat, sharp angles.

"Mr. Punch," Eliot said. "I did not realize you were still here."

"Just Punch, please. Do I understand correctly that you are searching for new ways to fatten your purse?"

"I beg your pardon?" Eliot was stunned by the offensive question.

"Mr. Calvert, I have come to speak to you on the matter of money. These are difficult times. Money is in short supply, but I can be most helpful in this regard. You have indicated that you want more of it, have you not?"

Eliot had occasionally discussed his financial concerns with those shopkeepers and merchants whose discretion he trusted, but now it was clear to him that his worries had not remained a secret. He was not as shocked as he might have been at what Punch claimed to know, but the man's boldness was inexcusable.

Eliot grabbed the door handle. "Your question is most inappropriate, sir. I must ask you to leave."

"It is why I waited until closing, Mr. Calvert. You will find that I value prudence above all else. Have I been misinformed as to your present needs?"

Eliot hesitated. "How dare you presume to speak to me of my needs?"

"Boston is not so large a city, my friend. You have made inquiries. Those inquiries have made their way to others, and some have made their way to me. You can certainly understand that a man of business must pursue opportunities when they arise."

Eliot regarded Punch with suspicion. The man looked more like a pugilist than a merchant, and he did not at all resemble the sort of men with whom Eliot usually dealt. Still, opportunity often presented itself in unlikely forms. Punch was more eloquent than Eliot had reason to expect, and he spoke with a wheezing assertiveness.

"Am I to understand," Eliot said guardedly, unsure why he did not insist that the man leave, "that you wish to make a business proposition?"

"Indeed. I suggest that you expand your offerings."

Punch hefted the canvas bag onto the counter and tugged at the drawstring.

Eliot held up his hands and shook his head. "I already carry a wide range of books. I daresay you'll not find better-stocked shelves in Boston."

"Heh." Punch's laugh squeaked through his flattened nose. "I've seen your stock, Mr. Calvert. I'd say there is room yet to augment your trove."

Eliot stepped toward the counter to see what Punch carried in the dirty canvas sack. "I can assure you, my shelves have not an available inch of space."

"The items that cannot be displayed on

your shelves," Punch said, "will likely demand a higher price than those that can." He snorted, then glanced around the empty shop and grabbed the bottom of the sack by its corners. The open mouth gaped dark and mysterious. Eliot was intrigued.

Punch lifted the bag, spilling a jumble of cards and papers tied in bundles, small pamphlets, and several thin books.

Eliot shook his head. "I already carry chapbooks and card games."

"Mr. Calvert, I doubt that you carry items such as these."

Eliot grabbed a stack of cards tied with string, and as soon as he saw what was pictured his jaw went slack. The top card displayed a hand-colored etching of a bearded man reclining on a plush couch of red velvet. At his feet, a golden-haired woman knelt in devotion, and in her hands she held his bright pink penis.

"Good God!"

Eliot dropped the cards and they scattered across the counter. He saw that another card displayed a man and a woman en-twined in the unmistakable act. In the corner was stamped "No. 16." The other cards displayed different numbers and a seemingly impossible array of contortions.

Punch grinned as he collected the cards,

retied them with string, and rummaged through the pile on the counter.

"Lest you think me unlearned, Mr. Calvert, please note that I am also a purveyor of the written word." Punch handed him a pamphlet, flipping the pages as he did so to show that there were no illustrations. "I have found that there are men who prefer something more in the way of, shall we say, *narrative*. For some it serves as an entertainment — for others it provides much needed instruction."

Eliot scanned the pamphlet's first page and immediately identified a half-dozen words that he had never heard spoken except in the company of men. He should have been disgusted by the filth spread over his counter, but something kept him turning the pages of the pamphlet. Eliot looked out over the properly stocked shelves of his bookstore, and then let his eyes drop down to the cabinets behind the counter, where he stored his extra stock.

"Where did you acquire this rubbish?" Eliot asked sternly.

"Rubbish never commanded so high a price as this, Mr. Calvert."

"I assume that you are the artist of these" — Eliot searched for the right word — "portraits."

Punch squeaked again through the flattened nostril. "You flatter me. I have not the skill, but I know talented artists in need of money. Men do what they must to meet their debts. And know this: you will be able to charge your buyers *twice* what you pay me for these items."

Eliot noticed that his hands were trembling, and he was angry that he had permitted this man to make him feel that he was not so worldly as he liked to think. "Look here, I have a reputation to maintain. I cater to respectable clientele. I cannot possibly permit these . . . *things* . . . in my shop."

Punch bared his brown teeth, wide and blunt as toenails. "The men who want such items are not the sort to pass judgment. Honest men recognize their honest desires."

Eliot grabbed the edge of the counter to keep his hands from shaking. "Do not think that you can teach me about honest men."

Punch scowled and began stuffing the books and cards back into the dirty sack.

"I will not play this game with you, Mr. Calvert. I see what you are up to. You think that you will shame me. And then, once you have made me feel that I am your inferior, you think you will dictate our terms. I am no fool. There are others, wiser in the ways of the world, who understand that your so-called respectable clientele will pay dearly for this."

Eliot watched Punch stuff the cards and pamphlets into the sack, and in the fading daylight he caught a sparkle from a long crack in one of the shop's windows. The pane of expensive tinted glass would need replacing.

"Wait, please," Eliot said softly.

Eliot picked up the stack of cards that remained on the counter. "No. 47" showed two lovers entwined with heads and feet at opposite ends. He thought of the shutters that were currently being repaired on Beacon Street. He thought of the broken flue in the chimney that would need mending before winter arrived. He thought of the spidery brown water stain that had mysteriously appeared on the ceiling of his bedroom. Eliot looked at "No. 52," where three bodies were, improbably, tangled in positions that did not strike him as at all productive. He thought of the expensive medicine that Margaret had begun needing for her headaches. He thought of the patterned china that she said could not possibly be used for another season of entertaining. And he thought how Josiah Edward, now five years of age, had already begun to show an interest in the scientific microscope that his grandfather kept as a novelty for examining small, squashed insects.

"You say that these men will actually pay for such things?" Eliot asked.

"Men pay dearly for what they desire, Mr. Calvert." Punch drummed his fingers presumptively on Eliot's countertop. "Dearly."

Eliot knows he should not allow these pointless ruminations to distract him from his business in Concord. He steps into the street in front of the old cobbler's shop, then turns and watches the blur of smoke spread above the distant treetops like a dark thought. He would gladly purge his life of men like Punch and Seymour Twine and forgo the added income their wares have brought, even if doing so necessitated moving into a smaller home, one less expensive to maintain, one that required no servants. But he knows that Margaret's father would not hesitate to intervene if he perceived that they were in financial difficulty. And the truth is, Eliot admits to himself, he has come to enjoy the idea that he is the kind of man who can afford expensive comforts. He has grown used to the unexpected luxuries that surround him. And what was wrong with that? He does not ask anything of anyone. Patrick Mahoney had provided him with a home and a business, but Eliot can point to his own labor as the sole source of his family's continued contentment. He is about to open a second bookstore; he is very nearly finished with the final draft of *The House of Many Windows,* and it seems that he has at last found a place for it onstage at Moses Kimball's Boston Museum. His ambitions have survived undiminished. Has he not remained true to himself, after all?

Eliot watches as the wind smears the looming dark cloud against the sky, and still no one seems to pay it much attention. He assumes the people of Concord are accustomed to farmers burning off their fields, or whatever it is they do this time of year. He knows it would serve him well to learn from their wise indifference. It has done him no good to be so easily distracted by his own restless memories. Eliot turns away from the smoke and walks toward Wright's Tavern at the town's center. Every man has his employments, he thinks, responsibilities enough to occupy him for a lifetime without having to seek out new worries. He has an ample store of his own, and today meeting with Seymour Twine heads his list.

17
CALEB

Caleb knows exactly how he has come to this.

And the fire assures him that he is not mistaken.

He crawls from under the tent of his wool coat, and he sees that it is still there, distant in the woods, little flickers of brilliance intimating greater things. He leaves his coat draped over the crumbled foundations of the farmhouse, and when he stands his long white surplice catches the wind. His followers concluded soon enough that the fire was no talisman of celestial reckoning. Caleb knows what they must have thought: if the Almighty so decreed that the woods should burn, who were they to countermand the wishes of heaven? They had no cause to find anything remarkable about a world consumed by flames.

But there is more to it than they can possibly understand, he thinks.

With the black-lacquered pipe clenched between his teeth, Caleb looks around the plot of land as if he were seeing it for the first time. Then he begins pacing its perimeter, crunching the spiky stalks of last year's weeds beneath his feet. The fire confirms that Providence has been at work all along, feeding his doubts, leading him into blasphemy, all so that he — Caleb Ephraim Dowdy — might willingly sacrifice himself in executing the plan that will bring proof of God's existence to a corrupt and ignorant world. Why else would the Concord Woods be aflame on this day of all days? Surely the universe was not so accidental a place.

Caleb stares at his feet as he walks, entranced by the rhythm of his steps. He draws on his pipe, feels the hot, bittersweet smoke seep into his lungs, and he circles the property a second time. From the corners of his eyes he recognizes groupings of stones he passed before, only now he perceives patterns, illegible messages arranged in characters native to the soil. The fire shows him a new way of seeing, shows him that there is a divine cause behind every act, every trial, every doubt that has accumulated in his memory, and he realizes that he has led a life composed of parables. Everything in his experience has happened

for his instruction: his mother's early passing, the flaw in the stained-glass window of
his father's church, the dead Irishman in
the woods, the blind indifference of his first
congregation, his visits to the Leverett
Street Jail, even his dealings with fallen souls
like Esther Harrington and Amos Stiles. He
circles the ruins and recalls, with a renewed
sense of purpose, the causes that have
brought him here.

Doubt had always been with him: the first
syllable of a query, a hard kernel of desperation ready to torment him in his idle hours.
It had not begun with his stumbling upon
the dead Irishman, but the worm-hollowed
skull did give substance and shape to his
already nascent misgivings. He saw the rotted face staring at him in his dreams, mock-
ing his attempts to believe that something
more awaited the sons of men. He held the
preachers of the New World responsible for
permitting so wicked a thing as incertitude
to gain purchase in his mind; it was a
consequence of their carelessness, a symp-
tom of their failed vigilance. He counted his
father among them, another impotent leader
of insouciant believers; he thought his father
too ready to forgive, too eager to dispense
the promise of redemption, as if his church
were an apothecary for the soul. The great

stained-glass window held out hope for the perfectibility of this world, but the sparkling flaw half hidden in the highest pane was a constant reminder to Caleb of man's ir-redeemable failings. If so beautiful a cre-ation as the window could harbor such a defect, Caleb reasoned, why should he not suspect that the erudite orations of his father and the other ministers of New England hid errors of reasoning in the depths of their well-turned phrasings?

Toward the end of Caleb's final year at Harvard Divinity School, his father pro-claimed that marvelous revelations had begun appearing to him in his waking hours, fiery pinpoints of light crackling in the periphery of his vision like mute and skittish angels. The intermittent visions ceased altogether after several weeks, but they were succeeded shortly thereafter by a massive epiphany that knocked Marcus Dowdy to the cobblestones as he strolled along Tremont Street, robbing him of speech and infusing his limbs with tremors. Months later, slurred and slow, he described the searing radiance that had felt as though it clove his skull in two. He struggled for words, grunting through the living half of his mouth, and with heroic effort he was eventually able to convey that, like Saint

Paul, he had been struck down so that he might look upon eternity, and he rejoiced.

Marcus Dowdy accepted the physician's conclusion that his powerful revelation had brought on an apoplexy from which it was unlikely he would regain his former vigor. His left side, the doctor informed him, had ceased to function, and Marcus took this as confirmation that man's earthly mold was a poor vessel to convey the full glory of heaven. Marcus could not return to his ministry, and the day after Caleb completed his studies, in the spring of 1830, he stepped into his father's pulpit in the Court Street Unitarian Church. Caleb envied his father's epiphany; he would gladly have sacrificed speech and motion in exchange for a glimpse of what lay beyond this world.

But Caleb understood the immediate significance of what had come to pass. Providence had stricken his father in order that Caleb might introduce the reforms so desperately needed. For guidance, he looked to an earlier generation of preachers who sermonized when the New World had not yet slid into decadence; he sought to revive Christianity's former glory from the days before the Revolution. He renamed his father's church, and in the Court Street First Reformed Unitarian Assembly he began delivering the kind of uncompromising sermons that had not been heard in Boston for a hundred years.

But neither this reformed liturgy nor his father's recurring epiphanies — which delivered to Marcus visions of increasing brilliance — assuaged Caleb's pernicious misgivings. Whenever his mind was not fully occupied, the doubts crept back. Caleb gnashed his teeth in his sleep. He dreamed of bottomless chasms. In idle waking hours, he saw the dead Irishman's face staring back at him black and empty. Caleb despaired and prayed for guidance until his clasped hands cramped around each other. And he labored. Like an indentured servant working off impossible debts, Caleb toiled until he could not tell where his calloused hands ended and the work began. He tended to the sick. He walked dark streets preaching to the indigent; he visited infirmaries. He exhausted his body in order to quiet his mind, and when acts of charity were not tiring enough he saddled his horse, stowed the blue-handled hatchet that he had found years earlier next to the rotting corpse in the woods, and rode into the trees beyond the city.

Sometimes he composed sermons while he chopped, swinging the hatchet ferociously, as if he thought the Devil himself resided in the trees. Caleb worked until the pain in his arms and shoulders overwhelmed whatever part of his brain occupied itself with his distress. Sometimes he returned from the woods empty-handed; sometimes he returned with a cartload of split logs ready for the hearth. He chopped wood for elderly widows; he hauled cords to the Sisters of Charity at the Female Asylum, to the School for the Feeble-Minded, to the City Lunatic Asylum and the House of Industry. And once, after he had chopped enough for those in need, he envisioned how he might employ the overgrown American forests in the salvation of his followers. Caleb amassed a great pile of firewood behind his church, and he engaged a carpenter from his congregation to install a large cast-iron stove behind the altar, where it would not be seen. No other church in Boston was equipped with so indulgent a comfort as a stove, but comfort was not at all what he had in mind.

Caleb still takes satisfaction in recalling how profusely the worshippers in the Court Street church sweated as he delivered a three-hour sermon on one exceptionally cold Sunday in 1832. He knows his mother would have admired his cleverness; she had always praised his resourcefulness as a boy, his small successes at silencing a creaking chair with a bit of twisted wire or leveling a table with a flat slice of shale. She had told him that these little deeds bespoke greater achievements to come. Caleb remembers how the bitter January morning squeezed New England in its petrified fist, how the immense icicles beneath the eaves of the small church caught the pale sunlight and spread thimblefuls of wan color into the nave, how the fat beads of perspiration glistened on the pink, round faces nearest him. He watched the men in the first row unbutton their coats and tug at the stiff shirt collars half hidden beneath their heavy jowls.

The wealthy paid a handsome rent for their private boxes at the front of the church, where every Sunday they sat closer to God than their fellow worshippers, stoking the hot embers of the foot warmers they had brought from home. As Caleb sermonized in front of the blazing stove, he imagined the envy they must have felt for the less fortunate seated on their drafty, open pews in back, their hot bricks long since cooled. Caleb surveyed the prominent men and women on display in the pews nearest him — Silas Tooke, Edmund Meade, Albertus Crowe — and he imagined the flaws they concealed beneath their respectable cloaks: *adultery, fornication, onanism, gluttony.* Their wives were no better; even the staid widow Harriet Crane, swaddled in her black shawl and lace, harbored venial secrets, he was sure of it. He watched Elijah Harwood, of Magnus-Harwood Shipping and Transport, open the narrow door to his family's box to let out the hot air. Caleb scowled and drummed his fingers on the pulpit, a sign for the boy behind the altar to cram another log into the overheated stove.

Caleb wanted to make his congregants feel the punishing heat that would percolate in the veins of the condemned. He did not shout like other preachers he had heard, did not try to force his way into the hardened skulls of the unrepentant. He spoke with restraint, trusting in the power of his words to convey their awful truth:

You may think the time is distant, but I assure you that the flames burn even now. Already, the match is struck for the wicked man yet to be born. The torch is lit that will scorch the feet of some here among us today. If you do not live every hour in holy dread of Judgment, then you do not understand that the fire is even now being

> stoked. It has burned for a thousand years
> and will burn for all eternity. Oh, everlast-
> ing misery! Before this year is out, it is
> likely that one of you here among us will
> feel this heat. We know not the hour, nor
> do we know who in this church today will
> be recalling these very words in hell. But
> we know this: the fires are burning even
> now.

Caleb looked out over the flushed faces,
watched sinners remove their gloves and
loosen their shirt collars. He felt his contempt for them rise in his breast; he could
summon no compassion for those who
would seek first to alleviate physical discomfort when they should be contemplating the
dire state of their souls.

> Do not think that you can snuff the flame
> already kindled for you. Do not think you
> can escape its heat. The only reason you
> do not already languish in the fires of hell
> is that God's merciful hand has held you
> up.

Caleb felt no pity for these pious dis-
semblers, ingratiating supplicants meek and
stupid as dogs; they were the font of the
New World's moral decrepitude. He felt
impatient with God for not casting them

into the fire at this very moment. Caleb drummed his fingers, heard the creak of the stove door, and felt a burst of heat strike the back of his head. Sweat poured from his skin. He searched their faces but did not see the terror necessary for their salvation. Caleb returned his gaze to the soft chin of Elijah Harwood, and watched in disbelief as the man let his jaw drop open, apelike, into an unencumbered yawn.

And then Caleb almost gave voice to the dread that nightly fed the fire in his blood: *And if it is not your own condemnation you fear, then fear this: what if there is no hell, no heaven? What if, as some in this New World would suggest, God is nothing more than the wind whistling through the trees?* Let them contemplate that! Let them contemplate an eternity rotting in the earth like so many fallen trees, fattened in life only to provide a nest for pulsing maggots. How could he make them understand that by dreading eternal torment they purchased the re-assurance of a touchable eternity, a proof of something beyond death's door, even if that something was unending pain? Caleb would show them that fear gave stronger testimony than hope. He would show them the com-fort to be found in hell's everlasting fire, for those flames consumed all doubt that this life might constitute the sum of all being.

But there were other things he could not tell his congregants. He could not reveal to them that, if forced to make the choice, he would find it preferable — a blessing, even — to suffer for all eternity rather than to cease being altogether. He could not tell them that what he feared more than the irrevocable certitude of death was the possibility that nothing at all came after.

When Marcus Dowdy learned how his son had abused the Court Street congregation, he wrote a reprimanding letter in the runic blotches that issued from his crippled hand. He encouraged his son to think on God's grace, on the promise of forgiveness and the power of redemption, and he gently urged him to soften what he called his "unforgiving ministry." Caleb tossed the letter into the cold stove but did not burn it.

At the time, Caleb thought it a shame that he would never again put the stove to use, but now he understands. It is clear to him at last: all that followed from that day has been necessary, else he would not have found himself here, in Concord, at this moment. It had all transpired in accordance with God's will.

As he circuits the skeletal remains of the

abandoned farmhouse, Caleb mulls over his disappointments at Court Street. He takes another pull on his pipe, welcomes the vapors easing his senses into blessed confusion. The ground beneath his feet grows more distant with each step, but he detects no diminishment of reason. Every confounding inhalation improves his clarity of thought, he believes, even as his body seems to break apart and scatter like so many dried leaves.

His congregants at Court Street, he recollects, had not been at all like the followers who assembled before him this morning. Poor, desperate, ill clad for the chill, most shuddering from the cold, some from lack of drink, they huddled around him today as if he were their last chance to touch the face of God himself. Their incontestable fallenness was almost proof enough for Caleb that a time and a place had been appointed already for meting out their interminable punishment. Caleb realized many years before that only among the fallen could he hope to find the absolute certainty that something more waited beyond this world, for they had every reason to be confident of eternity. And there was no better place to find a man assured of his damnation — and equally certain of the hour and the manner of his end — than on the scaffold.

So, in the summer of 1833, Caleb began visiting the Leverett Street Jail. He did not minister to the petty thieves and drunkards who occupied the large communal cell. He came only to speak to the vilest criminals, those who were sentenced to swing by the neck, for he hoped that by staring into the eyes of those who looked upon the prologue to everlasting misery he might catch a glimpse of eternity himself. Where his father had seen pure light, Caleb would content himself with a glimpse of smoke and fire, as long as they evidenced the eternal. In Leverett Street, there was no need to rely on a currency so nebulous as faith, Caleb thought, for here man had created his own narrow universe of truth.

At first, though, disappointment was his lot. Despite the certainty of their damnation, despite the heinous crimes they had committed without remorse, the condemned were too eager to repent on the scaffold; the uncertain hope of redemption clouded their eyes, mitigated their fears, and obscured any view that Caleb might have caught of the fires that lay beyond. Caleb nearly abandoned his quest, but on a suffocating July morning he came to Leverett Street before sunrise to spend a moment alone with a man calling himself Desmond Boone, a man condemned to hang for crimes that none dared speak aloud.

Caleb made his way through the dark prison, an hour before Boone was scheduled to hang, and he had nearly reached the office where the condemned man waited when he felt the clutch of bony fingers at his arm. He had been walking closer to the bars of the common cell than he realized.

"Please, sir." The voice reminded him of the rats he had seen scraping over the stone floor.

In the weak light of his lantern, Caleb found a face round and flat as a saucer, framed by a dirty bonnet unable to contain burst springs of rust-colored hair. The woman's pink eyes sat deep beneath her brow. She pressed her forehead against the bars of the cell, as if she thought she might slip through.

"I ain't eaten for two days, and I've no money for the guards," she begged.

Caleb caught a powerful whiff of gin and tobacco and sweat, and he raised his lantern so that he might take relief in the oily fumes.

"Are you intoxicated?" he asked.

"I come in that way, and it ain't worn off," she said. "Did you bring a drop with you, perchance?"

"I bring the word of God."

"A reverend? You come for the wretch what's about to hang, haven't you?"

Caleb tried to leave, but she held his jacket tight.

"Consider the state of your own soul, woman," he said, reluctant to touch her hand and pry the grubby fingers loose.

"My name is Esther Harrington, and I done nothing to hurt nobody. Least no killing," she said proudly. "That one is gettin' what he deserves."

"As will we all," Caleb said. "Which is why it would be wise for you to concern yourself with your own sins."

"You're a kind man to come for him," she said, showing him her rotten teeth. "He don't deserve no good words at the end, but I see you're a merciful man."

Caleb knew what she was after. He jingled the coins in his pocket, but left them there and leaned closer to the bars. "It is not for me to show mercy. We are spared only by His grace alone," he said. "Just as your own wretched soul now dangles precariously above the flames, suspended from God's hand by the thinnest of threads."

Esther Harrington let go of Caleb's sleeve and put her hands over her ears.

"Why do you say that?" she screeched. "I

done nothin' to hurt no one!"

Caleb could have walked away, but he kept talking, pleased by the effect of his words. "Can you feel the heat, Mrs. Harrington? Even now, in this damp place, can you not feel the hot flames licking at your feet, waiting for God to let you drop?"

"I didn't hurt nobody!"

"Think on this when you have sobered. You know not the number of days you are allotted, but each day that you waste in dissipation God's hold on you slackens." Caleb spoke just above a whisper, as if imparting a holy secret. "Tell me, Mrs. Harrington, have you ever awakened drenched in sweat?"

"Yes, yes! I am soaking even now! Feel this."

Her arm flew out between the bars. She grabbed his wrist and pulled his hand to her breasts, which hung heavy and hot beneath her damp clothes.

Caleb recoiled in disgust, but the woman would not let go. He felt sharp fingernails dig into his wrist.

"That sweat," he said, "gives evidence that you have felt the flames in your dreams, flames brought ever closer by your misdeeds."

"Oh Lord! Oh Lord, no! I thought it was just the fever."

"What is a fever, Mrs. Harrington, but a taste of the eternal torment that awaits? You cannot save yourself. You must put your trust in God, and swear off the foul intoxicants."

"I will. I will. I swear it. What else?"

Caleb was impressed by the ease with which she settled into her fear, and he wished he could fill his church with souls so easily transported.

"Leave me to tend to my business," he said, "and come to me when you have sobered."

Caleb pulled free, and she tumbled backward. He heard some hard part of her slap the stone floor. In the dark recesses of the prison, other women called out for her to be quiet.

Even in her drunkenness, Caleb thought, Esther Harrington was right about one thing: the wretch at the far end of the corridor, the man who was about to be launched into eternity, was beyond forgiveness. There were two guards in the office when Caleb arrived, and the inevitable slow dawn was already leaking through the windows. Caleb did not see the prisoner at first, but one of the guards motioned to a chair in the dark corner where the sluggish morning light did not yet penetrate. There sat a large man, barefoot and dressed in tattered clothes that did not reach the ends of his limbs; his black skin was almost indiscernible from the shadow that still filled half of the room. Caleb hesitated in the doorway. He had not been informed that Desmond Boone was a Negro.

The guards nodded without speaking and stepped into the hall. Desmond Boone stared at the blank wall opposite. Caleb was relieved to see that the man's thick wrists and ankles were shackled with heavy chains. He looked strong enough to be capable of snapping a neck one-handed.

"Have you prepared your soul?" Caleb asked.

The man ignored him. He continued concentrating on the wall, as if trying to identify a face in the shadows, and Caleb could not help following his line of sight to see if something was there, watching him.

"Desmond Boone, I asked if you have prepared your soul!" Caleb took hold of the man's heavy shoulder, tried to make him turn to face him, but the man was immovable as stone. "Look at me."

Desmond Boone sat straight in the chair, the posture of a man unburdened by guilt. Caleb studied the man's broad face. His wild black hair stood stiff with filth; his cheeks shone in the faint light from Caleb's lamp, and in his eyes Caleb saw defiance. It obscured everything else. His face seemed swollen above the cheeks, but if there were bruises they were hidden beneath the indigo sheen of his skin. Caleb wondered if the man was a runaway, unused to obeying laws without the constant threat of the lash. That would explain the savagery of his crime, he thought.

"Tell me how you have come here," Caleb said.

"I am a free man." Desmond Boone's voice was deep and strong. "Bought and paid myself. Done nothin' wrong." There was no hint of the quivering fear Caleb had so often heard from the condemned.

Caleb spoke slowly, unconvinced that Boone was not a fugitive. "Slavery, like deceit, is but one of many sins for which men must answer in the hereafter. Neither is justification for the other."

Boone struck his broad chest with his fist and repeated, "Free! I own my own self. I will die as a free man."

Caleb studied him. He wondered if the man's confidence came from some trust in the pagan lies of his forefathers. He squatted next to Boone and spoke softly into the curled dark shell of his ear. "Tell me then,

335

Desmond Boone, what have your false gods promised you after this life."

Boone leaped from his chair, knocking it to the floor and nearly toppling himself as well. His chains rattled and scraped against the floor as he regained his balance. The guards looked through the doorway, but Caleb waved them away.

"The Devil sent you to me!" Boone said fiercely through clenched teeth. "I am a Christian!"

Caleb stepped back and held the lantern between them; he saw outrage on the man's face, but nothing more. "If you are a Christian, then you know that only by confessing your sins can you hope to enter heaven." Caleb needed to get him to admit what he had done. Only then would this man look upon his eternal punishment with certainty. "We must first despair," Caleb prodded, "before we can find hope."

"I ask for no forgiveness," Boone said. "Lord Jesus knows I laid no hand on those boys." Boone swung his head from side to side, as if looking for an exit. "God won't punish me for what I never done."

The guards returned, and Boone resisted when they grabbed him by the arms. They led him into the hall, past the common cell, and into the prison yard, where the scaffold waited. Caleb followed close behind, marveling that they were able to navigate the powerful man, until he noticed the dagger that one of the guards held at the small of Boone's back. Aside from the warden and the other guards gathered under the jaundiced sky, the yard was empty, and Caleb thought it regrettable that the scaffold was no longer wheeled into the Common for public executions.

The two guards struggled to hold Boone steady while a third readied the noose. Caleb stood to the side and watched as Boone squeezed his eyes shut, and he grew incensed to think that this man would deny him what he sought. Caleb opened his Bible, and the words he read felt sour as they spilled from his lips. He laid his hand on Boone's shoulder and was surprised to see the man begin weeping. Caleb stood near as the noose was secured, and then Boone opened his eyes and spoke.

"I do repent my sins," he said quietly. "I swear I am good. Will you ask God to receive me?"

Caleb considered the power that he held at this moment, the power to fortify this despairing man with an invocation of God's saving grace. But never had he heard an appeal so baseless as this. Caleb wanted to draw back the veil of hope that so often clouded men's eyes at the end, to force this wretch to look clearly upon the inescapability of his damnation.

Caleb leaned in close to Boone's ear and answered, "No."

Boone did not at first understand, and then the realization struck and his face seemed to fall from his skull. His eyes widened, and Caleb saw a blur of animal terror as the trapdoor swung open and the doomed man's cry was cut short by the drop.

Once the death spasms ceased, Caleb climbed beneath the scaffold and looked closely at the protruding eyes, pupils tight as pins, whites ringed red and shot through with burst vessels. In a short time, the dead man's face, with its swollen tongue bitten purple and black, would look no different from the rotting skull that Caleb had found in the woods as a boy. But in his final moments of life Boone had given Caleb the glimpse that he sought, for Caleb knew that what he saw captured in the dead man's eyes was the undiluted awe of seeing eternity for the first and possibly last time.

When Caleb explained to his father what he had done and what he had seen, the right side of Marcus Dowdy's face exploded in frantic twitches, as if to compensate for the limp expression of the left. He sputtered incoherently, his lips unable to move rapidly enough to convey his righteous fury. His right hand grabbed the pencil he kept tied to a long string looped around his neck, and when he could not find the notebook that usually sat at his bedside he snapped the string in anger and threw the pencil at Caleb. It was the last time they spoke, though Marcus Dowdy lived on in his half-sensate body for eight years more. Marcus later made overtures of reconciliation, but Caleb would have none of it; the struggle to redeem mankind in the New World allowed no leniency for the preservation of polite civilities between ill-advised fathers and stalwart sons.

Despite the coldness of their relations, Caleb felt the stab of his father's spiritual infelicity one final time. In the last year of his life, the Reverend Marcus Ezekiel Dowdy fell under the spell of Ralph Waldo Emerson, and Caleb received a dictated letter, in neat, balanced script, in which the influence of Concord's gleeful pagan was all too clear.

April 5, 1840

My Dear Caleb:

I would speak to you while we both yet inhabit this earth, but even had I as yet the power of speech, how difficult it would be to break the silence that has isolated us for these many years. A father and son should not be, as we have been, islands to one another. We are of the same continent though the waters of disagreement may flow between us. We are one and the same a part of God's creation, and it is a blasphemy that we have sundered ourselves thus. Perhaps it is the greening of the natural world at the coming of another spring, perhaps it is witnessing this surge of life as I feel my own draining away, that makes me realize that one great soul imbues all things; it vibrates in the world around us and in ourselves. It is not in fear that I make my way into the winter of my being, for I take comfort in the knowledge that, like the trees of the forest, a spring awaits my soul. My son, I implore you to think on this, to reflect on the virtue of the natural world and attune yourself to it. Mr. Emerson has said, "Whenever the pulpit is usurped by a formalist, then is the worshipper defrauded and disconsolate. We shrink as soon as the prayers begin, which do not uplift, but smite and offend us." My son, it is not too late for you to make yourself receptive to the "beautiful sentiments" in this world, before seeking them out in the next.

Caleb was aghast. His father had certainly gone mad. *A vibrating soul?* Had the old man mistaken his own palsy as proof of pantheism? Caleb took no joy in the thought of sharing his soul with a tree, as if the soul were some sort of transparent rodent, equally at home in the woods as in its human nest. Once men like Emerson and his friends were shown that forests were nothing more than unharvested timber destined to frame the cities of the New World, there would be no more worshipping of trees.

Marcus Dowdy died a month later, and during the funeral Caleb studied the red glow of the stained-glass fire and thought of the hidden flaws in the window, a mockery of the perfection it was supposed to represent. He thought of his father's letter and its assertions that austere piety and Puritan dogma had no place in the New World. "Their creed is passing away," his father had again quoted Emerson. Caleb could not forgive his father's conversion to Mr. Emerson's blasphemy. Yet he could not stand the thought that his father might suffer the eternal torment he had seen in the eyes of Desmond Boone. Nor could Caleb bear the idea of his father's flesh rotting from his bones to feed blind worms, no better than the dead Irishman in the woods. Caleb desperately sought a reason that his father might be pardoned for his obvious failures; he prayed that God might show mercy on his soul, and then he was ashamed of himself for having done so. He knew that his weakness was brought on by his failure to remain true to the path he had chosen. Caleb knew he must show himself no leniency; he needed to purge his world of the distractions that had led him astray. Desperate to return himself to the proper path, Caleb walked into the church of the Court Street First Reformed Unitarian Assembly alone on a Saturday night, seeking guidance.

The sound of shattering glass brought the first witnesses early the next morning, and when the rest of the congregants arrived they found their minister, hatchet in hand, face red, shirtsleeves rolled, standing amid the ruins of what had once been their beautiful church. Caleb had saved the smashing of the great window for last, and he was still sending shards of fire and clouds flying about the nave when they arrived. He had worked through the night, chopping away at the benches until there were no pieces too big to fit into a stove. The walls were rent with deep gashes. He had smashed the pulpit as well, and he had very nearly smashed his own foot when he toppled the heavy altar. He had left not a single pew intact. If they want to sit, he thought, let them sit on the splintered remnants of their pride.

He expected their anger, but he was surprised when this did not give way to a deeper understanding of what he had done. He watched the faces of the men and women as they arrived, one by one; he watched as they realized that his weekly tirades against wealth and indulgence had not been metaphors for spiritual renewal. Caleb expected the poorer members of the congregation to stand up in his defense, but even those who usually sat on the exposed pews nearest the drafty doors expressed as much outrage as the rest.

And then the truth struck him. In this new world of unlimited possibility, the poor were willingly misled by the perversity of material ambitions. The meek would rather look upon the decadence of the wealthy as a sign of what they might one day attain on earth; they would prefer to covet these beautiful lives than follow the stark path to salvation. Caleb left his old congregants weeping among the wreckage of their church. Under one arm he carried his Bible, under the other his hatchet.

After what happened in Court Street, Caleb expected that no church in Boston would open its doors to him. He looked to the west, where he thought he might live as a hermit or preach to savages in territories unknown. Following the Concord Turnpike, Caleb carried his Bible and his hatchet into the untamed world beyond Boston. He spent the night in the woods and found nothing in the experience to suggest that there might be a spirit among the trees, as his father had insisted. He could not see how his father or Mr. Emerson or any of their deluded contemporaries could think it right to seek God in the dwelling of maggots. Caleb slept with pine needles for his bed and a pile of leaves to cushion his head, and he awoke to find a dozen members of his former congregation standing around him as if he were dead. They had come looking for him, they said. He recognized them from among those who sometimes stood at the back or hid in the corners of his church, and he had always suspected that they were in attendance only to seek shelter from the cold. They said they knew he could not return, but they begged him not to leave them, and Caleb understood that they needed his strict teachings the way a dog needs its master's cane. He knew then that he had found his mission.

He sought out new followers from among their acquaintances, the city's most despairing. In the alleys of Boston, he told the hopeless about his reformation in the woods. He carried his message to the prostitutes in Mount Vernon, to the beggars around Mill Pond, and to the thieves at the Leverett Street Jail, and he was always surprised to see a new face nearly every Sunday when he hung his hatchet from a tree and opened his Bible on a tall stump he had hewn into a crude lectern. At one of his meetings, a farmer who shared his disgust for the tree-worshippers of Concord came forward and offered him a place to stay and the use of his barn. Caleb preached in the barn on Sunday mornings, just after the cows had been milked, with the scent of manure and masticated grass hanging in the air. There were no private boxes, no cushions or foot warmers, no ornaments of gold or lurid stained glass.

On a bright Sunday morning in spring, after nearly three years of meeting in the barn, Caleb concluded his sermon by announcing that the time had come at last to build a church. He knew it might take years to accomplish, since many could contribute only pennies at a time, but he knew they would not waiver. They were being called to rekindle the light that had once adorned the city on the hill. He told them that they would succeed where their forefathers had failed.

After the sermon, Caleb stood in the open barn door as his followers filed past and readied themselves for the long walk back to Boston. They shuffled out from between the long wooden benches that Caleb had built himself, and the last two men in each row remained to carry the benches to the back of the barn. Within the hour, the cows would be led back in, lowing and belching.

From among the departing worshippers a woman dressed in black, face half hidden by a shawl, detached herself and waited until the benches were moved away. Then she grabbed a broom and began sweeping the ground with exaggerated zeal, as if the ferocity of her strokes might undo things long since done.

Caleb approached her and placed his hand gently on her arm.

"Mrs. Harrington, there is no need to do that. This is a barn, after all."

"It's as good a church as any when you're doin' the preaching."

Esther Harrington put her head down, swept, stopped, and looked back at him. She opened her mouth, revealing fewer teeth than she had when they first met, then rubbed her chin in deep contemplation. Caleb had seen her do this at least once every Sunday.

"Have you remembered today, Mrs. Harrington?" Caleb asked.

"Not today. I suppose the Lord will remind me when the time comes."

Caleb nodded as she scurried off with her broom. As if the Lord did not have concerns more worthy than the restoration of a drunken old whore's memory, he thought. Esther Harrington began appearing at his services a year earlier — somehow she had found him — and ever since her reappearance she claimed to have some important news. She could never remember what it was, but she was sure that it would be of great interest to him.

"Look here, Reverend!"

Caleb turned wearily toward the dry, cricket voice to find another drunkard he had recruited from the gutters of Boston several months earlier. The man stood close, right arm outstretched, hand flat, palm down, inches from Caleb's chin, close enough for him to smell the heavy scent of old tobacco. The man's fingers shook, and his face revealed that this feat was taking considerable effort. Caleb tried to remember the man's name.

"You said I ought deny myself drink, and I done it."

No matter how long or fiercely he preached, Caleb thought, it was never enough for these people. He wanted to transport them with his words, to send them into holy convulsions, to bring on fainting spells, but they just sat there during his sermons, waiting to speak to him afterward about their ailments or visions or moral confusions.

"See? Hardly no tremors at all, Reverend. Not half as bad as last month."

"You've abstained from the drink . . . Mr. Stiles?" Caleb asked. He remembered the man now, Amos Stiles, a drunk and a former pickpocket.

"Nary a drop in two months," Amos Stiles swore. "I count myself an improved man."

"Pride, Mr. Stiles. Beware of pride. And what of the other thing?"

Amos Stiles lowered his arm, and he spoke less confidently than before.

"I have touched no liquor or beer. No cider even. And no tobacco. Hardly."

"And the other?"

Caleb waited impatiently as the weak man struggled to admit what Caleb already surmised. The man wore the mark of his sin in his heavy-lidded eyes. It amazed him how the same men who were capable of committing the darkest acts imaginable would, when pressed, find themselves unable to utter the words for what they had done. What was this strange power of language?

Amos Stiles scratched his trembling arm in a raking motion from shoulder to wrist. "I did not think it was forbidden in Scripture."

"Mr. Stiles, excuses are the Devil's logic. Many are the wicked deeds not explicitly forbidden. Can you think it any different with the foul, intoxicating weed you put in your pipe?"

"I am trying to be a better man."

"Pray that His protecting hand does not release you into the flames before your transformation is complete."

Stiles paled and his jaw worked dryly, as if

he were gulping from an empty flask. "I'm most sorry, Reverend. Indeed I am. I'll get back to stacking those benches."

He watched Stiles lope about, dragging the splintery benches against the wall with misplaced zeal, atoning for his transgressions through a surfeit of frenetic activity. Caleb retrieved his Bible from the top of the stump that still served as his lectern, and he grabbed the hatchet that leaned against it. He slipped the Bible under one arm, collected the loose pages on which he had written his sermon, and hefted the hatchet to his shoulder. The hatchet was the sole ornament he would allow in his new church, he thought, and he envisioned a new building rising at the edge of Concord, austere, simple, righteous.

Caleb left the dusty shadows of the barn and walked out into the sunlight. He felt the bright warmth on his face and heard the soft swarming gnats rushing past his ear; his pulse quickened and he was stunned by the powerful urge that suddenly overcame him. For a moment, he was seized by the peculiar thought that he might be content to lie down in the grass and contemplate this beautiful creation without the incessant clawing after truth that marked his waking hours. He thought of another infuriating reference to Mr. Emerson in his father's final letter: ". . . one mind is everywhere active, in each ray of the star, in each wavelet of the pool . . ." Caleb turned away from the sun, tried to ignore the blue sky and the green scent that filled the air, but the feeling would not leave him; he sensed a buzzing in his limbs, as if something had been awakened, as if he could actually feel a trembling spirit infusing his mortal veins. He looked at his forearm, saw the feral pulsings beneath the skin, and he tightened his grip on the hatchet. He would not allow himself to be misled by the temptations of this new Eden. If his arm offended him, he thought, he would willingly cut it off. He heard someone calling his name, and he turned slowly toward the sound.

"Reverend Dowdy! I remember now!"

Caleb rubbed his eyes, as if emerging from a dream, and he saw Esther Harrington hobbling toward him from the barn. Her left leg lagged behind, and her earnestness seemed to transform her limp into a graceless ballet.

"What is it, Mrs. Harrington?" Caleb braced himself for some incomprehensible tale of dissipation and revival.

"The confession, did you hear about it?" Esther Harrington asked, out of breath.

"You'll have to be clearer, Mrs. Harrington. I have heard many."

"The scoundrel confessed to doing those terrible things."

Caleb shook his head, uncomprehending.

"Remember?" she said. "Another says he done the same things."

"What same things, Mrs. Harrington?"

"The buggering!"

There was no limit to the blackness of men's souls, Caleb thought. Everywhere one looked in the New World, moral decay was evidenced a hundredfold. Even this woman seemed to delight in the reporting of such crimes.

"No doubt the villain was under the influence of a terrible intoxicant." Caleb tried to sift the lesson in the tale. "You would do better to concern yourself with the state of your own soul and avoid those poisons that we were never meant to imbibe."

Esther Harrington was undeterred. "Listen, Reverend, this villain was hanged for the same deed, a year or two after. I was surprised you weren't there."

Caleb sighed. "I cannot minister to every soul in need."

Caleb turned and began to walk away, but he felt the familiar grip, the cold hand on his arm. The old woman seemed about to scream but could not summon the sound.

"Mrs. Harrington, please." He nearly pulled the woman from her feet as he tore his arm away. "What else can I offer? I am confident the miscreant received justice."

She grabbed his arm again, and this time he felt the fingernails at his wrist.

"Ain't I makin' myself clear?" she cried. "The man what confessed, he went by the name of Hus. Søren Hus. He confessed to the crimes they said that Negro did."

Caleb let the hatchet slide from his shoulder. He held on to the bottom of the handle and rocked the hatchet head on the ground, as if trying to work something loose.

"Boone?" he asked quietly, unwilling to believe it was possible.

"The one they thought did them same perversions," she insisted. "The one you ministered to before he hanged."

Caleb saw the face racing toward him. He remembered the dead eyes and the swollen tongue. "Boone," he mumbled. "Desmond Boone."

"That's the one. Didn't do it at all, they said."

"You must be mistaken. Perhaps they were in league?" Caleb asked.

The old woman cackled. "Far as I apprehend, buggerin' don't take much help."

Caleb felt a chasm open before him. He ran his tongue over his teeth and rocked the hatchet head back and forth in the dirt. A bitter taste crept into the back of his mouth. His final word to the innocent man echoed in his ears. *No.* What power had resided in that simple utterance? Had it condemned the man to eternal torment? Had it countermanded heavenly Providence? And, if not, were his words utterly without meaning?

Esther Harrington appeared delighted at the success of her brittle memory.

"Least he's in a better place," she said.

Caleb could not speak. The sunlight was suddenly blinding, and he thought he could hear the clicking and chewing of the manifold insects burrowed in the earth. He stepped forward unsteadily and felt the wooden handle of the hatchet slip from his fingers. The hatchet balanced on its head for a moment, shadowless under the high sun, before teetering over like a felled sapling.

18
ELIOT

The more Eliot thinks on it, the more obvious it seems that Seymour Twine should be found in a tavern at midday, stupefied by drink, when other men are hard at work. If he were staging the scene of their meeting for the Haymarket Theater, a tavern is exactly the setting he would have chosen: a sinister door hidden in a narrow street, a dark interior, heavy wood timbers in the ceiling, the air visibly laced with tobacco and greasy fumes from shanks of lamb and pork hissing in the open hearth.

When Eliot finds Wright's Tavern, though, he is disappointed. The pleasant two-story building sits at the corner of Main and Lexington, right in the middle of town, where its handsome façade might easily be mistaken for someone's home. Eliot lingers in the doorway; the interior proves not at all as dark as he would have liked. The walls are bright, the tables clean, and there is no meat cooking at the fire, no heavy smell of grease in the airy rooms.

There are only a few patrons, and Eliot quickly spots his man slumped by the hearth; there is no mistaking such men, he thinks. One of the man's heavy arms is wrapped around an overturned tankard. His forehead rests on the table before him while a long shock of his stringy dark hair soaks in a shallow puddle of ale. A thickset woman in an apron smiles at Eliot, and he holds up two fingers and points to the brute. As she reaches for two fresh tankards, the woman's smile turns upon itself, becoming more smirk than smile. Eliot is pleased. Everyone, it seems, knows Seymour Twine.

Eliot does not hesitate further. He approaches the large man boldly.

"Mr. Twine, you have kept me waiting," he says, standing over the half-slumbering drunkard.

The brute lifts his head and rolls the bleary eyes that Eliot has come to expect from such men. Up close, he is much larger than Eliot at first thought.

"Bugger off!"

Other patrons look up from drinks and break off conversations at the sound of the man's angry growl. Eliot tries to imagine what the hero of one of his unfinished plays would do if faced with such an antagonist. He clenches his fists and sets his feet.

"Look here. I am not a man to be —"

With astonishing speed, the giant leaps to his feet and strikes Eliot square in the chest with the heel of his palm. The blow is clumsy, but it sends Eliot sprawling backward onto the floor. In the next second, the giant is standing over him.

"You got no business with me," he growls.

For the moment, Eliot cannot breathe. He puts his hands in front of his face, shielding himself from the filthy boot heel hovering above his chin.

A voice behind the giant reins him in. "Briggs! Leave him be!"

Briggs lowers his foot, though whether at the insistence of the man who has shouted his name or in response to the fact that the barmaid has just brought over two sloshing tankards Eliot is not sure. The giant takes both drinks in his thick hands while Eliot struggles to his feet, winded. His breastbone aches, and he prods his chest gently, wondering if he has broken a rib. The man who called off his assailant is sitting at a table in the corner, next to a partition from which hangs a variety of cooking pots. Thin and pale, dressed in a long black coat, white shirt, and cravat, he sits stiffly with hands flat on the table, as if he is afraid of wrinkling his stiff clothes. He motions Eliot closer by wiggling a lanky index finger without lifting the hand. With the same finger, he motions to the attentive barmaid.

Eliot obeys the finger. "I am in your debt, sir," he says, brushing his sleeves, looking for damage along the seams of his coat.

"Indeed," the man says casually. "He would not have hesitated to crush your jaw."

"I thought I knew the man," Eliot says, wincing, finding that it hurts to breathe.

"I would choose my friends more wisely," the man advises. "Please have a seat — a blow such as you've received can disorient a man."

The man's gray hair is cut close, covering his head tightly like a skullcap. He wears a pair of half-moon spectacles, which give him the look of a physician. As Eliot lowers himself into the chair at the table, he notices a black leather satchel on the floor just before a sudden wave of dizziness comes over him. He sits down harder than he intended. He wonders if he should ask the man to examine his ribs.

"I recommend a mild drink," the man says. "Something to fortify you after your ordeal." The man studies Eliot with concern, as if he were examining a patient. "Did you injure your head?"

Eliot rubs the base of his skull where it struck the floorboards. "I was told Seymour Twine was to be found here," he says distractedly. He removes his hand from his head and examines it, checking for blood. "Apparently, he is not a man to be relied upon."

"I should think not," the man says, chuckling, as his eyes continue their survey of Eliot's features. "May I ask what business you have with this gentleman?"

"I cannot say for certain. I have never met the man."

The thin man finishes his examination, and his eyes come to rest on Eliot's chest, as if he had decided where to make an incision. "I take it, then, that you are Mr. Eliot Calvert."

"*You?*" Eliot cannot hide his shock. "We were to meet at noon."

"What time is it now?"

"It is already three-quarters past the hour."

"And so we are meeting." Twine's face does not reveal emotions of any sort.

"Do you always show such disregard in your business dealings?" Eliot asks.

Seymour Twine's small mouth flickers into a tight smile as the barmaid sets two pewter

359

tankards on the table. She steps to the hearth, wraps a cloth around one hand, and from the coals retrieves an iron rod with a red-hot ball at its end. Eliot cringes at the thought that the implement might easily be employed as a weapon.

Twine nods appreciatively. To Eliot he says, "The secret to a good flip is in the beer. I have no taste for the eggs and cream that others use. Start with a good spruce beer if you can get it, molasses, and a half-gill of rum, and watch that the loggerhead is not left in too long."

The barmaid thrusts the hot iron rod, ball end first, into one tankard and then into the other, holding it in each hissing mixture until Twine wiggles a finger to stop her.

"Nothing better to warm body and soul on a day such as this," he says, as he curls his sinewy fingers around the foaming tankard. "Drink up, Mr. Calvert. Its inebriating effects are quite minimal, unless you are wholly unaccustomed to spirits."

"I have not come to discuss the merits of flip with you, Mr. Twine."

With the tankard at his lips, Twine mumbles before drinking, "I seriously doubt that your customers crave my goods in the full light of day."

"If we are to do business," Eliot says,

ignoring his steaming drink, "I must insist on a certain propriety in our dealings." He knows he must put Twine in his place first.

"Propriety?" Twine lowers his tankard and licks the froth from his upper lip with a pale, sharp tongue. "I do not allow my customers to dictate terms, Mr. Calvert. I knew you would find your way to me. Your sort always does."

"If you are going to presume knowledge of my *sort* —" Eliot says, and before he can continue Twine interrupts, spitting the froth from his flip as he speaks.

"And yet *you* would presume to know *me* well enough to think that a drunken animal like Briggs was *my* sort. A fine hypocrisy, is it not, Mr. Calvert? Did you honestly think I would meet you in the street in the middle of the day?"

"Mr. Punch informed me that —"

"I am sure whatever that lout told you bore little resemblance to my instructions."

Eliot is dumbfounded. He knows that handling such men requires one to act the ruffian, and he is not unfamiliar with the role. He sits back and folds his arms across his chest. "There are others with whom I might do business," he says.

"Then go to them."

Twine finishes his drink and points to

Eliot's full tankard. Eliot reaches for it and absently swallows a mouthful of the warm, heady concoction while Twine retrieves the black physician's satchel from under the table. He pulls out a wooden box the size of a serving tray. He stares at Eliot through his half-moon spectacles.

"But before you go, Mr. Calvert, you should see what you will miss. I assure you, never before have you seen the like." Twine lifts the hinged lid, revealing a square of green felt.

Eliot has heard this kind of talk before, and he is not impressed. But when Twine draws back the green felt covering the stacks of glass plates beneath, Eliot cannot keep his eyes from betraying his astonishment. Twine begins placing the glass plates around the table, holding them carefully by their edges. He looks up to make sure that his actions are hidden by the partition hung with the cooking pots.

"No man who sees one ever refuses to see more," Twine says flatly, without looking at Eliot.

Eliot has heard this before, too, but he cannot disagree, cannot help but stare in amazement.

Twine smiles. "Please, Mr. Calvert, do not let your flip grow cold."

Eliot saw nothing like this in Punch's sack. The glass plates bear the real shapes and shadows of living bodies entwined. He holds one at an angle to bring out the full details of the ghostly images, black and gray and silver, floating on the shimmering surface. Twine explains the elaborate process required to make the smoky images: the calculated exposure, the long poses, the silver-nitrate and mercury vapors, the darkened rooms. Each plate guarantees that the image is more than just the suggestion of an act. It is a captured reflection, physical evidence that the act actually occurred.

"Where did you get these?" Eliot murmurs.

"Someplace where a man of your *sort* cannot."

Eliot rubs his bruised breastbone where Briggs struck him, and beneath the dull pain he feels a discomfort of another kind. He thinks of his father marveling over the volume of Goethe in his bookshop.

Twine finishes the dregs of his flip, dabs at the corners of his mouth with a handkerchief, and pulls a scrap of paper from the box. From a pocket he fishes a nubbin of pencil with the letters OREAU NO. 2 stamped on the remaining bit; he writes a number on the paper and slides it over to Eliot.

"What is this?"

Twine smiles. "The price men will gladly pay for one such portrait."

Eliot stares at the number. He thinks of the house in Boston, where there is never a quiet room. He thinks of his plans for an office above his new bookstore, a simple space with a desk and a chair, and perhaps a small platform for rehearsing soliloquies. He pulls out his watch and checks the time, and he rubs the watch chain between his fingers. Eliot feels queasy, as if the room had suddenly begun to tilt.

"I'll need to think on it," he says. "It is no small financial commitment."

He senses another set of eyes on him. The man called Briggs is looking at him and grinning, as if they were old friends. The queasiness beneath Eliot's throbbing breastbone solidifies and drops. He realizes that the air has grown darker, heavier, full of the smell of cooking meat. He peers around the partition and sees the barmaid smirking at him. She is not as attractive as he first thought. Her skin is splotchy; the cut of her blouse hangs lower than seems proper. Eliot wonders what he is doing here. What kind of man has he become? He looks over toward the hearth, where hissing shanks of lamb and pork have materialized on the spit, and he feels an inexplicable urge to run over and stick his hand on the hot, sizzling meat, to feel the grease burn his skin and rouse him from his complacency. He needs to alter the fundamental order of his life, but it will require something drastic, something swift and furious and decisive.

"I don't know . . ." Eliot says uncertainly.

Twine begins to respond when the door flies open and the bright light catches him full in the face. Twine's pupils narrow as if retreating into his head; the whites of his eyes flash. Eliot feels himself to shrink from the light.

From the bright doorway a dark silhouette bellows a single, shattering syllable.

"Fire!"

The first thing Eliot notices when he exits Wright's Tavern is that the streets of Concord have awakened. Shouts, the clatter of hooves, and the staccato crunch of wagon wheels fill the air. A crowd is gathering at the intersection of Main and Lexington, a few strides from where he stands, and from all directions men rush toward the center of town with a sense of urgency, some carrying shovels, some cradling hatchets in their arms. Women run behind them, holding kerchiefs over nose and mouth. Eliot did not notice it before, but now he hears a bell tolling loudly nearby, and in the few seconds it takes him to cross the street a dense, foreboding haze, more brown than black, slides across the face of the sun. It appears to Eliot that while he was absorbed in conversation with Mr. Twine the world beyond Wright's Tavern underwent a startling metamorphosis.

Eliot spots Otis Dickerson in the crowd. Red-faced and puffing, the man hugs the handles of a dozen new shovels against his chest. Their gleaming blades clank and scrape against each other as he hobbles through the crowd, offering the tools to the few men who have arrived empty-handed. Eliot calls out, but Dickerson ignores him until Eliot reaches his side.

"May I be of some help?" Eliot asks, gesturing toward one of the shovels teetering from Dickerson's embrace.

Dickerson adjusts his burden and hugs the shovels tightly, like a mother protecting her children. "If you take one, they'll all go."

Eliot hears the distrust in the man's response.

"Did you find your associate?" Dickerson asks, speaking directly into the blade of one of the shovels.

Eliot thinks carefully. "He is not the man I thought."

"I see." Dickerson lets the shovels slide to the ground; they stand upright on their handles, corralled by his arms. He looks at Eliot thoughtfully before making up his mind and pushing a shovel toward him. "Here. We'll need every man if we're to save Concord."

Eliot accepts the shovel, though he does not think the situation so dire as Dickerson claims. "Is the town truly at risk?"

Dickerson points toward the center of the crowd, and Eliot puts on his spectacles to better see the man standing on a barrel, speaking to the gathering. His face and clothes are blackened with ash, and he is describing the fire in the woods with great sweeping motions of his arms, as if he were trying to take flight.

"The way he tells it," Dickerson says, "we'll all be standing in ashes by nightfall if this wind does not abate. Nothing more than a few hundred acres of dry forest stands between Concord and the flames."

"Does he know how it began?"

"Says it was an accident. That's Squire Hoar's son, Edward Sherman, a trustworthy fellow."

More men arrive, and Edward Sherman

Hoar continues to describe the height of the flames and the speed of their advance, but he offers no thoughts on how to combat it. A man in overalls at the front of the crowd nudges him from the barrel and climbs up in his stead. This man shouts in a commanding voice, suggests that the women and children of Concord, and anyone else incapable of swinging a shovel, should be sent out of the path of destruction.

"He's right," Dickerson says to Eliot. "We ought to empty the town, before the fire does it for us."

Eliot pictures the Concord Road jammed with horses and wagons, carts piled high with valuable belongings. "Surely it will not come to that."

Dickerson swings his boiled head to indicate the homes along Main Street. "I reckon there are almost two thousand souls hereabouts," he says, "and if the fire comes — the plague could do no worse."

Eliot imagines the homes of Concord ablaze, pictures the Shakespeare Hotel collapsing under the heat and smoke; he thinks of his own impotent attempts at describing such a blaze in *The House of Many Windows*. And in that moment he can hardly believe this fortunate turn of events. It is no wonder that he has not been able to realize his vision for the play's final scene. The problem is suddenly clear to him. Eliot wants the audience to feel the heat of the fire, wants them to experience the dismay of his hero, Marcus DeMonte, but he cannot hope to describe what he has never experienced for himself.

While the men of Concord debate how best to attack the fire, Eliot envisions the scene from *The House of Many Windows* as it should appear onstage. In the foreground, DeMonte wrings his hands, frozen in agony. The entire set will be destroyed and rebuilt every night, a massive endeavor, but Moses Kimball has convinced him that the Boston Museum Theater has handled bigger spectacles than this. Eliot must simply finish the play. He pictures DeMonte summoning courage to enter the burning house and rescue his infant son. He thinks he might allow DeMonte a soliloquy at the end as he stands before his ruined home, a poignant reflection on his unexpected freedom from material possessions. Eliot revises the title in his head: *The House of Many Windows; or The Second Chance.* Concord must be saved, he thinks, but there is valuable experience to be garnered first.

Eliot clutches the handle of the shovel from Dickerson's shop and watches the men in the crowd argue over the best course of action.

"People need to be more careful with their blasted lucifers," Otis Dickerson says. Eliot nods in agreement, and then quietly slips back through the crowd, taking the new shovel with him.

19
ODDMUND

Just before Odd reaches the center of Concord, he sees a stranger approaching him with long, deliberate strides. In the presence of such men, Odd feels something shrink behind his rib cage. Even as he tells himself that they are no better, no more deserving than himself, he feels his breath diminish, as if to acknowledge that he has no claim to their air. The man before him looks like a wealthy merchant, with his bright yellow vest and the rectangular spectacles balanced on his nose. He carries a bright new shovel, cradling it in his arms as if he were unsure how to put it to use. Odd puts his head down and scuttles sideways, but the man is on him in an instant and their paths meet next to a narrow wooden watering trough. Odd studies the bottom of the empty trough, avoiding the man's stare.

"There is a conflagration in your forest,"

the man tells him. He speaks loudly and punctuates his words with the handle of the shovel.

Odd sucks in a deep, undeserved breath. His tongue finds the little black tooth. His news is already old, his trip wasted. He smiles nervously and again tries to step past, but the man slips in front of him once more.

"I shall not tarry while your townsmen deliberate. With each passing minute, another acre disappears into the fiend's gaping maw." The man raises his shovel like a sword and waves it at the horizon.

"This fire," Odd says, looking at the man sideways, "it is *utstrakt* . . . ah, most very large. It is more than one man can do, I think."

"Then you intend to wait for the others?" the man says. "Well and good. Each man must choose according to his will. I am a man of action, and today I shall act."

The man taps the handle of the shovel to his forehead and marches off. Odd wonders if he has any idea what he is headed into. He watches the man stride away in the direction of the unfurling ribbon of smoke, the blade of the shovel shining over his shoulder.

The men Odd has come to inform are already gathered at the center of town.

There are a hundred or more, as far as Odd can tell. Odd knows most by sight and a few by name. They are arguing quietly, trying to restrain their panic.

"We must stop it before it reaches the town," someone shouts. "If it comes here, it will go to Boston."

"We must surround it."

"Get to its source, strike at its heart."

"I have shovels enough for all."

Between each comment, murmurs and nods float through the crowd. Odd knows that he should return to Woburn Farm at once. These men do not need his help, and he feels foolish now for having left Emma unprotected.

"We'll need more axes," someone yells. "Who'll collect more axes?"

Odd watches the crowd grow denser, pressing inward with the utterance of each new idea. Then he is startled by a voice that materializes an inch from his ear.

"Mr. Hus, what do you expect to accomplish empty-handed?"

Otis Dickerson stands beside him, perched on his toes, holding two rust-spotted axes, one of which he apparently has been trying to give him. "I've no more shovels. You'll have to content yourself with one of these. Not so dull as they appear."

Odd takes one of the axes without looking at it, and Mr. Dickerson shakes his head in mild exasperation.

"What were you dreaming about?"

Odd feels his face redden. It is his apology for simply being here. He blushes the way that some men block punches. Odd steps away, but Otis Dickerson places an avuncular hand on his shoulder.

"You ought think only of *what* you are doing *when* you are doing it. Dreaming will get you killed in that fire. I've seen a man swallowed whole in a house fire, and what we're facing is tenfold in size."

Odd nods. He thinks of Emma and he feels foolish for having left her in danger. He thinks of the usual errands that bring him into Concord, thinks of the simple lists written in her careful script, the beautiful smudges of her thick fingers in the damp ink: *soap, flour, salt, beans.* The thought of living out his days on this narrow path of austere intentions makes his throat constrict with happiness. Then he thinks of what Dickerson has just described to him, and he pictures Emma trapped in the burning farmhouse, waiting for rescue.

"Odd!" Otis Dickerson startles him from his thoughts and seizes his arm behind the elbow. "You had better stay close to me. Do what I do, so you don't get misplaced. You don't want to be caught in the fire alone."

Odd imagines the size of the fire loose in the woods, and the vision fills him with dread.

"I cannot go into the fire," Odd blurts out.

"Why have you come if not to help beat down the inferno?"

Odd cannot argue with the man. Why has he come? He has done so for the same reason that he does most things. He is here because Emma asked it of him. She asked him to come to town to tell the people of Concord what they already knew. He should have realized before leaving that the smoke would have alerted everyone long before he arrived. He should have realized that, once here, it would be impossible for him not to help. These men will rush into the fire, when the sensible thing would be to run away, as far as the ocean if necessary. Odd feels the shiny, scarred flesh on his forearm tighten. He hopes that Emma has sense enough to run before the fire reaches her.

He turns to tell Otis Dickerson that he truly cannot help them, that he is needed back at Woburn Farm, that he will not know what to do when he encounters the fire, that a man who has already been burned is the last man he should want standing beside him when the flames advance. But when Odd turns to plead his case he finds that he has somehow been swept into the midst of the army of volunteers. Otis Dickerson is a half step behind him, pushing him along with a gentle pressure on his elbow. The men have already begun to move, and Odd is moving along with them.

20
ELIOT

Eliot follows the rising plume of smoke as far as the road out of Concord takes him, and then he turns into the woods. The fire is not here yet, but the smell of the burning is everywhere. Flurries of white ash drift through the untouched trees like snow. If the men do not act soon, he thinks, the fire will certainly fall upon the town. Eliot walks quickly, but the smoke is an elusive guide, shifting direction, coiling and uncoiling above the trees. Eliot pretends he is tracking the slithering tail of a dragon, the kind of mythic beast that the modern world lacks. The great quests have all been undertaken, he thinks, oceans crossed, continents discovered; there are few means left by which a man might prove himself. The untamed expanse of the American continent promises adventures, but not of the kind once embraced by explorers of uncharted seas; the Western territories promise only the opportunity to contribute to the slow, inevitable population of inhospitable land.

Eliot is not entirely certain what he will do when he reaches the fire. The stupendous clouds of smoke confirm what the quiet man at the watering trough has just told him: the fire is surely too large for a single man to inhibit its progress. But Eliot wants to stand alone in front of the maelstrom, to let its heat and thunder wash over him, before the other men interfere. After today, he will understand what it means to confront this most elemental force of nature.

Eliot thinks of his play as he tramps through the woods; he envies DeMonte. His hero will lose everything to the flames, but he will gain the opportunity to start anew. Eliot imagines himself standing next to Margaret and their children, watching the house on Beacon Street crumble to ash, and suddenly another possible ending for *The House of Many Windows* comes to him. Eliot stops walking, drops the shovel, and pulls out his pocket memorandum and pencil. DeMonte, he decides, will announce his transformation through a courageous soliloquy. Eliot writes quickly, with the taste of smoke at the back of his throat: *"I am a man simplified! Through the accident of the purging flame, I have discovered the benefit of*

*reducing life to elemental wonders. Simplify!
What other men see as tragedy, I view as a
miracle."*

This fire in the Concord Woods is more
than an accident, Eliot thinks; it is evidence
of the Fates in action, and he knows he is
meant to take a lesson from it. Eliot has
spent too many hours studying his ledgers,
paying bills, filling invoices, satisfying one
need only to create new ones. He wonders
if he might convince Margaret that they
really do not need the large house on
Beacon Street. At the very least, perhaps he
can make her see that they do not need so
many servants. He thinks he could surrender his carriage, or purchase a smaller
one. If he cannot render his life as simple as
DeMonte's, then he will strive to make it
less complicated. He will find a way. The
fire will show him how to rework the final
scenes of the *The House of Many Windows*.
Once he faces the heat and smoke, he will
better understand what DeMonte should
feel, what he should say and do. Eliot knows
that Moses Kimball is impatient for the
finished manuscript, but once he has seen
the revision he will understand why it has
taken so long.

Eliot had always intended that *The House of*

Many Windows would reach its climax with the burning of DeMonte's home, but he had thought the effect might be achieved simply through a combination of foot lamps and undulating scrims of painted flames. He had not considered setting the entire stage aflame, not until he had spoken to Moses Kimball of the Boston Museum and Gallery of Fine Arts.

Eliot had not set foot in the Boston Museum until the day he met with Mr. Kimball. In fact, he had avoided the place since its opening in 1841. Eliot had heard enough about the cheap entertainments to be found inside. Aside from the occasional operetta or tableau vivant, the venue mostly offered diversions of a non-theatrical sort, but by 1843 Mr. Kimball had decided to begin showing full-length plays. Eliot had reason to be hopeful. It seemed a likely possibility that a new theater looking to establish a regular audience might be open to the work of an untested playwright.

The museum inhabited a large building at the corner of Tremont and Bromfield Streets. On the day that Eliot brought the pages of his unfinished manuscript to Mr. Kimball, he found the entrance to the museum plastered with faded placards advertising past appearances by "Mary

Gannon the Juvenile Delineator," "Wyff
Kloff the Russian Giant," and "P. T. Bar-
num's Japanese Mermaid." Eliot understood why Mr. Kimball might need to rely
on such attractions to underwrite his theat-
rical productions, and he could find no fault
with a man who sought to turn a profit. A
sign above the entrance to the museum announced:

Admission 25¢
Grieving a Beloved Pet?
Taxidermy While You Wait!

Art must make concessions to commerce,
Eliot thought. He took another look at the
crude drawing of the simian mermaid,
stuffed his play resolutely under his arm,
and stepped through the doors.

There were no visitors to the museum this
early in the day, and Eliot's footsteps echoed
off the high ceiling. In the foyer, a twelve-
foot-tall giraffe greeted him with an em-
balmed smirk. The vast space was crammed
with cages, each promising a curiosity more
astounding than the last. Glass cases bore
rows of greasy smudges: at bottom, smears
of little palms and flattened noses; higher
up, the demonstrative prints of large fingertips. Behind the glass prowled lifeless beasts

featuring exotic colors and strange deformities: an orang-outang, a grounded flock of dodoes, a dog with an extra foreleg, a cat with two heads. Shelves and pedestals held jars of cloudy brine in which floated pickled creatures one would never encounter in the forests or rivers of New England.

And there were humans on display as well, figures cast in wax. A kneeling woman pleaded for her life with a trio of red-skinned savages, all of whom shared the same drooping, glass-eyed indifference. Next to this, a more grisly scene of madmen drenched in gore: "The Pirates' Cabin — A lesson to discourage the young lads of Boston who would play at being pirates on the river Charles." Between these displays sat a replica of a pneumatic railroad and a functioning model of the gigantic cataract at Niagara.

Eliot sidestepped the spears of sunlight reaching from the tall windows near the ceiling; motes of dust eddied around him as he made his way to the back office. His knock went unanswered, and when he looked around the edge of the half-opened door he caught his breath and nearly dropped his manuscript. At the desk slumped a man, his head lolling back at an impossible angle, his throat cut from ear to ear, eyes white, shirt soaked through with blood. A whiskey bottle protruded from his coat pocket, and his lifeless hand still clutched a bloody knife.

Eliot jumped away from the door and stumbled into Moses Kimball himself. The man laughed and slapped him roughly on the back.

"Our newest display!" Kimball said proudly. "We're calling it 'The Drunken Reward; or The Deadly Fruits of Dissipation.' Church folks love this kind of thing. Can't get a penny from them for a play, but dress up a moral lesson and they'll gladly give over a silver eagle to look on the bloodiest predicaments. You must be the man with the new play. Calvert, is it?"

"Eliot Calvert." Eliot was surprised by just how deeply the bloody figure had affected him. He tried to laugh good-naturedly but succeeded only in clearing his throat.

Moses Kimball was ordinary-looking, with a high forehead and a sharp nose, but he wore his dark, thick hair unusually long, and he was dressed entirely in black: boots, breeches, coat, shirt, cravat. He stepped around his desk, pulled up an empty chair, and motioned for Eliot to take a seat across from him. Kimball's office was jammed with displays in need of repair. A giant bear spilled straw from its hindquarter, and next to this a fragile landscape of the city of Dublin rendered in paper and wood four inches high, bore the large, unruly imprint of a child's foot at its center. Eliot noticed that the naked wax figure in the corner bore a woman's head, and he hurriedly turned his eyes back to Kimball.

"Well, let's have it," Kimball said. He flipped through the hundred-odd pages Eliot handed him and sighed. "The gist, man. The gist! I haven't time for tedium."

Eliot gave his best summary, half wondering if he was expected to evoke some approval from the bloody figure seated next to Kimball.

"A fire, you say?" Kimball's eyes were shut, his forefingers touched at his nose.

"At the end, yes."

"There's no language in this, is there?"

"I beg your pardon?"

"Curses, man! Blasphemies. We'll have none of that at the Boston Museum. If there are objectionable ejaculations — *O, Providence! O, Heaven! O, lud! O, paradise!* — you'll have to cut them right out."

"Of course not." Eliot fiddled with the buttons on his waistcoat. "So am I to take it that you are, in fact, interested?"

"What do I know of plays? But the fire

you mentioned, now *that's* something!"

"It's in the last scene."

"I've wanted to stage a conflagration for some time. Joan of Arc, or a Hindu funeral pyre. But this is better. An entire house! You don't extinguish it, do you?"

"No, well, I mean . . . I don't know."

"You don't know?"

"I haven't quite finished the scene."

"Let it burn. Right in front of the audience — we'll burn an entire house to the ground. Think of the spectacle, Calvert! We'll fill every seat in the hall."

Kimball drummed his fingers on the manuscript, lifted it between thumb and forefinger as if trying to gauge the thickness of the paper.

"We'll need to shorten this a bit. No sense making people sit through what they haven't come to see. Once the fire is done, they'll want to leave."

"It's at the end."

"Then we'll shorten the beginning, but not too much. We'll make 'em wait a little bit, build the suspense."

Eliot watched Kimball riffle the pages and divide them in half like a deck of cards.

"There's your edits. I should think that these remaining pages will provide dramatic tension enough."

Eliot struggled against the urge to rescue his manuscript. "I'm flattered by your interest, but I'll need to mull this over before I can give you a final answer."

Kimball returned his forefingers to the tip of his nose and studied Eliot from the apex of the little pyramid. "Let's not dally, Calvert. We both know why you've come. You've taken this play to every theater in Boston. And you've been turned down every time. I am your last resort. Am I right?"

Eliot fiddled with the chain to his watch and looked at his fingers. When he looked back at Kimball, the man was adjusting the stiff collar of the bloody wax figure seated next to him.

"Here at the Boston Museum," Kimball said, as if speaking to the wax figure, "we paint our drop scenes in broad strokes. I know my customers. They have no curiosity for fancy speeches. We'll need a moral, a lesson. Have you got one?"

"Well, the main character is a man enslaved to his own prevarication."

"What does that mean? You need to think Old Testament, Ten Commandments, or, better yet, Benjamin Franklin, *Poor Richard's Almanack* — you need a moral that people already know by heart. Reassure them there's nothing new they need to learn. You get the idea."

"I'll work on it."

"Good man. Now, let me show you something."

Kimball leaped to his feet and led Eliot back through the foyer to the exhibition hall where the play would be performed. By the stage was a device resembling a pipe organ.

"It's called an orchestrion," Kimball explained. "With this I can replace an entire orchestra. We'll have a score written for *The Burning House.*"

"It's called *The House of Many Windows.*"

"*The Burning House* is better. I'll have lyrics written as well. People want songs. You see, Calvert, with a device like the orchestrion I need not argue with temperamental musicians. It does just what I ask. No grumbling. It cost me a fortune, but it's repaid me time and again. I always spend wisely. Do we understand each other, Calvert?"

"Certainly."

"We'll divide the profits fairly. Which brings us to the important matter of expenses. If you intend to burn an entire house in my museum every night, there will be considerable expenses . . ."

After jotting down his new thoughts for the

play's conclusion, Eliot puts away the memorandum and pencil, picks up the ax, and continues his march toward the fire. He looks up through the barren branches and sees that the smoke has changed direction again, curling around itself, doubling back the way it has come. Eliot traces the new shape against the bright sky. He alters his course and picks up his pace. He knows he must be getting closer, but he feels that he is walking in a broad arc.

Certainly, he thinks, Margaret will agree to some of the small changes he has in mind, though it might require substantial effort to persuade her. He is encouraged when he thinks of the freedom he would purchase simply by reducing their expenses. Patrick Mahoney will not be pleased with his decision, but Eliot also knows that once his play is successful, once it is performed to packed houses, his father-in-law will understand, too. There are not really so many obstacles to his happiness as he once thought. All he needs is a quiet room, a chair, and a small table. He can make his life as simple as this and still count himself a man of infinite riches.

Eliot emerges from the trees at the edge of a sloping field and sees that something is not right. He puts on his spectacles and discovers that the trail of smoke he has followed for nearly a mile has misled him. On the far side of the field, a coal-black plume snakes over unmolested treetops, weighed down by its darkness. Eliot traces its source to where the smoke swallows a slice of the horizon. In the distance, at the bottom of a rocky hill, rows of blackened trunks stand like limbless sentinels before a fierce, menacing glow. The blaze is much larger than Eliot expected. Even from a distance he can tell that this fire is a wild, angry thing. Eliot grips the shovel resolutely and trudges toward the green hill he sees rising through the distant smoke.

21
EMMA

Emma listens to the far-away skillet clang of the bell in Concord's town hall, and it is a relief to her to know that Oddmund has delivered the news, though now she wishes she had not sent him away. The smoke has grown heavier since he left, and her chickens have all returned to the coop, fooled by the darkening sky. She does not want to imagine the monstrous things taking place in the woods. She stands at the back of the kitchen, in front of the last open window in the house, and tries not to worry.

Mr. Woburn said he would not be away long, but still he has not returned, and Emma dislikes being alone. Sometimes when she is left to herself she can feel her worries gorge themselves on the empty space around her. She closes the window to keep out the smoke and goes to the basket of unfolded bedclothes sitting on the kitchen table. Then she remembers the undergarment she left hanging on the line to dry. She is sure that it already smells of the burning and will need to be washed again before she can try to wear it. She considers fetching it, but she is afraid to go outside; the sight of the black clouds, rolling toward Woburn Farm like a blight from the heavens, would be too much for her to bear. She knows that she ought to fold the laundry and tend to the mending that awaits her needle and thread, but her mind is so full of worry, she thinks it best to distract herself for a few moments with the new book tucked behind the others on the top shelf of her bookcase.

A few weeks earlier, Emma had overheard two young women in Concord discussing a book by Allan Poe. She heard the women say that his book was filled with stories of murder and spirits and mysticism, and when they said that it was a wholly inappropriate book for ladies she could not help but find her curiosity stirred.

She asked Mr. Woburn to purchase the volume for her the last time he traveled into Boston, since she knew that any respectable bookseller would have refused her outright, and recommended that she purchase the latest volume in the *Eclectic Reader* series instead. And she also understood that

Concord's new library would never afford her the opportunity to run her fingers over the scandalous pages, for the venerable Squire Hoar — whose conversion to novels, it was said, came only after he found himself snowed in at a distant tavern with nothing to occupy his time but an abandoned copy of Sir Walter Scott's *Ivanhoe* — would never approve of the inclusion of Mr. Poe's work. Emma was not overly fond of frightening tales, but she simply could not stand the idea that a book might be forbidden to her, whatever the reason.

Under her bed, Emma kept a jar of coins earned from the piecework she still took in, and out of this she purchased books once a month for her little library. Despite Mr. Woburn's promise before they wed, he regularly grumbled about the money she spent on books that she could barely read. He complained about the time she wasted staring at the pages as if the words might suddenly announce their meanings to her. Emma seldom asked him to buy books for her, but she had handed him the money with a slip of paper bearing the title, and she was surprised that he consented to purchase Mr. Poe's book after only a brief show of displeasure.

She has not looked at the book since Mr.

Woburn returned with it last week, and now, she thinks, it might be just the sort of thing she needs to take her mind off her worries. She stands at the bookcase, retrieves the little volume, and runs a penknife under the first set of uncut pages. This is her favorite moment with a new book, cutting open the pages to look on the fresh ink seen only by a handful of people. The title page of Mr. Poe's book holds three lines of poetry in a language that looks to her like German, followed by the name "Goethe." She turns to the opening story and slowly mouths the first words, expecting to be appalled from the start. But in the first few dozen lines there is no mention of murderers or ghosts or demons of any kind.

Emma cuts the next set of pages to see if there are any illustrations, and when she slides the knife through the open end a card slips out and flutters to the floor. At first Emma thinks it is an etching that has come unglued, but there does not seem to be a missing space on the front or back boards. She retrieves the card from the floor and finds a skillful drawing of two men threatening a kneeling woman with short, curved daggers, a scene no doubt spawned by Mr. Poe's grim imagination. All three of the figures have heavy-lidded eyes, dark hair, and dusky skin. The men grin like devils, and the woman appears frightened, as one would expect. But Emma can tell that something about the scene is not quite right.

She takes the card to the window to study the picture in the gray-filtered sunlight, and then she realizes that what the men are clutching are not daggers at all. She feels the blood rush to her face. The shock of what she holds settles in slowly, but her curiosity will not allow her to put it down. The men wear short robes that stop at their waists, and below this they wear nothing at all. The woman's robe is thrown back over her shoulders; her small breasts stand out straight, the nipples pointed like darts. One of the men wears a little hat with a limp tassel. For some reason, the inclusion of the tassel strikes Emma as supremely ridiculous.

Emma's hands are trembling, and she wishes now that she had decided to tend to the laundry. She stares at the smiling woman until the two men fade away and all that remain are the woman's face, her unreasonably pointed breasts, her round hips, and the hidden ends of the men's impossible curves. Emma stares at her face, trying to puzzle out the expression she finds there. At first glance she thought the woman was frightened, but now what Emma sees on her face is not fear but something else, a kind of pleasure, perhaps, for which she can find no words.

These are not acts that Mr. Woburn requires of her, she thinks. He never makes any demands other than that she lie still while he dutifully grunts above her once a month. In his exertions she can hear the expectation that his joyless efforts will again prove fruitless. She knows that he blames her for their childlessness. Once, in a drunken rage, he went so far as to tear her precious books from their shelves and scatter them across the floor, telling her that too much reading had rendered her barren. After that episode, she made him swear that he would never again touch her books, and he promised to cease his indulgence in drink, though she could tell he did not mean it. She knows he keeps bottles hidden in the barn, and she suspects that today's business has led him to a tavern. She has learned to tolerate his drinking, but she promised herself that she would never again suffer his abuse of her books.

Emma checks the bookseller's stamp inside the cover: "Eliot Calvert, Bookseller, Boston." There is no stamp on the card. She imagines her husband's dirty, blunt fingers clutching the vulgar illustration and she quickly slips the card between the pages and places the book back on the shelf. Her face burns as if she has done something wrong; she knows she should not have looked at the etching for so long, and she cannot keep from thinking of it and wondering if the smiles were genuine, if the depicted figures were indeed happy to be coupled thus. She thinks of the woman, naked and unashamed before two men. What other varieties of bliss, Emma wonders, would be forever unknown to her? She has learned not to want kind words or caresses, but sometimes she cannot help but wish that the grunting might go on a bit longer.

The card is Mr. Woburn's doing, she knows, but she blames herself. He would never have set foot in a bookstore in the first place were it not for her. Emma had hoped that his willingness to purchase Mr. Poe's book signaled a softening of his feelings toward her, but the card suggests otherwise. She realizes that he must have had his own reasons for visiting the bookshop, and then it at last occurs to her that this is probably not the first time he has purchased such things. She looks around the room and through the doorway into the next and she takes note of the many nooks at every corner, dark places that she has never noted before. And she wonders, then, how many cards just like this one may already be secreted within the paper-thin crevices of her home.

22

ODDMUND

The chatter of the angry men, the bump and jostle at his elbow, the gritty scrape of shovels and ax heads dragging in the dirt — none of this keeps Odd's mind from drifting elsewhere. Odd knows he must take greater pains to concentrate on matters at hand. He looks around at the men briskly walking toward the fire. If he were to allow any of them close enough to eavesdrop on his errant thoughts, he knows they would surely have him pilloried. Odd trudges along in the middle of their little army, but even now, with the danger before them and the town of Concord in peril, his thoughts return to the undergarment on the clothesline, to the image of Emma's breasts giving substance to its shape. He sees her bending low to brush away the chickens pecking at her feet. In his mind he peers into the shadowy cleft at the scoop of her dress. He thinks of her lying on her back.

There are too many scraps like this in his memory, and with each passing year he finds it harder to separate the real from the imagined. Things he has witnessed sometimes prove more peculiar than what he invents. The images of things he should never have seen creep along the dark folds of his brain: his father disappearing in a flash, his mother looking up at him from the burning deck, the deific heart engulfed in flames, his uncle's grin before the rope goes taut, Emma's full lips rounded open in pleasure, her eyes hidden in dark shadow, his own wet hair plastered to his forehead and the feel of a splintery window frame beneath his fingers. Images overlap in his mind. Faces displace other faces. He manufactures memories from fragments that have no bearing in the world: his father and mother walking the streets of Boston, his sister fully grown and playing with her children, Emma on board the *Sovereign of the Seas,* squeezing his hand, surrounded by flames that do not consume, the ship turning from America back to the open sea. It is foolish to desire the world other than it is, but he believes there have been moments when he might have rendered the present more tolerable had he simply looked away, for no amount of regret can excise the hard lump of memory.

Odd had once clung to the pallid hope that Emma's marriage to Cyrus Woburn was just a convenience, a partnership built on sweat and chaste respect. There were no children, and Odd let himself think the marriage was unconsummated. It was a simple fiction to attend, since he already found it unlikely that people actually did the things he imagined them doing when they were alone. He dared not ask after Emma's happiness and had not the boldness to confess his feelings for her, but it mattered little. He has always known that they would never be together; it was the one certainty in his world. From the first time they met he understood this, simply by the way that Emma sprawled on top of him in the mud. He could tell she was familiar with the immediacy of other bodies; she sank into him unashamed, even as he felt his own skin retreat from the intimacy.

One of the men walking in front of Odd begins to chant a marching song about a forlorn lover, but no one else joins in and he gives up after the first stanza. There is some nervous laughter, then silence, and then the angry chattering resumes. Odd's thoughts wander back to the night, a few months earlier, when he had allowed himself to hope for something more between himself and Emma. Mr. Woburn was not at home the night that Emma stood in the rain and knocked on Odd's door to ask him to carry a load of firewood onto the porch. It seemed a strange request. Odd thought he had brought in plenty that afternoon, but Emma felt that the stormy night called for more. The rain had soaked through his clothes by the time he was finished, and she insisted that he sit by her fire until he dried. Mr. Woburn was not expected until morning, she said, and she did not wish to be alone while the storm raged. The thunder shook the windows and the lightning made the shadows of trees dance along the walls like shuddering marionettes. She asked that he stay until the storm weakened, and Odd could not refuse. He followed her inside and stood cautiously by the fire. Emma removed her wet bonnet and shook it out. She draped her wet shawl near the hearth, and Odd saw how her pale arms shown through the clinging damp sleeves of her dress. Her skin shone like fire in the orange light. She insisted he remove his boots and jacket, and she placed them near the fire next to her shawl. Odd allowed himself the fantasy that they were behaving as husband and wife.

"Do you play whist?" she asked Odd, as

she crossed to the other side of the room. She came back holding a deck of cards decorated with bluebirds and little blue boats.

"I don't know."

Emma laughed. "You don't know? Have you ever played cards before?"

"I don't think so."

"Well then, Oddmund Hus, let's find out."

She pressed several cards into his hands; the cards were covered with perfect red hearts on one side. Emma's fingers felt soft against his palms. He listened to her patient explanations.

"Really, we're each supposed to have a partner for whist," she said, "but I think we'll do just fine by ourselves."

He showed her the cards he was supposed to keep hidden, and he listened to her laugh at his mistakes until he felt an ache behind his ribs. To hear her laugh like that, he would have been content to make a lifetime of errors. She showed him how to fan the cards, and when he could not master this simple skill she placed her fingers on his and spread the cards for him.

They were still sitting by the fire, Odd's wet jacket dripping from the screen in front of the hearth, a blanket hanging from Emma's shoulders, when Mr. Woburn unexpectedly returned. He stood silently before them, lit by the fire and framed by the blackness of the open door. A flash of lightning made him double in size for a second. He held his fists at his side, and swayed slightly, as if he were trying to contain the building rage that flickered across his face in the firelight. He mumbled, stopped, then sputtered.

"Bloody hell."

Odd did not move, Emma pulled the blanket tightly over her bare arms, and Mr. Woburn stared past the two of them at the fire. He leaned forward and stepped toward Odd, then seemed uncertain, as if he thought the floor might be dropping away in front of him. He stepped back and almost fell over.

Emma stood slowly. "Mr. Woburn, come to the fire. You look ill."

It occurred to Odd that he had never actually heard Emma call her husband by any other name, and now he wondered if such informality existed between them. Mr. Woburn removed his dripping hat and dropped it where he stood while he groped the air for support. Emma stepped forward and grabbed his arm. At the same time Mr. Woburn reached out, looked Odd straight in the face, and cupped his wife's breast roughly, as if he were appraising its heft. Emma slapped his hand away.

"Not here."

Her voice took on an edge that had not been there a moment earlier. She turned Mr. Woburn around and led him away from the fire while Odd clumsily pulled on his wet boots and grabbed his jacket. His hands moved like bricks as he thought about what Mr. Woburn had just done, and he fumbled hopelessly with the tangled sleeves of his jacket. Emma smiled at him over her husband's shoulder and nodded toward the door, but before Odd could hurry off Mr. Woburn spun about on his heels and bellowed.

"Hussss!"

"Sir?"

Mr. Woburn broke free from Emma and charged toward him. Odd backed toward the open door, nearly tripping as he stepped out onto the porch. Mr. Woburn kept coming, and he caught the edge of the door to keep himself from falling. Odd could smell the liquor on his breath.

"Mnninthellbrrr! Dvillivll!"

Odd said nothing. He looked past Mr. Woburn's swaying form and caught Emma's eye before she cast her gaze to the floor in shame.

"Many thanks, Hussss! Looking after mis-sussss. Devil's night out."

Mr. Woburn leaned heavily against the door, slamming it shut, and Odd heard the bolt slide into place on the other side.

Odd remembers the restrained elation he felt once he stepped out into the rain, a feeling like a trapped bubble that seemed to lift his feet from the earth. *She had slapped his hand and called him Mr. Woburn with a voice that sounded as distant as last year.* Odd had never known hope like this. *Mr. Woburn was a drunkard.* All he needed from her now was a sign that she was waiting to be rescued. *They still had no children.* He had no idea how he would go about it, but he felt as though a door had been thrown open to him, a possibility existed where he had felt no reason to expect one.

Then he heard a crash and a muffled scream from the back of the house, and Odd's fleeting hope collapsed. It had not occurred to him that he ought to be worried for Emma. Her husband had returned home, drunk, to find her sitting by the fire with another man. What would any husband likely think? The rain splattered his face and ran down his neck. He heard another cry and made his way around to the back of the house, sick with himself for allowing his desire to push aside the concern he should have kept foremost in his thoughts. He should never have allowed his selfish wants to jeopardize Emma's safety. What husband would not react violently to any man who so poorly concealed his feelings for his wife?

Odd sank to his ankles in the mud as he crept alongside the house, and he crouched low when he reached the window, where the cries were audible through the bubbled panes of glass. He hesitated, and hated himself as he did so. Emma cried out again. He knew what he was likely to see — Mr. Woburn, the drunken brute, striking his wife for her disobedience. But what should he do? Break down the door? Crash through the window and run to her aid? Would that not make matters worse? What if, in the gallant act of rescuing Emma, some evil that lingered in the blood of the Hus family drove him too far? What if his rescue turned to murder? Emma's cries soared louder, and Odd grabbed the splintery wood of the window frame and peered into the room.

At first, he could not see Mr. Woburn at all. The room was dimly lit by a single lamp on a bedside table. The rain ran into Odd's eyes, and he held his hands at his brow and saw that Emma lay on the bed alone beneath a dark shadow. In the narrow slice of watery lamplight he saw that her head was turned away from the window, facing the sputtering shadows on the wall. Then he realized what was happening. The shadow was Mr. Woburn, still in his wet coat and boots, hunched over Emma with his breeches at his knees, his hips thrusting awkwardly. Emma squirmed; she swung at his jacket and grabbed at the bedclothes.

Then Emma turned her head toward the window. Odd clutched the windowsill and tried to pull himself closer. He heard her cry out again. He pressed his forehead against the glass and saw her face half hidden by shadows, saw her neck curved back, and saw her lips, dark red and rounded, in what he could only guess was the inscrutable shape of pleasure.

23
HENRY DAVID

The wind surges and stutters, and in the gaps he hears the faint progression of tinny hiccups that an unfamiliar ear might mistake for the remote clatter of pots and pans. The bells tell Henry that news of the blaze has finally reached Concord, and he imagines Edward reporting their carelessness to the gathering crowd, though it is possible, he thinks, that word may have come to them by some other means.

Henry sights his hand against the leaping flames on the horizon and tries to measure the expanse of the burning between thumb and forefinger. More than two hours have passed since he and Edward attempted to cook their chowder. He knows men are readying to battle the flames, but it will take time for them to assemble, time to gather weapons and plan the assault and march from town. And the fire knows this, too. For now it rejoices unthreatened. It flows like water, eddying, swelling, carrying along forest detritus in its path, burning waves of flotsam. Fierce plumes surge in extravagant display. Great arms of flame reach out and sweep over treetops. Henry watches as the fine needles of a towering pine, hundreds of thousands of green spikes, ignite all at once and leap from their branches, tracing thousands of fiery tangents, swirling erratically like the swarms of locusts he saw in New York City the previous summer. Those buzzing mammoths helped persuade him not to remain in New York — if locusts were content to frequent the city once every seventeen years, he reasoned, the same would do for him.

Henry closes his eyes, senses hot red fingers pressing against his eyelids, starbursts of orange, gold, the unexpected colors of ripe fruits and vegetables: pumpkins, squashes, melons, carrots, tomatoes. The wind comes in hot blasts, propelled by the pressure of the flames. Henry smells the calamint that covers the hill in scraggly patches, its crisp scent released by the heat. From deep within the woods, a loud rumble sends tremors through the ground, then there is a flash, another roar, another thunderclap — the fire makes its own weather; it is both part of and opposed to the natural world.

The fire hesitates when it nears the bottom of Fair Haven Hill, like a weary traveler contemplating a steep grade. It pauses, deliberates, decides. It splits and moves around the base of the hill, consuming grasses, bushes, small wind-bowed trees. Henry knows what it is doing. A dense massing of trees stretches from here to Concord, but the fire must be clever. It must move slowly, consume gradually, portion out its fuel if it wants to unleash its destruction on the dwellings of men. The possibility makes Henry shudder. He places a hand on a stone next to him and finds that it is growing warm on one side.

His legs feel rested, but they are still unfit to challenge the flames; he might easily be overtaken, or crushed by a falling tree, or suffocated by the blanket-thick smoke. Or he might break a leg in the soft terrain of ash and cinders. Even if it were possible to run away, he dares not leave his post for fear that the fire's boldness will only increase once it realizes it is no longer being watched.

One by one, the trees submit to the burning as if this process were merely the rampage of another season. Henry has trod through the muffled gray of winter, witnessed the jubilant eruptions of spring and the riot of summer, felt the brilliance of autumn quicken his blood, each season bringing outrageous transformation in answer to the season come before. But what answer would follow *this* transformation? Every season in nature destroys to transform, Henry thinks, but the season of man brings destruction alone.

Henry has always felt welcome among the trees, not as a visitor who comes for sport but, rather, as one returning home after long absence. But he wonders if some portion of the woods will understand that it was his careless hand that struck the match. Is recollection a faculty of man alone, or do all things in the world bear the imprint of what has come before? The mark of his deed, he thinks, might forever reside in the deep-ringed memories of the woods, entombed in the striated record underfoot. And after the fire — *his fire* — has finished its rampage, will the blackened survivors of this once green expanse ever again welcome his homecoming? Henry spots charred clumps of grapevine hanging dead like tangled fishnets from scorched maples and alders. He sees ospreys and teals, winged titmice and shelldrakes careening through the smoke in mad flight, their iridescent

411

feathers dulled with ash. They who sit in parlors, dreaming of acreage and wilderness unmapped, cannot imagine the terrible loss.

Is there a way, he wonders, that he can make reparation or atonement, a way that he might prove himself solicitous on nature's behalf? Perhaps he might raise a tent amid the ruins and sit in wake beneath the shriveled branches. He could return, he thinks, and make the poverty of this ravaged place his own, join the dumbfounded animals in their homelessness. Or, better still, he will build a small cabin with his own hands, a simple structure assembled from dead limbs, to stand like a forgotten guardhouse in a plundered city. The cabin will have no adornments, not so much as a doormat, so that he need not waste in housekeeping time better spent documenting nature's slow recovery. His door will be open to the mice and squirrels and woodchucks whose dwellings have vanished; his roof will offer its perch to birds searching for stolen boughs. He will make these creatures his neighbors by encaging himself in their midst.

As penance, he will sleep on a bed of ashes, cover himself with boards instead of blankets, and wake to soot-filled mornings, a parent nursing a sick child through long nights of slow healing. He will watch the grasses return, blade by blade, and he will rejoice when the first sapling forces its way through the charred forest floor to seek alms from the sun. And he will remain the patient guardian of this vulnerable world, a steward content to spend his days in penitent isolation.

Henry reclines on the crest of Fair Haven Hill and imagines this new life. After months of loud confusion, thought contesting thought, he feels some small relief in knowing what he must do. In the midst of chaos, he is suddenly calm. The patch of sky directly overhead is a pale, translucent blue, the color of glass buttons he once saw used for a doll's dress. When he closes his eyes, the fire returns. He sees its dark ghost, and he envisions its aftermath. Fire purges all, leaving only the things in themselves, stripped of former attributes. With eyes shut, he senses a presence, a spirit from the woods, bringing forgiveness and seeking his protection. It touches him, then seizes his forearm; the grip is strong, and it yanks him forward from his back onto his knees.

"You are saved, sir!" proclaims a voice that is, unfortunately, very real.

Henry opens his eyes, sees the pale blue sky roll past, and then the face of a man, bespectacled with tiny rectangles of glass

413

that flash orange in the reflected light. Henry winces from the slingshot of pain in his neck. He sinks back from his knees and sits on the ground.

"Your terror is at an end," the man says. "I have come to your rescue."

Henry's surprise fades into annoyance. He raises a hand to block the glare of the fire and to better view this assailant who has interrupted his epiphany. The man stands with one hand at his hip, the other atop a shovel upright against his leg like a staff. The man thrusts his chin forward, as if he were trying to appear as large as his thoughts. It is all too common a sight in the city, Henry thinks, except for the shovel. He assumes that the man has lately arrived from Boston, though why he is now standing above him is less clear.

"Do I strike you as one in need of a savior?" Henry asks.

The man seems confused. He points in the direction from which he has come and says, "You are exposed to the flames, and very nearly surrounded."

"And now, sir, so are you."

Henry watches the man rub the soft line of his jaw, watches the toll of understanding exacted.

"Oh . . ."

The man drops to his haunches but does not sit. He squats with his weight on his toes; the tips of his boots crush the strong-perfumed calamint and press it into the earth.

"How long have you been on this hill?" the man asks.

"I cannot say," Henry replies, rubbing the back of his neck. "I exhausted myself trying to contain the blaze."

"Alone?"

"The fire was in its infancy." Henry shows him the blackened soles of his boots.

"The town is coming," the man says. "A hundred men or more. And they are equipped."

Henry tries to hide his disdain for this man who has intruded upon his solitude. He hopes he will return to the others and leave him to finish his thoughts.

"I suppose there is nothing for us to do but await their arrival," the man says. "You needn't worry. I should think them no more than a quarter hour distant."

Henry watches the man survey the burning expanse with a hand at his brow, like a general reviewing his troops. The man smiles and nods, as if to express his satisfaction at having brought himself so close to the line of battle.

"I confess I had not expected the fire to be quite so impressive as this," the man says. He pats his coat, pulls out a small book and a pencil, and begins writing.

"You might obtain a better perspective over yonder," Henry suggests, pointing to an outcropping of rock fifty yards away.

The man does not hear him, or perhaps ignores him altogether. He continues writing, then says, waving his pencil, "I must beg your indulgence. I am a writer and, as such, a willing slave to the Muse. When inspiration arrives, I must obey."

"I fear I have burned my muse," Henry says under his breath. But again the other man does not look up from his earnest scribbling. Henry rotates his head slowly, rolls it against his chest, feels the tendons click and pop at intervals of discomfort. He sends an exploring finger to the back of his neck and identifies the troublesome spot, a point of focused pain like a railway switch.

Henry has given up hope that the intruder will leave him. He watches him gnaw the pencil's blunt end and offers advice. "You wouldn't do that if you saw what we put into their manufacture."

The man looks at the name stamped on the pencil and regards Henry with sudden appreciation. "You are John Thoreau and

Company?"

"His son. Henry David."

"What strange fortune! Your father makes excellent pencils indeed. My best customers write with nothing else. I am Eliot Calvert, of Calvert's Bookstore, in Boston."

Henry nods and rubs the knot of pain at the back of his neck.

"I could wish the circumstances of our meeting different," Eliot says, pointing to the fire. "Although it is another of fortune's curious turns, I am only in Concord today because I plan to open a second bookshop. Otherwise, I might have missed this spectacular conflagration entirely."

Henry is surprised to feel suddenly possessive of the fire. Moments ago he had wanted to share its beauty with another, but now he feels jealous of this man's admiration for the flames. He does not want to discuss the fire further, knowing where such a conversation will inevitably lead.

Eliot writes in his little book and then muses aloud, "I should hope there will still be a town remaining in which to open my shop, when all of this is done."

Henry wonders if Eliot has any idea that he is speaking to the person who started the fire, which — if indeed it reaches Concord — may have no small effect on his business.

But then Henry asks himself what claim this man has to bring his business to Concord, and he grows more annoyed with him still.

"I have little to do with bookshops," Henry says, trying to contain his irritation.

Eliot rolls his pencil between his fingers. "That is a peculiar statement for a man who makes pencils."

"Why should I give money for a book containing thoughts that occur as freely to its author as they do to all men?" Henry had not meant to speak quite so vehemently, but then he sees that his words have little impact upon Eliot Calvert, who looks at him blankly, as if he were a bit of fauna waiting to be classified. He wonders if the man has willfully ignored his point.

"You do not read, then?" Eliot asks.

"There are libraries," Henry says.

"Certainly there are books you might care to possess."

"Why would I want a book once I am finished with the reading of it?"

"I am at a loss, Mr. Thoreau. This is not an argument I have ever needed to make." Eliot chews his lip, thinking. "Books — they make a fine ornament for one's shelves."

"I have no shelves," Henry replies.

"You might lend them."

"My friends can afford their own books."

"There must be books that you cannot find in your library."

"I find what matters to me." By way of illustration, Henry pulls a book from his breast pocket. Its battered leather binding is held together with a strap that fits into a tiny silver buckle.

Eliot accepts the book Henry offers, turns it in his hands, and wipes away a sooty thumbprint on the spine.

"Catullus? If I am not mistaken, this is a valuable book, Mr. Thoreau. What library allowed you to remove it?"

Henry reaches for the small volume and squirrels it away in his coat again. From deep within the woods there issues another loud rumble, like logs rolling downhill.

"I have a way with librarians," Henry explains. "I consider it my one true talent."

Eliot watches Henry pat the pocket hiding the valuable book.

"When I am done with this book, I shall return it," Henry says, "and I need no longer concern myself with its care."

Eliot nods appreciatively. He puts away his memorandum, slips the gnawed pencil back into his pocket. He sits and straightens his legs before him and watches the rising pillars of smoke just long enough, Henry assumes, to show the solemnity of his contemplation.

"I see you are a simple man, Mr. Thoreau."

Henry shrugs.

"I myself am not so complicated a man as I may appear," Eliot says.

Henry thinks of the leather-covered memorandum the bookseller has just returned to his pocket. He observes the man's fine clothes, dusted with ash, takes note of the expensive-looking boots and the watch chain at his waistcoat pocket, and he imagines the gold timepiece nestled within. He watches Eliot frown as he inspects the lenses of his spectacles, rubs them on his sleeve, and checks them again. Owning such fine things, Henry thinks, must encumber this man's days with tedious cares; he no doubt consumes precious hours with polishing his boots, winding his watch, arranging the books on his shelves. Henry's agitation gives way to pity. He has seen this sort of man before, and he is suddenly seized by the urge to warn him of impending disappointment, but he realizes he can offer no solution. What direction can he provide, when lately he has done little more than distract himself — from his own true ambitions — with the making of pencils? Henry resists the impulse to lecture Eliot and instead tries to think of gentle advice.

"There are many ways a man might content himself," he says.

"True," Eliot says, brushing ash from his sleeves and lapels. "Opposing these advancing flames, for example, shoulder to shoulder with the good people of Concord and" — he gestures toward Henry — "with the maker of America's finest pencils. What greater expression of manhood can there be?"

Henry finds that he cannot bear to meet this man's gaze. And after you have finished with this adventure, he thinks, you will go back to Boston. You will return to the safety of a big house and the comforts of fine possessions and your business and the thousands of meaningless little tasks that consume your hours, and you will regale your friends with embellished tales of how you fought the great fire in Concord. The memory of this one day will supply vitality for the thousands of lifeless days to follow. You are mired in a life of desperation, Mr. Eliot Calvert, and do not even know enough to remain quiet about it.

"Simplicity" — Eliot nods solemnly in response to Henry's silence — "it is all a man need pursue."

Eliot pulls at the cuffs of his trousers and

takes hold of his heels. Henry watches as the bookseller removes his boots, and he becomes conscious of his own feet, hot and damp and swollen. Henry pulls off his boots as well and soot pours forth like sand. His dark stockings are covered in gray ash, and he sees that there are more holes than there were when he dressed this morning. He places his feet side by side, misshapen lumps in ragged green wool. Even in his stockings, it is easy to see that one foot is missing its big toe, the result of a childhood accident. If his young hand had dropped the hatchet an inch to the left, Henry thinks, he might have lost half his foot. Even had he survived such a grievous injury, his life would have followed an altered path; he most certainly would not have had means to foster his love for nature. How could he have explored forests or clambered up mountains, how could he have tramped through snow and mud and fallen leaves with little more than a stump in his boot for balance? But then at least, he thinks, the Concord woods would not be burning.

While Eliot writes again in his little book, Henry picks up a stick, scratches a broad rectangle in the dirt, and draws a lopsided triangle inside it, estimating the area of the woods that have already burned. In the crude drawing, he and Eliot are just beyond the triangle's base. He marks their position with an X. Henry is trying to sketch the swath of the devastation when Eliot snaps his book shut and emphatically places his hand in the middle of Henry's drawing.

"I have come to the awareness," Eliot announces, "that if a man would reclaim his life he must remove all that is extraneous to the living of it." Eliot looks down when he has finished this pronouncement, and he sees that he has accidentally erased part of Henry's map.

Henry redraws the lines, then crosshatches the triangle and adds to its length by increments, scratching out the X as he does so. He hears Eliot's comment, but it makes no sense to him. Who is the man so careless that he would fail to claim his life as his own in the first place?

Eliot grabs a stick, too, and begins adding to Henry's sketch. He scratches in the new Fitchburg rail line and draws another snaking line to indicate the Concord River. Henry flinches as Eliot's meandering stick comes close to the triangle's apex, where the hollowed tree stump should be marked, but Eliot takes no notice of his reaction. "I believe the proximity of the present danger has focused my understanding of things,"

Eliot says. "In life, as on the stage, a tragedy can expunge the extraneous diversions that so often muddle one's mind. I think it possible that some good may come of this."

"No good will come to the former tenants," Henry says, without looking up from the map.

"The trees will return," Eliot says. "The woods might become stronger than before, and as for the *tenants* — assuming you speak for the people of Concord — well, after great loss one is always more appreciative of what remains."

Henry sighs. He cannot make this man understand what has been lost. He puts down his stick and explores the toe that has poked through a hole in his stocking. He picks a tiny sliver from beneath a thick toenail and says quietly, "If you would appreciate what has been lost, then you must return and live among the ashes."

"I have no doubt," Eliot muses, "that a week in nature's bosom — a trip on the river, perhaps — would elicit a deeper understanding of its beauties."

"That is not my meaning," Henry says. "I do not propose that you return for sport. Rather, come to this very spot and build your home from the blackened timbers. Feed yourself with what meager fruit struggles up from the scorched earth. Live."

Eliot fumbles. "I might find such an exercise useful for my own reflections, and certainly it would provide much desired opportunity for writing, but I fear my wife and children would find such privations intolerable."

"Then leave them," Henry says, rubbing his feet. He looks at Eliot and watches him search for some sign that he has made the comment in jest.

"I understand the thrust of your arguments, Mr. Thoreau," Eliot says slowly, "and I cannot disagree." Henry listens as Eliot thinks clumsily out loud, and he is reminded of having once seen a bee struggling in the oozings from its own hive. "If I am truly to simplify my life," Eliot continues, "I must find ways to pare down that which I truly do not require. Of course, I cannot ask my family to abandon civilized life, but we might secure more modest accommodations. And under reduced conditions we might still find means to afford some small comforts, which would be all the more enjoyable for having required no greater sacrifice of time or labor."

Henry picks up his stick and gouges a divot at the apex of the triangle to mark the point where the fire began.

"Mr. Calvert," Henry says, sighing, "a man cannot simplify halfway."

They are plotting strategies in the dirt with the pointed ends of sticks when the fire-fighting Concordians arrive shouting plans of their own. Henry sees a hundred men or more come through the woods from the north, waving shovels and axes and hoes, a host of warrior angels in need of flaming swords. They run at the fire, shouting and catcalling, as if they believe they might intimidate the flames. The assault quickly turns to slow retreat. The determined Concordians set up a moving line of defense; the men with hoes align themselves first, thrusting their heavy weapons into the burning underbrush and raking it forward, stamping it underfoot. Behind them, men with shovels set about digging a ditch several yards ahead of the flames; they dig like dogs, hurling the loose soil into the burning grass to bury the fire alive. But this arrangement is flawed.

The flying dirt showers the men on the front line, stones bounce off their raking shoulders, and one man stumbles backward into the shallow ditch. They reorganize and stagger their positions. The men with the shovels form the front line. The men with

426

hoes stand at either end of the line; some move back to rake the unburned brush, exposing dry earth, clearing an unburnable space behind the men with shovels. Farther back, the men with axes set about removing the trees next in line for destruction, depriving the flames of their food. The men can only hope to claim the trees before the flames reach them. The fire forces the men to fight it on its own terms. They must destroy what they would save.

In the chaos the men work together, though some have arguments; flying elbows and empty boasts reveal prior tensions. Henry and Eliot are still perched on the spine of the hill, hurriedly pulling boots onto swollen feet, while the men below switch positions a second time, trying to find workable arrangements.

"The essence of heroism," Eliot observes, as if what is passing below them is evidence of a theory he has recently proposed. As Henry squeezes his feet back into their boots, a fat blister bursts and he can feel the sticky liquid seep between his toes. It does not hurt, but the thought of it — the torn onionskin bubble of flesh — makes him flinch. A wound, a breach of any kind in the body's ramparts, leaves it vulnerable to invasions that might carry off a digit, a limb, a whole person with the indifferent necessity of natural cause.

Eliot leaps to his feet and shouts, "Let us to battle!" Then he picks up his shovel and runs down the hill toward the other men.

Henry delays. He knows the unexpected results of rash acts. He will not rush the seething cataclysm. Henry watches as Eliot reaches the skirmish, inserts himself between two men raking burning brush on the left flank, and joins in the frenzy, crushing the flames underfoot, a whole line of men seized by Saint Vitus's dance, hopping, jerking, shouting. More men arrive from the direction of Concord, some armed only with intentions. The fire calls upon reinforcements of its own. Forced back upon itself, the blaze seems to burn faster now, hissing and smoking indignantly. It tries to outflank the men on the left, reaching around with long arms, but there are no longer trees there, no underbrush, no fuel to support the maneuver, so it retreats, regroups, and launches a new assault on the right but again finds nothing to burn.

And then a tree collapses across the line of men. No one is injured, but the fire crosses this bridge to new quarry and the flames spread to the trees flanking the men. Henry sees a dismal proof in this. Nature will not be outfoxed so long as chance is her ally. Men exhaust a disproportionate sum of energy in a vain effort to prevent nature from doing what she will: damming rivers, filling swamps, leveling hills, clearing fields, claiming land from the sea. The cities of America are the hosts of gratuitous transformation, aberrant changes that, once left unguarded, will revert to what was. Attempts to bend nature's design are merely pointless acts of hubris. Nature — brutal, beautiful, beneficent nature — will prevail in the end.

Henry is convinced that his efforts to combat the fire will be as impotent as those of the other men, but he cannot divorce himself from the desperate spectacle. He pushes himself to his feet and, empty-handed, picks his way down the hill toward the roiling flames.

24
CALEB

You will build here a church of bones, yes?

It is clear to him, now, that the flames slithering through the distant trees portend the end of things. Caleb stands at the edge of the woods and pokes the sputtering dregs in his pipe with a twig. The fire tells him its intention to advance on Concord, and he divines that it will not stop there; the burning will lay waste the town and then descend upon Boston. Caleb rejoices that heaven has at last grown weary of the wickedness of the New World, and he is pleased to have played no small role in at last moving the palsied hand of Providence.

All fortunes, he thinks, good and bad, betide with purpose: his doubts, his defiance, his revelations and blasphemous rantings. It becomes obvious to him that the two old women appeared this morning as shepherds of the flames, witches sent to announce the arrival of the end. It is very likely, he thinks, that he has been visited by others like them in his life, messengers he failed to recognize. Esther Harrington, Caleb can now see clearly, is most certainly a witch as well. He should have uncovered this truth before. It was she who delivered the news about Boone's innocence; hers was the voice that revealed to him that his words, his prayers, his blessings, meant nothing. And he knows in his heart that she is in league with Amos Stiles. Together, the two have led him to this day; they have shown him the path to self-destruction, and he had no choice but to take it. Even if he had discovered their true nature earlier, he could not have resisted their direction, for everything comes to pass as God so wills.

After Esther Harrington's revelation that he had condemned an innocent man — a Christian, no less, who had once already escaped the Pandemonium men had created on earth — Caleb expected his own punishment to be swift and fierce. Only a cold, indifferent universe, he thought, could allow his terrible deed to pass unanswered. Caleb waited, and when God's wrath did not immediately descend upon him his old doubts returned. If there truly existed a just and righteous God, how could he not have damned Caleb for so rank an offense?

Perhaps, Caleb thought, it was impossible for him to have condemned Desmond Boone; perhaps there was no burning lake into which he or any man might be cast; perhaps Caleb had merely darkened Boone's final conscious moment in this world before sending him into the void. He thought of the Irishman's body in the woods. He thought of Boone's eyes and tongue, straining to leave his skull, and he thought of the lifeless faces that haunted him, visited his dreams, mocked his yearning to believe that something more than this meaningless putrefaction awaited all men. As long as he escaped castigation, Caleb would have no answer, and thus it became clear to him that he must seek out punishment on his own.

Caleb's followers presented no deficit of imitable transgressions that he might willfully heap one upon the other to awaken heaven's justice. After weighing their sins, searching for what might be most offensive to the Almighty, he decided to seek direction from Amos Stiles. Despite his many faults, Stiles seemed wholly unperturbed by the damnation that he certainly knew awaited him. He clung to the hope of redemption not with an outward show of desperation but, rather, with the inconsequential eagerness of a dog begging at his master's table.

Caleb was intrigued by the thought that Stiles's transgressions, while increasing the burden of guilt with each repetition, might actually deaden him to its weight. Caleb had never tasted spirits, had never sampled the tobacco or hemp leaves that he suspected Stiles still imbibed despite his protestations that he was reformed, but Caleb knew that he might easily enough trick the lapsed sot into showing him how it was done and where such intoxicants might be obtained. So Caleb followed him one night into the cramped lanes snaking around Boston Harbor, winding cow paths long since covered by cobblestones now slick with filth, and found him at a tavern lacking any discernible name. The portrait of a white bird above the door was all that distinguished the entrance from the other low doorways.

Caleb waited outside the dark door for half an hour, wrestling with his conscience, before he finally entered. He found Amos Stiles half-asleep at a long table with a smoldering clay pipe cradled in his open palm. He opened his eyes when Caleb nudged him, but he did not appear to recognize him at first.

"It cannot be you," Stiles said, waving his hand and sinking back into his seat.

So sunken were the man's cheeks that it looked to Caleb as if his eyes had swollen to the size of walnuts beneath their lids. Caleb nudged him again.

"Go away," Stiles mumbled.

Caleb stood above him and tried to sound commanding. "Mr. Stiles, I have come to taste of your weakness, that I may show you the path to strength."

"Aye?" Stiles rubbed his eyes and waved away the smoke between them. "What's this, then?"

Caleb felt foolish for trying to engage Stiles in discourse, but he was determined not to turn back. He would find a way to partake of the man's wickedness.

"Together we will outsmart the Devil, Mr. Stiles, but you must help me to understand how the Devil leads you astray."

"The Devil?" Stiles awakened with a start. He did not move, but his eyes opened wide and seemed to reach for Caleb. "How do I know you ain't himself, the Devil, come to tempt me? You might take any shape you please in these shadows."

"Mr. Stiles —"

"Away! I am a man redeemed!"

"The fact that I have found you here

confirms my suspicion that you are no less fallen than before."

The pipe rolled onto its side in Stiles's palm, and he jumped from the touch of the hot bowl. He looked up and smiled slowly in recognition, and Caleb counted no more than three brown teeth tucked behind the man's lower lip.

"Reverend Dowdy? Is it you?" Stiles wondered aloud, trying to sit up straight. "You make me doubt my very eyes."

Caleb sat down across from Stiles and folded his hands in his lap. He stared at him sternly; he knew the man would never comprehend his true reason for coming.

"It disappoints me to find you here, Mr. Stiles."

"But not entirely, eh? Otherwise, you wouldn't have come looking."

"Don't make light of your sin."

Stiles's stupid smile faded, and he came back to himself, suddenly serious.

"It's the poison in me, Reverend. It falsifies my logics."

Caleb watched Stiles examine the pipe as if it had suddenly materialized in his hand.

"Look here, Reverend," Stiles said, tapping the pipe on the table. "I'm going to cast this off. To testify to my efforts."

"Wait. Show me."

Stiles struggled with the idea before putting the pipe eagerly to his lips, like a child happy with permission to misbehave. After inhaling, he spoke in a small voice.

"And then you have to hold it for a while, like this, so you can drink it in."

Stiles blew a steady stream of smoke across the table and smiled. Caleb's mouth watered. He wanted desperately to taste of something that might bring him relief from guilt and doubt, from the nightmares and the waking visions. He wanted to flaunt his weakness before heaven and call down upon himself the punishment that was his due.

"Give it here, then."

Stiles froze. He cocked his head sideways and stared at Caleb. Stiles started to speak but was distracted by the coil of smoke that drifted over his face when he opened his lips. Caleb noticed that some of the other men huddled in the dark room clutched larger pipes, pipes connected to thin tubes, pipes of polished wood decorated with precious metals that sparkled in the dim light. Stiles's pipe was gray and crooked and looked as if it had been fashioned from mud.

Stiles seemed to remember something, then said, "I cannot let you do that, Reverend."

Caleb saw how the other men reclined on

benches, hunched over tabletops, asleep or barely conscious, and he looked enviously at Stiles's half-opened eyes. It angered him that these worthless men had found blissful release from their cares while he still struggled under the crush of uncertainty. If they could so willingly embrace their damnation and reap the rewards of sin while yet on earth, he would do the same.

"Give it to me at once!" He snatched the pipe from Stiles, who stared at his empty palm for several long seconds before looking up.

Caleb put the gritty opening to his lips, inhaled, and choked on the sweet smoke. It burned his tongue, and he thought he tasted blood. Caleb tried again, and forced the smoke down his throat into his lungs. He tried to exhale slowly but could not control the coughs erupting from his chest.

"Slowly," Stiles said encouragingly.

Caleb found that the third pull went down smoothly, and his head seemed to expand. To his surprise, the first sensations came almost instantly, a dizzying feeling of having been suddenly transported to the rafters.

"Powerful stronger than laudanum or that Brown Mixture," Stiles said. "Never much liked the licorice medicines myself."

"Marvelous strange," Caleb said appreciatively.

Caleb inhaled again, placing the rough end of the pipe a little farther into his mouth this time, disregarding the disgusting wet sheen he saw on Stiles's lips. He took another long taste from the pipe and watched with curiosity as Amos Stiles dissolved right in front of him; the man's gray face smeared itself over the space between them. If only the visions haunting his dreams would dissipate so easily, Caleb thought, the death mask, the black eyes, empty sockets and swollen tongue, his own mother's face, wasted with sickness. Caleb could stand the visions no longer. If God had not the courage to strike him down, then he would erase the visions himself with whatever weed Amos Stiles could stuff into his pipe.

Stiles began laughing, flaccid shudders that rippled along his arms. Caleb felt the intoxicant take a stronger hold, but he was not giddy. He felt somber, a bit dulled, as if he had been sealed inside an enormous glass jar stuffed full with rags. Caleb held up the crude pipe and looked into its bowl at the black ball glowing red at its edges, like a distant planet or a flaming comet. Caleb sniffed the hot fumes rising from the bowl and he felt a calmness suffuse his veins, even as his nostrils burned. Stiles laughed again, sluggishly.

"I had not thought your foul weeds to have so remarkable an effect," Caleb said, closing his eyes, sinking deeper into a confounding quietude.

"Reverend," Stiles mumbled, sounding as if he were drifting along the edges of a dream, "this is no weed. This is opium."

The wind comes in strong gusts, lifting Caleb's coat from the crumbled foundations of the farmhouse, tumbling it through the ruins, like a dog seeking shelter.

There will be no church after all, Caleb thinks, neither bricks nor bones. The lingering words of the old women cut through his opium haze and prick some remote part of his brain as yet unaddled by the soporific poison. He can see their wizened faces and the deep-set eyes, one dark pair, one faded pair already dead in their sockets. He watches stalks of light poke through the distant trees, illuminating swarms of tiny gnats floating above the shorn fields. Tongues of orange flame flutter from branches like autumn leaves. Most trees have not yet bloomed, and in their nakedness they seem more vulnerable than the few already dressed in riotous spring attire. Caleb knows it is a foolish thought. Fire shows neither preference nor deference; it consumes the living and the dead with equal fervor.

Nearby, a dormant sycamore rustles the parchment leaves it has stubbornly clung to since October, a thousand stale petitions for which April now has no use. Caleb does not share his fellow New Englanders' enthusiasm for the golden days of autumn. It is a season more piteous than beautiful, a prolonged dirge for insensate organisms incapable of understanding death's inevitability. The season of bountiful harvests is nothing more than a rusty-hued death rattle — stately oaks and maples so desperate to cling to life, so uncertain of what lies beyond the long winter to come, that they eat the green from their own leaves to eke out one more day. The brilliant reds and yellows of that cruel season are evidence that brute life, unguided by reason or faith, will willingly cannibalize itself just to purchase another hopeless hour on earth. To be sure, in Caleb's experience the forest reawakens every spring, but how can the trees of October know that? To a penumbral mind of pulp and bark, the dark clouds and arctic winds rolling in from the north are dire heralds of an infinite void. And each year there are, perchance, a scattered handful of otherwise hardy-seeming oaks and maples and birches and pines that prove unable to parry the bitter thrust of January and the vicious stab of February. *Evergreen* is a misnomer of the highest order. No wonder the coppery leaves do not release their grip like the heavy fruits of summer but cling tenaciously to twig and branch until the last is torn away by the first nor'easter of the season. Each tree dies a hundred little deaths without knowing which one will be its last.

It is no different for man. It was no different for Desmond Boone, clinging to the last few seconds of life even as he dangled at the end of a rope. Which moment was his last? There was the drop, the dangle, the gasp, the fierce struggle, the bright red of burst vessels, and the fluttering descent. Was his autumn any less glorious? And would he have a spring?

You will build here a church of bones, yes?

Caleb kicks the crumbled foundations and sends a fist-size stone into the stubbled cornstalks. Desmond Boone was once alive. Then he was dead. That was it. No prologue. No epilogue.

Caleb remembers his mother's gaunt cheeks, but he had not seen his father's face at the end. Already four years in the grave, does his father's face look now as it did in life, he wonders; is any part of it still recognizable as the man he knew? Caleb examines the expired ashes in the bowl of his pipe; he licks a finger, wipes it around the bowl, and touches the blackened fingertip to his tongue. He tastes smoke, a tang like burnt sugar, and he feels a deadening calm smooth out the wrinkles in his logic. He cannot know the fate of his mother or his father — *their* salvation had not been within his authority to dismiss — but he himself condemned Boone to the flames. Caleb looks into the woods, sees the fire motioning for him, and suddenly realizes that there is only one way to find out if the man's soul lives on. He must look for it. He will go and seek out Desmond Boone's spirit among the very flames to which he condemned it. Caleb sucks once more at the empty pipe and tosses it into the field. He will need it no longer. A peaceful feeling suffuses his limbs, the confident serenity that precedes knowledge soon to be acquired.

Caleb pulls his arms into the sleeves of his white robe, points himself toward the Concord Woods, and treads lightly through the dry field. Each step seems to catapult him skyward. He tries to measure his gait so that he does not fling himself over the treetops out of sheer eagerness. He keeps his eyes locked on the fire peeking at him from between the trees. He hears the flames calling to him, roaring in his ears. He steps carefully, bouncing, floating, giddy and terrified at once; he reels from the sublimity of truth too quickly imbibed. He realizes that his first impression earlier in the day had been absolutely correct. He should never have doubted his own insight. This fire is indeed for him, specifically for him alone. This is precisely what he has been waiting for. These flames are to be his salvation, or his doom, his affirmation or condemnation. There is only one way to find out.

25
ODDMUND

He is not prepared for the certainty of the flames.

On the way from Concord they watched the smoke unfurl overhead, a procession of phantoms grasping for light, opaque one moment, translucent the next. The men approached the fire from the opposite side of Fair Haven Hill, and they shuddered together as the wall of crackling heat slammed into them. Odd was stunned by the enormity of the sound. The men fell silent as they took in the extent of the fire, and then, weapons raised, courage renewed, they charged.

Odd fears that they are outnumbered, for the fire is not one enemy but many, thousands of individual flames, chewing through trees, taking possession of the woods as if this were their inheritance. During the years Odd lived alone in his little cabin, he had come to suspect that trees and plants and animals — and all else that relied upon sun and soil and water — were inhabited by a gentle spirit that seemed to tremble beneath the surface of living things. And now he imagines the ghosts of what has burned gathering in the dark ribbons of smoke and fleeing skyward. Odd feels helpless to save them; he inhales, tries to draw the dissipating life into his chest, and doubles over coughing.

This is what it means to be haunted, Odd thinks. He has heard others speak of ghosts as half-glimpsed shadows in forgotten corners, but Odd knows that they are more sensation than presence, an ache, a stirring. He has sometimes felt their earnest touch — a flutter in his stomach, an acrid finger at the back of his throat. The first time he visited his family's gravestone at Copp's Hill, Odd discovered that the spirits of the dead did not haunt places at all; they haunted people.

The gravestone sat in the overgrown weeds at the back of the burying ground, near the spot once set aside for slaves. A grieving Boston family had paid for the stone, and they allowed the grass around it to grow tall like the seaweed shrouding the relatives who did not make it to the New World. Odd's family was not buried there, but they shared the memorial with the forty-three other passengers from the *Sovereign of the Sea* who also were not buried there. Together, their bones mingled on the ocean floor, dressed and undressed by shifting sands. Odd used to worry that the ghosts of his mother and father and sister would be unable to breathe underwater, but when he visited the gravesite he understood: from the moment he flew from the ship's deck on the expanding ball of heat, he carried their spirits with him. The fire in his lungs should have been a sign to him that he was to be the vessel of their haunting. The vacant grave at Copp's Hill was marked by a thin rectangle of slate topped by a jawless, winged skull. Odd studied the hollow sockets and the empty grin of the half-bird, half-death's-head image etched into the brittle stone. He pressed his fingers into his cheek to feel the hidden contours of his own skull grinning back from behind closed lips, and he knew that he, too, for a time, had had wings.

A shovelful of dirt hits Odd's shoulder. Otis Dickerson yanks the ax from Odd's hands and pokes the handle of a shovel against his ribs.

"Wake up, man! If you're going to stand here, you'll need this instead."

Odd nods. He takes the offered shovel and starts digging.

Otis Dickerson shakes his head and carries the ax back to the men who are chopping down the trees behind them. Odd helps the men nearest him dig a shallow trench in front of the flames like a long, snaking grave. He tries not to stand too close to the others. Beneath grunts and coughs there are darker complaints, muttered between strokes and swings, as if their thoughts must be kept secret from the flames.

"This will carry on to Concord."

"If Concord goes, the forests at Walden will go next."

"We'll hang the devil that brought this down upon us."

Odd fears that their anger is directed at him, that each man has somehow already intuited that he is responsible for this. They fling the dirt into the burning woods, trying to bury the fire alive. Odd digs faster than most. He is strong, and the loose black earth yields easily. He feels his muscles settle into a comfortable rhythm of exertion, expanding and contracting across his rib cage, yanking the bones of his arms forward and back. His shovel bites into the soil, tears up grasses, rips out spindly, tangled roots and hurls them into the fire, feeding and killing the monster at the same time. He calls on the anger that he feels over the fire's certainty and lets it flow through his limbs, lets it energize him with a sense of purpose.

The smoke is thick, and more than once Odd throws a shovelful of dirt into the back of someone's head. At times it is impossible to see, but Odd is convinced that some of the other men are looking at him, watching him for some sign that he is the cause of this blaze. The very thought makes him feel guilty. He wants to shout that this fire is not his. He shovels faster, as if to prove his innocence. Around him, bodies materialize and vanish. Men grow large against the flickering light and shrink back into their own skinny shadows. Odd listens for accusations but hears only angry shouts and the steel thump of axes and shovels above the din in the trees. Each man seems lost in his own repetitive task, but through a break in the smoke Odd sees a man staring at him, a dark shadow among shadows, and after a wave of smoke passes the man reappears in a different place. Odd thinks he has seen the man in these woods before, but he does not know his name.

He feels a hand on his shoulder and turns

to find Otis Dickerson at his side once again. "Look here!" the shopkeeper yells, though they are standing only inches apart. "What are you doing? We're trenching this way!"

Odd looks once more at the man he thinks is staring at him, and Dickerson follows his gaze before a cloud of white and gray smoke engulfs them and moves on.

"You acquainted with that one?" the shopkeeper asks.

Odd shakes his head.

"If you've no cause to speak with him, I wouldn't recommend it. Strange fellow." The shopkeeper rests for a moment, props himself on the handle of his shovel. His face is smeared with sweat and soot, and Odd can see a network of thin veins in his cheeks, bright red beneath the filth.

"He's taken to calling himself Henry David Thoreau," Dickerson says, "though he was christened David Henry. Pointless, that. No less an idler now than he was before he rearranged himself."

The shopkeeper hefts the shovel with both hands, steps forward, and attacks the gnarled underbrush. Then he turns back to Odd and adds, "He makes a fine pencil, I'll give him that, but I came upon him once in the woods, completely without clothes.

Now, what kind of a man does that?" Dickerson resumes digging with a fury that seems to reflect his disdain for the man who dared to change his name. Odd does not find Henry David Thoreau's conversion unusual. People remake themselves in ways more troubling than merely switching their first and middle names. Whole families erase entire histories every day simply by stepping off ships and announcing themselves to the New World as the Smiths or the Coopers. Even Cyrus Woburn is a man remade, though Odd doubts that Emma herself knows as much as he does about her husband.

Odd came upon this knowledge by accident. It began with a spotted rabbit that had made a nest for her squeaking babies in the feed bin. When Odd lifted the lid, the mother blinked at him with surprised black eyes, shamed by her failed instincts. Odd knew Mr. Woburn would order him to fling the babies into the dirt, so he dragged the wooden bin to the garden beside his own lodgings, certain that he would be able to find extra chicken feed somewhere in the barn. What he found instead was a bottle of rye whiskey hidden beneath a worn-out saddle.

When Odd turned around with the bottle

in one hand and a half-empty sack of chicken feed in the other, he saw Mr. Woburn outlined in the bright morning light, tamping powder into the long barrel of his rifle. He was not wearing his hat, and his wild tangle of gray hair was swept back from his forehead and stuck out behind, making him look as though he were leaning into a strong wind. Mr. Woburn withdrew the rod, slid it back into place along the barrel, and peered at Odd through one eye, taking aim without his gun.

"Morning, Odd."

The bottle felt suddenly slippery, and Odd dropped the feed sack so that he could better cradle the whiskey with both hands.

"I was looking for feed . . . for the chickens."

"Did she send you back here?" Mr. Woburn asked, holding the rifle lengthwise. He wore only trousers and an unbuttoned vest over his nightshirt, and Odd could see dark circles of sweat beneath his arms. The cuffs of one trouser leg were half tucked into one of his boots.

"I did not see Mrs. Woburn this day," Odd said carefully. "I will tell her nothing."

Mr. Woburn shrugged to show that he had nothing to hide. "Why don't you help yourself?"

"I will put it where it was."

"Come with me, Odd. And bring that bottle."

Odd could not take his eyes off the loaded rifle.

"We're going to rid the back field of those damned turtles once and for all," Mr. Woburn said. He threw the satchel with powder and balls to Odd. "They ruined the pumpkins last season. I've thought on it, and I'm certain it was the turtles. Damned nuisance."

By the time they crossed the field, Mr. Woburn had taken several pulls from the bottle and had begun speaking in a loud voice that reminded Odd of the rainy night when he found him sitting next to Emma in front of the fire. The old man seemed to have forgotten entirely about the incident, or at least he never spoke of it. Odd kept a nervous eye on the rifle just the same. He had never liked working alongside Mr. Woburn, and since that night he had avoided being alone with the man altogether. When they reached the creek, Mr. Woburn sank down onto the grassy bank and teetered backward before righting himself with his legs straight in front. He motioned for Odd to take a seat beside him. Odd noticed the white beginnings of a beard in the deep crevices of Mr. Woburn's cheeks and neck, where he could not be bothered to guide his razor.

Mr. Woburn's aim was lousy, but the turtles were easy targets. They sat sunning themselves placidly, shells glistening black and brown and yellow, hooked beaks turned toward the sky. A line of stinkpot turtles perched head to tail on a fat log that jutted above the stream. Snapping turtles floated in twos and threes on the slow-moving water. Odd wanted to warn them. He cringed at the sharp report of the gun, the sickening crack of the turtles' shells, and the voluminous spray of red.

Between curses and pulls on the bottle, Mr. Woburn reloaded. He was in no hurry. When he fired, he usually sent the ball cracking through the shell of the turtle next to the one he was aiming for. He might have achieved the same results with a heavy club and a net. He might have set traps or spread poison where he believed they nibbled at his crops, but he seemed delighted by the flying shards and plumes of red, each little explosion suggesting that the turtles were packed into their shells under great pressure. Odd could not understand why they did not all swim away at once. The shots scared off a few each time, but most only withdrew into their shells, and those that fled returned moments later, poking their creased, leathery heads above the water at the worst possible instant. Odd strained against the urge to help them. He sat holding the open bottle by the neck while Mr. Woburn fired lazy shots between swigs.

"I forswore the drink ages ago, Odd my boy. I'll tell you, it near delivered me to self-destruction. This bottle here, it's only for the pain in my back. Go on, a tipple will do you good."

Odd put the bottle to his mouth and let only a trickle pass before he felt as though his tongue had been set on fire. Mr. Woburn pulled the trigger without raising the gun from his lap, and another turtle disintegrated into a shocking red cloud. He saw Odd gag and pulled the bottle away, placed it to his lips, and tossed his head back. Odd watched three coppery bubbles float up through the churning liquid as Mr. Woburn gulped.

"See how it's done? Don't let the baldface sit on your tongue. Whole point is to put the fire into your gullet."

While Mr. Woburn drank, Odd saw movement from the corner of his eye. Three painted turtles surfaced near them, creating ripples of overlapping light. He could see the shadows of their feet, paddling quiet little circles underwater while fragments of shells floated past, black and pink. Odd saw Mr. Woburn's eyes tighten with the act of swallowing, and before he lowered the bottle Odd ran a hand through the grass, found a stone, a pretty one with a vein of black jagging through smooth gray, and sent it skipping across the water. The turtles darted below the surface.

Mr. Woburn cleared his throat and kept one eye squeezed shut as he spoke. "Moderation, Odd. Try again. Take a good, long drink."

Odd held the bottle upright, kept his lips closed, and pretended to swallow until he could feel his Adam's apple working dryly in his throat.

"It softens the unpleasantness of things, it does. No reason to tell Mrs. Woburn about this, you understand."

Odd nodded.

"Good man. She won't understand, and I don't need her worrying. Terrible nervous woman she is. Good cook. Terrible at the rest of it. Wifely matters."

Mr. Woburn winked at Odd and then took a shot at a small turtle floating nearby. The ball skipped over the water's surface, and the turtle slowly turned and paddled calmly in the other direction. Mr. Woburn reached for the powder horn and spilled gunpowder down the barrel, onto his lap, dropped in two balls instead of one.

"Never tell a woman what you don't want to hear again and again. A woman can't let things be. Doesn't know how to take unpleasant news and lock it away."

By way of illustrating his point, Mr. Woburn rapped the barrel of the rifle against his temple. "Take all this." He flung his arm over his head in a broad circle. "If she knew what happened to the farm before, ach, imagine the state she'd put herself into."

Odd saw another doomed turtle rise to the surface, and he leaned into Mr. Woburn's line of sight. "What happened to it?"

Mr. Woburn held up the half-empty bottle and swirled the contents, staring at the spinning threads of sunlight with reverence.

"Damn fine piece of land. Came all the way to New England to start over. But a man can always start over in this country. New farm, new name — a new wife, too. Ha, there!" Mr. Woburn suddenly threw his arm wide, tossing the bottle clear and knocking Odd onto his side, and with his other arm he pointed the rifle and fired. A large turtle on the opposite bank burst open and the fragments skipped across the creek's surface. The recoil sent the rifle flying from Mr. Woburn's hand.

"Damn!"

Clutching his hand, Mr. Woburn fell onto his back, and when Odd tried to help him up he began laughing hoarsely. "I think it's broke." He laughed, squeezing his forefinger, not yet acknowledging the pain. "Oh, we mustn't let the old girl get knowledge of this predicament, Oddie my boy."

Odd wonders if Mr. Woburn, drunk or sober, is fighting the same fire right now on its other side. If the flames are already this close to Concord, surely they must have reached the edge of Woburn Farm. Odd and the other men force the fire back over what it has already burned, and they reclaim a little strip of charred earth. The fire moves to their flanks, lunging at them with bright spears, looking for a way around their assault. Odd is growing tired. His shirt is soaked through with sweat. His throat is dry and his arms are heavy; he feels his efforts begin to slow. After each shovelful of dirt, Odd gazes deep into the burning trees, looking for some indication that this is not *his* fire, that it was not a spark from *his* burning that spawned this beast. He tries to ignore the growing sense of guilt, and each time it rises up he shovels more furiously.

No matter how hard he works, though, he cannot keep himself from wondering if he has caused this. The brush he cleared that morning burned differently; at times it seemed almost reluctant, and Odd needed to coax it with forkfuls of brush to keep it going. But this fire soaring above him destroys with impunity, as if destruction were its right, and in response Odd works his shovel in the soil, striking the ground with enough force to rattle his elbows. He does not understand the anger that hardens in his chest, but he lets it guide him, lets it shift his center of balance forward so that he might dig more efficiently. Heat and effort drench his shirt. Some of the men curse under the burden.

Odd sucks at his dead tooth, forces his shovel through a thick root, and sends the twisted mass flying into the fire. He glances about before stepping sideways to start on a fresh patch of earth, and he finds the sight at once noble and pathetic — the wall of flames towering over bent backs, swinging arms, blackened faces. The thick smoke obscures the sun, but the fire casts its own sideways light, intense and focused. Odd hunches over his shovel and resumes digging. Behind him, his wide shadow dances on the rolling smoke, stretches out along the earth, and touches the laboring shadows of the other men.

26
HENRY DAVID

Many have come to quell the convulsing wrath among the trees. Henry looks for Edward among their number, but the smoke is thick and the men are spread along the front of the blaze for a half mile or more. Some of the men are experienced, and they shovel and chop with the rhythm of fights remembered. Some clearly have no inkling how to battle a fire and they display curious tactics. One man, marked by a great shag of gray beard and a dazzling crown of gray hair, attempts to smother the flames with a heavy blanket, singeing the shadows of leaves and vines into its fuzzy nap but achieving little else. Another kicks at the flames as if he were driving a stubborn mule. Within minutes his trousers ignite and he is set upon by the other men, who shovel dirt on him until he is extinguished. He rises, a wiser man, and resorts to clearing unburned brush by hand.

They are too far from the river to form a line of swinging buckets, but a number of men have come straight from the tavern, bellies full with drink. They realize at once — as if through some unconscious concordance — that they have, each of them, brought ample stores of water, and with no women present they are free to make public use of private resources. One man and then another puts idea into action; laughter erupts; trousers drop. A dozen men take part, and the nearest flames spit steam under the insult. The foul streams slacken, and the fire marches back over the barely dampened earth. The men retrieve themselves and fight on.

Some of the men tire quickly, starved for air, stunned by the intense heat. Henry accepts a shovel from one of the exhausted men and joins in the digging. More men continue to arrive from town and, each in turn, they show a gaping admiration for the size and ferocity of the blaze before they attack the fire with undiminished assurance. All exude the same empty confidence that Henry found so abrasive in the bookseller he met on the hill. Where, he wonders, do these men find this powerful consistency to look upon the world as if they owned it, as if they held the answers to its every dilemma?

Nearby, Henry notices a trio of Negroes, dark as the smoke itself, hacking at trees with long-handled axes. He has seen them in Concord before, Africans brought to the New World to advance the dreams of white men. The tallest of the three, Douglas Jackson, directs the other two. His head is shaved smooth and on either side his ears rise to shriveled points, razor-clipped as punishment by the Georgia master from whom he eventually escaped. The fugitives Henry has encountered each bear some horrid deformity, testimony to the unfathomable creativity of vicious men — branded faces, missing fingers, split noses, and worse — silent injuries punctuating the discourse between savagery and hope. The Underground Railroad brought these men to freedom, and Henry knows they have witnessed trials far graver than this. As a modest protest against the evils of slavery, Henry has begun withholding his annual poll tax from the state of Massachusetts, but thus far no one seems to have taken notice of his resistance, and he wonders if a single man can ever expect to affect the mass of men. America, Henry fears, will always be a brutish home to noble ideals.

The blaze devours all things equally. Grass, shrub, and tree are reduced to cinders in its wake. The ground becomes a black sameness, and no one notices when they cross the invisible line marking the boundary of private property. Through the trees the men see a half-plowed field, a farmhouse, a barn, stables, and tall haystacks dry and inviting. The fire does not hesitate to trespass. It consumes private trees, crawls over private grasses, hobbles over the stubble of last autumn's harvest, slinks along parched fence posts. The woods seem to shudder as the fire heaves, coughs, and catapults a part of itself — a sparkling oyster flickering weightless through the air — onto the roof of the nearby barn. For a moment, the men stop and stare in disbelief as a solitary shingle smolders, glows, and pops into flame. The fire races madly from shingle to shingle, spreading along the roof edge before beginning its steady march up the incline to the weather vane; the copper rooster points northeast, as if showing the fire the fastest route to Concord. Within minutes, the entire structure is engulfed.

From the burning barn a farmer in a frayed straw hat comes running toward them, waving his arms, barely able to shout. His clothes are scorched from his futile efforts to save his barn. When he reaches the men, he wrings his hands and bursts into sobs. He cries that they are trespassing in his woods and, in the same breath, begs them to rescue his doomed trees. Narrow shoulders quivering, the weeping man stands useless among the firefighters, wiping his eyes with the back of sooty wrists, indicating places where the fire seems to be advancing, pointing out heroism for other men to undertake. He offers no assistance, so absorbed are his energies by his despair. The weeping man removes his broad-brimmed straw hat and smacks the frayed edges against his thigh, and Henry recognizes him as the first man he encountered on his search for help, the man who refused him aid.

In the weeping man's anguish, Henry finds further cause for dismay, for here he sees the narrowness of men's lives defined. He knows that Concord brims with farmers who will labor for the better part of thirty years — an entire lifetime — to pay for their land and the house that sits upon it. In this, Henry thinks, the Indian proves far wiser, for he would never exchange his wigwam for a mansion if it so ransomed his life. The weeping man no doubt has taken pains to draw a map demarcating the extent of land he possesses, but his map, like all maps, is an illusion. Draw as many maps as he will, a man no more owns this land or these trees than does the blackbird that alights here in search of insects.

Henry sees the weeping man collapse on a charred patch of earth, his head hanging between raised knees, black holes in his straw hat where flying embers have penetrated. "I am ruined. I am ruined," the man moans, and Henry feels a twinge of guilt, a criminal remorse distinct from the regret with which he regards his thoughtless act at the pine stump. But Henry knows that he has committed no crime against man. His carelessness may have brought about this calamity, but no one can accuse him of being anything so common as a thief. He has not taken what was not his. He has not caused the destruction of anything that a man might rightfully possess. He has done nothing more than unleash a natural force; the flames, after all, are but consuming their natural food. The weeping man may believe he has suffered great loss, Henry thinks, but a man cannot lose what he has no right to own; nor can any man be robbed of what was never his.

Amid the chaos, something catches Henry's eye, a figure laboring apart from the rest, a solid and powerful-looking man, fair-skinned, white-haired. The man stands considerably shorter than the others, but his quiet self-reliance nonetheless marks him as a fine specimen of Young America. Something about his demeanor, a certain stutter that haunts his gestures, suggests that the man mistrusts his own abilities, and Henry feels a flicker of kinship to see uncertainty registered in so sturdy a frame. Henry hears shouts, and turns to discover the weeping man running back toward his doomed barn; he does not get far before a pair of men tackle him and drag him back to safety. The fire exhales a cloud of thick smoke, and for a moment Henry is surrounded by darkness. He hears men coughing in the impenetrable gray, and he stumbles forward with arms outstretched. The fire inhales, the smoke dissipates, and Henry finds himself next to Young America, who is wildly shoveling dirt onto the retreating flames.

The man acknowledges him with a silent nod and flings another shovelful of blackened dirt; he spits, wipes grit from his lips, and grimaces, revealing a tiny, dead tooth perched on a row of remarkably white teeth. Henry is transfixed by the sight; he had lost the first of his adult teeth several years earlier, and he recalls how swallowing the tooth seemed to render him lame and vulnerable, as if he had been missing a limb or a piece of armor. At the time, he could not hold his head up in the presence of other men, but since then he has lost more teeth through accident and rot. He understands the inevitability, and he realizes that he will probably be altogether toothless before long. It is a sad curiosity, he thinks, probing the gaps in his mouth with his tongue, how something as simple as the loss of a tooth seems to leave his soul a little more unprotected each time. Henry sees Young America work his tongue at the black tooth. It appears to be a source of shame to him, a reason not to smile at kindness shown. Henry almost envies his unusual white teeth, even though the man seems wholly unaware of his prize.

He watches Young America regard the smoldering ground with sensitive eyes, and he thinks that he sees a blunted longing there. Henry has had his fill of confident men, with their bold plans and overreaching ambitions, men who would transform the land that will soon cover them. The look he sees in this man's eyes, a trepidation that cannot contain its want, gives him hope. The new nation might yet outgrow the old ways of men, but it will require something stronger, a different kind of animal, descendants of Young America, perhaps, or others like him. Henry thinks he would like to converse with him when the fire is done, and at that very moment the man looks deep into the woods, where the fire as yet holds sway, and he mutters, "I know it is not mine."

It sounds more like an angry exhalation of words than actual speech. Henry assumes he is talking about the land, and it amazes him that they may have been thinking the same thing. Henry leans in close so that he can be heard over the roaring flames.

"A man might come to woods such as this," Henry says, "to live on his own. Only then might he claim some dominion."

Young America starts, as if he had forgotten that Henry was working next to him. He stops shoveling for a moment, seems to take Henry's suggestion seriously, and at last responds.

"I did."

It is Henry's turn to be surprised. "You have lived in the woods, alone?"

When Young America nods, Henry can only marvel that this man has already accomplished what he has only dreamed. His unrealized ambitions litter his mind with thoughts of things undone.

"I ought not have left her," Young America mumbles to himself as he resumes his shoveling, and Henry understands his regret. If he were finally to go off to live alone in the woods, Henry thinks, he might never find reason convincing enough to leave, might wish to remain forever as nature's guest and protector, living in accordance with the seasons until he passes as quietly as autumn passes into winter.

Young America kicks at a tongue of flame pushing up through the ash. He remains focused on the rhythm of his shovel strokes, and Henry hears him whisper, "She is in danger."

Henry stomps at the flames. He thinks he knows on whose behalf Young America fears. He places a hand on his strong shoulder, feels the taught muscle beneath, and leans close. "Nothing in nature is ever endangered. She alone always is."

27
ELIOT

The heat is far greater than he expected. It seems a thing in itself, a glassy surface, malleable and shimmering, pressing upon him with the force of a solid object.

And the business of fighting the fire strikes him as far less heroic than he thought it would be. His hands and face are black with ash. The air is thick with it, and he feels the grit in his collar. His eyes burn and his tears mix with the soot, caking his lashes. He licks the coarse powder from his teeth. He is certain that his lungs are coated with a greasy paste he will cough up for months to come. The first thing he will do upon returning to Boston, he thinks, is invite Dr. Samuelson to call, and then he will go straight to the apothecary to see what purgatives the chemist might provide to flush the filth from his body. These thoughts bring him solace.

A visit to the tailor would not be entirely

out of the question, either. Eliot looks sadly at the sleeves of his coat. The expensive dark blue is streaked with ash, like shooting stars. His yellow vest is torn and stained. It cannot be helped. Errant cinders swirl about him, landing on his arms and shoulders, burning scores of little holes ringed with hard crusts. Instinctively, he reaches inside his jacket for his memorandum to record this last thought, but then pauses, reluctant to smudge the creamy pages with sooty fingerprints. He will not forget the observation. He decides that he will save his ruined clothes and put them on when he resumes work on *The House of Many Windows.* He looks at his boots, scorched beyond the rescue of rigorous polishing. A visit to the cobbler will be in order as well.

Eliot pauses and leans on his shovel. More men than he can count have gathered in the woods, and more keep arriving. He can feel their desperation and wonders how he might capture and convey this emotion on the stage. Around him the metallic complaints of shovels and axes and saws compete with the rushing howl of the fire. And that is something else Eliot did not expect: the symphony of noise. Eliot wonders if Moses Kimball can re-create the sound with his orchestrion. The fire thunders and moans, as if the underworld were breathing its last in one long, continuous exhale. Were it not for the other men, Eliot might have cowed under the pressure of the roar alone. It surprises him that he takes comfort in their presence. He had briefly thought that he might distinguish himself from the society of men in this fight, but they sought him out and made him one of their own again.

And then a curious thought crosses his mind. He wonders what would happen were his bookshop to catch fire. Would so great a number of men arrive to extinguish the flames? It would take little effort to start a blaze in a building crammed from floor to ceiling with paper: just a spark, an over-turned candle, a dropped cigar. And if it happened at midday, when the streets were too crowded for the horses to bring the pump engines, or in the middle of the night, when no one would notice until it was too late, in either case the shop would be beyond rescue in a matter of minutes. His father-in-law would have money enough to finance another such business, but would he still have the will, once he had seen how vulnerable such an operation was to the capricious whims of chance? Eliot imagines his proud bookstore a hollow shell, the fine volumes reduced to ash, the lewd illustrations cooked to cinders in their secret tin boxes. A man might agonize over decisions for years, and in a single moment decisions might be made for him by a sudden turn of circumstance.

The pencil-maker is a fool, Eliot thinks. From the moment he first saw him, he thought the man's eyes were set far too deeply beneath his prominent brow to be trusted. Eliot suspects the man has neither wife nor children of his own to care for, else how could he so easily have suggested that Eliot abandon his family. *Then leave them.* The phrase floats through Eliot's mind, halfway between impossibility and temptation. Clearly, Eliot thinks, the pencil-maker must be a bachelor still, to have leisure to sit in judgment and make proclamations about the world and the lives of others. For those men who must actually live in the world as its owners, driving and shaping it, the choices are not so plentiful as they may seem from without. A happy accident is their only hope for liberty.

Eliot rams his shovel into the earth and the handle twists from his hands as the blade strikes something hard and unyielding. In the crook between thumb and forefinger, a purple blister rises beneath the tender skin. Eliot crams the affected area into his mouth. He looks to see if anyone has noticed his clumsiness, then retrieves his shovel and flings another futile load of dirt into the flames.

He cannot stop thinking about Henry's suggestion. *Then leave them.* Could he return to Boston, blistered and soot-covered, and tell Margaret that he was retiring to the woods to write for a week, a month, a year? Could he announce this to her father? What would he say to their children, and how would he explain this to their friends? He knows that undertaking such a humble quest would not endanger his family's finances. And he would not, after all, abandon them forevermore; he would return a wiser, happier man. Men left families every day to pursue fortunes in the new territories out west, and no one thought the less of them for it. Men left wives and children in terrible circumstances and sailed across the ocean in search of advancement, and no one thought this reckless or selfish. The men building America had not hesitated on the shores of the Old World, so why should it be different for him?

And yet it *was* different. Eliot knew that he could circumvent the opinions of his wife and his father-in-law, and he need not worry about his youngest children, who were too busy reeling from the countless innocent insults of childhood to notice their father's tribulations. But he could not deceive his oldest son, Josiah Edward, a perceptive boy teetering on the brink of reason. Josiah Edward — keenly aware that adult expectations sometimes exceed the still inexplicable world — would know his father was crippled by doubt. Eliot knows that Josiah has already begun to suspect that his father is not the hero he needs him to be. Eliot tries to hide his weaknesses, but his son seems always to see through the charade with quiet disappointment. Josiah possesses a preternatural ability to turn the appearance of a thing into an argument against the thing itself. The night before Eliot left for Concord, the boy had disarmed him with just such an observation.

Eliot often wrote late at night, long after everyone else was asleep. It was the only way to find solitude in a house bustling with children and servants and frequent guests. Since moving into the house on Beacon Hill, he found writing to be less a conversation with the Muse and more a struggle to shut out the world. He cursed his predicament quietly in those late hours, pulling at his hair when the pages were blank, burning those that displeased him, muttering self-disparaging oaths. He did not want his children to witness any of this, did not want them to see that their father, at some rudimentary level, was unhappy.

But last night Eliot had failed to notice the door to his study open slowly, and he was startled when his son finally spoke.

"Papa?"

Eliot covered the pages with his hands and turned to find his son standing in the shadow of the hallway, rubbing his eyes. He had no idea how long the boy had been standing there.

"Josiah! What are you doing awake at this hour?"

"I cannot sleep."

Eliot smiled gently. "Have you tried closing your eyes?"

"Both of them. But I am seeing things."

Josiah often ignored Eliot's quips, but Eliot suspected that it was not that his son misunderstood. The boy seemed predisposed to lure his father into making pithy statements, only to reveal that he, the child, was several cognitive steps ahead. Eliot looked at this boy, a creature possessed of the good and bad parts of himself; he watched him rub his eyes with soft-knuckled fists, took in his sandy hair, the curve of his small ears, the narrow shoulders, and the bare feet just visible below the hem of his nightshirt.

"Where are your socks? The floors are frightfully cold."

"My feet have to breathe."

Why did Eliot always feel outwitted by him? He never had a satisfactory response at the ready. "I think there might be some milk left from supper. Let's have some milk, and then it's back to bed."

"What are you doing, Papa?"

"Writing."

"Why?"

"Because I cannot sleep, either."

"Are you going to have some milk, too?"

"Perhaps I will. Yes."

"Are you writing letters?"

"No." Eliot never knew how much to tell the boy. "I am writing a play, Josiah."

Eliot watched his son think. Josiah made it look like a physical activity, as if thinking were a meticulous finger-tracing of a large catalogue, page by page, a marshaling of relevant facts.

"Will you read it to people, like Mama reads to us?"

"Well, no. Actors will read it, in a theater. And they will pretend that they are the people in the story."

Eliot watched Josiah consider these new facts, his small features squeezing together in an unconscious performance of concentration.

"Come on, Josiah. Let's see about that milk."

Eliot stood and led Josiah down to the kitchen. The boy's small hand rested in Eliot's, clutching the base of his thumb, where the muscle swelled faintly bluish into the palm. Eliot might have made a fist then and crushed the fragile bones. Josiah looked up at him, and Eliot felt his own hand go protectively limp, felt his body assume its instinctive defense, protecting the boy from his father's errant thoughts.

In the kitchen, Josiah pulled himself onto a chair while Eliot fetched the half-full pitcher of milk from the cold room at the back. Eliot thought about the expensive blocks of ice that were dragged here in March, and the worthless puddles that would cover the floor by May. In the heat of summer, the cold room was almost as warm as any other room. A worthless luxury. Eliot poured two glasses, and took a seat across from his son. This was a good moment, he thought, and he immediately wished he had not had the thought. He wished he could stop thinking about every moment as if it were a rough draft of a much better life that would never be realized.

"Will you make them dress up?" Josiah asked, after a mouthful of milk.

"Who?"

"The people that are making pretend. Remember. You said."

"Oh, the actors — well, yes, they do, yes."

"And they pretend they are other people, because you tell them to?"

"You could say that."

"Why do you tell them to?"

"Well, because people like to watch other people make-pretend."

"Why?"

Eliot was determined that this time he would not wither under the boy's inquisitiveness. "It makes them laugh, sometimes. And sometimes it makes them sad."

"Why do people want to be sad?"

"They're not really sad."

"They're just pretending?"

"Yes. The actors pretend to be sad, so that the people watching them can feel sad without really being sad." Eliot knew it sounded preposterous and immediately wished for a better explanation.

Josiah drank more milk, swishing it around in his cheeks, and thought about this.

"So all the people are pretending to be sad?"

"Yes. Unless the play is a happy play. Then the people watching it are happy."

"They are pretending to be happy?" Josiah asked.

"Well, yes."

Josiah swished another mouthful of milk between his teeth and swallowed.

"Why don't people pretend to be happy all the time?"

Clever boy. Eliot saw traps at every turn. How could he answer without revealing that the world into which he had brought this child was a disappointing place where adults spent precious time trying to escape their ordinary lives? How could he offer an explanation that did not sound like an apology?

"Well . . ." Eliot proceeded carefully, watching his son's trusting eyes, wanting to offer a bit of wisdom that the boy would carry with him and draw on in future crises. "People don't need to pretend all the time. They just do it a little bit, every now and then, because they find it amusing."

Josiah thought about this. He tilted back his empty glass and waited for the ghostly film of milk along the sides to collect and trickle into his mouth. In any other child, the thought would have fled by now, the target of interest shifted. But Eliot knew that Josiah had taken in all that was said and was kneading the information, working and reworking it, looking for the hard lump in the argument. Josiah finished the creamy dregs and smached his lips in what struck Eliot as a deliberate parody of lip-smacking. Still holding the glass in both hands, his son looked at him and smiled.

"That was good milk."

Then the boy set the empty glass on the table and for a moment assumed the startling gravity of an adult in possession of uncomfortable news.

"Papa?"

"Yes, Josiah?"

"Papa, I don't think that people should ever make-pretend at all."

28

ODDMUND

Odd sucks at his little dead tooth while he shovels. His eyes sting from the bright heat. The pencil-maker, who rechristened himself Henry David Thoreau, works beside him. He does not strike Odd as so strange a man as Otis Dickerson seemed to think. When Henry learned that Odd had lived alone in the woods for a time, he showed great interest and asked about the construction of the cabin and its location and the number of seasons Odd had spent divorced from the company of men. Odd did not know how to explain that he had never felt comfortable in the company of others and so had felt no deprivation. But the fire allowed little chance for talk, and they soon turned their full attention to driving back the surging flames. It seems to Odd that the fire is growing angrier, and he can just make out a snarling beneath the roar. A shower of swirling red embers rains down upon them, and

Odd thinks he hears Henry say something about finding beauty in this.

Staring into the blaze, Odd tries to see it. The brilliant gushings of copper and gold and the shimmering air boiled silver; these may mimic the shades of beautiful things, he thinks, but there can be no beauty in a thing that destroys for no reason. He thinks of the flicking torch in his father's hand, and of the flash and the great ball of red heat devouring the *Sovereign of the Seas.* It seems to him that beauty belongs to what is fragile and vulnerable, forever in need of protection. He thinks of Emma.

Odd can find nothing in the fire but tragedy. He watches Henry push his shovel through the ash and pull it back, making a little powdery hump of smoking embers. Between intermittent waves of smoke, he sees the man whose barn and woods have burned. He sits in the dirt, face buried in his hands. Odd wonders if this farmer has ever done something to deserve punishment — *shooting turtles for sport, drinking himself senseless, deceiving the woman he should protect.* No one is supposed to suffer needlessly, not in the New World, and this suspicion tempers Odd's sympathy for the man.

Henry makes a shallow stab at the dirt

with his shovel and wheezes. The smoke is beginning to wear on all of them, Odd thinks. Several men have collapsed, coughing and sputtering oaths against whoever started the fire. Odd tries to take small breaths, tries to defeat his own thirst for huge quantities of pure, cool air. He wonders what it is like to suffocate, to drown, to gag at the end of a rope, and then he wonders if these men will insist on punishing someone for causing this calamity. He worries that they will learn of his small fire on Woburn Farm and accuse him of losing control of it. What is the penalty for carelessness?

The progress of the men is visible now. The fire is still devouring new territory along its flanks, still sending out armies of hot cinders, but it is clearly in slow retreat, and they are forcing it back onto scorched land, where there is little left to sustain it. Where the fire seems to have surrendered, dark patches of brush smolder insolently; here and there the fire chokes on its own smoke, waiting to revive.

Odd wipes the grit from his eyes. He hopes Emma has shown the good sense to flee the flames, which have surely already crossed the fields of Woburn Farm and reached the farmhouse. Odd knows that

Emma does not understand his aversion to fire. He has worried that his refusal to kindle his own hearth might seem a ploy so that he could eat his meals at her table. He turned down her invitations as often as he thought necessary. Still, at least once a week he found himself sitting between Emma and Mr. Woburn at the small table in their warm kitchen, shrouded in the comforting smells of baking bread and roasting meat.

When he sat at her table he tried not to let his gaze wander where it didn't belong, and whenever he caught himself following the line of her forearm — plump beneath her white sleeve, up to her elbow, her shoulder, the milk-white skin of her neck — he forced his eyes back to the table. He tried to keep them on the steaming heaps of food that she put before him on the heavy pewter plates. Great mounds of steaming potatoes towering over shanks of meat, bright vegetables boiled to creamy softness, crusty rolls piled haphazardly beneath a striped linen cloth, dark stews so thick they might have stood on their own outside their crocks, and swollen pies pregnant with fruit. It was hard to believe the amount of food she prepared for three people, and yet, at the end of a meal, there was seldom a bite left, especially after she had prepared Odd a basket to carry back to his cabin to make sure that he had food enough for breakfast.

"You do not eat enough, Oddmund Hus," she would often say. "I cannot understand why you don't take every meal with us here."

"I don't like to impose."

"There is food enough. And we have no one to share it with."

At such comments Mr. Woburn would always look at her sharply. "That's enough. Let him be. The man likes to have some time to himself."

"Everyone enjoys having some company with their meal," Emma would insist. "It's no good to eat alone, and we have plenty for a whole *family*."

"Some don't need to be talking all the time," Mr. Woburn said, his mouth filled with potato.

"It's a shame for food to go to waste," Emma said. "And it's not as though we have children to feed."

"Then you should cook less."

The conversations at dinner were usually the same. Mr. Woburn did not seem to mind having Odd at his table; he just felt no need to talk about it. Odd figured out that this simple rule governed Mr. Woburn's approach to the world: nothing was unbearable, so long as a man spent no time discussing it. Odd seldom had much to say, but he could have sat for hours listening to Emma chatter on about the weather or the color of the sky at noon or the strange behavior of one of the chickens, pausing only to laugh self-deprecatingly at an example of her own foolishness. Emma would talk about anything, just to keep the semblance of conversation alive, sometimes going so far as to respond cheerily to her own idle questions when her husband refused to answer. There was one thing, though, which she spoke of only to Odd, and she did so only when her husband was not present.

Some afternoons, when Mr. Woburn was in town, Emma would insist that Odd join her for tea on the wide front porch, and together they would admire one of her new books. Sometimes she asked him to read to her from a passage she could not decipher on her own. She would offer him the rocking chair that matched hers, not realizing that by making him sit in her husband's chair she made it impossible for him to resist the fantasy that this was his house, his farm, his wife. Emma always looked uncomfortable, her thighs pressing against the confining armrests, stretching the seams of her dress. The seat was too narrow for her, and she had to hunch forward with her cup and saucer balanced on one knee. But she smiled as she sipped her tea and laughed apologetically at the occasional creaks that issued from the overburdened chair.

"My husband does not approve of me spending money in this way." This was how Emma prefaced almost every new book she showed to Odd. "But I cannot help myself. Have you read this one? It is by a British poet, a young man named John Keats."

Odd held the small book and rubbed the whorled leather cover, smooth and shiny like healed scars. Emma sipped her tea, a fat pinkie extended from the tiny cup like a little sausage.

"There is one poem so lovely that I have already memorized the first bits," she said. " *'Season of mists and mellow fruitfulness . . .'* That's how it begins. Isn't that wonderful? *'Season of mists and mellow fruitfulness . . . close . . . close bosom friend of . . . of . . .'* Well, I don't remember what comes next, but then there is a part about fruit swelling with ripeness, and plump gourds. I have only made out a few of those words so far. So much beauty in so few words; it makes me want to curl up inside them and fall asleep. Isn't that silly?"

"No," said Odd, tonguing his dead tooth.

"Not at all."

"You're sweet for saying so. You can borrow that if you'd like. I cannot put it on the shelf just yet or Mr. Woburn will notice. I'm not supposed to buy more than one a month, and I already bought a blank book to practice my letters in. But the pages are empty, so I don't think it should count."

Odd felt the small book suddenly grow heavier in his hands, and he leaned forward in his chair, as if pulled off balance.

"This poet," Odd said, wanting to say something appreciative, "he must be a very happy man, I think, to make such beauty with words."

"Oh, no. I was told he had a very sad life and died right after he wrote this poem. That's what Mr. Fields told me when I bought it in his shop."

Odd opened the book and closed it. He thought about autumn and swollen pumpkins, and about the unembarrassed way that Emma recited the word *bosom.*

He looked at Emma as she sipped her tea, and then said quietly, unable to stop the words that spilled out, "I would let you buy as many books as you wanted."

Emma put down her tea and held a plate of shortbread toward him.

"Oh, you *are* a sweet man, Oddmund Hus."

Odd hears the pencil-maker wheeze loudly. Henry's eyes are red-rimmed, and he places a hand on Odd's shoulder to steady himself. Then he rubs his eyes, stares, and points. Odd follows Henry's skinny finger and assumes that his own watering eyes have begun projecting visions onto the terrible landscape. What he sees is impossible. A white shape, a ghost or an angel, materializes in the distance and glides toward them, indifferent to the danger, floating unharmed over burning logs, passing fearlessly beneath flaming trees ready to topple. From a distance, the figure seems to have wings amended to human form. The other men see the specter, too, and they call out in disbelief; they shout warnings, as if the strange creature were unaware of the danger. The apparition heads directly into the heart of the fire, armed with neither ax nor shovel. Then Odd and the others realize that it is not an angel at all but something even more improbable, an ordinary man clad in white robes. The man is not floating but stumbling and staggering deeper into the fire. The men yell at him. They urge him to turn back. One man starts to run after him, but another man restrains him, warns him that the doomed man will drag him into the flames the way a drowning man will sink his would-be rescuer. The poor fool has no doubt been driven mad by the heat, they say. The men yell louder still, until the white robes grow dim and disappear into the smoking woods. An awed silence falls over them.

"The man is touched by madness," Henry explains to Odd, breathing heavily. "The natural elements can powerfully disturb the finite mind."

Odd clutches the handle of the shovel tightly and wonders what Emma is doing at this very moment. He pictures her alone, facing the flames that have driven a man mad, ruined a farm, a barn, and an untold number of trees. And what of her sensitive mind? Could her worries drive her to the kind of distraction that the pencil-maker has just described? Odd thinks of the expensive books on her shelves, the pages of beautiful, flammable words. She would never abandon them to the flames.

Henry clasps Odd's shoulder again for balance; Odd feels the subtle transfer of weight as the man leans more heavily against him. Henry churns something up from his lungs, spits, and clears his throat. Odd looks around and sees that the other men are beginning to flag in their efforts as well, unable to withstand their growing exhaustion.

"We need to keep going," Odd says. He wrestles his shovel through roots and stones and tries to read the fire's next move, tries to listen to the strategies whispered by one flame to the next, but he cannot fight back the pestering image of Emma trussed up in her enormous, elaborate undergarment, wielding an ax before a looming column of flames.

29
CALEB

The Reverend Caleb Ephraim Dowdy swims happily through the burning sea.

The fires part before him and the flames touch him not. Trees fall, shaking the ground with powerful tremors. Caleb shouts passages from Scripture, barely able to hear his own voice over the thundering fire. *"I am come to send fire on the earth; and what will I, if it be already kindled?"* Great spires of bright orange heat tower above him. Billowing clouds of soot and ash swirl around him, lift him off his feet, propel him onward. If this were indeed the anteroom to hell, it is infinitely more glorious than foretold. The image on his father's stained-glass window had never come close in intensity. Searing heat and tumultuous rumbling. No mere abstraction, this. There truly is nothing in God's creation that does not possess some form of beauty, however mysterious. He walks calmly through the maelstrom, descending deeper, level by level. If these glories are but the furnishings of purgatory, he can only shudder in anticipation of what waits at Pandemonium's heart.

Moments ago, Caleb passed legions of the condemned, toiling and suffering in the heat. Men half consumed by the fires, swinging useless implements, shovels and axes and hoes, condemned men sentenced to perform these vain tasks again and again, in infinite torment. But among them he did not see the damned soul of Desmond Boone. He saw a man weeping, and one whose clothes had been burned from his waist, his exposed torso shimmering in the heat. All around, men choked and gasped. He saw a giant, bald devil, skin black as night and ears pointed, ordering the men to work harder, sending them into the flames where they were hottest. Two more dark-skinned demons stood at his side, and their exposed arms and chests glistened in the flickering light, their muscles swelling with effort as they labored like men possessed. And these poor souls called out to Caleb, crying out for his aid, but he ignored their pleas. He is not of this place, and cannot countermand the sentences they serve.

He has left them behind, but still he can hear their desperate cries as he plunges deeper into the horrifying depths. *"Be not afraid of them that kill the body, and after that have no more than they can do. But I will forewarn you whom ye shall fear: Fear him, which after he hath killed hath power to cast into hell; yea, I say unto you, Fear him."* Caleb sees through the flames, sees through the burning to the bodies ablaze, the curling bark and smoldering skeletons of trunk and branch and limb. What is the body of man but a rootless tree, as readily devoured by flame and beetle alike, as fit to feed the hungry soil as any piece of rotting offal.

He cannot find Desmond Boone, but this gives him hope of another sort. One way or another, he will have his answer, he will demand his epiphany. He plunges on into the bright darkness, ignoring the intensifying heat, ignoring the cinders that land in his hair and scorch his scalp, ignoring the flaming branches that scratch his arms and tear at his robes; he can smell the hot fabric, heated to the point of combustion. He will have his punishment. He will demand it. If there is justice, then it must befall him now. He will not be deprived of the damnation he deserves. The heat bores into him. He can no longer hear the tormented cries of the other sufferers, only the thunderous rush of burning, like the crashing of waves at the ocean's edge. But he does not stop. He will not be deterred. He alone will move the hand of God. He will have his proof. And then he hears a crack, like the snapping of a giant's neck, and from above he sees it coming, a mighty tree towering no more, plunging to the earth, falling toward him with the speed of denunciation, and Caleb closes his eyes, thinks of the jawless skull crushed beneath the rotted trunk, and waits for the obliterating impact.

30
HENRY DAVID

Henry cannot believe it, though he sees its beginnings, the clumsy-slow retreat, the fire a dying beast, enraged and indignant. Nothing goes gently. The men are encouraged, but they do not rejoice. They are familiar with nature's deceptions. They have seen April blizzards mock naïve buds, have watched May frosts reap tender crops. The men have been fooled to hopefulness by abundant spring showers and outbluffed by late-summer droughts. They know that the diminishing flames are not finished raising havoc. The weeping man's barn has collapsed into itself, a blackened heap of lumber, more bonfire than building, and his haystacks glow red-black like spent coal. The weeping man is still among them, despondent, staggering aimlessly, as if drunk. His horses and cattle have run screaming from the flames and are nowhere to be seen. A few of his chickens remain, stupid curious, pecking at the falling soot and staring at the barn's glowing flinders. His portion of the woods is completely lost, the unharvested timber ruined, and his fields are buried beneath smoldering ash like a blanket of filthy snow. The fields, Henry thinks, will not bear fruit this season.

The men have worked at a brutal pace without respite. They can almost believe it true that Concord will be spared this destruction, but they do not allow this relief to slow their efforts. These men are happier now than they have been for some time, Henry thinks, because today they are men of action. The fire has offered them much sport, and yet he knows that they will not abandon their need for retribution. The woods have been steadily disappearing for decades, but no one has ever suggested that farmers and carpenters be judged criminals. No one has proposed levying a fine against the engineers of the Fitchburg rail line for carving a path through the peaceful forest and filling in the extremities of Walden Pond. No guilt has ever fallen upon the people of Concord for the loss of the wild green world where their town sits. But Henry knows that the men who have fought the fire here today will persist in punishing the author of this conflagration, and it is because they do not like to be awakened to themselves.

Henry works his shovel in the hot soil, flings steaming piles of dirt onto the flaming brush. His sweat mixes with soot, traces salty, acrid rivulets into his eyes and mouth. The wooden shaft is heavy as lead in his blistered hands, and he feels his motions grow stiff and sluggish. Henry watches in admiration as Young America plants his shovel deep and leans on the rounded end of its worn handle. He observes how the man's short, broad chest heaves from the exertion, how his rolled shirtsleeves, soaked with sweat, cling to the tapered swells of his shoulders and biceps, and he winces at the sight of a scarred forearm, smooth and taut. Henry is suddenly conscious of a heaviness in his chest. His breaths come short and labored, full of smoke that feels solid in his lungs. He thinks of the string of fish gasping in the bottom of their boat that morning. He doubles over, hands on knees, coughing, wheezing.

Henry feels a steadying hand on his back.

"Sit a moment," Young America says, the tip of his tongue hiding the little black tooth.

Henry shakes his head, flaps his arm. His lungs are too greedy for breath to allow him to speak. He swallows mouthfuls of air, wishes he could open his jaw wider, and then he spots a man coming toward them through the smoke, barking something indecipherable. Not until the man is upon them does Henry recognize him as one of the champion pissers from the earlier contest. The man lumbers under the weight of his paunch and uses his long-handled ax as a crutch.

"Ho there, Mr. Oddmund Hus!" says the pisser. "I am surprised to find you among us."

Henry sees Young America acknowledge the seemingly unworthy name, sees his eyes flicker left and right, as if looking for an exit.

Another man comes forward, stooped and exhausted. Henry can barely distinguish one man from another; the fire has rendered them all the same, crusted with soot and ash, looking like unfinished sculptures. The stooped man pulls at his suspenders, reveals white shadows beneath, claps a thick hand on Odd's shoulder and gives him a hearty shake.

"It helps to have a few sober men like Mr. Hus here in the fight, Mr. Addington."

The stooped man taps the handle of his ax against Addington's paunch. The fire has momentarily glazed over the petty skirmishes and disagreements, but even in this cauldron brittle impurities of former tensions flare up.

"Well, Mr. Merriam," Addington says, knocking the ax handle aside, "had you relied on the likes of Mr. Hus alone, I wager you'd be sifting through the ashes of Concord by now."

"What I find a true wonderment," Merriam replies, "is that you and your tavern friends have not belched yourselves aflame."

"Bah!" Addington grumbles. He spits a rubbery strand of tobacco juice that leaves a black paste on his chin and hisses when it hits the ground. He wipes his mouth with his thumb and looks at Odd.

"If we get our hands on the cussed imp who started this," Addington says, "come morning he'll be swinging from a tree."

"Might have been a brushfire what started it," Merriam says.

"Who'd be fool enough to burn their fields on such a day?" Addington growls, spitting again from the endless supply swelling his bottom lip.

Henry has kept quiet during the exchange, but now the direction of the bickering worries him. The men are tired and angry. Assigning blame for the fire while it still burns can come to no good. The men will not think clearly or charitably if called upon. Henry tries to get Oddmund's attention. He hopes they might slip away while the other men argue.

"Lightning," Oddmund suggests quietly. "Lightning may have done this."

It sounds like a reasonable enough possibility, but Henry is disappointed that the man he prefers to think of as Young America does not speak more forcefully.

Addington laughs. "Lightning? From this sky?"

We ought not pass judgment on the cause just yet, Henry thinks, and he is not sure whether he has said this aloud to himself. He holds up his hand and interrupts. "The wind and the trees dry as kindling and no rain . . . I should think all, to some extent, are accountable for this."

Henry sees the other men look at him as if he himself had suddenly burst into flames. He tries to explain his reasoning, but before he can say another word they hear a shout and together they turn to see if the fire has broken through the line of trenches and the swath of cleared earth. The weeping man is sounding an alarm, but not about the fire. Wandering in despair, he has stopped a few yards away and is staring at Henry from beneath the frayed brim of his straw hat. A shadow of recognition briefly crosses the man's blackened face and passes, as if he had already confirmed its impossibility. Then the shadow returns and the man's red eyes grow wide.

"There he is!" the weeping man shouts. "That's the man! Vandal! Idiot! Criminal!"

Henry sees Oddmund drop his shovel, retrieve it, and point toward the path of the fire's retreat, a tunnel of swirling heat and smoke.

"We must go to it," Oddmund says, and without waiting for them to concur he breaks into a run over charred roots and fallen branches, running not like a man in pursuit but like a man in flight.

The weeping man is running at Henry now. He throws his frayed hat to the ground and balls his hands into fists. The other men stop him and push him to the ground, thinking that he means to hurl himself into the fire like the madman they witnessed earlier. The man is furious. He can barely keep from choking on the despair-turned-rage that has lodged in his throat. As Young America disappears into the flames, the weeping man points at Henry from the ground, his arm rigid and trembling with intent.

"He's the one! Wastrel! Villain! Woodsburner!"

31
ODDMUND

Odd runs west through the trees. Those that have already burned stand mutely iridescent beneath their charred husks, like glowing pillars of coal. Odd knows the weeping man was pointing at him. Through the trees he can still hear him shouting, "Woodsburner!" But as Odd penetrates deeper into the fire these cries are gradually swallowed by the roar of the flames, which will not be outdone. Odd wonders if this is to be the moment that history at last catches up with him. He has slipped from its grasp before, but those escapes were dearly purchased. When fate could not take him from this world, it gladly took from him those parts of the world he loved most. His feet catch in the fire's tangled leavings. It has finished on the ground, but it is everywhere above, a fiery canopy dropping burning debris upon him in thick, slow clumps. Odd knows he cannot push on without setting himself aflame, but he cannot retreat; surely the men, spurred on by the weeping man's accusation, would pounce upon him, and Emma would find herself alone and unprotected. Fate would again take his world from him. Odd curses his stupidity; he should never have left Emma's side that morning.

Odd dodges the falling clusters of fire and continues running. He understands the fire in a way that the others do not. For most of the day, a steady wind has spread the flames north and east, and now the men with their shovels and axes and hoes think they have stopped its advance. They believe they will beat it back slowly, suffocate it inch by inch until they can crush its last thrashings underfoot. But Odd knows better. The fire will not burn itself out. It is a living thing, but it will not be bled to death. It will deceive them. Like a serpent cornered, it will only grow fiercer as it loses ground, coil onto itself and lash out if they do not strike at its heart.

Odd runs over seething ashes, past the Andromeda Ponds. He heads toward the concentrated flames, hurls himself straight into the dead forest covering Shrub Oak Plain. The fire slithers back, curls between black trunks already burned, looking for a place to hide. The air grows hotter, and the smoldering underbrush bites at his legs. He passes little outcroppings of flame and keeps going, ignoring the hot air that stings his eyes and burns in his throat, willing himself to suck in deep breaths to keep his legs pumping. His chest tightens and he grows dizzy. He thinks he hears voices amid the howling flames, and then realizes that the other men are pursuing him, calling his name, demanding that he return.

He passes through a stand of burning trees and continues running. Blazing eyes wink at him from the blackened woods. The fire retreats, outflanks him, and retreats again, teasing him, drawing him in. He ignores the blazing columns that sprout left and right and continues forward, swinging his shovel at the burning brambles in his way. There is a loud crack and a tall tree topples behind him, spewing flames in all directions. He is deep inside the inferno, cut off.

Odd leaps over a burning log and keeps going. He thinks of Emma, wonders if she has fled to safety or remained behind to protect the house and her precious books. He imagines the flames reaching the barn, exploding in the dry hay, running along the clothesline, engulfing the porch of the house, the door, the roof. He pictures

Emma running from door to window, unable to escape. He sees her bright orange hair and flames all around. Odd runs faster, head down, arms pumping, and he feels a sickening crunch beneath his foot and suspects what it might be before he recognizes seared fur and red skin. He stops and examines the charred lump more closely. It is an animal of considerable size, though hardly recognizable — a small deer, perhaps, a fawn. The carcass shudders, the legs twitch; the animal has not finished dying, but it is close. Then Odd notices the other blackened carcasses scattered over the ashes, caught in the underbrush, trapped beneath fallen trees, and tangled in the blackened branches. He cannot move without stepping on something dead or dying. Here the trees stand close together and the fire must have spread especially fast. It took what it wanted and moved up into the branches. Small flickerings underfoot reveal that the fire has left sentinels behind, hiding in the ashes, waiting for someone to return. Odd looks up and sees that the sky is blotted out by dark smoke and bright flames. He hears the flames cackle all around as he scans the ground for other bodies. Squirrels, birds, woodchucks, skunks, raccoons — he is unable to distinguish their charred and shrunken forms.

Odd cannot move. The forest has become a peculiar landscape. The trees are little more than phantoms, but some appear to have life in them yet, hidden away in untouched limbs. These trees might yet heal themselves, ooze sap over their grievous wounds, extrude great whorls of scarred bark, thick and knotted like permanent scabs, signposts to past tragedies. Odd knows that at this very moment some of the trees are exhaling invisible pollens, dropping bundles of cones that will open in the intense heat and laugh at the fire's futile rampage. The forest will return, populated by a greener, softer version of itself. The new trees will toughen over time. More complicated creatures, however, are not so resilient. These dead animals littering the ground will never live again. Their skeletons will not sprout tender new limbs, nor will their descendants spring from desperately scattered seed. Animals will again roam these woods, but they will be the descendants of animals fast enough to have escaped the flames and fearless enough to return and breed faster, wiser creatures. That is what the New World requires, Odd thinks; if it is to survive the intrusions of the Old World, America needs stronger animals.

Odd wonders what his father would have done had he made it to America. Men can leave their homes and their families, but no man can leave his past. Søren Hus was proof enough of this. Where could a man go to start anew, to purge himself of what runs through his veins? Crossing an ocean is not enough. Something more powerful is needed to bring about such a change, something more corrosive.

He grows conscious of the heaviness in his arms and legs, and realizes that he has not moved for some time. The muscles in his shoulders tug at one another for balance. The fire screams in his ears alongside the rushing beat of his own blood. He knows he has made a terrible mistake. He should not have separated himself from the other men. He should not have left Emma alone. The fire mocks his indecision, dances left, dances right, a center without substance. It drops on him from above. How could he have thought that he might slay it with a single, well-timed thrust? Odd steps forward and then back. The fire mirrors his movements. Odd moves forward again, and he feels the heat of the flames like sunburn on his cheeks. He steps back, and the heat bites into his tired shoulders. The fire closes in slowly, surrounding him with indifferent patience. Odd lifts his shovel and waits.

A flood of visions rises from his memory. He recalls how quickly his father became a swirling cone of flame. One moment his father was standing with the burning scroll in his hand, and in the next moment the expanding ball of red heat was lifting Odd from the deck of the *Sovereign of the Seas,* suspending him above the shocked, up-turned faces of his family. There was his mother beneath him, a large, self-possessed woman of generous proportions, shorter than his father but twice as broad, anchored to the earth by the confidence of her girth, and she stared up at him with a complex spray of emotions across her wide cheeks: terror and sorrow and hope — a hope, perhaps, that he alone might escape the horror. And in the next second the fire consumed all.

Odd remembers the cool, clear blue above him and the feeling that he was being pressed flat against the dome of the sky. He remembers holding his breath as he rose impossibly high on the blast of hot air. Far below, he saw his mother waving at him, not in farewell but in warning, and he thought that he heard her voice encouraging him, reminding him, urging him: *breathe.* He inhales and chokes on searing heat. The fire has come for him again. Through the smoke he sees an impertinent flame nibbling at the cuffs of his trousers. It has tracked him from the Old World, pursued him across an ocean, determined to carry out his sentence.

And then he hears the voices of the men. They have broken through and can see his predicament. They shout to him. They tell him he is burning and they urge him to act. They have not come to apprehend him; they have come to help. And then Odd smells something sharp and sees the flames scurrying giddily up his trouser leg. He drops to his knees, onto his back, rolls, smothers the flames, and he is back on his feet. He feels a stinging in his eyes, sees the blistered skin on his arms, and is angry. It is a euphoric outpouring of anger, and he lets the feeling carry him forward.

All at once, the understanding comes to him: he is supposed to be here. He can see that this has been his destination from the moment he washed up onto the beach at Boston Harbor. Odd puts aside the fears that he will not be able to convince his pursuers that he did not bring this fire here. It is no longer of any consequence; this fire will not be his ruin. He determines to put an end to it, regardless of how it started. He will not swing from a scaffold simply because that is what fate has decreed. His blood will not rule him as it ruled other members of the family Hus.

He attacks the fire wildly, screaming at the flames. He swings his arms above his head and brings them down, smashing the blade of his shovel onto the many-headed beast. He hammers so powerfully that the wooden handle splinters under the blows. He tosses the broken parts into the fire and does not need to call for another; an ax materializes in each hand, brought forth by the men dumbfounded by his ferocity. Two axes now, one in each hand, and his arms fly over his head and down, smashing flames, scattering brush and branches. The men join him, following him into the heart of the fire. They shovel dirt over the flaming detritus that his flying axes spew in his wake. Some of the men pause in disbelief, and then resume, spurred on by the sureness of Odd's advance, arms spinning, chewing through the fire. They cheer their looming success. Odd does not look back, does not check to see if they are following. He knows where he is going and what he must do. The fire will not escape him. It will not dictate his end. It cowers, tries to flee, but he is on it, crushing it beneath his boots. Flames scatter and dwindle before him, and the men fall in line behind their new leader. Odd feels transformed, tempered by the intense heat. He feels the blood in his veins come to a boil. He has become a different animal — something stronger, something entirely new.

32
ELIOT

Eliot is in trouble, though he is slow to admit it.

It happens so quickly, it seems a temporary thing until it is not. He moves to the right when the others move left, and the fire, seeking opportunity, comes between.

He is not certain how it begins, but he watches them run, one after another, until there is no one left around him. Like madmen, they breach the very battlements they have constructed and follow one another into the heart of the blazing woods: a useless display of courage. Eliot stands at the end of one of the shallow trenches that extends as far as the fire to his right. They were to continue digging, to join this trench to the other. For hours the men labored, chopping trees and clearing brush. Before him stretches a blackened expanse where they have beaten back the flames; behind him, a denuded strip of earth runs alongside the trench and stops, unfinished. Certainly the fire cannot cross these barriers, Eliot thinks. There is no need to pursue, no need to fight on; all that remains is to let the flames burn themselves out.

But he hears the men shouting for those ahead to return, and then he hears them calling for him to follow. Eliot shouts to no one in particular, and the sound is meaningless to his own ears. He yells simply to match the cacophony around him. Something in his chest tugs at him, makes him feel that he should run after them. But he cannot summon the courage, and with each passing second they grow more distant. He knows there is another group of men somewhere to his left; he can hear the clank and scrape of their shovels, the clap of their axes as they work their way toward him, to join their work to his, but he cannot see them through the thick smoke. He shovels faster, flinging dirt onto the licks of flame that creep forward toward the trench. He is suddenly gripped by an overwhelming desire to rewrite the scene in which he finds himself — a playwright should never place characters in circumstances so inextricable. The stage dictates that there always be a way out: a door unlocked, a hidden closet, a forgotten weapon ready at hand. An audience, Eliot knows, has little patience with the reality of undeserved, inexorable doom.

The fire surges in the distance and the smoke surrounds him as he looks for a way in, a way to follow the others, but he cannot move. He cannot reach the men who have run forward, and he cannot find those who have stayed behind. He knows he is nothing like DeMonte; he is not the hero he would write. Before him he can see only fire and smoke, and he is terrified. He cannot understand how these sensible men could plunge headlong into it. And now, in their absence, the fire creeps toward Eliot in fits and starts, trying to reclaim the ground, useless earth it lately conceded to the swinging shovels and axes.

The heat makes him squint until the bright flames become flickering diamonds between his eyelashes. And that is when he sees it, a wink, a sparkle in the dark smoke that fills him with a chilling realization: *it knows what it's doing.* The fire studies the barrier the men have constructed, looking for a way around it. Eliot watches flames stagger toward him, searching for unburned bits of terrain, anything to sustain them long enough to make a last-gasp attempt at the true prize — Concord — and he understands that he alone stands poised to stop the fumbling attack. The fire lunges toward him, and Eliot hurls dirt in wild sprays, stepping backward with each desperate shovelful. He wants to move forward, to follow the other men, who surely need his help more than ever. Instead, he thrusts his shovel into the bottom of the trench and leaves it standing upright in the blackened soil as he backs away across the firebreak. A billowing mass of gray smoke rolls over him like an open hand.

Eliot can no longer hear the shouts of the men digging and chopping their way toward him on his left, only the howl of the flames, and through the smoke he sees the winking eyes telling him that the fire is there, too. The fire seems for a moment to change its mind, to retreat unsteadily, and then Eliot understands that he is the one retreating, carried backward by his own uncertain steps. The fire prods him, mocks him, forces him to follow his heels blindly.

This is not at all how Eliot envisioned that the fire would behave in *The House of Many Windows.* He had not given any thought to the powerful confusion of heat and smoke. He understands now that the burning of a house onstage might cause the bonnets of the women in the front rows to burst into flames. And what would keep soot and ash from raining down upon the entire audience? And the roar of the flames — he had not thought of this at all — surely that would drown out any dialogue. There would, in fact, be little for the actors to do save run about the stage in a pantomime of distress. The grand conflagration at the end of the play had not been his idea to begin with, and he realizes now that if it were an impracticable effect after all, then he truly had no idea how he would end his play.

Reworking *The House of Many Windows* to suit the requirements of the Boston Museum proved far more difficult than Eliot had expected. He attacked the manuscript with a vigor bordering on vengeance. He had heavy curtains made for the windows of his study, so that he might work in the darkened room during the day, but the sunlight still found its way in around the edges. On warm days, he could feel the heat radiating from the other side, the curtains squarely haloed by sunlight.

One Sunday, a few weeks after Eliot's meeting with Moses Kimball, a soft knock at the door interrupted his editing.

"Eliot?" Margaret searched for him in the shadows. "I thought you might be in here.

What on earth are you doing sitting in the dark?"

Margaret made her way to the curtains and pulled them back, allowing the bright day to flood the room. Eliot held his hands to his eyes and saw flashing blue squares fluttering where his stack of writing paper had been.

"Margaret, please."

"Eliot, you look terrible. And our guests will be here soon."

"Guests?"

"It's *Sunday,* Eliot. We're having dinner, remember?"

Margaret finished tying back the heavy curtains with braided tassels, and smoothed the folds of her dress. "There. That's better. Isn't that better?"

"When are they arriving?"

"Father is already here, and he has brought Mr. and Mrs. Durham with him. I will entertain them until the rest arrive, but you must get yourself ready at once."

Eliot looked at the manuscript before him, littered with *x*'s and marginal scribblings. On many pages he had crossed out all but one or two lines, and a few pages had not fared as well. He rubbed his eyes. He wore his spectacles only to see at a distance, but lately even words at arm's length had begun to seem a bit blurred. He no longer knew how many years had passed since he penned the first page. It sometimes seemed he had been at work on *The House of Many Windows* for most of his life, since before he had married Margaret, since before he had become a father, since before he had worn spectacles at all, and now the only way he had found to save his troubled masterpiece was by undoing it.

"Eliot. Are you all right, dear?"

Eliot did not know that he was going to ask the question until the words had already fallen from his tongue. "Why did you marry me, Margaret?"

"What?" Margaret stared at him, hands at her hips. "Why did I — Eliot, there is hardly time for this now! We have guests below."

"Please. It should be easy to answer." Eliot looked at his butchered manuscript, and he thought of the conversation he and Mr. Mahoney had had so many years earlier. He had never asked Margaret if the bookstore was her idea, and she had always pretended that it was a surprise.

"For all of the reasons you can certainly imagine," Margaret said with a tight, indulgent smile. "Because I love you and respect you. Will that do?"

"Yes, but why?"

"Oh, Eliot, really. It is because . . . you have a quality that so many men lack. You are a practical man."

"Practical?" Eliot felt something shrink inside him. "I thought you believed in my work — in my writing, I mean."

"Well, of course I do. It is what first distinguished you from all the boorish, moneyed men that Father so often introduced to me. And your devotion to your art still distinguishes you from such men. But, more important, you are not the sort to sacrifice the practicalities of living to airy dreams that may never come to fruition. You have always provided for your family, and you are a good father to your children. You are a *reasonable* man, Eliot. It is a most uncommon quality. Father approves, and so do I. Will that do for now? I have left Father alone with the Durhams. . . ."

Eliot nodded. He had expected something more, but he was not entirely disappointed; instead, he felt a relentless sobriety wash over him. His eyes were still adjusting to the piercing bright light, and when Margaret crossed the room she seemed to him to be pushing her own shadow. He saw her come toward him, then saw her turn abruptly toward the door.

"Father!"

"Those stairs are a fright." Mr. Mahoney stood in the doorway, balancing his bulk forward with both hands on the head of his cane.

Margaret rushed to her father's side, but he waved her away. "You shouldn't overwork yourself like that," she said. "Where are Mr. and Mrs. Durham?"

"Terrible company," Mr. Mahoney grumbled, "but what would half of the coffee merchants in Boston do without Mr. Durham, eh? What are you doing, Eliot? Working on a Sunday?"

"Eliot is working on one of his plays, Father."

"Excellent recreation. Just the other day I wrote a poem about my cat, right after balancing the accounts for the week. You can tell us all about it over sherry. Unless it is unsuitable for the ladies."

"Really, Father." Margaret laughed, moving toward him. "Eliot would never write such rubbish. Come, we should give him a moment to prepare for our guests."

"I believe I can suffer the Durhams' company for another quarter hour," Mr. Mahoney said with mock resignation. "Then we'll talk of the coffee trade, Eliot. Impressive profits to be had."

Margaret gently prodded her father from

behind. "He'll join us soon," she said, smiling, and looking at Eliot she mouthed, "Hurry up."

Eliot heard their voices recede down the stairwell, and then heard Mr. Mahoney's booming laugh greeting the Durhams as if they had only just arrived. He felt his face grow warm on the side facing the bright window. He sometimes pondered what would happen if he opened one of the windows and walked out into the light. Even when the room was dark, he wondered: if he were to pull back the curtains, crank open the windows, and step confidently into the bright air, would the solid shafts of sunlight support his steps so that he might walk about freely above the city of Boston? The thought always brought him a momentary thrill.

And now Eliot is wondering much the same thing as he faces the burning woods alone. Would it be practical — *reasonable* — to run into the flames as the others had done? He knows that the men who have thrown themselves into the conflagration need his help. They will need every available pair of arms that can swing an ax or shovel, but Eliot's arms hang limp as he imagines the terrible things that are happening where the other men have gone. If he were to follow them now, it is entirely possible that he might never sit at his desk again. He feels the ground shudder as a massive tree falls somewhere behind the impenetrable curtains of smoke. Eliot shuffles sideways, tracing a close circle in the black earth.

Those men are fools, Eliot thinks. He watches the flames scatter, sees them test the edges of the trench, searching for something to burn, something to take them to the other side. Little points of flame hop toward the trench, lurch for the clearing where Eliot stands, and expire in midair. The fire cannot cross the divide, but it does not give up. It is possible, Eliot thinks, that a shift in the wind might send the flames skipping east to the Walden Woods, and a strong enough gust might launch the flames over the trench into the trees that stand on the other side of the firebreak. If that were to happen, there would be no one here to help him. Eliot faces the flames across the divide, and he feels suddenly vulnerable.

A few feet away, Eliot sees the wooden handle of his shovel begin to smolder in the heat where he left it stuck upright in the ground. He has been treading steadily backward without realizing it. He knows he can hesitate no longer. He decides. He takes a deep breath, gathers his courage, then pivots on his heels and runs away through the dark clouds, toward the clear, cool air of Concord.

33
HENRY DAVID

Young America is gone. Henry watches him disappear into the fire like a man fleeing the specters of his own conscience. Some of the men pursue him, hesitantly at first, and then moments later the rest follow, with Henry swept along in their midst. No one can remain behind when one of their number dares to move forward.

The fire closes behind the men in front of Henry, and he calls to those nearest him to fan out over the charred ground. They swing their axes at the crippled half-burned trunks, felling trees left and right. They cut a fresh swath the fire cannot cross. There are more shouts, more orders; in confusion each man seeks to direct the action of another, but in the end they only narrate their own deeds. For a half hour more, they labor without pause. And then they stop, and wait, and watch.

The fire makes several attempts at crossing the new void they have carved. It marshals its forces, hurls itself skyward, aims at the treetops across the divide, lurches hopefully toward the distant, tantalizing rooftops of Concord. But each effort diminishes its intensity.

The men stop chopping, stop shoveling, devote themselves to selfish gasping. There is no cheering, no triumphant slapping of backs. Their victory is gradual. It is, Henry thinks, an anticlimax, a slow dawning. It affords no moment that one might celebrate as *now*. Portions of the woods as yet lie under siege, but the men have halted the main advance. They stand wearily in the firebreak, leaning on handles, watching the fire eat itself, and as the smoke thins, new scenes emerge: ghostly shadows, blackened trunks, tall sentinels stripped of bark and branch and leaf, a giant forest of silent spent matchsticks.

Never has Henry been so relieved to see a creation of his own hands approach its end. He has mangled his creations before. He has torn apart drawings of flawed perspective, blotted out the malformed poems that sometimes issued from his pen, but the relief then was for embarrassment avoided. And, now that the enemy has been halted, the murmuring begins anew. There is talk already of pecuniary losses, of recrimination and restitution, as if a man could assign a price to the soil and the sky and the living woods. But, in fact, men can and do. There will be estimates of lumber lost. There will be the untallied damages to shovels and axes and hoes and boots and clothes. There will be complaints of chickens unable to lay for months because of the disturbance, and together these losses will accrue considerable sums. When weighed against what might have been suffered — the possible destruction of Concord, the potential loss of life — the sums will seem small, but when considered alone the amounts will amaze. Already someone points out that even the felled trees at the firebreak will be of no use to the carpenter, smoke-damaged as they are.

Henry at last sees Edward Sherman Hoar among the others. Edward sees him, too, but they do not acknowledge each other. They keep their distance, not wanting to invite further suspicion or accusation. The weeping man has returned to his ruined farm, and no one has yet asked Henry about the man's accusation. They will not believe it until the story is repeated, until Henry confesses to the deed as Edward no doubt already has. It occurs to Henry that it may prove some benefit to count Edward Sherman Hoar as his companion in this misadventure. Fortunate accident, that. In deference to Edward's esteemed father, Squire Hoar, there may follow a willful forgetting, just short of forgiveness. But Henry knows that he will not smother his sorrow, will not ask forgiveness from men. He will tend and cherish his regret, until he finds himself restored. He will remain behind after the men have left; he will find his way back to the beginning and finish the excursion begun that morning. Perhaps he will spend the night here, alone, among the ashes.

And these men, Henry thinks, have stood for a moment on the brink of something greater than themselves. These men have had a precious opportunity to act as men, and now they will return to their groveling lives. They will return to the ordained destruction of land and living things that pretends offense at accidental loss. As towns and cities expand across the continent, woods like these, vaster tracts by far, will disappear beneath ax and saw and the other engines that men will devise to quicken the clearing of what brought them here. The railway slicing through the woods at Walden will bring more men to help topple solitude's slow reign. More and still more will distribute themselves far and wide across the surface of things; each day they will extend their numbers over the untouched land, while their individual lives remain as shallow as ever. In all mythologies, a forest is a sacred place, but those who arrive on America's shores will continue to bring with them the old displacing fables, until one day they will voice disdain for the new world that can remember no legends of its own.

■ ■ ■ ■

II
AFTER

NEW ENGLAND
SPRING, 1844

■ ■ ■ ■

The fire, we understand, was communicated to the woods through the thoughtlessness of two of our citizens, who kindled it in a *pine stump,* near the Pond, for the purpose of making a chowder. As everything around them was as combustible almost as a fire ship, the flames spread with rapidity, and hours elapsed before it could be subdued. It is to be hoped that this unfortunate result of sheer carelessness, will be borne in mind by those who

may visit the woods in [the] future for recreation.
— *Concord Freeman,* May 3, 1844

That night I watched the fire, where some stumps still flamed at midnight in the midst of the blackened waste, wandering through the woods by myself; and far in the night I threaded my way to the spot where the fire had taken, and discovered the now broiled fish, — which had been dressed, — scattered over the burnt grass.
— *The Journal of Henry David Thoreau,*
1850

34

ANEZKA AND ZALENKA

Three days after the fire is extinguished, the forest still smolders, mourning its loss. At night it glows, its blackness punctured by thousands of glittering orange eyes blinking angrily beneath the ashes. Sometimes a small fire breaks out, but with nothing left to burn it struggles against its own rapacious hunger and vanishes as quickly as it appears.

On the third day, Zalenka and Anezka go searching for wood. Many others are doing the same. Summer is coming, but the cold New England nights are far from over and winter will come again soon enough. Anezka complains that she does not expect to live through another winter, but she says this every year.

It is Zalenka's idea. She says it makes sense to take what advantage they can from the misfortune. There is plenty of dead wood to be had, she says, and the men who fought the fire cut down many trees that did not burn. Even charred logs will be of use once they scrape off the blackened bits. Anezka does not want to go. She says that Zalenka only wants to see the damage, like the rest of the silly tourists who arrive each day from Boston to gawk at the forest that is no longer there and take away handfuls of ash as keepsakes.

Anezka taps her temples with a crooked finger.

"The eyes, I do not miss so much sometime. Not to see bad thing, is good thing."

Zalenka hitches their mule to the old, rickety cart that looks like it has given up hope of ever being repaired. She helps Anezka up onto the narrow bench and then climbs up next to her. The mule pulls gently, as if he were afraid of pulling the cart to pieces. Like the cart, Zalenka found the mule among the cast-off belongings of others. The poor creature had been beaten and abused and left for useless. Zalenka named him Václav, fed him from their garden, and bandaged his suppurating wounds, which formed thick scars along his haunches like knots in a tree trunk. Václav's hide is dark brown, but, like everything else in Concord now, it is speckled with the gray soot that falls like spring snow whenever the wind blows through the skeletal trees. Although the women live almost a mile from the site of the fire, they need to keep their windows shut against the loitering clouds of floury ash.

The ground is still warm when Zalenka and Anezka arrive. Václav, disconcerted by the smell, refuses to leave the road, so Zalenka pulls a sled from the back of the wagon and drags it in her left hand and Anezka in her right. As Anezka predicted, there are already people in the burnt woods, but fewer than they expected. Some well-dressed visitors stand on an elevated patch of ground, surveying the destruction and making soft noises of amazement from under the brims of fancy hats. Local people sift through the ashes, sleeves rolled, trousers tucked into boots, looking for what can still be burned, hunting for wood that might yet be useful as lumber. Zalenka sees a man pushing a wheelbarrow piled with small, blackened animal carcasses, and she declines to ponder his intentions. Here and there thin wisps of smoke issue from the ground, as if the earth were breathing in troubled volcanic gasps. Zalenka's nose and eyes burn, and she sees that Anezka's milky eyes are watering as well.

"We should go, maybe," Zalenka suggests.

Anezka wipes her useless tears and squints at the pale shadows she just barely discerns against the dark horizon. "Pshh! Now, after we are come here?" Anezka coughs. "Take what we need. Tonight I will make nice tea for the throat."

The air is hazy, as on a humid summer afternoon, but there are none of the gnats or swarming flies that usually herald warm weather. Aside from the voices of human scavengers, the woods are quiet — no chattering or barking or twittering or buzzing of any kind.

Zalenka walks into the woods, scanning the ground. Anezka stands with the reins of the sled in one hand, and she looks so much like a child with a toy on a leash that it makes Zalenka's heart ache. Zalenka stoops to pick up a charred branch and smiles. She cannot help it. She still finds the world a wondrous, capricious thing: cruel and unjust, it can become inexplicably, unexpectedly generous. It has, after all, granted them these years together, a whole lifetime to be lived at the end of a life. Already, Zalenka begins to think of the tea that Anezka will prepare later, some unique creation of local herbs and roots that she will blindly identify and measure out with sensitive fingertips.

When they first arrived in Boston, penniless, hungry, it was Anezka who turned whatever they stumbled upon into something edible. Dead birds and rodents and rotten vegetables became, in her hands, a feast. Too old for factory work, and too clumsy to pass as a seamstress, Zalenka eventually discovered that people beyond the reach of city physicians were willing to pay generously for an experienced midwife. Zalenka put her skills to work, setting bones and cleaning wounds and pulling rotten teeth for farmers. And after Zalenka found work Anezka continued to seek out new ways to coax startling flavors from the simple garden behind the abandoned cabin they had adopted and redeemed.

It was an odd cabin they found, far from the road, a solitary outpost in the woods. The cabin had no stove, and the small, poorly built hearth looked as though it had never been used. It held no other comforts, but it seemed as if it had been left specifically for them, as if the world were trying to meet their simple needs in recompense for the deprivations it had visited upon them in the Old World. On the floor at the center of the room, they found a pile of small, colorful stones, veined with contrasting minerals. They wrapped them in a cloth bag and put them aside, in case the previous owner returned for them one day. Zalenka surprised herself with the repairs she ably made to the roof. Generous souls in Concord helped, gave advice and supplies, lent tools. A young man arrived unexpectedly, a white-haired Norwegian with a gentle smile and a black tooth, just passing through the woods, he had said, though he seemed surprised to find them there, as if he had been expecting to spend the night in the cabin himself. He reassured them that the man who had once lived there was not intending to return. He asked if he might have the colorful bag of stones, and in return offered to build them an extra room for a kitchen. While he was at it, he extended the porch as well, so that Zalenka and Anezka could position their rocking chairs to watch the rising and setting of the sun through the trees at any season. It surprised Zalenka to learn that men had once debated the meaning of the sun's shifting path, when they needed only to accept it as a fact and adjust their perspectives accordingly.

Zalenka sifts through the ashes on the forest floor and considers the good fortune they have enjoyed in recent years. The world still surprises them with so many things to savor. Zalenka feels at times that she wants to do something to repay its belated kindness. She spots another branch poking up from the ashes, and when it proves too big to carry she snaps it into smaller pieces over her knee.

A few yards away, Anezka pulls the small sled over fallen branches, slowly feeling her way into the ruined forest. She is not as helpless or fragile as Zalenka likes to think, and she occasionally feels the need to prove this, though she knows that her weakness appeals to some deep-rooted need in Zalenka's nature. The details and colors of the world dropped away years ago, but she can still see vague shadows enough to keep from walking into objects that honestly present themselves. It does not bother her, the loss of vision. She has seen enough of the world in the first half of her life to know that some things are best seen in black and white, while other things should not be looked upon at all.

She sifts blindly through the ankle-deep ash with her toes and clutches the reins of the sled, as if the thin leather strap anchors her to the rest of the world. She is reminded suddenly of a small toy that her father made for her when she was scarcely old enough to speak, a little wooden dog that she had pulled around on wheeled legs. It was strange how these memories announced themselves, rising from beneath the ruins of other experiences too bleak to admit memory's grasp. The recollection makes her clutch the reins all the tighter. Zalenka sometimes upbraids Anezka for allowing her heart to harden, but Anezka can never find the words to express that this is not the case at all. Given the enormity of the past and the future, she simply finds that there is more to care about in the world than there are hearts to bear the weight; picking and choosing is a matter of surviving.

Anezka strikes something hard with her foot and retrieves a good-sized chunk of wood on her own, but she can tell by feeling along its length that it is burned beyond use. She hears the amazed voices of the tourists as they climb back into their carriages and set off. Strange, she thinks, how this new world, as yet inexperienced in the tragedies that wearied the Old World centuries ago, seems to inspire an insatiable hunger for disaster. These Americans seem to think that the horrors endured by others are spectacles for their entertainment. Their own terrors will come soon enough — terrors that will leave their storybooks and walk among them, through their streets, into their homes and bedrooms. She does not wish this sad knowledge on them, but she knows it is coming. She shudders when she hears men talk excitedly of the war they believe is on its way, a fight that will be waged not against a foreign invader but between the Americans of the North and the South. Some men say the fight is inevitable, though Anezka does not believe that the terrible things men do to one another should ever be thought of as unavoidable. If the New World does not grant men the freedom to rise above the dark paths mapped by fate, then what is the point of coming here?

Anezka squints into the darkness but cannot tell which of the shadows belongs to Zalenka. She starts to call out but stops. She knows Zalenka is there; she knows that she will never again be alone. Anezka ventures forward a few steps, dragging her feet through the ashes until they strike another fallen tree. She kicks along its side to determine whether there is a branch small enough for her to lift without Zalenka's help. Something seems unusual about the tree. She kicks it again, and her jaw falls open in amazement.

Too far away to see what Anezka has found, Zalenka drops her armload of wood as soon as she hears Anezka's shout and stumbles toward her as fast as she can, swinging her stiff legs over the blackened debris. It is not quite a scream but something closer to startled amazement. Zalenka finds Anezka standing next to the upturned roots of a large tree trunk half buried in the ashes.

"Co se děje?! Jsi v pořádku?!"

"I am fine," Anezka reassures her friend. "But please, you must watch. Amazing things. These American woods, they live."

Anezka reaches out for Zalenka's support, then she swings her right leg with as much force as she can muster and kicks the fallen tree. The mound of debris stirs and a weak moan rises from under the ashes.

Anezka smiles. "It is a miracle, this moaning tree, yes? An American golem."

Zalenka drops to her knees and claws through the charred earth until her fingers strike something soft in the soot. She pulls her kerchief from her head and wipes at the soft black mound until something pale emerges — a round opening that moves, opens and closes — a mouth — then a nose, a pair of eyes. The moaning increases, the eyes flutter open, and Zalenka sees in them the unmistakable shock of recognition. Zalenka grabs Anezka's arm.

"It is the priest."

"The priest for the new church?"

"He."

Together they dig through the ashes. Caleb Ephraim Dowdy is pinned under the massive tree, his right leg twisted at a telling angle beneath the weight of the trunk. At least one bone is broken, Zalenka can tell, but the size of the tree has saved him from the fire. Most of the heavy trunk is burned away, enough that Zalenka is able to rock it back and forth while Anezka pulls at Caleb's left arm until he is out from under it.

Caleb's lips work and he coughs; he tries to speak. He has not had a pipe in three days, and the effects on his brain are even more devastating than the hunger and thirst and pain that hold the rest of his body in thrall.

"The leg is broken," Zalenka says, examining the twisted limb.

Anezka disappointedly kicks the fallen tree a final time. "The tree, it is not living? Pity."

Instinctively, Zalenka has already begun to tie a straight branch around Caleb's broken leg with her kerchief. He writhes in agony as Zalenka works; a dry hiss issues from his lips.

"We must care for him," Zalenka says. "He will need food and drink, and much rest."

Anezka feels a heavy weight in her chest. "The church builder? No. To the road we can take him. Someone will find him."

"Anezka! How can you say such a thing? What would God in heaven think?"

"It is God who should worry what I am thinking," Anezka says, surprised at herself for uttering the thought out loud.

"I will not hear it," Zalenka snaps. "This is for us to do. We must repay the kindness we receive."

Anezka shrugs in submission. "You can help his wounds?"

"There are broken bones only, I think." Zalenka tightens the splint, and Caleb moans under the pressure, then he laughs deliriously.

"He is mad with the pain. We must take him home."

Anezka sighs. She will make room in her heart if that is what Zalenka wants. And she knows Zalenka is probably right, even if she is reckless with her sympathy. If this new country is ever to escape the nightmares of the old, its new inhabitants must become a kinder race, recklessly so.

Together, they drag Caleb onto the sled and secure him with the ropes they brought to tie down their firewood. He moans but does not struggle. His body lies slack as Anezka feels along the lengths of the ropes and checks the knots with nimble fingers.

"Here," Anezka says. "This one will come undone. If we are to help, we must not do worse."

Zalenka smiles as she tightens the sloppy knot. "You do not have the cold heart that you pretend."

Anezka grunts dismissively and fishes around in the sled for the reins. "I hope he will not be eating much."

The two women pull the sled back to the road, pausing several times to catch their breath. Caleb continues to mumble incoherently. Getting the sled into the wagon is a difficult business, and he cries out as they jostle him up the inclined gate.

"Can he live, do you think?" Anezka asks.

"There is not much bleeding, and there is yet color in his face. It is rest that he needs. To mend is all."

Caleb lifts his head far enough to look into the faces of the two old women, and then he begins to cackle weakly.

"At long last," he croaks.

"What does he say?" Zalenka asks.

Anezka leans closer to his face, picking out the shadows of features. "You are building the church of bones, yes?"

Caleb looks back and forth between Anezka and Zalenka, and his eyes roll wildly. Zalenka has seen the reaction before in desperately injured men.

"Is it true?" Caleb moans. "Am I come to hell?"

Caleb watches hopefully as the two women confer.

"We must be swift," Zalenka says. "He has a brain fever, I think."

"Am I come to hell?" Caleb asks again, weak laughter rattling in his parched throat.

"Ride with him," Zalenka says. "I will walk. Václav cannot pull us all."

Anezka climbs into the back of the wagon and Zalenka hands her a flask of water.

"Give him this."

Anezka dribbles the cool water over Caleb's lips, but he sputters under the flow, flinching as if the water were acid.

"Is this my punishment at last?" Caleb pleads as the wagon begins to move forward.

"Rest," Anezka says.

"Am I come to hell? Tell me!" Caleb stares at Anezka's milky eyes; the sinews in his neck strain like taut ropes as he struggles to hold his head up.

"Am I?"

Anezka considers the question for a moment and leans close to his ear.

"Yes," she says softly. "Yes. You are in this world still."

35
ELIOT

The fire is hot enough to blacken, and it
will burn if they are careless. The secret is
to regulate the temperature with distance
and motion. Constant motion. The boy
seems never to remember this last part, and
the skillet inevitably burns, ruining its valuable contents, filling the place with an acrid
stench approximating singed fur. Why is it,
Eliot wonders, that some edible stuffs seem
to demand inexact comparisons to what
they are not: animals, plants, seasons, feelings, an unnecessary surfeit of words? Eliot
will make it a point from now on to describe
things as they are, to eschew metaphors for
a more economic language.

"This way," he instructs his son.

Eliot feels the muscles in his forearm swell
against his rolled sleeves as he shows the
boy the circular motion that keeps the hard
yellow beans shuttling around in the skillet.
Then he hands it back.

"Have you ever tasted them uncooked?" The boy struggles with the heavy skillet.

Eliot nods. "I do not recommend it. It is fire that imparts the flavor."

Wearing a clumsy pair of thick gloves, Josiah holds the blistered iron handle in both hands. He is small and thin and probably weighs little more than the skillet he counterbalances by leaning back into his hips, projecting a center of gravity into the space in front of his knees. The skillet traces a tight ellipse above the fire as Josiah's narrow hips orbit in the opposite direction. Eliot barely keeps from laughing at the innocent, indecent dance; he doesn't want to confuse the boy. Roasting coffee beans is a serious task.

Sounds of hammering echo from the other side of the room, where workmen are installing tables and booths. In the middle of the room, a carpenter works on the empty frame of a new doorway to be set into the wall when complete. Eliot straightens and steps back from the fire. He sees tiny beads of sweat appear on the boy's forehead and watches his hips rock in wider circles, as if he were desperately trying to conjure a host of libidinous demons from the flames.

"I think I've got it, Mr. Calvert." So eager to please, this boy. They had agreed that it would be proper for Josiah to refer to him as Mr. Calvert while they were in the place of business, and Eliot has never had to remind his son, not once.

"You're doing fine, Josiah."

Eliot turns and steps through the rubble into his bookshop. He would have to remind the workmen again. They broke through the wall last week; more than ample time has passed for them to sweep up the debris. He is making changes, just as he promised himself. The shelves that once held books by Emerson, Hawthorne, Irving, Alcott, Longfellow, are empty now and the bare planks stand propped against the wall. There is empty space only where the shelves once hung, the brick wall punctured by a toothy hole opening into the building where Josiah gyrates with the skillet of smoking coffee beans.

Eliot looks in the boy's direction, but he is staring at the empty space itself. He has no plans to relocate the displaced American authors. None of Eliot's regular customers would miss them. Let them gather in Ticknor's bookstore with their pockets turned inside out and their heads full of idle thoughts. Let them chatter around Mr. Fields as if ideas alone had force enough to shape the world. The best literature has already been written. The best words were committed to paper well before literate men set foot on American soil. America does not need more books. The New World does not need to re-create the literary accomplishments of the Old. What it needs is commerce. It cannot survive on dreams and words alone. Trade, goods, business — these are the tangible things that will fuel the engines of America.

Eliot decided against opening a bookshop in Concord, but he found another way to expand his Boston business. What he needed was a change. Upon his return, he took the money he had set aside for producing *The House of Many Windows* at the Boston Museum, purchased the shop next door, contacted Mr. Durham at the suggestion of Margaret's father, and set about establishing a coffeehouse on the premises. The decision immediately proved to be a good one. There was always much to be done, and he threw himself into the distracting labor wholeheartedly. He has recently ordered a new sign, simpler though more prominent than the former: "Calvert Bookshop and Coffeehouse."

The expanded business requires a greater amount of his time than the bookshop alone ever did, but he fortifies himself with copious amounts of the stimulating black liquid, and he often works well into the night, long after other merchants have closed their shops. The new business means more of everything. More stock, more invoices, more bills, more employees, more profit, more worry, and dealing with coffee merchants was a far trickier matter than dealing with printers and publishers. Coffee beans are subject to the capricious whims of the marketplace, prices fluctuated wildly, and Eliot was forever on his guard against paying the inflated prices of yesterday or tomorrow. He hopes that the increased profit from the coffeehouse might make possible the country cottage that he and Margaret have talked about building near Walden Pond, a place where they might get away from the city and entertain friends from time to time.

The work is satisfaction in itself, and whenever his thoughts wander back to the plays that remain unfinished he works harder, medicating himself with the numbing exhaustion of labor. He learns to ignore the pointless yearnings that do little to advance his business. Lately, he has begun to feel an almost constant pressure behind his eyes, a black pain that never seems to dissipate. And at times he detects a heaviness in his chest, but these sensations he attributes to the misfortunes of age. Hard work is not without its penalties, and he knows he must accept the costs with the rewards.

Eliot returns to the room next door to check the progress of the roasting. He pushes his sleeves up to his elbows, exposing a shiny, scarred patch of skin on his right forearm. No one could accuse him of not being a man. Everyone knows that he fought the great fire of the Concord Woods; he runs not *one* but *two* businesses here in this modern Athens; he provides for his family, and he will leave a legacy. He is one of the bedrocks of America, a living force in its young economy. Eliot pulls out his pocket watch to remind Josiah of the appropriate time to keep the beans over the flame. He can see the boy's skinny arms trembling from the effort, struggling against their own weakness, and he feels a sadness mingle with his sense of duty. He will teach this boy about the world, about hard work, sacrifice, and compromise.

Margaret does not like that Eliot makes Josiah work like this. She does not think it at all appropriate, but there are things his son needs to know, lessons he must learn, and he is certain that Josiah will become a better man for it. Eliot will see to it that

Josiah chooses a narrow and definite path and remains faithful to it. He will teach him that the world demands arduous labor from men who would be successful, that every pleasure in this life must be earned. Eliot taps the glass of his watch and then indicates the iron stand where Josiah is to set down the heavy skillet once the second hand completes its agonizingly slow sweep. The red light from the fire flickers against the gold watch in Eliot's palm and, farther down, the light twinkles over the polished gold fob, shaped like an open book, that hangs decoratively from the chain.

36
HENRY DAVID

It happens again, almost exactly as before.

Only this time it is not lockjaw but fever that seizes him.

For a full week after the last flame flickers out, Henry is weak with it. He cannot determine the fever's cause, and he tries to keep his ailment secret. He places clammy fingers to hot cheeks. He wakes to cool spring mornings wrapped in sheets dampened to translucence by his own poisoned sweat. He marvels that he does not drown in perspiration; yet even these prodigious night sweats cannot extinguish the fire that he feels dancing beneath his skin, along his arms, down his legs, roiling within his torso. He cannot tell anyone. Not this time. His family has not forgotten the counterfeit symptoms following his brother's death. He cannot again call upon their sympathies until he is certain that this time his disease is real. But he feels that he is burning up.

He can hear the faint crackling of flames consuming his ligaments and tendons, feel his bones baking brittle, smell the faint wisps of cooked flesh issuing from his pores. He knows that his blood is very nearly on the point of boiling in his veins. He is convinced that the sharp pain in his head is the result of his brain, swollen with heat, pressing against the inside of his skull. But he tells no one. He drinks copious amounts of water to flush the fire from his body. He applies cool wet cloths to his forehead. He avoids exertion and keeps his breaths shallow, lest he fan the flames. He creeps into the cold room off the kitchen and sits on the block of Lake Concord ice purchased earlier that spring. He sits on the ice every night, letting it pull the heat from his body. For weeks, his family wonders aloud about the half-moons melted into the top of the block.

And then one morning, for no apparent reason, the fire in his veins abates, the fever breaks.

His health is restored, but little else changes. The world to which he returns is just as he left it. He learns that much of the devastated land in the Concord Woods is the property of A. H. Wheeler and the Hubbard brothers, Cyrus and Darius. The *Con-*

cord Freeman publishes a castigating article that does not mention Edward or Henry by name, but Henry takes offense that the editors of the paper think he merely sought recreation in the woods. Edward Hoar tells him that his father has promised to make restitutions on their behalf, though it is not enough to cover the loss in its entirety, and it cannot restore what has been taken.

The signs of the fire are everywhere. A heavy smell of charred wood, the bitter tang of immolated flora and fauna, drifts into Concord from the desolate forest and lingers in the air. Even when the wind blows away from town, the smell has so permeated carpets and curtains and clothing and living trees that the evidence of his guilt is discernible. People carry kerchiefs held to nose and mouth like bandits. The townspeople of Concord are grateful to have been spared, but their gratitude is soon overtaken by anger. Henry cannot walk the streets of Concord without suffering icy stares and hearing behind his back the angry, accusing whisper: *woodsburner.*

People come from Boston to witness the damage and carry black smudges back to the city with them. People come to scavenge. In every home, at every hearth in Concord, a visitor is sure to find a pile of firewood already blackened. Carpenters and cabinetmakers come to the woods and take what little can be saved. The soot makes its way onto hands and faces, shirtfronts, jackets, skirts, and hats. The patrons of Wright's Tavern complain that the taste of their beer is sorely tainted, acrid, and smoky on the palate. For months, even the cleanest Irish whiskey tastes like scotch.

And in the unburned world there are still pencils to be made.

Henry returns to his father's factory, but he knows he must do something more. *Woodsburner,* they call him. He hears the accusations in his dreams. *Woodsburner.* The whispers are everywhere, like the drifting ash. *Woodsburner. Woodsburner.* Henry thinks at first that he will immerse himself in work. He and his father become so successful at concocting their lead mixtures that other pencil-makers demand it. Soon the selling of lead itself becomes more profitable than the tedious manufacturing of pencils. They become lead salesmen, purveyors of the blackest bits of earth.

A pencil made with lead from John Thoreau & Co. is a writer's delight. But that does not save Henry from the scorn of his own conscience. Henry knows that every act is itself a cause, a link in a chain, germinating future effects unforeseen. There is a debt to be paid — for what is taken, for what is lost, for what is carelessly thrown away. Henry thinks of the string of uneaten fish, a sacrifice for no purpose. America is not so stalwart a place as it may seem. The bountiful stores of plumbago and lumber and coal and fish and fur and all the other incomprehensible riches of the continent, riches waiting for industrious men to come along and scoop them up — these things are not endless. Once gone, they are gone for good. Even lifeless clay, taken from the ground, leaves only a hole in its stead. Man's inability to conceive of the world's limits does not render the world limitless. And there is no longer a new world for the empty-handed to flee to from here.

The vast wilderness that covered the shores of the New World seemed impenetrable until they built a city. The hills and rivers of Boston seemed immovable until they leveled and filled them. Concord was an outpost in the wilderness until it grew to devour its landscape, like an actor kicking away his props. And then the fire took its portion of what little remained. Henry David Thoreau knows he must atone. He has seen the swiftness and finality of loss. There are wildernesses still, and what was lost at

Concord might yet return, if it knows that its return will be safeguarded. Henry cannot live among men now, cannot give his time — always in short supply — to those who call him *woodsburner* as if this were all he will ever be. He will seek out what is not yet lost. He will help other men grasp the limits of the seemingly infinite; he will look to nature for instruction.

There is nothing left in the blackened woods to sustain a man, Henry thinks, but there is another place he might go. Adjacent to the devastation, the woods at Walden Pond did not burn. Through those green and budding trees, he might watch the lonely charred trunks nearby, offer meek consolation as they wait for the spring that will not come. Together, Henry and Waldo have often mourned the distressing number of trees felled each year at the pond, and Waldo has hinted that he might purchase a parcel of the land himself in order to protect the beautiful surroundings from further abuse. Walden, Henry thinks, would serve as good a place as any to settle down by himself. The privacy and stillness might even grant him opportunity, at last, to make a book from the notes and sketches he collected with his brother during their trip on the Concord and Merrimack Rivers. Henry knows what he must do. He will turn his back to those who would call him *woodsburner*. He will build a simple cabin near the pond, perhaps, and study nature's infinitesimal beauties, as frail as they are profuse. He will commiserate with displaced creatures, tend to the injured woodlands until they revive. And, if they will have him, he will become their steward.

37
ODDMUND

He will build them a fire, unafraid.

They are running through the trees with no sense of urgency or fear. Their footfalls are light, their course without direction. West, perhaps, is their general heading, but they have sacrificed their bearing to giddiness. Euphoria consumes any sense of direction that might have guided their steps. They run as if in chase, though pursuer and pursued are the same, roles they exchange through embrace or glance; to catch and to be caught reaps the same reward.

It is Emma's turn to follow now, and she runs with a lightness that surprises. She holds her arms around herself to support her bulk, but does so more out of habit than need. Beneath her dress she wears the undergarment that she fashioned out of a dismembered corset and her husband's old handkerchiefs. The tight lacing and the whalebone do her hugging for her, hold her bosom close as she hops gracelessly over a rock. Then he reaches back for her, grabs her elbows, and slingshots her forward. They switch places, and it is her turn to lead them nowhere.

Odd does not care where they are headed. Almost any direction, any direction but east, will take them someplace new, someplace to start over.

Emma's final vision of her husband will fade. The word itself is already foreign to her: *husband.* Will its meaning transfer to wherever they are going, or can time and distance divorce the word from its object? She can see Cyrus Woburn in the fading image she carries. She imagines him still sleeping where she left him, stupefied by drink in the chair by the fireplace, the fire in the hearth an unusual color, more blue than yellow, his watery eyes half open and not seeing, an empty bottle on his lap, and in his hand the last of her expensive books. In the fire, the doomed pages of a splayed book curl into ash, one at a time, as if the flames were taking the time to read what they consumed. Around the chair and in his lap are the dozen or so cards with lewd illustrations that Emma retrieved from their hiding places and flung in his face when he staggered into their home so drunk that she could not fathom how he had made the trip without leading his horses into a ditch. When she confronted him with the cards he struck her, for the first and last time, and then he lurched toward her bookcase as she cowered in a corner and wept.

Emma will never know what she might have been driven to do after her husband had fallen into the chair by the fire, insensible at last. She might have flown into a rage, reached for the nearby poker, dragged his feet into the fire, grabbed the empty bottle and smashed it over his head. Not until Odd arrived did she realize that her shaking hand was clutching the kitchen knife so tightly that she had cut her own palm. She might have committed any number of irreversible deeds had Odd not come at that very moment, clothes torn and scorched, bleeding, blistered, wild-eyed. She noticed straightaway that he stood differently and walked toward her as if his feet owned the places they trod. He touched her gently.

Without hesitating, he said quietly, "We will go now."

Odd had not known what he would find when he arrived, but he knew what he wanted. He had walked through fire to embrace those wants, and he was confident of the consequences. He had no right to hope for success, but he knew what he must do. He knew he would start over, though there would be no need to cross oceans or change names. They are running, but not fleeing.

Emma is happier than she has ever been. She has never run like this, has never known what it is like to be chosen by someone who does not expect her to be grateful for the choosing. She can barely keep from leaping in her stride, weightless with happiness. Odd knows where he is going. He pretends he does not, but she knows him better than that. He is a careful man, a man to be trusted, though she has never seen him look so reckless or exude such boundless energy. He said something about being a "stronger animal" now, and she is happy to wait forever for an explanation. They find a clearing where they will spend yet another night in their journey. Emma has lost count of the days and does not care. The fire Odd builds is larger than what they require. Logs stacked in a pyramid, a skeleton of right angles beneath the bright, flickering skin. In the dark night, leaves appear overhead in flashes as the flames leap and lick at the high branches overhanging the clearing. Odd is not worried. The fire will do what he wants it to, for he is the author of its world.

From a distance, anyone watching might think this a pagan ritual, two dark figures dancing without rhythm around a bright fire in the blackness of the night. Anyone who cared to come closer would see and hear that they are neither chanting nor clapping. They clasp hands, embrace, break apart and come together again, but without discernible pattern. They are not dancing but jumping for joy, like children so overwhelmed with happiness they must pound it out of themselves. And this is all that they will take with them into the New World: this happiness, and these stronger children of their former selves.

AUTHOR'S NOTE

Woodsburner is a work of fiction that draws upon a number of real events. On April 30, 1844, Henry David Thoreau did indeed set fire to the Concord Woods during an excursion with his friend, Edward Sherman Hoar. In July of the following year, Thoreau took up residence in a simple cabin at Walden Pond, thus embarking on what would come to be regarded as one of the iconic undertakings of American literary history.

For details of what happened on the day of the fire, I have, for the most part, relied on two primary sources: the newspaper report in the *Concord Freeman* of May 3, 1844, and, of course, Thoreau's own journals. It is interesting that Thoreau does not mention the fire in his journal until an entry in 1850, in which he describes the event at length. By Thoreau's own account, he was attempting to cook a fish chowder in a pine stump. Driven by strong winds, the fire quickly grew out of control and spread north from Fair Haven Bay. By the day's end an estimated three hundred acres of the Concord Woods lay in ruins, and were it not for the efforts of the people of Concord, the flames might have reached the town itself. Meteorological records confirm that the early months of 1844 were exceedingly dry, and on the day of the fire a strong wind was blowing out of the south. Had the winds shifted, the fire might have spread to the nearby Walden Woods, though it is likely that the new railway to Fitchburg would have, ironically, provided a firebreak.

Most of the burned land was privately owned, and Edward Sherman Hoar's father paid reparations to the owners, which dissuaded them from taking legal action against Edward and Henry. For months afterward, the residents of Concord complained of the lingering effects of smoke and ash, and it appears that the sudden loss of woodland may have also bolstered their growing sense of the natural world as a place in need of protection from careless adventurers. A modern-day visitor to Concord might be surprised to learn that deforestation was already a concern in the early 1800s as rapidly growing cities, towns, and farms spread across the land. The first half of the nineteenth century saw two concurrent developments in the way that Americans viewed their new world. Increasingly, as Americans flocked to cities, they began to view the countryside as a thing apart from where they lived and worked, a separate place to be visited for recreation. And at the same time, many were growing conscious of the natural world's vulnerability; it should come as no surprise, then, that among Thoreau's contemporaries, the seeds for the modern environmental movement were being sown.

ACKNOWLEDGMENTS

Many thanks to all who generously read the unpolished manuscript and offered advice: Marsha Moyer, David Liss, Amanda Eyre Ward, Dominic Smith, Caroline Levander, and Ted Weinstein.

For research, I owe thanks to the Concord Free Public Library, the A. Frank Smith, Jr., Library at Southwestern University, and the libraries at the University of Texas at Austin. A number of texts were essential to this work, especially *The Days of Henry Thoreau: A Biography,* by Walter Harding; *Thoreau: A Life of the Mind,* by Robert D. Richardson, Jr.; *The Pencil: A History of Design and Circumstance,* by Henry Petroski; *American Literary Publishing in the Mid-Nineteenth Century: The Business of Ticknor and Fields,* by Michael Winship; and, of course, the writings of Thoreau himself, especially *A Week on the Concord and Merrimack Rivers*

573

and his incomparable *Journal.* The following organizations and Web sites were invaluable resources as well: the Walden Woods Project (www.walden.org) and the Thoreau Society (www.thoreausociety.org).

I can hardly find words to describe my indebtedness to Marly Rusoff for believing in this project, and I am awed by the finesse with which she and Michael Radulescu piloted the manuscript through the shoals and eddies of publication. With great insight, enthusiasm, and thoughtful critique, Janet Silver embraced the manuscript and helped me find my way to its full realization. And I will be forever grateful to Nan A. Talese for welcoming me to Doubleday and enlisting the expertise of Luke Hoorelbeke, John Fontana, Sean Mills, Greg Mollica, Pei Loi Koay, and so many others.

In the course of writing this book, I came to know many talented authors through the Writers' League of Texas. Every writer should be so fortunate as to have access to such a vibrant writing community (www.writersleague.org).

I am especially happy to be able to acknowledge, at last, the boundless encouragement of my parents, John Paul Pipkin and Mary Frances Pipkin.

And, to be sure, without the immeasurable patience and support of my wife, Eileen, these pages would never have had the slightest hope of coming into being.

ABOUT THE AUTHOR

John Pipkin was born and raised in Baltimore, Maryland, and he holds degrees from Washington and Lee University, the University of North Carolina at Chapel Hill, and Rice University. He has taught writing and literature at Saint Louis University, Boston University, and Southwestern University. He currently lives in Austin, Texas, with his wife and son. He can be reached via his Web site at www.johnpipkin.com.